WORLDWIDE PRAISE FOR THE AWAKEN SAGA

"Ellis K. Popa (delivers) an amazing story full of mystery, intrigue and romance."

JOHN BENEDICT, BESTSELLING AUTHOR
OF *ADRENALINE*

"(Simply) one of the best books I've ever read."

HEATHER BROWN, BOOK GIRL BROWN
REVIEWS (US)

"A gripping and unforgettable read that heralds Popa as a rising star in the genre."

ELICIA MEIERS, NETGALLEY (US)

"This book is an adrenaline rush, with every twist sharper than the last."

ALEXANDRIA W, BOOKSTAGRAM (US)

"A fast-paced mystery with a strong, likeable protagonist to root for."

THE WISHING SHELF (UK)

"Go ahead! Go add this to your TBR!"

BOOKS WITH CATS (CYPRUS)

"(*Awaken the Dawn*) will have you hooked from page one."

NESSA'S BOOK REVIEWS (UK)

"This is an absolutely delicious book. I both devoured it in one day, and savoured every word!"

BLUE FAIRY BUGS BOOKS (UK)

"Kat was amazing and a kick-ass character."

KRITI, THIS READER GIRL (INDIA)

"(Popa) builds a world charged with grief, secrets, and the urgent need to uncover the truth."

JOHN RANDALL, POSTMODERNISM &
BEYOND (US)

"Popa's vivid prose (invites) readers to actively partici-
pate in the unfolding story."

ROGUE BOOK REVIEWS (US)

"(*Awaken the Dawn*) is unputdownable…"

JAME_EREADER, GOODREADS (US)

"The book thrilled me (and) I can't wait to read the
sequel."

SOPHIA, GOODREADS (CROATIA)

"The story is action packed involving dead ends, jeop-
ardy, (and) trying to keep one step ahead of the bad
guys."

HELEN FOX, LIBRARIAN (UK)

"The book was absolutely amazing and I couldn't get
enough of it. I can't wait to see what happens next."

SCARLET LE CLAIR, NETGALLEY (UK)

FIRST LIGHT OF DAWN

AN INTERLUDE NOVEL

THE AWAKEN SAGA
BOOK 1.5

ELLIS K. POPA

PUBLISHER'S NOTE

First Light of Dawn is Book 1.5 in The Awaken Saga. It's an interlude novel, picking up where *Awaken the Dawn* left off and giving a glimpse of things alluded to in *Dawn to Dusk*. Both Kat and Maksim are featured, but the story is told from Maksim's perspective.

We recommend reading *Awaken the Dawn* (Book 1) **before** this interlude novel. If you've already read *Dawn to Dusk* (Book 2), be sure to look for the "Easter eggs" sprinkled throughout this story. You can grab the first two books here...

Books2Read.com/Awaken1
Books2Read.com/Awaken2

EDITOR'S NOTE

The characters in *First Light of Dawn* originate from all over Europe and beyond. Conversations are presented in English, but *italicized* dialogue indicates a foreign language is being spoken.

A FINAL NOTE

First Light of Dawn touches on topics related to cybercrime. Although this type of crime happens online, it can have real psychological effects on victims (called cybertrauma).

If you or someone you know is the victim of a cybercrime or cyberbullying, there are trained professionals who can help. The nonprofit *Love in Action* is one such resource…

LoveInAction.ro

THE PLAYLIST

Listen to the playlists for The Awaken Saga as you read. Includes a character playlist for Miro…

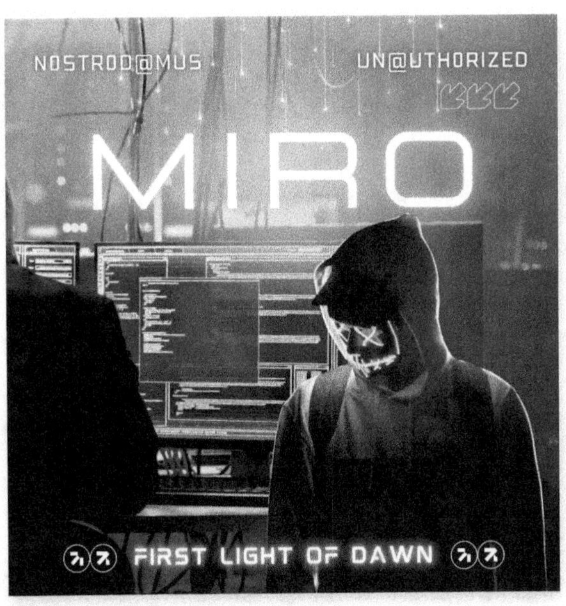

www.Linktr.ee/BookishMood

EPIGRAPH

Then the king returned to his palace and spent the night without eating and without any entertainment being brought to him. And he could not sleep.

At the first light of dawn, the king got up and hurried to the lion pit. When he came near, he called to Daniye'l in an anguished voice, "Daniye'l, servant of the living G-d, has your G-d, whom you serve continually, been able to rescue you from the lions?"

FROM THE KETUVIM (WRITINGS) OF THE
TANAKH

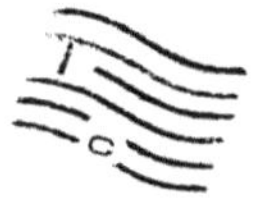

PART ONE

MAKSIM
SIBIU , ROMANIA
@NILEX_KA

CHAPTER ONE

MIERCURI, 12 IUNIE, 09:08 (WEDNESDAY, JUNE 12, 9:08 AM)

MODERN LED LIGHTS accented the reception area of Sibiu's premier private hospital. The glossy glow reflected off the sleek floors and highlighted the colorful bouquet in Maksim's hand.

Flowers for Kat.

A nurse peeked up from the reception desk. *"You were here very early this morning,"* she said in Romanian. *"Are you returning already?"*

"I am. I left to buy these." He showed her the bouquet.

"Ohhh. Ce trandafiri frumoși aveți." (What beautiful roses you have.)

Maksim replied with an easy smile—one of the easiest he'd managed in over a week. Kat's condition had been touch and go upon their arrival, but the worst was over. She was going to be okay. Dr. Rhyland had assured him of that.

Maksim left the nurses with an earnest *mulțumesc frumos*

(thank you very much) before rounding the corner. A smattering of people sat in the yellow chairs of a waiting area. The sign mounted in this part of the hospital roiled his stomach.

Urgenţe. (Emergencies.) This was the first place they'd brought Kat after airlifting her from Village Ksorba. He'd spent hours sitting in these same chairs, pacing this same hall.

But not today. Today, he was headed for Kat's private room on the third floor.

His smile widened despite a strong sterile odor that followed him through the hospital. The wait for the elevator didn't bother him either. This was the main lift used by patients, visitors, nurses, doctors. Normally Maksim would have taken the stairs, but today he decided to stand and wait with everyone else.

He smiled and nodded, greeting each person, showing off the flowers. All the while his anticipation kept building. He had an idea he'd been wanting to share with Kat, something that would involve spending more time together. He didn't know how she would feel about that, but he had remained patiently hopeful, waiting until she was well enough for the discussion.

Ten minutes later, Maksim was striding through the third-floor hallway. Two nurses exited a room. As Maksim drew closer, his ears tuned in to a familiar female voice. "… Madă has family here and arranged for us to stay with them." That was Kat's best friend, Brandy. She and her boyfriend, along with Brandy's father and younger brother, had all flown in after learning that Kat was in the hospital. Their efforts, especially their loyalty, had made a positive impression on Maksim. Unfortunately, he didn't think they felt the same about him. At least Brandy didn't seem to.

Brandy herself confirmed the suspicion, and her next words brought Maksim to an instantaneous halt. "…My dad ended up paying for Maksim's lunch. Does the guy not have a job or what?"

"Come on, Bee." This voice belonged to Dave, Brandy's boyfriend and Kat's other friend.

"What?" Brandy asked. "It's a fair question."

"He has money." This was Kat, but she spoke so quietly Maksim barely registered the words. "He probably lost his wallet when we were out at that village." She was talking about Village Ksorba.

Maksim, Kat, and Levi had made the long and treacherous hike out to that village, trying to solve the scavenger hunt Kat's father and grandfather had crafted before they died. Maksim's former colleagues—part of the Răzvan crime syndicate—beat them there, and the already dangerous excursion had degenerated into a hellish nightmare.

Maksim felt a deep pinch, center mass—but not because he was remembering those events. It was hearing Kat defend him with such quiet reservation. Her underlying doubt, the waver of uncertainty in her tone, took a hard swipe at his ego.

"In all fairness," Dave said, "Maksim turned down lunch. It was your dad who insisted."

Brandy harrumphed at that.

"He got the cheapest thing on the menu," Dave continued. "Some kind of soup with cow stomach. *Blech.*"

"Oh, so the guy's a saint because he ate cow stomach instead of rib-eye steak?" The comment—Brandy's ire as she said it—sliced into Maksim.

He redoubled his grip on the flowers and closed the gap to Kat's room.

"Seriously," Brandy was saying, "who lets the girl he *supposedly* cares about go off on some wild, crazy—"

Maksim cleared his throat from the doorway. A curtain of silence fell, and he allowed it to stay that way, letting his presence sink in.

And sink in it did.

As he entered the room, he found Kat and Dave cringing. Brandy, unremorseful, held her position in the visitor's chair—arms crossed, a scowl seared into her freckly features.

Kat was sitting up in bed, her expression stuck somewhere

between surprise and embarrassment. The red in her cheeks indicated she may have been experiencing more of the latter.

Dave, who stood beside Brandy, forced a smile. "Hi," he said, offering a polite nod. "Good to see ya."

Maksim answered with a courteous nod and then focused on Kat. Her hair had been piled into a high, loose knot that showed off her delicate ears and revealed the slender lines of her neck. Her pink hospital gown hung loose, and Maksim couldn't keep his gaze from brushing along the pale curves of her shoulders.

She was beautiful. Even like this. Even in this place.

He was nearly to the bed when her embarrassment gave way to a smile. Her eyes shifted toward his arm, and she pulled a tiny gasp that was more visible than it was audible. "You're not wearing the sling."

"I've been making use of the physiotherapy department." Maksim followed her gaze. "The therapist wants me to move normally, without the sling, as often as I can. I'm currently up to two hours."

"That's amazing. I'm so proud of you." Her attention shifted to the bundle in his hand. She blinked out a hint of shyness that seemed to say, *Is that for me?*

Maksim answered by extending the flowers.

Her eyes lit up. "These are gorgeous." The paper crinkled as she turned the bouquet one way and then the other, examining the spray of teacup roses. "Thank you."

"I came to tell you…" He chanced a glance at Brandy, and the pinch inside him returned. "I'll be gone for a day or two," he said, changing course.

Kat sat up straight. "Why? Where are you going?"

"An errand, one that's time critical. I'll return as soon as I'm finished." This errand involved a secondary matter related to his big idea, but it wasn't the idea itself. That, he decided, would truly be best discussed when Kat was alone.

"Actually, that's why we're here," Brandy interjected.

"There's no need for you to keep coming if you have other stuff to do."

"Bee." Kat leveled a horrified stare. "What the actual hell?"

"Sorry. I wasn't trying to be rude." There was no apology in Brandy's tone. "You're doing better than anyone expected, babe. Dr. Rhyland didn't think you'd be able to fly for weeks, but your injuries are healing so fast she's gonna discharge you in a couple more days."

Kat sent a startled look to Maksim. He felt a bit startled himself. The oxygen therapy accelerated recovery, but Kat's injuries were healing at breakneck speed.

Just like the injury Émilien had inflicted on her cheek. That one had healed overnight.

"Babe. Are you listening?" Brandy leaned closer, her eyes wide with excitement. "Do you know what this means?"

"Um, yeah." Kat withdrew her gaze from Maksim. "I'll be back to normal soon."

"It means we can go *home* soon." Brandy took Kat's hand and gave it a squeeze. "You don't have to be in this hospital for weeks on end like we thought. Isn't that great?"

Kat's attention made a return trip to Maksim. Her expression held a question—for him, perhaps, or for herself. *Is it great?* And in the physical sense, the answer was a resounding *yes*. Her speedy recovery was the best news Maksim could have hoped for.

Except for the part about going home. He probably should be happy for her, and yet…

He turned away. "I'll try to be back by tomorrow night."

Silence followed him to the doorway.

He paused, his stare flicking to Kat before falling to the colorful bundle. A sadness he knew but had long since buried rose from the grave—a monster that might very well consume him should he permit it.

Kat gazed at him, and he detected a glossy sheen coating her eyes. But she said nothing.

He curbed his thoughts and all of his feelings and exited the room. Brandy's voice flowed into the hallway. She was speaking to Kat, but Maksim didn't break stride to hear the exchange.

He bypassed the elevator and entered the stairwell. He no longer had the luxury of time, and the present circumstances had stolen any normalcy he'd allowed himself to experience. He had to run that errand—today if possible—and get his ass back there before Kat was gone.

If he could get back there.

CHAPTER
TWO

15:14 (3:14 PM)

MAKSIM'S CAB idled in a long line of Bucureşti traffic. Glass buildings sprang up around him, stretching into the sky and standing guard like the princes of old.

Maksim peered up at the skyscrapers. Living in Pipera afforded him many luxuries—nice streets, modern buildings, fine restaurants—and yet he longed for the old-world charm he'd left behind.

He wanted to be in Transilvania. With Madă and Daniel. With Kat.

The cabbie's voice drew Maksim out of his thoughts. *"Unde mergeţi?"* (Where are you going?)

Maksim found a pair of eyes staring at him through the rearview mirror. The driver had been asking for an address since the moment they'd left Sibiu. It'd been a long drive—nearly four hours—and Maksim had managed to sidestep the question each time.

No doubt the man thought he was going to be stiffed.

Maksim replied in Romanian. *"Don't worry. We're almost there."*

The cabbie's mouth drilled down into a frown. *"What is this? Do you have money now? I'm tired of you being so secretive."* His Romanian popped hard and fast, lighting the words on fire. His underlying anger doused the blaze in lighter fluid.

Traffic started forward. The driver stayed put.

Maksim did a quick assessment of his surroundings. Hyper-awareness was second nature to him—checking for threats, police—but as his attention returned, he realized he now looked guiltier than he had a moment ago.

The cabbie's glare burned into the rearview mirror.

Maksim leaned forward. *"I will pay for this ride—four hundred euros, as I promised."*

The driver rolled his eyes. *"But?"*

"I stepped on someone's lightbulb. He's furious with me, and I don't want to risk encountering him." Maksim wasn't referring to a real lightbulb. It was a Romanian saying. To step on someone's lightbulb meant to make a mistake.

Honks went up in the line of traffic. Maksim's expression morphed into pleading.

The cabbie snorted a laugh. *"You're selling me doughnuts, aren't you?"* Another colloquialism.

"No. I'm not lying. I need some things from my apartment, and I prefer not to encounter this person." Now *that* was quite an understatement.

The cabbie muttered and started forward. *"I suppose this is why people pay four hundred euros for a ride instead of taking the bus."*

"I'll give you an additional one hundred for the trouble." Maksim lifted an eyebrow in time for the driver to see. *"I'm asking only that you remain discreet. Nothing more."*

"Who is the person you are avoiding? Your landlord? Do you owe him money, too?" The cabbie shook his head but ultimately didn't argue. *"Tell me where to go."*

Maksim explained where his apartment was. *"On Strada Baia*

de Aramă. I'll show you, but we must drive past the building. Don't stop. Remember, we must be discreet."

The driver proceeded through the traffic light and continued to the next block. Strada Baia de Aramă curved to the left and then to the right while simultaneously narrowing. Parked cars lined both sides of the tree-lined street, and the first of several high-rise apartments came fully into view.

The road widened a moment later. The apartments in this section were modern and colorful.

"Slow down, please," Maksim said as they passed a building with bright red panels running along the exterior. *"A little slower, actually. But don't stop."*

The cabbie obliged.

Maksim lived in one of the yellow apartments at the end of the street. As they approached the colorful high-rise, Maksim sank down in the back seat. He'd chosen this cab because of its tinted windows, but they weren't so dark that he was invisible.

He forced himself to relax, hoping to look like a normal passenger. Meanwhile he scanned. He recognized several parked cars on the street, but there were others he'd never seen before.

White BMW.

Gray Peugeot.

Blue Dacia.

Smooth lines in black and silver captured his attention. His insides twisted. *My bike.* He didn't normally park so close to his apartment, but he had the last time he'd used it.

Out of everything he owned, his beloved—and very expensive—motorcycle was going to be the most painful to leave behind. He was going to miss cruising through București, weaving through traffic on Calea Victoreie, riding alongside the glowing fountains of Piața Unirii. But it wasn't simply that he would miss those things. It was that he would never be able to do them again. For Maksim, there was no returning to București. He could never come home.

He cursed himself for the distraction and dragged his focus

to the other parked cars. He had to get this right. His life depended on it.

Gray Dacia, new.

White Dacia, old.

Yellow taxi, parked, no occupants.

Black Mercedes-Benz, brand new with high-end rims.

An old Yugo in faded rust-colored red.

Maksim took note of these vehicles, being careful to observe their license plate numbers. Often the license plate told more of a story than the vehicle itself.

The DRPCIV—Romania's version of the DMV—used a coding system for plates. Those belonging to diplomatic vehicles, for instance, consisted of the letters CD followed by two sets of triple digits. The first set always referenced the country of diplomacy, and Maksim had dedicated all of those numeric codes to memory. Were he to see any vehicle with diplomatic plates—specifically for Russia, Georgia, Montenegro, or any other country where Vladimir held major operations—that would have been a red flag.

Thankfully, Maksim didn't see any. He did, however, see two license plates that seemed suspect. Both began with IL—the abbreviation for Ialomița, a county east of București.

A town called Țăndărei was located in Ialomița, home of the Țăndărei mafia, one of the biggest human trafficking operations in the world.

The EU and UK had been making inquiries for years, but the investigations always came to nothing, and no one—not the detectives or police or media—understood why.

But Maksim understood. Because Vladimir Răzvan, the man who had murdered Maksim's parents so long ago, was the money and influence behind these trafficking rings. While the Țăndărei mafia was being investigated, it was Vladimir operating in the shadows… and it was Vladimir who had paid off the right people to make the investigations go away.

As soon as Maksim saw IL on those license plates, he knew

the vehicles likely belonged to Vladimir's men. The fact that both vehicles were parked *and* had male occupants confirmed his suspicions.

Maksim dipped lower as his cabbie passed the first vehicle—a top-of-the-line Mercedes. He noted a driver, a passenger, and at least two other men, possibly three, in the back seat. It was hard to tell through their tinted windows.

The second vehicle—an old communist-era Yugo—contained a driver who appeared to be reading a newspaper. Whether he was actually reading it or merely pretending was unknowable, but the man very distinctly looked up when Maksim's cab drove past.

Maksim's attention shot to his cabbie. Relief overflowed when he discovered the man gazing up at the high-rises. At least he hadn't been looking at the Yugo.

"Continue to the next street. Go slowly, and then turn right."

The cabbie executed the instructions while Maksim twisted around, keeping low. Both cars remained parked. Maksim saw no movement, no indication the engines had been started. Chances were good the men hadn't noticed the SB—code for Sibiu—on this taxi's plates.

Maksim faced forward, still crouching, as a flash of red rolled past. A Poşta Română delivery van had turned onto the street, heading in the direction Maksim and his cabbie had come from.

The van stopped beside an apartment building. The driver stepped out, carrying a package

That was all Maksim saw. His cab turned right, following another curve, and the van disappeared from his line of sight.

"Well?" The cabbie's gaze flicked to the rearview mirror. To his credit, he did not move his head, making him appear to be focused on the road.

Maksim stayed low and kept scanning. He needed a way into his apartment, but how? Anyone attempting to enter that building would be under a microscope, and those men wouldn't hesitate to open fire the moment they recognized Maksim.

Pedestrians trickled out of the neighboring buildings. What if someone could access the apartment on his behalf?

He discarded the idea. Even if he could find someone trustworthy enough to do that, he would have to convince them, coach them on what to do… the whole thing was too risky. For them *and* for Maksim.

All right, then what about a decoy? Maksim figured he could pay a couple of teens to run past the vehicles—or throw rocks at them?—while he snuck into the building.

But… no. If even one of the men failed to take the bait, Maksim would be finished before he got started.

The road straightened out, and his street grew distant behind him. He rubbed his eyes and squeezed his fingers together at the bridge of his nose. *Think. Think!*

His mind returned to the delivery van. He pictured the driver climbing out, walking up to the building, delivering the package. A hundred people could have been watching, and no one would have questioned a thing. The guy was simply doing his job.

What if Maksim could do that job?

The first inkling of an idea sparked. Levi had shared a story about Kat's father, Nicolae, who had been trying to warn innocents of an impending raid during communist times. Nicolae had dressed like a produce vendor to throw the Securitate—Romania's secret police—off his scent.

Could Maksim do something like that? What would it require?

"Sir?" The cabbie's eyebrows lifted high, flagging Maksim through the rearview mirror. *"Where do you want to go?"*

"The mall." Maksim sat up straight. *"I need to buy something, and then I'll show you where to park."*

CHAPTER
THREE

A POSTAL WORKER emerged from the mall wearing the standard issue uniform—blue polo, black pants, gray ball cap, matching gray windbreaker.

Except this wasn't really a postal worker. It was Maksim, and he was faking this uniform with clothes he'd purchased from the mall.

The real Poșta Română uniform would have been trimmed in yellow, and their logo would have been stamped on the polo's breast. Nevertheless, the faux uniform was passable. As long as no one looked too closely.

Maksim hustled to the cab and dropped into the back seat. *"That way,"* he said, pointing. *"The way we came. I'll show you where to park."*

The cabbie twisted the key. His engine purred, and he pulled out of the parking space. *"I should perhaps receive another fifty euros."* The man kept his eyes on the road. *"You never mentioned any of this when we agreed upon the price."*

Maksim fought the urge to roll his eyes. *"Fine. Add fifty to what I owe you."*

"The mall was an extra stop." The man shrugged. *"I had to wait, and it's very hot today—"*

"Bine, bine. (Fine, fine.) How about seven hundred euros? But that's the total, for everything, and we don't repeat this conversation."

The man gave a firm nod while fighting a smile. Clearly, he had no idea the risk he was taking—being caught by Vladimir's men, yes, but also being paid. Maksim's entire plan hinged on his ability to access the apartment. Without that, there was no money.

The neighborhood supermarket took up the corner between two streets. Maksim prepared to exit. *"Aici."* (Here.)

The cabbie slipped into a parallel space twenty-five meters from the store. Colorful apartments stretched to the left. A vacant lot occupied the right.

"Stay here. Don't look around too much. Act like you're taking a break."

The driver turned. *"Am I James Bond? Why do you tell me this?"*

"Pretend that I'm James Bond, and a villain is looking for me. That's the best way I can explain it."

The man's face widened.

Maksim offered a weak smile. *"I need a few things from my apartment, including the cash I've promised you, but this man I told you about is determined to make me miserable. Please."* He placed a reassuring hand on the cabbie's shoulder. *"My acquaintance will never know we're here if we simply remain discreet. This is all I ask."*

"Înțeleg." (I understand.)

A security guard balanced on a stool inside the supermarket. Maksim smiled—nothing that could be construed as fake, just a polite greeting. *"Bună ziua."* (Good afternoon.)

The security guard didn't smile, but his reply seemed friendly enough. *"Bună ziua."*

Maksim tugged on his ball cap, ensuring it rode low on his forehead, and pushed through a metal turnstile. He bypassed the fruit and vegetables and angled for the dry goods. Grocery shelves created neat lines across the store, and he turned down the aisle with school and office supplies.

A four-pack of document mailers plucked at his vision. He

selected that along with bubble mailers in various sizes—small to extra large—and a handful of letter-size envelopes. Mailing labels would have been helpful, but Maksim only had enough cash for one more item.

Well, hopefully he had enough. He was about to find out.

He grabbed a stack of copy paper and strode for the checkout. Sweat drizzled beneath his cap as the clerk scanned the items. Maksim counted out the Romanian lei in his pocket. He only had small denominations, but they were just enough to pay for everything, including the plastic bag. *Thank you, Daniel.*

Maksim exited the supermarket, putting himself out of the guard's view, and began prepping his items. First, he crumpled several sheets of copy paper and stuffed them into his new mailers. For the envelopes, he simply folded the paper and slipped the blank pages inside. His thoughts traveled to the labels he'd forgone. Those would have aided in authenticity, but, from a distance, he hoped these faux parcels would work.

The afternoon sun cooked him as he crossed the street. He ignored the stickiness on his skin and sealed each envelope and mailer. He then situated everything, carrying the items in a more intentional way, and strode through the neighborhood as fast as he dared. Vladimir's men may have established a wide perimeter. They could have been watching from one of these buildings.

Maksim had no way to know, so he kept his gaze down and his ball cap low, using the faux letters to shield his face. Every so often, he followed a walkway that led to one of the apartment buildings and pretended to deliver a faux parcel.

Pain plucked at his right arm. His clothes rubbed against his scars, and a burning sensation spread beneath his sleeve. Desperation rose up. He pictured himself stripping off the windbreaker, giving his arm a chance to breathe—but he absolutely could not do that right now. So instead he clenched his jaw and focused on the task before him. He visualized what needed to be done and mentally rehearsed himself doing it.

The pain, the weakness, the fire all drifted into the background.

He reached the curved road that led to his street. This was where he'd noticed the delivery van, but the vehicle had since moved on.

"Ce dracu." (What the hell?) He'd spent only six minutes at the supermarket, but his trip to the mall had taken much longer —five minutes there, sixteen minutes inside, another five minutes to reach the supermarket. All in all, forty-two minutes had passed. He hadn't been fast enough, and now he was running low on the phony parcels.

He slowed his pace, thinking through contingencies. His original plan had been to approach the delivery person, ask a question, and discreetly knock the man out. Such a move would have been bold, risky, but with the van in his possession, Maksim could have parked beside the building and walked straight in. The vehicle would have served as additional cover.

Now what was he going to do?

He veered onto his street, situating the two remaining parcels —an extra-large bubble mailer and a manila document mailer. He held those close to his body while clutching the last three "letters."

The air felt heavy, thick. Sweat broke across his brow and dripped down his neck. *Act natural. You're just a delivery person. Nobody of importance.*

Pedestrians crossed paths with him. He pretended to be absorbed in his work, splitting his attention between the parcels and the buildings. His attention flicked ahead. He glimpsed the rusty Yugo and immediately hung a left, following a walkway to a yellow apartment block. This wasn't his building, but he was getting close.

Upon reaching the entrance, he used the envelopes to fan himself. He couldn't linger, he knew that, but he needed a moment to assess the current situation.

He leaned against the alcove wall and peeked around the corner. Vehicles lined both sides of the street, including the two he'd spied earlier. He couldn't see past the tinted windows of the Mercedes, but the Yugo had a clear view. There were now two men in that car—the driver with the newspaper and a passenger. Neither gave any indication they'd noticed him.

Movement drew his attention up the street. A car cruised past, followed by another. He needed to go now while he had a chance.

He wedged a blank letter in the door and strode up the walkway, slouching as he went. That should have shaved about three centimeters off his height. With the oversized windbreaker, he might get another two out of it. Would that be enough to hide his imposing frame?

Probably not, so he made sure to adjust his gait as well, shortening his stride and forcing more of his heel into each step.

He crossed paths with two teenagers as another car motored past. Maksim didn't let his gaze wander, not even a millimeter, toward the men in the parked cars.

He squinted, pretending to study the last of his parcels and envelopes. His attention flicked toward the next building. *His* building.

Almost there.

A car honk blipped somewhere behind him. He kept his focus on the walkway. *Twenty-five meters.*

Twenty.

Fifteen.

Another honk blared, longer, and concluded with several short bursts. Dread exploded through him. The tangos had spotted him. That had to be what was going on.

But he knew many of Vladimir's men. He'd worked with them, and although a handful were trigger happy, most relied on the element of surprise. So then who the hell would have been honking? One of Maksim's neighbors? Had an acquaintance recognized him?

Maksim couldn't imagine more of a nightmare scenario... until he cast a backward glance and saw a red delivery van cruising up the street.

It was the postal worker he'd seen earlier. The guy was honking at Maksim.

CHAPTER
FOUR

MAKSIM STIFFENED, muscles engaging. He had to run. Now.

Bad idea. He'd never outrun two cars with four to six men in pursuit. There could be a dozen more stationed around the neighborhood with overwatch and snipers.

Running wasn't an option. He would have to socially engineer his way out of this one. Somehow.

The van pulled alongside him and stopped. Maksim hurried toward the walkway, intending to get as close to the building as possible. This would prevent Vladimir's men from hearing whatever elaborate lie he was about to tell this postal worker.

I'm new. My uniform isn't ready yet.

I was attacked by a stray dog, and my uniform was torn. I'm wearing plain clothes until I receive the replacements.

I forgot to wash my uniform. Please don't tell anyone. I'll lose my job.

That third option seemed the most plausible, and perhaps the worker would take pity on a young man who'd made a mistake. There was no guarantee, of course, and if the worker didn't believe him—or if he didn't give a chicken's ass about a vulnerable fellow worker—Maksim would be screwed.

"Hei!" A door snapped shut and footsteps bore down on Maksim.

Eight more meters to the walkway.

Five...

The postal worker caught up to him. Maksim stiffened by reflex, his free hand folding into a fist—but to his surprise, the worker wasn't there to question him. *"I asked you something. Are you deaf or what?"*

Maksim broke stride. He chanced a look and noticed the van parked precisely where he'd envisioned it for the original plan.

His attention snapped to the postal worker. The man held a brown corrugated box, and he was explaining something. *"...I'm already late. Will you take it?"*

Maksim processed all of this in a flash. He was being asked to take an extra delivery.

Had the man taken a moment to observe Maksim, he would have noted the phony uniform. But the postal worker seemed to be in a hurry, and Maksim knew he needed to snap up the opportunity.

"Desigur." (Of course.) Maksim took the parcel. *"Ah,"* he said, skimming the label. The recipient lived in Maksim's building. *"I have another delivery for this address. I'll deliver your parcel, too. No problem."*

"Thank you."

"With pleasure." Maksim powered toward the entrance. He had ten, maybe twenty seconds before the van pulled away, and he wanted to be inside the building by the time that happened.

He managed to cross half the walkway before the van's door shut. He broke into a jog, reached into his pocket, and yanked out his key card—one of the few belongings he'd found after the incident at Village Ksorba.

The hum of the van's motor grew softer, more distant. The postal worker had pulled away. Maksim knew it without looking. He also knew several sets of eyes were locked on him. The stares penetrated his being like heat from a fire.

Don't look. Be casual.

Maksim clutched his key card, hiding it under the envelopes. His bubble mailers and the real parcel remained in his arms as he pushed through the main entrance. He angled for the mailboxes, sending a casual glance over his shoulder.

The men he'd seen in the Yugo now stood outside the vehicle. No one had exited the Mercedes, but the doors were ajar. Maksim's adrenaline coursed. The men hadn't crossed the street, but they would.

Except they didn't.

Maksim squeezed a fist, steadying himself, and pretended to search for a mailbox. The entryway wrapped around to a side entrance. He followed the path and peeked through the glass door on that side, searching for anyone who may have been stationed outside.

He didn't see anyone and began to withdraw.

A flash reeled him back. Maksim lifted his gaze to the high-rise next door. A man stood at a window on one of the upper floors. Maksim could barely detect his faint outline, but the sun had reflected off the man's binoculars.

Maksim did a quick count. That window landed on the eighth floor, putting the man directly across from Maksim's apartment. There was no reason to do that unless they had line of sight *into* the apartment. And if they had that, there was nothing to stop a sniper—Vladimir's preferred method of hit job —from eliminating someone who entered.

No wonder the street-level surveillance had been minimal. As soon as Maksim walked into his apartment, he'd be a sitting duck. *Well-played, Uncle.*

He scolded himself for using the term "uncle." Maksim was not related to Vladimir Răzvan. The whole thing had been a hoax, albeit an elaborate one, and the sooner Maksim stopped thinking of himself as a Răzvan the better off he would be.

But then who was he? Who was Maksim Răzvan without the Răzvan?

Maksim shoved the thought aside and entered the stairwell. He didn't have time to ponder these things. He needed to retrieve his go-bag and get the hell out of here.

A plan formed in his mind as he jogged up the stairs. He clutched the parcels, unwilling to leave them behind—a precaution in case the men decided to investigate.

A fresh layer of sweat skidded down his face by the time he rounded the fourth floor. He stopped and nudged the door to the hallway, which led to the apartments on that floor. *Clear,* he thought when he didn't see anyone.

He did a visual sweep, searching for anything out of place—doors partially open, cameras mounted along the ceiling.

He saw nothing and proceeded through the doorway and down the hall. He stopped at apartment 429. Not his apartment, obviously, but a friend's. He rapped on the door. *"Distribuireon."* *Delivery.* He deepened his voice, adjusting the timbre.

His ears registered movement inside the apartment. The footsteps were clunky, but not necessarily heavy. Maksim breathed a sigh as the door swung open.

Thirteen-year-old Mihai stood in the doorway. His jaw fell slack as he took in the imposter delivery person. *"Ce..?"* Mihai began. (What..?)

Maksim interrupted. *"Are your parents here?"*

Mihai shook his head.

"May I come in?" Maksim peered down at himself. *"It's urgent."*

"Yes, Mr. Răzvan. Of course."

Maksim decided not to correct him about the name. How would he explain these things to a thirteen-year-old?

He couldn't. Not without expending valuable time. So he let it go and slipped inside the apartment. *"Lock the door."*

"Huh?" Mihai blinked. *"Why—?"*

"Please, Mihai. I beg of you."

Mihai retrieved a set of keys and slid one of them into the

lever-style handle. He twisted until the locking mechanism engaged.

"Have you noticed anything unusual these past days?" Maksim dropped the faux parcels on the kitchen counter. *"People you don't know? Strange men in the building?"*

"No, Mr. Răzvan. I mean…" Mihai gestured at Maksim's clothes. *"This is strange. What's going on?"*

Maksim spun toward the windows in Mihai's living room. The apartment didn't face the building with the overwatch, but he refused to take any chances. He curtained the windows and then returned to the kitchen. *"I need to enter my apartment, but—"* Maksim hesitated. Mihai was a boy, a child, and likely wouldn't understand a complete explanation.

Maksim changed course. *"How would you like to make some Bitcoin?"*

Mihai lit up. *"A whole Bitcoin? Mr. Răzvan, that's almost ten thousand euros!"*

"I didn't say a whole bitcoin. I was actually thinking half." The kid began to protest, but Maksim continued. *"That… and I won't tell your parents you swatted that kid from your school."*

Mihai's excitement fizzled out.

Swatting was fast becoming the most popular form of revenge pranking, especially in the gaming community. In essence, the swatter reports a "crime" serious enough for a SWAT unit to be deployed. and the police go in heavily armed, believing they're dealing with a high-level threat. In reality, the person being swatted is the victim.

Mihai had done this to one of his classmates, and he'd gotten away with it. He had no idea Maksim knew about the whole thing.

"I-I didn't swat anyone, Mr. Răzvan. I swear—"

Maksim held up a stern finger. *"Let your yes be yes and your no be no. Every lie you tell chips away at the trust between us."*

"You're right. I'm sorry." Mihai tucked his chin. *"The boy was a bully, and he embarrassed me in front of my class."*

Maksim eased off the scolding. Mihai was a good kid, smart. Too smart perhaps. His parents had asked Maksim to keep an eye on him, and Maksim had been doing precisely that—in person from time to time, but also online.

That was why—and how—Maksim had learned about Mihai's stunt.

"Please don't tell my parents." Mihai clasped his hands. *"I don't need the bitcoin, sir. But if my mom hears what I did, I think she will report me to the police."*

"I doubt your mother would do that, but… I'm in a predicament. I need help, and I would be willing to overlook this transgression if you will promise never to do it again. Also—" Maksim pushed out a breath that deflated his being. Was there any other way to go about this? Did he have any other options?

"Also?" Mihai pumped up an eyebrow. *"Is it something bad?"*

"Yes." Maksim yanked off his hat and pushed a hand through his damp hair. Sweat glazed his face and neck. *"There are dangerous men looking for me, and I need to use your computer to swat them."*

MIHAI WATCHED as Maksim stationed himself in front of the computer. *"What are you doing?"*

"Using Telnet to perform a knock sequence." Maksim opened a command line prompt. A black window with white text appeared.

"A knock sequence? For a swat?"

"Unless you have a burner phone." Maksim raised a questioning eyebrow.

"I had one. That's what I used to swat the boy from my school. But I threw the mobile away." Mihai hesitated. *"I wasn't anywhere near here when I made the call, sir. To be extra safe."*

Maksim rolled his eyes. At least the kid hadn't been dumb enough to make the call from his apartment. *"I need you to promise me you will never try to emulate what I'm about to do. It's a cybercrime punishable by many years in prison."* Maksim tapped out the first command, accessing the Linux side of Mihai's system.

"What exactly will you do?"

"I'm going to call the police from your computer using a backdoor into RoCom. I'll do it in such a way that the call can't be traced here."

Mihai's breath caught. *"You know of a backdoor into RoCom?"* RoCom was Romania's main telecommunications provider.

Their system had some of the most advanced security, and Mihai's reaction landed with equal parts concern and admiration. *"How did you find a backdoor into their network? Where?"*

"I didn't find it. I created it."

Mihai's already wide features doubled in size. *"Ceeee?"* (Whaaaat?)

"A year ago, I breached one of their routers using a server attack and a poison DNS re-direct. I wasn't stealing anything or delivering a malicious payload," Maksim added when Mihai grabbed his head. *"I never did anything with the backdoor. It was a precaution in case of an emergency. Something like what I'm facing today."*

"So you left the backdoor open."

"Quietly, yes, while keeping it hidden with the knock sequence. When I go to those ports — in a certain order, without logging in — the firewall will temporarily open a designated port. That's the way I set it up, so that only I can gain access. Like being let into a speakeasy by knowing the secret knock."

"Or a hidden door disguised as a bookshelf. When you pull the correct books, the door opens." The sides of Mihai's mouth curled up. *"The knock sequence gives you access while keeping the backdoor invisible to anyone else looking for a way in!"*

"Precisely, but it won't be invisible after today." Maksim flexed his fingers. *"Accessing it will signal to RoCom's cybersecurity team that there's been a breach. Standard operating procedure will be to take down the compromised router — I just hope they don't do it before SIAS arrives."* Maksim was referring to Romania's version of SWAT. *"I have one shot at accomplishing this,"* he continued. *"Then I lose access."*

Mihai's expression softened. *"And you're doing all this so the call won't be traced here? To me and my parents?"*

"Exact." (Exactly.)

Mihai set his jaw. A look of resolve overshadowed his hesitation. *"What do you need me to do, sir? Tell me."*

Maksim glanced at a game controller. *"Do you have any first-person-shooter games?"*

"Yes, sir. Many."

"Choose one that's realistic. The most realistic you have. Go into the settings and mute the music. We need to hear only gunfire. A lot of it."

Mihai grabbed his controller and exited out of a puzzle game he'd been playing.

Maksim began the knock sequence, which consisted of four ports reserved for common service providers. A welcome banner appeared each time, followed by a prompt for entering credentials. Maksim ignored the prompts and continued through the sequence.

When he finished, he logged into a double VPN and used a Linux WGIT command to download a specially patched version of an open-source VoIP client. This particular software would work with his backdoor to emulate a phone.

A stream of machine-gun fire blasted from Mihai's TV. *"I think this is my most realistic game,"* the boy said.

Maksim's attention shot to a speaker mounted in the corner. *"Switch to the stereo. Crank the volume."*

Mihai did so, and the volume increased.

"More," Maksim said.

The gunfire ramped up to painfully high levels.

"Is that the phone you will use?" Mihai shouted the question, attention shifting to his computer. A user interface with a telephone-style number pad filled the screen—just one more modification Maksim had made to the VoIP client.

He'd made other modifications as well, the most important being a voice modulator that made him sound like an elderly woman. That part was going to be critical, and Maksim now wished he'd done more testing on that particular feature. If there existed even a shred of error in his code, his real voice would be heard and recorded.

"I'm ready when you are." Mihai returned to the main menu in his game, and the gunfire ceased. *"What will you say if the*

dispatcher doesn't believe you? What if they perceive it's not real gunfire?"

"We won't know if they do or don't." Maksim hovered his pointer over the dial pad. *"This is going to be a one-way phone call. The dispatcher will hear us, but we won't be able to hear them."*

A stunned expression broke across Mihai's face. He rocked back, as if knocked off balance. *"How will we know if they're hearing the gunfire?"*

"We won't," Maksim said flatly. *"All we can do is hope."*

Mihai blinked away his shock and went into the audio settings. *"We should do a mic check."* He tinkered with the levels, speaking vocal cues, and the testing bar responded. *"Mic is good."*

"All right." Maksim inhaled slowly. *"Ready?"*

Mihai nodded.

"Go."

Gunfire blasted through the speakers in Mihai's room. Maksim used the mouse to dial 112—Europe's version of 911—via the on-screen keypad. Since the call was one way, they had no way to know if and when the call had been answered, what the person might be saying…

It was all guesswork.

Maksim shaped his fingers into a pistol and made like he was pulling a trigger. Keep shooting. That was the message.

Mihai complied while Maksim spouted off cries for help in Romanian. He pleaded with the dispatcher he *hoped* was listening and repeated the address many times over—but he did not provide the address for this building. Instead he gave the address for the building next door, the building where Vladimir's men—the overwatch and likely a sniper as well—lay in wait.

Maksim gave a loud, terrifying shriek. *"They are dead! My neighbors, everyone, they are dead!"* He held up a single finger to Mihai.

The boy ceased firing in his game.

Maksim panted into the phone, muttering in Romanian. *"I am hiding in my apartment. The man who did this is on the eighth floor. Hurry, please. I am afraid he saw me."* Guilt grated at him—like digesting a stomach full of gravel. He despised having to do this, but his go-bag was his lifeline. There was no way to disappear without it, no way to escape Vladimir's long-reaching tentacles.

Maksim couldn't tolerate this charade a second longer. He pleaded once more, hoping to God a dispatcher really had answered, and then disconnected the call.

Mihai shut down his game. *"What now?"*

"We wait and watch."

"Watch?" Mihai shook his head. *"How would we—?"* He gasped. *"The building's camera system!"*

Maksim stepped aside. *"You know what to do."*

Mihai cracked his knuckles and parked himself in the chair. His fingers flashed across the keyboard as he pulled up Telnet—exactly the way Maksim had—and used it to access another backdoor.

Their landlord was a cheap man, always making excuses for why he couldn't buy new cameras. When Maksim had asked about software updates, the man had responded with something like, "What software updates?"

Maksim realized the system was vulnerable to attack, and that created a security issue—for the tenants in the building, yes, but especially for Maksim. He'd offered to update the system and had inserted a backdoor during the process, giving himself a way to check the cameras whenever he wanted.

He'd then used the system to teach Mihai about cybersecurity and antisecurity. The kid knew how to access the backdoor, and he was now in charge of installing the updates.

Camera one appeared on Mihai's screen.

Maksim leaned in. *"It's live?"*

"There's a ten-second delay ever since the last update rolled out."

Camera One showed the side of the building. The lens

pointed down—toward the side entrance—and Maksim couldn't see the building next door.

"Go to camera two."

Mihai typed the command. This feed showed the opposite side of the building. There was no entrance. Just the meter, the recycling bins, and a walkway that led to the front. People used that walkway to bring their recycled items throughout the week.

"Camera three?" Maksim asked.

This feed showed the front entrance, but the camera angle didn't reveal much. Just the door and a sliver of the walkway.

Maksim wiped a hand down his face. *"Tell me you have access to the other camera, Mihai."*

"You have access to the other camera, Mihai." Mihai inserted a cheeky tone, echoing Maksim, and pulled up camera four. This feed streamed from inside the mailbox area, but it was angled in such a way that the video captured the entrance, the walkway, *and* the cars parked across the street.

Those cars were distant. But they were visible.

"That's them." Maksim tapped the screen, pointing out the Mercedes and the Yugo. *"The men are in those vehicles."*

Mihai squinted, trying to see the images, and worry cast a shadow across his features. *"Mr. Răzvan? I think we have a problem."*

Maksim leaned in for a closer look. He immediately felt the color drain from his face.

A man had exited the Yugo, leaving the door ajar, and was making his way to the building. Had they realized something was afoot? Surely the men had been wondering why the "delivery person" hadn't returned.

The man pressed his face to the glass, peering inside. Maksim swore.

"Can he get into the building?" Mihai looked at Maksim. *"Mr. Răzvan?"*

"I… don't know."

"What if our call didn't work? What if the dispatcher didn't believe

it was a real shooting?" Mihai's face paled. *"What if the SIAS doesn't come?"*

Maksim had no answers, only hope... and the last little bit faded when he remembered the ten-second delay. That man might have already entered the building. They all could have.

Regret choked Maksim. He shouldn't have come here. He'd placed this family in danger.

"I'm going to my apartment." He squatted beside Mihai. *"Whatever happens, whatever you hear, do not leave this room."*

"Sir—"

"Forgive me for coming here, Mihai, for involving your family." Maksim stood and crossed the room. *"I'll do what I can to ensure you remain safe."*

"But... Mr. Răzvan, look!"

Maksim returned his attention to the television. What he saw made him pause. The man was still standing at the entrance, but his attention had shifted toward the street.

Movement stemmed from the Yugo. A second man had stepped out of the car and was waving manically. The man at the entrance cupped his mouth, appearing to call out.

"I wish we had audio." Mihai zoomed in. *"I can't read their lips either, and I want to know what they're saying."*

A laugh no bigger than a puff of air escaped from Maksim. *"The police are coming."*

"They are?" Mihai's attention snapped toward Maksim. *"How do you know?"*

"Pay attention to the man by the Yugo." Maksim pointed. *"He's waving at his partner, beckoning him. Now he's pointing down the street. Either he sees police lights or hears their sirens."*

"You really think—" Mihai's response broke off as distant sirens seeped into the quiet room. His features widened. *"It worked!"*

Maksim and Mihai watched as the man sprinted to the Yugo. Meanwhile, the Mercedes whipped onto the road and bolted down the street. The Yugo followed five seconds later.

The sirens grew louder as Maksim rested a grateful hand on Mihai's shoulder. Mihai peered up at his mentor. *"We did it, Mr. Răzvan."*

"Yes, we did. Thank you, Mihai." His attention wandered to the doorway. *"I must go. For your own safety, you cannot tell anyone about any of this. Find a rag. Wipe down your keyboard, your chair, anything I came into contact with. I'll take the faux parcels with me. We need to make it look like I was never here."*

Mihai jumped up, ready for action, but then hesitated. *"Uh, sir? Could you please not forget about the bitcoin? I really want to buy a new gaming rig."*

CHAPTER SIX

MAKSIM WOUND his way up the stairwell. He carried the remaining fake parcels, watching for anything out of the ordinary.

He rounded the sixth floor. Then the seventh. Sweat soaked his head as he reached the eighth. The door that stood between the stairwell and the hallway appeared before him. He levered the latch, tugged, and peered through the opening.

Apartment doors spanned the hallway. At the far end, a large window overlooked the street below. Sunlight warmed his neck as he entered the hall and started toward his apartment.

He moved at a fast clip. Many of his neighbors were at work, but not all of them. Housewives and remote workers would soon trickle out of their apartments, wondering about the sirens. Maksim couldn't risk an encounter while dressed like a phony postal worker.

He dug out his key, jimmied it in the handle, and twisted. On the second rotation, the lock disengaged. He held his breath, readying himself for whatever waited on the other side of this door. More of Vladimir's men? Or perhaps…

He tensed. Perhaps the door had been rigged with explosives. That kind of thing would draw more attention than

Vladimir usually preferred, but he'd done it before, and these were extenuating circumstances. The moment Vladimir learned of Ștefan's death—the death of his only son—the man would be capable of anything.

Maksim levered the handle and paused, waiting for a click, a tick, a ping, or anything else that might precede an explosion. He registered nothing and opened the door a crack. Again he went static, listening. If anyone was inside, they were certainly being quiet.

"*...they sound like police sirens. I will try to discover what is happening.*" The male voice, muffled by a door, stemmed from down the hall.

Another voice, this one female, responded. "*There could be a fire. Ask the little grandmother on the second floor, will you? She knows everything.*"

"*She is visiting her children in Iași these days. I will discover who is home at this hour.*"

The voices belonged to Maksim's neighbor, Radu, and the man's wife. Maksim ducked inside his apartment and listened as Radu began to knock on one neighbor's door and then another.

Maksim's awareness jerked to the space around him. He pivoted, observing his surroundings. The living room had been ransacked. Gashes marred his couch, the cushions tossed, stuffing strewn into patches of synthetic snow.

And the blinds. They'd been torn from every window, giving the overwatch a clear line of sight into Maksim's place. If any snipers had taken up position on the roof, they too had a clear line of sight.

Maksim dropped to the floor and high-crawled over books, paperwork, stuffing, other miscellaneous items. The whir of an engine grabbed his attention. A helicopter approached, the blades circulating in a steady rhythm.

Maksim high-crawled to the nearest window and peeked out. A sleek black helicopter drew close to the building next door. If there really had been a sniper, the person had very likely aborted the mission.

No longer feeling the need to crawl, Maksim pushed up and entered his bedroom. He went to his closet first. Clothes had been pulled down. His shoe rack had been tossed. Hat and belt boxes lay open, and all of his cufflinks had been stolen. But he didn't care about any of that. He didn't even mind the incisions in the floor—knife marks from where the men had been checking for loose boards.

They'd been searching hard, looking for anything that might be valuable to them or their boss.

Maksim slid a hand over the top shelf. His fingers brushed leather, and he took hold of an empty duffel. He would have grabbed one of his spare laptops, but Vladimir's men had confiscated them.

He grabbed whatever clothing he could, ensuring his picks were practical and versatile, and stuffed all but one of the outfits into the duffel. He shed the phony uniform and changed into a classic button-down and chinos. He kept the cap, which could prove useful, and tossed it into his bag.

Now for the kitchen. He was headed that way when a knock at the front door halted him. He stilled himself.

"Răzvan?" Another knock. *"Are you home?"*

The voice belonged to Radu—but Maksim's relief evaporated as he watched the door handle begin to turn. His neighbor was letting himself in.

Maksim dropped his duffel and dashed forward. The door was open wide enough for a small child to fit through before he reached the entryway. *"I'm here."* Maksim thrust himself in front of the door, using his foot as a stopper. *"Radu, my friend. How are you?"* Maksim forced a smile. *"How may I help you?"*

Radu seemed disappointed, though not entirely surprised. He'd been dropping hints that he wanted to see Maksim's place, but Maksim never permitted anyone, especially neighbors, to enter his apartment. Only occasionally did he enter theirs. It was a small boundary, but an important one due to his profession.

Former profession. Soon-to-be former. If he could get the hell out of here.

"Something bad is happening," Radu said. *"In the neighborhood."*

"I heard, yes. The sirens." Maksim redirected his attention to something inside his apartment. He held up a finger, as if telling someone to wait, and then re-attuned himself to Radu. *"I have to be honest with you, friend."* Maksim poked his head outside a little more. *"I'm, uh, entertaining a guest."*

Radu maintained a blank stare.

"She's a friend." Maksim arched an eyebrow. *"We've been… busy."* He pushed the eyebrow higher.

The insinuation, false though it was, finally computed in Radu's brain. *"Ohhh. I see."* The man nodded. *"My wife wants to know about the sirens. She is concerned about a fire."* Radu turned toward the elevators. *"I will go down and try to discover the answer. Perhaps the police will speak with me."*

"No!"

Radu wheeled around. His expression turned quizzical.

"That's not a good idea because… what if it's not a fire?" Maksim feigned a blasé shrug. *"There could be another type of danger. Perhaps a robbery. An escaped convict."*

Radu drew back. *"You think this is possible in Pipera?"*

"I know there's no risk of a fire." Maksim flitted a hand toward the sprinklers, sirens, and flashing lights in the hallway. *"This system would sound the alarm at the slightest detection of smoke or embers."*

"But—"

"I will go investigate and report my findings to you." Before Radu could argue, Maksim added, *"You had knee surgery last month, Radu."*

A glimmer twinkled in Radu's eyes, like the man hadn't expected Maksim to remember. *"I did. It's true."*

"Then please, allow me to go on your behalf." Maksim's mouth

tipped up. *"You'll be doing me a favor, helping me look like a hero in front of my date. But I'm most concerned about your knee, of course."*

"Of course!" A smile broke across Radu's face. *"Good. Okay. I'm convinced."* The man angled toward his apartment. *"Do you promise to report your findings when you're finished? My friends in the building will be interested to hear the news."*

"You can count on me." Maksim glanced over his shoulder and proceeded to lower his voice. *"Allow me to explain the situation to my date. Then I'll go."*

"Thank you, Răzvan. You're a good man."

If only that were true. The guilt that had been grating at Maksim intensified. Maksim covered it up with a smile and a wink and then closed his door.

This time he locked it.

His heart thudded furiously as he snatched up his duffel. He did so with his right hand, and the sharp pain that stabbed his arm was a cruel reminder of his current state. Émilien and Drago had beaten him badly. "Tortured" might have been a better word. Maksim would need weeks, possibly months, to regain his former strength.

He switched hands, carrying the duffel with his left, and moved to the kitchen. The cabinets lay open, and one of them had been emptied. Maksim reached inside. He was searching for a nylon go-bag that contained a cache of emergency items—a Walther PPK .380, a passport, some cash, some flash drives, and a journal with bug-out plans. There was also a hardware wallet with a handwritten seed phrase and a folded-up note that read *BACK UP! DO NOT LOSE!*

Maksim would have normally detected the nylon bag with a single swipe of his hand. Today he felt nothing, and a smile touched his lips. *It worked.* The bag had been a decoy, a fairly obvious one, but the men had fallen for it.

The pistol was in poor shape mechanically. No loss there.

The passport corresponded to an identity he'd burned last year.

The bug-out plans were false, but they were detailed enough to expend a good amount of time and resources.

The cash was infinitesimal—five grand in euros—and when they restored the hardware wallet using the seed phrase he'd written down, they would get access to five thousand more. Not exactly pocket change, but significantly less than a person would need to change their identity and go into hiding. Hopefully Vladimir's men wouldn't realize this.

And then there were the flash drives…

The smile tugged harder at Maksim's lips. Those drives contained a virus courtesy of a Serbian hacker he knew. They had been made to look like they contained important information—passphrases, addresses, names, account numbers.

This would appear to be a great find, and all the while Miro's virus would be quietly burrowing into whatever system they were using. From there, Maksim would be able to collect valuable information about them, their system, their communication, even their location.

All of this would be contingent on Maksim being able to build a new rig. *That* would have to wait until Belgrade.

An authoritative voice pealed through an external PA system outside. *"We are the police. You are surrounded. Exit the building holding high your hands."*

Maksim crash-landed in the present. He needed to get out of there, or he'd be going to jail along with Vladimir's men.

His tools had apparently been confiscated, but Maksim managed to find a hammer in one of the kitchen drawers. That was all he needed.

He entered the pantry, slid out the bottom shelf, and hammered into the drywall. Dust plumed. Maksim held his breath as the drywall disintegrated under his blows.

A moment later, he was yanking out a garbage bag that contained the cache he'd come here for…

A Glock 19 with two full mags.

Two flip-style burner phones and one smartphone he'd set up to work as a burner.

His Romanian passport—not one he could use anymore, but not one he could leave behind either.

Two other passports with alternate identities. These alternates would be critical for accessing his safe deposit boxes.

A flash drive that held digital tools, apps, drivers, and everything else he would need to set up a new system.

Laundered cash of various denominations—about forty thousand euros in all.

He stuffed the entire trash bag into his duffel and zipped up the bag. As he reached the front door, he let his gaze linger on the apartment one more time. This place had become a refuge, a place of safety amid the chaos of his life. Now that refuge, along with his love for this city, had been blown to smithereens.

He no longer had a sanctuary. He was homeless.

Maksim closed his eyes and settled into his resolve. When he finished, he buried the sadness and walked out of his apartment for the very last time.

CHAPTER SEVEN

22:07 (10:07 PM)

NIGHTTIME RESTED ON the city as Maksim grabbed his duffel and climbed out of the taxi. He'd made his cabbie take an alternate route from București, which had helped to avoid traffic —and the police—but the journey had taken much longer due to poorly maintained roads.

This had spurred a slew of objections from the driver, but Maksim soon realized that if he passed a ten-euro note to the driver every time they hit a pothole, the man's complaining would cease. At least until the next event.

Maksim had expended most of his tens by the time he was dropped off on this shadowy side street.

STRADA DOCTOR ȘTEFAN STÂNCĂ

The cabbie rolled down his window. *"No tip?"*

Maksim responded with a sharp look.

"What? It's an earnest question." The man took in their

surroundings. His brow creased. *"Do you know where you are?"* He gestured ahead. *"This is a cemetery."*

Maksim said nothing.

"Fine, fine. It's your life." The cabbie rolled up his window and shifted into gear.

Maksim waited until he was gone before shouldering his duffel and beginning his trek. Madă's cousin lived a few streets over, but, as a precaution, he had asked to be dropped off elsewhere.

His cabbie had been harmless. Nevertheless, Maksim wasn't taking any chances.

He reached an intersection and turned right, inspecting parked cars as he went. He checked their plates and peered inside each vehicle. So far, there'd been nothing out of the ordinary. The cars he passed were empty, and they all had Sibiu plates.

His awareness heightened at the next block. He was nearing his destination, and the muscles in his back and shoulders tightened. His head turned on a swivel. He, Daniel, and Levi had asked Mircea—Madă's cousin—to show them around the neighborhood on four separate occasions.

Morning.

Afternoon.

Evening.

Late night.

Each time, Mircea had pointed out the cars he recognized and those he didn't. There'd only been four of the latter, and each time they'd been food delivery or taxis. The rest had been neighbors or someone who knew those neighbors—friends, family, colleagues. One such vehicle belonged to the mistress of a man whose wife had gone to visit her parents. *"This isn't the first time he has committed this sin,"* Mircea had explained. *"I tried to go to the man's wife, but she refused me. She could not believe what I said."*

The situation was unfortunate, but Maksim's only concern

was whether the car could belong to one of Vladimir's people. It had not, and so his worry had been assuaged.

The road widened. Maksim recognized Mircea's house ahead, but instead of veering toward the entrance, he continued up the sidewalk. As the road curved, a graffitied gate appeared on his left.

Side entrance. It belonged to Mircea's neighbor, as did the grassy area the gate opened onto, but Mircea had a decades-long friendship with the man, and Maksim had been given full permission to use this entrance whenever he wanted. There was only one caveat.

"The handle is rusted," Mircea had warned, *"and the gate is very difficult to open. This is why my neighbor doesn't use it."*

That would have defeated the gate's usefulness as a secondary exit point. So his first night, Maksim had taken a wire brush to the rusted sections—everything associated with the opening mechanism—and greased the hinges. The gate still dragged after that, so Maksim had borrowed Mircea's tools and re-tightened the hinges and screws.

Maksim paused at the gate, lifting the handle and giving a slight push. The gate opened quietly and easily, and he let himself into the grassy yard that ran between the two properties.

Darkness cloaked the neighbor's house. Mircea's house was dark as well, but a light drew Maksim's attention. Hushed voices reached him as he peered inside the kitchen window.

Daniel and Madă stood at the counter, speaking softly while an electric kettle heated. Maksim pushed out a breath. Adrenaline had been masking his pain all day, but fire suddenly smoldered in his arm.

He grimaced and gave the window a double tap. Daniel and Madă jumped.

Maksim gave a reassuring wave. *"Eu sunt."* (It's me.) He ducked beneath a clothesline and met Daniel by the laundry room.

Daniel opened the door, and Maksim slipped inside. *"Son."* Daniel took the duffel. *"We've been waiting for you."*

"I'm sorry I'm returning so late. My burner phones aren't set up, and I had no time to sort anything."

"You're safe. That's the important matter." Daniel placed a gentle hand on Maksim's shoulder. Unfortunately it was Maksim's bad shoulder, and he recoiled.

Daniel withdrew his hand. *"You have an injury."*

"Not a new one, thankfully. I didn't wear my sling today, but perhaps I should have." Maksim locked the door, and then he and Daniel crossed the laundry room.

Madă was waiting for them in the kitchen. *"Where is your sling? Do you need me to retrieve it?"*

"It's at the hospital. For now, I need a shower." He looked down at himself.

Madă's attention fell to the drywall that dusted his pants. *"Would you like me to wash those? Mircea has a new machine that washes and dries. I can have them ready by lunchtime tomorrow."*

The pain in Maksim's body fought against the smile he offered her in return. *"Thank you, but there's no hurry."* He set his duffel on the floor. *"I have multiple sets of clothes now."*

"Maksim, tell us what happened." Worry overflowed in Daniel's voice. *"Did you discover anyone at your apartment?"*

"Not inside. But Vladimir's men were watching."

Madă gasped, crossing herself. Daniel muttered a prayer.

Maksim gave a filtered account of what happened—sans any details that might have given them heart attacks.

"And how were things here? Did you notice anything unusual?"

"Nothing so far." Daniel wandered over to the kettle. *"But if anyone wants to bring harm to you, I would say Brandy is a top contender."*

"Daniel." Madă paired his name with a scolding look.

"You don't need to convince me." Maksim pushed a hand through his hair. *"Brandy blames me for what happened to Kat, and she's right. I'm to blame for all of this."*

"You are the reason Kat survived. And Levi, too." Madă joined Daniel. *"I cannot bring myself to imagine an outcome where you had not been with them."*

"Nor I." Daniel removed the kettle from its base. Bubbles surged, and he poured himself a mugful of boiling water. *"Would you like tea? The chamomile will calm your nerves and help you sleep."*

Maksim couldn't afford to take anything that would decrease his alertness, even something as mild as chamomile. *"I appreciate the offer, but I'm fine."*

"You know…" Madă took the kettle from Daniel. *"Levi shared with us everything that happened at Village Ksorba."* She sent a sidelong glance to Maksim as she filled her mug. *"He said Kat was determined to finish the treasure hunt with or without your help."*

"Without anyone's help," Daniel corrected, *"or so it seemed to Levi. He said he understood your decision to accompany Kat, because he felt the same compunction."* Daniel tugged on his teabag string, and the water began to darken. *"You all needed each other out there. If any one of you had been absent, the results would have been different. Things certainly would have ended tragically for Kat."*

Maksim looked away. *"Then why do I feel guilty?"*

"Could it be because you love her, perhaps?" Madă sang the question teasingly. Maksim's eyes flashed toward her, and she slipped into a mischievous smile.

She held up a hand—her left hand—and wiggled her fingers. Specifically her ring finger. Maksim's thoughts landed on his wallet, which rested in his back pocket. That was where he'd stored the ring. He hadn't thought of it all day.

"What I believe Madă is trying to say"—Daniel sent a warning look to his wife—*"is that we know you care for Kat. Caring is a form of love, and there's no shame in expressing it."* Daniel carried his mug to the kitchen table. *"We just don't want to see her leave without her knowing your true feelings."*

Maksim kept his thoughts to himself. He had many, specifically about this subject, but it was late, and he wasn't inclined to delve into this level of discussion. *"I badly need a shower. When I'm done, could one of you drive me to the hospital?"*

MAKSIM TREADED DOWN the staircase with his duffel in one hand and his dusty clothes in the other. A lock of wet hair flopped as he reached the bottom.

He raked his hair back, ignoring the droplets chasing down his neck and face, and handed the dirty clothes to Madă. *"Mămică."*

She brightened at the Romanian for Mom. *"Îngerașul meu,"* she said, holding a tender hand to Maksim's cheek. (My little angel.)

Maksim was no angel. Daniel and Madă were fully aware of that, but they'd never been able to have children, and they thought of Maksim as *their* little angel. As their son.

Daniel appeared with the car keys. *"Ready?"*

"I need one more thing." Maksim handed the duffel to him. *"It's in the room I was staying in before Kat's friends arrived."*

"Levi and Eugene are sharing that room. But I believe they're asleep."

"The item belongs to Kat. I plan to speak with her first thing in the morning, and I'd like to be able to give it to her."

Daniel gave a conciliatory nod. *"I'll go start the car."* He took the duffel and angled for the front door.

Shadows encased the upstairs. Maksim pressed the wall switch and light flooded the hallway. He bypassed two closed doors and eased open the third.

Snores spilled out of the room. "Levi?" he whispered, peering inside.

The room was dark, but he could make out Eugene Ballerini on the left side of the room. Levi occupied the bed on the right. Both men appeared to be asleep.

Maksim slipped inside. His boot collided with something on the floor, and a disgruntled moan followed.

Maksim opened the door wider. As the hallway light stretched deeper into the room, he found Brady Ballerini—Brandy's younger brother—sleeping on the floor. Surprise flickered through Maksim. The boy was supposed to be sleeping in the basement guest room.

Brady sat up.

"Sorry to wake you." Maksim squatted. "I need to get something."

Brady grabbed his pillow and blanket and scooted over. Maksim whispered a "thank you" and stepped past him.

The room was wide enough for two single beds with a nightstand in between. The nightstand held a pair of glasses, a cell phone, and a wallet—likely Eugene's since they were on the left side. Maksim set everything on the floor, along with the lamp, and eased the nightstand away from the wall.

He lifted. The table tipped back, and he reached underneath. His fingers connected with dented metal.

He grabbed the lockbox and then re-lowered the table. The snoring behind him tapered off as he replaced Eugene's personals and the lamp.

"Good morning. Or should I say 'good evening'?"

Maksim turned. Levi lay on his side, his eyes brightening under the hallway light.

"How was your time in București?" he asked in Romanian. *"Did you find any trouble?"*

"Not too much." Maksim forced a smile. *"Forgive me for the intrusion. I'm going to the hospital, and I need the lockbox."*

"You will deliver the item to Kat?"

"Exactly."

"Well, then," Levi whispered, switching to English. "You won't want to forget this." He turned away and fidgeted with something.

A grunt drew Maksim's attention to Brady, who was leaning against his father's bed. "Almost finished," Maksim said.

The kid huffed a sigh.

"Here. Take this." Levi rolled over, hand extended, and Maksim accepted a wooden cross with a tiny Christ figurine. The crucifix hung from a familiar leather cord.

"This belonged to Kat's father," Maksim whispered.

"Indeed." Levi settled against his pillow. "Will you tell her the story I shared with you? How the crucifix had once belonged to her grandmother?"

"I will. Certainly."

Levi offered up a sleepy smile and returned to their native language. *"Pa. Noapte bună."* (Bye. Good night.)

"Pa pa." Maksim stuffed the crucifix in his pocket. As he passed Brady, he made sure to ruffle the boy's hair. "Tell your father I'm sorry for moving his things."

"It's fine," Eugene Ballerini mumbled from the bed. "Don't worry about it."

"Thank you, sir. Pardon the disturbance."

Mr. Ballerini waved him off. Brady reclaimed his spot on the floor as Maksim left.

———

THE HOSPITAL WASN'T FAR from Mircea's. Then again, nothing was far. Sibiu was a small city, quaint, with cobblestone streets and Medieval architecture. By that time of night, the roads were clear and the drive was quiet.

"Did you find everything you needed?" Daniel asked, glancing at the duffel. *"From your apartment?"*

"All that I could have expected to find."

"And you don't need me to hold anything for you?" Daniel flagged him with an eyebrow, making it clear he'd meant any illicit items.

"I wish I could let you have everything. It's a lot to carry, and my shoulder is sore." Maksim unbuckled his seatbelt as the car rolled to a stop. *"But this is my go-bag, and I need it with me in case..."*

"In case something bad happens," Daniel finished for him.

"Yes." Maksim hoped like hell nothing went sideways, but if it did, he needed everything with him. *"This duffel contains the bare minimum I would need to survive."*

"I understand." Daniel pressed the unlock button, and the doors disengaged. *"There's a security guard who stands watch at night. I'm sure you remember. What will you do if he wants to search your bag?"*

The Glock wasn't Maksim's only concern. The duffel contained forty thousand euros, three burner phones, and three passports with three different identities. That was more than enough to warrant a phone call to the police.

"I suppose I'll have to socially engineer my way out of the situation." Maksim conjured up a reassuring smile. *"Pray for me."*

"Madă and I both will."

An unarmed security guard stood by the reception desk, speaking with a lady in scrubs. Maksim didn't recognize the woman from Kat's unit, but nurses throughout the hospital took turns manning this desk at night.

The security guard broke away from the conversation when Maksim entered. The man's gaze flicked to the duffel, and he held up a finger as if to tell Maksim to wait.

"Good evening." Maksim polished his smile and turned his attention to the redhead in the scrubs. *"Hi, how are you? It's good to see you again."* He blanketed his greeting in warmth and added a double dose of familiarity.

Confusion blossomed in her expression while a hint of pink dusted her cheeks. *"I am well, sir, thank you. How are you?"*

"I'm well, thanks. Did you see Dr. Rhyland today?" Maksim leaned against the counter. *"I arrived early this morning, but I didn't find her."*

Understanding overshadowed her confusion. *"Oh, the American doctor."* Her mouth stretched wide. *"You're her special patient, aren't you?"*

"That's me." Maksim directed his smile to the security guard. *"Dr. Rhyland has made special arrangements for me, since my physical therapy is early in the morning. She has me doing oxygen treatments, and I'm sharing the chamber with another patient—"*

"Yes, yes, yes." The woman flitted a hand, dismissing the explanation. *"You're staying at that floor. We know all about it."*

The security guard *didn't* appear to know about it, based on his bewildered expression, but he didn't contradict the woman.

"It's so nice to finally meet you," the nurse said. *"I am working the overnight shift, so perhaps I will see you again soon."*

"I hope so." Maksim held fast to the smile. The response was a bit flirtatious, but he needed to ensure the guard wouldn't intervene.

He didn't, and as the nurse blushed, Maksim turned and continued through the lobby. The elevator came into view, but he aimed for the stairwell. He wanted to be sure none of Vladimir's men were lurking about, and taking the stairs wouldn't leave him boxed in the way an elevator would.

He began his ascent…

First floor, clear.

Second floor, clear.

Third floor… He nudged open the door that led to the third floor. Bright lights filled the hallway. He registered white noise, but nothing unusual. The stairwell and hallway were clear.

He entered the hall and turned left, trekking for the main hallway. The white noise grew louder—typing, beeps, a phone ringing. Voices sprinkled the mix, but they were soft and few.

Whatever switch existed in Maksim, enabling him to go from engaged and cautious to totally relaxed, activated. He was in social engineering mode again.

You've seen me. You know me. I'm not a threat. This is just a bag with clothes, nothing illicit, not suspicious. The thought expanded from deep within him until a bright smile—but not too bright, because normal people weren't perky at this late hour—shined across his face.

He passed the *postul de asistente* (nurses' post) and took note of the staff. One nurse sat at a computer while taking a phone call. Another with sleek blond hair stood nearby.

The blonde looked up from her clipboard. Her attention shifted to Maksim. He sweetened his smile, tilted his head, and let that same familiarity he'd expressed to the other woman seep through. *"Oh, good evening. How are you tonight?"*

"I'm well, thank you." She matched his sense of familiarity, a smile shining through in her eyes. *"Are you staying the night again, sir?"*

Perfect. She already remembered him.

"I am, and with proper sleep clothes this time." He lifted the duffel as if to show the woman. *"Don't worry. I never wear anything too revealing to bed."* He added a wink, and the nurse giggled.

She didn't give the duffel a second glance.

Maksim headed for the physical therapy room. Dr. Rhyland had arranged for him to stay there, which was ideal since it was on the same floor as the oxygen chamber—and the same floor as Kat's private room—and there'd been plenty of space to set up a cot.

He hit the lights and closed himself in the room. A special treadmill attached to a heart monitor sat against the far wall. Other PT stations were scattered about the area.

Maksim crossed the room and stopped in front of the lockers. These weren't full size. They were shorter, only reaching to waist level, and a supply shelf with bandages, wraps, and braces had been installed across the tops.

Maksim moved the medical supplies and set his duffel on the shelf. He pulled out an undershirt, navy tracksuit pants, fresh socks, and his trainers—his sleep clothes for the night. The undershirt was sleeveless, leaving his arms exposed, but nighttime was the only time his old scars had a chance to breathe.

His pale, crinkly skin, which spanned shoulder to elbow on his right arm, drew far too much attention. In order to avoid the usual gasps and stares, he would need to get inside Kat's room stealthily, without encountering any nurses or doctors.

He folded the rest of his clothes into neat stacks and placed them inside one of the lockers. Hiding forty thousand euros wasn't the easiest task before him, but he managed to do it, breaking up the bundles into smaller, flatter groups and tucking them between the clothes. He did the same with his hardware wallet, the burner phones, his passports…

He was about to add the crucifix when he remembered the ring.

Maksim pulled out his wallet, its leather scuffed and scratched after the incident at Village Ksorba. He'd been blown up, beaten up, and very nearly killed; and if that hadn't been bad enough, someone had then stolen his cash before Levi could gather their belongings.

The wallet had stayed that way—empty, useless—until Madă gave him the ring she'd been alluding to. It was the centerpiece of her grandmother's jewelry collection, and it had been buried in their garden for decades—ever since the communists took control of Eastern Europe after World War II. The courts restored the property to Madă's family only five years ago, and Daniel had managed to dig up the jewelry based on instructions passed down through Madă's mother.

Maksim retrieved the ring and held it up. The overhead lights broke across the sapphire solitaire, casting a glossy shine each time Maksim turned the ring. The halo of diamonds glimmered. After the Village Ksorba excursion had gone sideways, Daniel and Madă insisted on driving to Sibiu to be with Maksim and Levi. Moments prior to their departure, Madă had felt compelled to bring the ring. *"Don't worry for Kat,"* she'd said upon their arrival. *"I had a dream. Everything will be okay."*

Kat had been wearing the ring in this dream, and everyone had clung to the hope that it meant she would survive. She had, but now Maksim didn't know what to do with the precious piece of jewelry. There was no casual way to give her something like this.

He tucked the ring into its hiding place and slipped his wallet and the crucifix under a stack of neatly folded clothes. Everything else, including his duffel, went into the second locker. He locked both doors, stuffed the keys into his pocket, and gathered his pillow and medical sling.

Time for phase two.

CHAPTER
NINE

THE NURSE he'd conversed with had disappeared by the time he walked out of the room. The other staff, including a doctor, didn't notice him. Precisely the way he preferred it.

Maksim let himself into Kat's room. She didn't stir even as the hallway light followed him in. This space was smaller than the PT room, but since he couldn't turn on the overhead lights, he did a perimeter sweep, checking her bathroom, then walking the room's exterior.

There were no hostiles lurking in the shadows, no one tucked away in a corner. *Kat's room, clear.* He exhaled his tension. Kat was safe, but how long would she stay that way? How long before Vladimir learned she was there? Maksim and Kat were responsible for the death of Vladimir's son, Ștefan, and Vladimir was going to be set on vengeance.

The thought of Ștefan unwrapped a secret, hidden pain in Maksim. He hadn't let himself think about what happened at Village Ksorba... and he couldn't now. That would have to wait until Kat went home. After she was out of Vladimir's reach.

Maksim settled into the visitor's chair. The cot would have been more comfortable, and he'd considered setting it up in here, but he hadn't wanted to draw more attention than necessary.

Further, he hadn't wanted Kat to know he'd been guarding her so closely. She needed to focus on getting well rather than existential threats that may or may not be imminent.

For the time being, Maksim had decided to keep his presence low key. He gripped the chair handle and tugged. The leg rest lifted while the back reclined.

That might have been a generous description, actually. The chair reclined about as much as an airplane seat.

Maksim pushed away his discomfort and situated his arm in the medical sling. The strap went over his head, and his forearm rested on his torso. This was the most painful part of the day, the time when his body attempted to heal the damage done by Ștefan's crew.

Ștefan. Why did Maksim keep thinking of him? He never allowed himself to become distracted by physical pain, and he couldn't become distracted by emotional pain either.

Maksim tucked the pillow under his head and focused on the sounds around him…

The hum of white noise that stemmed from the nurses' station.

Kat's breathing—soft, steady—coming from the bed.

His own breaths, which began to quiet as his adrenaline settled.

The rhythm of his heart…

The thump of his pulse…

He settled into the sounds until they became something of a song in the background. Just the other day, he would have heard the beep of Kat's heart monitor, but she'd been taken off that machine. Her IV drip had been removed as well.

She was in observation status now, likely to be released soon. As Brandy had already mentioned.

Maksim sank into the thought. Kat would be gone soon. Would he ever see her again? Speak to her? Even if he called or emailed from time to time, in what capacity would he be doing so? As a friend? He couldn't be more than that. Not realistically.

A dull ache accompanied the thoughts. He cleared his mind and tried to focus on the present. That helped with the emotional turmoil, but the pain in his arm persisted, developing into a throb that grew sharp and tingly. The medical sling helped take a load off his shoulder, but it did nothing for the rich, colorful pain wailing in his biceps, triceps, joints, and tendons.

He swore under his breath. Everything hurt, and his scars—the nerve damage he had because of them—amplified the pain. *Focal point. Find a focal point.* He closed his eyes, pushed out a breath, and began to run through worst-case scenarios—ambushes, sneak attacks, a kidnapping, an assassination attempt. What maneuvers would he need to execute in each scenario? Where would he need to go?

Three meters to the door. Ten more meters to the PT room.

Four seconds to get inside. Another five to open the locker. Plus seven to draw the pistol, seat the mag, and chamber the first round.

Allow for possibility of adrenaline rush—tachycardia, shakes, tunnel vision, sweaty palms.

Account for enemy combatants, weapons, lethality.

Account for innocents—nurses, patients, their last-known whereabouts, the third-floor layout, alternative exits…

The mental rehearsal brought a level of comfort to Maksim, and he found himself relaxing. Sleep overtook him.

———

*M*AKSIM *GASPED, water running down his face. He tried to sit up. A rope held him in place.*

He was lying down. Why was he lying down?

He shook his head, blinking, gasping hard for air. Ștefan came into view first. He had tipped Maksim's chair back and was holding it so that Maksim was at an incline.

Ștefan's stare remained bland, almost blank. Maksim opened his mouth, intending to ask—no, beg—his cousin to lift the chair.

Vladimir appeared, his frigid blue eyes spearing into his nephew's. "Again," he said matter-of-factly.

Maksim's twelve-year-old heart exploded into a gallop. He didn't understand the physical feelings that struck him, but he would later learn these symptoms—the shallow breathing, the uncontrollable shaking—were all part of an adrenaline spike.

He didn't yet know how to take control of his respiratory system, and this caused him to panic even more. His expression grew wide. He divided a horrified look between his uncle and his cousin.

Before he could speak, a hand—with a dense rag—covered his mouth and nose. Maksim jerked his head from side to side, trying to pull one more breath as cool water began to pour. The rag was already saturated and quickly formed a seal. Maksim attempted to do what he'd been taught—focus on his escape plan, visualize everything he needed to do.

He only managed to do that for about ten seconds, until his lungs burned and his throat closed. Breathe. I need to breathe. *But he couldn't.*

He convulsed, gagging. Darkness bled into his vision. His thoughts blurred.

The water stopped. The rag lifted, and Maksim's chair righted. He gasped, still gagging and now coughing violently as well.

"You are weak," his uncle said. "How can I trust you when you will break under the slightest pressure?"

The rope dug into Maksim's arms and chest. He gulped air, his lungs desperate for oxygen. A mix of water and vomit spilled from his mouth, rendering him unable to answer. What would he say anyway? He had no response.

His uncle gave a disgusted shake of his head. "Again."

Ştefan flicked a look to Maksim. "Father—"

"Again." Vladimir stepped forward, asserting himself.

Ştefan was Vladimir's biological son, and at twenty-two he was a man, not a boy. But he wasn't nearly as imposing as his father, and he instinctively shrank back.

Vladimir raised his large hand—a threat, but not against Ștefan—and brought it crashing into Maksim's face.

Maksim cried out.

The hand collided again. This time it was a fist. Fire burned in Maksim's jaw and spread to the bone beneath his eye. The punches moved to Maksim's torso, expelling any remaining breath from him.

"Weak!" More punches. "You will never survive under duress." He finished with a hard blow between Maksim's ribs.

Maksim opened his mouth, and a river of vomit flowed.

"Waterboard him again." Vladimir was speaking to Ștefan. "Do not make me repeat myself."

Maksim coughed and wretched every last bit of fluid in his stomach. Then he felt his chair tip back. Horror filled him. "No! Uncle, please!"

The rag came down, and the water poured. He gurgled a scream.

JOI, 13 IUNIE, 05:57 (THURSDAY, JUNE 13, 5:57 AM)

Maksim jolted awake. The first hints of dawn appeared, illuminating a tree outside Kat's window. Birds fluttered and chirped.

He turned and discovered the door ajar. One of the nurses had likely stopped in, checking on Kat. That was normal, but Maksim should have heard the movement. The fact that he hadn't startled him.

He gripped the chair handle and returned his makeshift bed to the upright position. Then he stood and made his way out of the room. An influx of light blinded him in the hall.

He carried his pillow, still wearing the sling, and cast a sleepy look toward the nurses' station. New faces had replaced the ones from last night; though, he did recognize the blonde entering a patient's room.

Nightshift was finishing up. Dayshift would be taking over soon.

He closed himself inside his makeshift room and re-opened the cabinet. Nothing appeared to be out of place. He moved his boots and found the pistol precisely where he'd left it.

He stripped off the sling, changed clothes, and sifted through his toiletries. He hadn't brought cologne, so he merely freshened his deodorant and ran a brush through his hair.

After locking the cabinet, he rolled his sleeves into neat folds at his elbows and grabbed what he needed to brush his teeth. That was about all he could manage for a morning routine. Going for a run was out of the question, and he had no way to take his usual morning shower.

"Soon," he reminded himself, envisioning his soon-to-be life —early morning runs along the Costa Brava, afternoon swims in the Mediterranean. He would have all the routines he wanted, old and new, and ample time for his body to heal…

If he could just get there.

CHAPTER
TEN

MAKSIM LET himself into Kat's room and found her turning one way, then the other. He wondered if she had always been a restless sleeper or if this was a new development. It had certainly been the case since she'd been in the hospital.

The lockbox in his hands rattled as he walked forward. Kat made a noise, almost like a soft gasp. She opened her eyes.

"Bună dimineaţa," he whispered so as not to startle her. (Good morning.)

She stiffened, clutching her thin blanket. Early morning light trickled into the room, and Maksim did his best to find a patch large enough to illuminate him. Recognition dawned across her features.

"Maksim." Kat said his name in a sleepy voice that released a flush of heat through him.

He ignored the feeling and helped her with the recline controls on her bed. An electronic hum broke the stillness as the bed raised Kat into a sitting position. Her curls, black as midnight, spilled down her shoulders and framed her delicate face. She had a litany of pillows, which would have seemed ridiculous had he not known the reason for them.

Kat's worst injury had been a shrapnel strike to her right shoulder blade. Lying down had been difficult for her, but the nurses had found a way to prop her up so that she could lie at an angle.

"I'm so glad you're here. I know you said you'd try to be back tonight, but—" She paused. "Honestly I wasn't sure you'd come back at all."

Maksim smiled, thinking of all the trouble he'd gone through to ensure he *would* come back. "I didn't want to risk missing you in case—" He lowered himself to her bed, keeping close to the edge.

"In case Dr. Rhyland discharged me?"

He reached over with his free hand and tucked a tendril behind her ear. "And because I've missed you, and I've wanted time to talk with you."

"I'm really sorry about Bee. She was there for all the stuff with my mom, and she's way too protective."

"That's good to hear." Maksim forced a smile. "I know you'll be in good hands when you go home." The statement crushed his windpipe.

"About that." Kat tucked her bottom lip between her teeth, a nervous habit she seemed to have. "Brandy is, um— She's booking our flights for Sunday. Early in the morning, first flight out."

If his own words had choked him, Kat's very nearly finished him off. Sunday. They were leaving on *Sunday*? What about her inheritance? Did she no longer care about retrieving that?

An army of thoughts barraged him. He refused to say them aloud and instead placed the lockbox gingerly on her lap. Another gasp followed.

"No way." She picked up the small metal box. "Where did you find it?"

"Two villagers found it. They were the ones who cared for me after I was—" He stopped short.

"Tortured?" she finished. "Maksim, I saw everything."

Maksim's thoughts trajected him into the wilderness, to the tragedies that had befallen their group, and everything within him turned cold.

He swallowed. The reaction was louder than he'd intended, and he tried to cover it up by clearing his throat. "Vadoma and her husband attempted to rally the other villagers against Ştefan. Their efforts failed, but when they heard the explosions, they made the trek to the hill themselves. Vadoma happened across the lockbox and delivered it to Levi."

Kat had many questions. They went back and forth, talking about what had happened, until finally she said, "Why are you still here? You could have taken this"—she set the lockbox aside —"and stolen the money, and I would have never known."

There had been a time where Maksim might have been capable of such a heinous act, but now? He could never.

No, Maksim had accompanied Kat to Village Ksorba because… why? The answer fluttered outside his reach until Daniel's voice broke through. *Caring is a form of love.*

Maksim cared for Kat. That was why he'd gone. Certainly not because of the lockbox.

"I have plenty of money," he said matter-of-factly. "I simply won't have access to most of it until I'm out of the country. That's what I've been hoping to discuss with you." He scooted closer. "If you desire to claim what's rightfully yours, I would be happy to escort you—and your friends—to Germany before you depart for the States. That would give me a chance to access my own funds, and it would be better—safer—than booking flights that depart from Romania."

"Wait, we're not safe? But Brandy might have already booked our flights. I-I didn't realize—"

"Shhh, it's all right." He reached for her. "I think everything will be fine," he said, caressing her cheek. "Even if she did book them."

"Are you sure?"

"Not one hundred percent, but Émilien is in police custody, and both Levi and Daniel have been contacting Interpol and following up with EU authorities. That should prevent the police from quietly or 'accidentally' releasing him."

"What about Vladimir?"

"With so much heat coming down, he will likely stay in the shadows. That's my hope, anyway, at least until we can get you home." Maksim left out a fair bit of detail. There was no sense in frightening her. Soon she would be out of Vladimir's reach, and then she would be safe.

As he considered her impending departure—not merely from his country but from his life—a deep ache mushroomed within him. He wanted her to get home safely… but he didn't want her to go.

The ache morphed into sadness. Maksim responded by leaning forward and planting a kiss on her soft, delicate cheek. Bruises speckled her face, neck—probably other parts of her body as well—but he found a clear spot that wouldn't hurt even if the kiss hadn't been so tender.

As he pulled away, he placed the crucifix in her hand and closed her fingers around it. She drew her next surprised breath and sat up straight.

"That was among our belongings," Maksim explained. "Levi discovered it at the village after you and I were taken away on the rescue chopper."

She clutched the crucifix that had once belonged to her father and gazed into Maksim's eyes. "I don't want to go home," she whispered.

His ache returned, deeper now, heavier. He covered her hand, giving a gentle, reassuring squeeze. "Vladimir's network is vast. He has too many connections in Europe."

"What if you escort me to Germany like you said, and then we could… I don't know, disappear?"

He dismissed the idea so quickly his thoughts were already transitioning. If Kat agreed to his offer, he could bypass

Belgrade, perhaps hit the cache in Paris... but how would they get there? Hitchhiking was out of the question with Kat's friends in tow. A bus would be too risky. Perhaps he could put them on a flight and meet them there...

"Not forever," Kat continued, "but maybe until... I'm not sure. All I know is that Bee and Dave—they love me, I know they do, but they don't understand what I've been through. You do. You were with me through this whole thing."

Her explanation finally took root in his mind. He straightened. She wanted to be with him. She was *asking* to be with him.

The epiphany ignited an electrical charge that originated between his ribs and ballooned outward. He withdrew his touch, startled, and directed his gaze to the window. Dawn pressed forward, painting the morning in tea rose pink, and a healthy dose of light began to pour inside the room.

What would it be like to disappear with Kat? To *be* with her? Completely, and with complete freedom. Something in him longed to know, and so he posed the first question that arose in his mind. "Where would we go?"

Silence stretched. After a moment, Kat said, "I... don't know. England? It's not part of the EU anymore, right?"

"Vladimir has too many connections in the UK." Maksim wiped a hand down his face. "Some of his operations are based in London."

"Oh."

The next blanket of silence fell. Maksim knew he shouldn't do this. It was a bad idea, just as the club had been a bad idea— but everything had worked out in the end, hadn't it? She'd been okay after all, and they knew each other more deeply in part because of what had transpired.

"Where else?" He slid a look to her. She was stunning in this light, her hospital gown emanating the same pink as the dawn that enveloped her.

Her breathing seemed to speed up at his question, her chest rising and falling beneath the gown. "Germany?" she asked quietly. "We could stay there after I claim the account in Frankfurt, maybe go to a different part of the country."

"That's not far enough. We would have to go to Western Europe and stay off the grid." Dear God, what was he saying?

"How far off the grid?" She clutched her father's crucifix. "Like, stockpiling guns and food? Or taking precautions?"

"Precautions. Many of them." His mind grew distant, his thoughts racing as he contemplated the scenario. "We couldn't use credit cards. Your friends couldn't know our location. Nobody could know, not even…" His voice trailed off.

"Levi?" Kat said.

"I was thinking of Daniel and Madă. I'll have to limit communication with them. God, they may be in danger. How would I do this?" He hadn't meant to say half of that out loud. His gaze flicked to Kat, and he detected a hint of reticence in her expression.

He shoved a hand through his hair, pushing it straight back and then raking it down. This was a bad idea. Very bad.

But then, to his utter shock, she said, "This is why we should stick together. At least until we figure things out."

Maksim's mouth slipped open. *Not a good idea. You know it's not.*

"Maksim?"

"I wish I could agree with you, *dragă*, but there is too much uncertainty." He closed his eyes and pinched the bridge of his nose. "There are things I need to do, connections I must sever, before I can be free of this life. I don't know how I could do that *and* be with you." It wasn't the full explanation, but it was the best he could manage in summary.

Worry twisted through him… and then pain as he pictured himself parting ways with her, saying goodbye, never seeing her again.

"We're in this together," she said, slipping her hand into his. Her eyes shone with hopefulness, and his emotions swelled. "You remember?"

Of course he remembered. How could he forget? She'd had the opportunity to escape when they'd been out in the wilderness, but she had refused to go. For his sake. And for Levi's.

His gaze fell to their hands before returning to her face. Her eyes sparkled like sapphires in the morning light, and whatever coldness he'd been harboring warmed another degree.

"I want to go somewhere with you," she whispered, tugging on his hand. "Anywhere."

His emotions softened. He scooted closer.

"And when the time comes for you to sever those connections you mentioned," she continued, "I'll go home. You can come visit me when you're done."

Desire overtook him—a stampede of horses running wild within him, and there was no corralling them. He leaned in, head tilted, and brushed his lips against hers. Her softness radiated, and a spark of heat tingled.

As she closed the connection, pressing their mouths together, fire engulfed him. His body longed for hers, and his mind wandered to that place—the thought of holding her, of feeling her body pressed against his. He wanted all of it. All of *her*.

But then a stray thought doused him in ice-cold water. He pulled away, breathless. "I don't wear glasses," he blurted.

Kat's eyes were partially closed, her lips searching for his. She blinked and shook her head. "What, you mean... the grandpa glasses?"

"Those and others. I use them whenever I tail someone. Then if the person sees me again, looking as I normally do, they're less likely to remember from where."

"Oh."

"Kat, I have many secrets such as this. I'm willing to bring them into the open—the ones I can—but there are certain things you can never know."

She reached out and touched his face. "Okay," she said, running her fingers over the stubble.

He sent a glance to the doorway. The bustle and buzz of the

hospital filtered into the room. "Can you slide over a bit?" he asked, refocusing on her.

She scooted over while he lowered her incline partway. Then he settled in beside her and tucked one of her many pillows beneath his head.

"Hey." She grinned. "I was using that."

"Use this." Maksim offered his arm, motioning toward the space between his shoulder and chest. Discomfort arose in this position—a painful reminder of his injuries—but he wanted to hold her. He needed to.

His pulse drummed as she settled against him. It felt incredibly natural, and he instinctively pulled her closer. "The less you know about my world, the better it will be for you. I don't want you to be entangled with the people I associate with, and I'm not sure if you would understand the things I'll be required to do."

"That might be true. I might not understand everything. But I would try. Maksim, you're worth trying for."

He tightened his hold—more than he should have, probably, but she didn't protest.

They stayed that way, entangled, talking. She had more questions, and Maksim added a heavy filter to his answers, guarding her from the things she shouldn't know, those that were too heavy for an innocent to bear. She persisted as she often did, but he quieted her with another passionate kiss.

The heat once again sparked, and they both tumbled headlong into the fire. Maksim found himself consumed, whispering to her, mumbling in his native language. He understood the words but failed to comprehend where they had come from…

"*Mi-ai furat inima.*" (You stole my heart.)

"*Mă gândesc tot timpul la tine.*" (I'm thinking about you all the time.)

"*M-am îndrăgostit de tine.*" (I fell in love with you.) His thoughts landed on the ring, and a jolt of shock hit him. His lips stopped moving.

"I don't speak Romanian," she whispered, slipping into a shy smile.

He pulled away, breaking their connection. She hadn't understood him, but he should not have spoken such strong words.

Madă's voice, teasing, ricocheted through him. *"Could it be because you love her, perhaps?"*

PART TWO

CHAPTER
ELEVEN

DUMINICĂ, 16 IUNIE, 04:34 (SUNDAY, JUNE 16, 4:34 AM)

"HOW MUCH LONGER?" Brandy asked, sounding frantic. "We're gonna to be late."

Maksim turned in time to see her check the time on her phone.

"We were supposed to—" She caught Maksim looking, and her unease narrowed to a glare. "We were *supposed* to be there eleven minutes ago," she snapped. The comment was obviously directed at him, though she rotated toward Kat, who'd been sitting quietly beside her in the back seat.

"It's okay," Kat whispered, patting her friend's leg. "I think we're almost there."

"How do you know? And how much farther?" Brandy turned toward Dave, who sat on her right. "Did you ever start the map directions?"

"Hm?" Dave plucked out an earbud, and the distant sound of hard rock streamed through the tiny speaker. "Directions?"

Brandy responded with an eye roll. "It's not a hard question, y'all." She focused on Kat. "If we're almost there, we'll probably be fine. But if the airport is thirty minutes away, we'll have to haul ass to get to our gate."

"I realize that. Maksim does, too."

"Then why won't he tell us how much farther?" Brandy shoved a hand in Maksim's direction. The fact that she wouldn't say Maksim's name did not escape him.

He did his own eye roll from the front-passenger seat and watched the stucco and wooden homes of Sibiu breeze past.

"Someone's mustard has jumped off." Mircea spoke the colloquialism in Romanian—a reference to Brandy's ire—and peeked over at Maksim. *"What does she say?"* he asked, taking them through a roundabout.

"Nothing very important." Maksim turned halfway. His attention skimmed Kat, who sat behind Mircea. Her eyes had tightened along the sides as worry blossomed in her features. "Maksim isn't from here," she was whispering to Brandy, "and Mircea doesn't speak English."

"He could *ask* Mircea how much longer," Brandy said. "He just doesn't want to."

Kat's attention shifted toward Maksim. Her expression turned into a silent plea for help.

Maksim exhaled his annoyance and focused forward. *"Mircea."* He addressed the man more loudly than necessary. Loud enough so that Brandy could hear.

Mircea divided his attention between Maksim and the road. *"Da?"*

"Cât facem până la aeroport?" How long to the airport?

Mircea took in their surroundings. He checked the time on his watch and then on the dashboard. *"If we don't hit traffic... about ten minutes."*

Maksim twisted around.

"Well?" Brandy asked, finally acknowledging Maksim in a more direct way—though she still didn't speak his name. "What'd Mircea say?"

Maksim hesitated. Then a smile played across Maksim's lips. "That we're almost there."

Brandy clenched her jaw so hard a vein in her forehead bulged. Maksim watched a furious shade of red bleed up her neck and into her face.

Kat's jaw went slack. Maksim slid a look to her and winked. Her cheeks darkened to a lovely shade of pink that suited her complexion. Her lips formed a secret smile, and she had to clear her throat to hide a small laugh.

The streets widened as they reached the outskirts of the city. Mircea had been right about the timing. They arrived at Sibiu's airport less than ten minutes later. Maksim shifted into high alert, surveying their surroundings, inspecting other cars. A cab was dropping off another passenger, and airport security sat parked out front. Apart from that, there were no other vehicles.

Daniel and Madă pulled in behind Mircea. Eugene and his son, Brady, climbed out of the back seat while Daniel retrieved their bags from the trunk. Most of the Americans had brought carry-ons. Brady was the youngest at twelve years old and had easily made do with a backpack.

Maksim ambled over to the kid. *"Hei, ursuleț."* (Hey, little bear cub.) Brady Ballerini had been Maksim's shadow the past few days—watching what Maksim did, listening to how he spoke. They'd kicked around a football—what Brady called a "soccer ball"—in Mircea's yard, and the kid had insisted on learning as much Romanian as possible.

Brady Ballerini squinted through sleepy eyelids. "Hey, Maks," he mumbled, scratching his head. "Thanks for the Romanian lessons."

"Cu plăcere. (You're welcome.) Do you remember the plan?" Maksim gave a bounce of his eyebrows. "The one I shared with you last night?"

The kid perked up and nodded.

Maksim fished out the cash he'd brought, which he'd paper-clipped into thin stacks, and handed them over to Brady, who began to dole them out. He did so precisely as Maksim had explained—in secret, without anyone noticing.

"Dad." He tugged on his father's sleeve, keeping the cash out of sight. Eugene was talking to Daniel and Madă and didn't immediately respond to his son. "Dad, can I see your wallet?"

Eugene pulled out his wallet and handed it over without question. And without looking. Brady tucked away the first thousand and returned the wallet to his father's pocket.

Brandy and Dave were next. As they said their goodbyes to Kat, the kid had no problem delivering everyone's money. Brandy's went into her purse; Dave's into his backpack. Neither of them noticed.

Maksim grinned. He'd wanted to pay for everyone's flights, but he suspected Eugene wouldn't accept the offer. This was a good workaround, and young Brady had been eager to help.

"Don't forget yours." Maksim squatted, bringing himself eye level with the kid, and handed him the last set. "Remember, you're in charge of carrying that into the airport, but it needs to go to your father after you pass through security control."

Brady groaned. "Do I have to give it to him?"

"You do, but here." Maksim reached into his wallet and pulled out a one-hundred-euro note. Brady's face lit up. "You did well. Very discreet."

"It's not as good as a thousand, I guess." Brady shrugged. "But it works."

Maksim ruffled his hair. Then he held out his hand, and they did their new secret handshake Maksim had taught him.

They finished with a fist bump as Eugene strolled up to them. "Ready, kiddo?"

Brady was all smiles as he nodded.

"Great meeting you." Eugene extended a hand to Maksim, and they shook. "Take care of Kat. She and my daughter have been friends since they were little girls, and she's family now."

"I won't let anything happen to her, sir."

Eugene's mouth parted, as if he had more to say, but he

seemed to second-guess himself and angled for the airport's entrance. "You guys ready?" he called out.

Brandy, Dave, and Kat stood in front of the revolving doors. Brandy held up a hand to wait. Maksim couldn't hear what she was saying, but he managed to read her lips.

Brandy: *"I don't trust Maksim. I think he has ulterior motives."*

Kat held a pained expression. She turned her head, looking the other direction, and Maksim couldn't read her reply.

Brandy: *"He could be playing mind games, babe. Reverse psychology."*

Kat: *"Bee, stop."*

"Why won't you listen to me?" Brandy's volume spiked. "Kat, I don't want to leave you here. Please, I'm begging you, *don't* go off with this guy. You don't even know him."

The words landed with enough force to knock Maksim back a step. The movement caught Kat's attention, and she forwarded a sincerely apologetic look to him.

Maksim swallowed everything he wanted to say, any defense or justification he may have had, and wandered over to Mircea's car.

Mircea stood at the driver's side. *"I was called into work. They have an emergency production issue."* He gripped the door handle. *"Do you think Madă and Daniel can take you to the hospital? Will you ask?"*

"I'm certain they can." Maksim hugged him. *"Thank you for driving this morning. We couldn't have carried everyone in one vehicle."*

"You're welcome. I'm happy to help." He opened his door. *"I will see you tonight."*

"Bye. See you." Maksim gave the car a friendly tap. *"Don't forget to be watching for unfamiliar vehicles."*

Mircea nodded, dropped into the driver's seat, and drove away. By the time Maksim turned around, Kat's friends were filtering into the airport. Maksim half expected Kat to be with them, but she merely watched from the sidewalk.

Brady Ballerini waved, giving Maksim a thumbs-up. *"La revedere."* (Goodbye.)

Maksim grinned and waved as Kat ambled closer. "I guess you heard that," she said softly.

"Heard what?" He held fast to the smile, though his eyes, which had tightened along the edges, likely revealed his true feelings.

Kat's expression fell. "I'm sorry. She doesn't understand."

Was Kat *sure* she wanted to go through with this? Was she absolutely certain she didn't want to be with her friends? Maksim was a breath away from asking when she slid her hands around his waist and wrapped him in a hug. He melted against her, his body conforming to hers. Suddenly, he was reminded of their rendezvous the night before. Just hours ago, really.

He had slipped downstairs around midnight, planning to check on her. She'd been fine but, like him, was restless. When he'd gone to kiss her goodnight—a tender kiss he'd intended for her cheek—their lips had discovered each other. Soon, everything else had, too.

Every part of him that had been made for every part of her… met. In the quiet of the night. In secret.

Except maybe it hadn't been so secret. Perhaps Kat had confided in Brandy about it. That would have explained the redhead's extra-fiery demeanor. But with Kat nuzzling his chest, their bodies pressed firmly together, Maksim realized he cared exponentially less about Brandy's opinion. Kat was here, with him, and that was what mattered.

Daniel cleared his throat. Maksim snapped to attention. Kat pulled away.

"Uh, Maksim?" Daniel fought a bashful grin. "We noticed Mircea left."

"He was called into work." Maksim stationed himself beside Kat and slipped his hand into hers. She maintained a shy smile that hinted at something more.

She was thinking about last night, too.

Maksim focused on Daniel. "Would you mind taking us to the hospital? We both have appointments—"

Headlights dragged his attention away. Their small group stood outside the airport, and the approaching car was headed straight for them.

Another car followed. And another. The vehicles swung into the Departures zone. Maksim registered a ride-sharing sign in the first car. The next two were traditional taxis.

"Ow." Kat winced, trying to reclaim her hand. Maksim had been squeezing and hadn't realized it.

He released her. "Sorry."

"You both have appointments?" Daniel asked, reigning in Maksim's attention.

Maksim raked at his hair. "Kat has an appointment with Dr. Rhyland, and we both have physical therapy and hyperbaric sessions."

"We can take you. Of course." Daniel moved toward his car, and they all climbed in—he and Mada in the front, Maksim and Kat in the back. "I've been wanting to ask," Daniel said as he fastened his seatbelt. "When will you leave for Germany?"

"That will depend on Dr. Rhyland." Maksim buckled himself in. "Ideally, we'll be on the road by the end of the week."

"That sounds like a good plan." Daniel smiled through his rearview. As he started the car and pulled forward, he asked, "And when will you two be joining us in Brașov?"

Kat and Maksim shared a look. Maksim thought perhaps he'd missed out on a conversation, but Kat seemed equally confused.

"Is something wrong?" Daniel rotated the steering wheel, following a bend in the road. The airport grew distant behind them.

"We aren't going to Brașov." Maksim met Daniel's gaze in the rearview. "We can't return to Romania at all. I thought you understood that."

"I did. But I assumed since Kat would be with you that—"

Daniel shook his head. "Forgive me. I was being hopeful, I suppose." Daniel tried to inject enthusiasm into the response. His voice fell flat.

"Where will you go after Germany?" Madă twisted around to face Kat. "Are you well enough to travel so much?"

"I don't think we'll be traveling a lot," Kat said. "Not after we get where we're going."

"And where is that?"

Kat looked at Maksim.

Traffic was beginning to accumulate, and Daniel struggled to maintain focus, splitting his attention between his passengers and the road. "Maksim?"

"You know I can't tell you," he said matter-of-factly.

"But that was before Kat was accompanying you. Eugene will want to know. And Kat's friends—"

"They can't know either. No one can. It's a safety issue—for us and for anyone who would know our location."

"What does this mean?" Madă switched to Romanian, directing the question to Daniel. *"Why are they not safe when we know their location?"*

Daniel answered, trying to calm his wife. Madă would not be assuaged.

"Can't you tell them the country?" Kat whispered. "The general area of Europe? Anything?"

"No. I can't. If Vladimir ever—" Maksim paused as an invisible force, something akin to a magnet, drew his attention to the rear.

A car was behind them.

Maksim faced forward, but the magnet drew him again. The car wasn't merely behind them. It seemed to be pacing them.

The hairs on his neck rose to attention. "We need to get off this road." His sharp tone slapped shackles onto the present argument, and a weighty silence descended. Everyone went still.

The first hints of dawn had appeared, though not enough to light the landscape. Traffic continued to thicken, and the other vehicles had their lights on. Daniel did as well. So did the car behind them—but that driver was using their brights.

By accident? Or intentionally?

Daniel activated his left blinker and moved into the left lane. The other driver shadowed them, and alarm bells sounded in Maksim's intuition. They had picked up a tail.

CHAPTER
TWELVE

"VEER RIGHT," Maksim said.

Daniel's gaze flicked to the rearview. "We're turning left."

"Not anymore." Maksim spotted bright lights ahead. "There. Pull into that petrol station."

Daniel activated his blinker.

"Pay attention to this guy behind us. *Without* turning around." Maksim waited, giving Daniel a chance to assess. "Well? Am I paranoid?"

"His blinker is off, but he appears to be slowing down with us." Daniel squinted. "And his high beams are on."

Maksim swore. "Park by the entrance. As close as you can get."

Madă muttered a prayer as Daniel turned in. Kat sat frozen.

The cover of darkness they'd had dissipated under the petrol station's lights. Maksim tensed, hoping the car behind them would continue on.

The driver pulled in behind them. Maksim's adrenaline cranked. "Act natural. Stay facing forward."

Nobody spoke. Nobody moved apart from Daniel, who was navigating the parking lot. A work truck was filling up at one of the pumps; a hatchback pulled away from another.

Daniel skirted the truck and made his way to the store's entrance.

"Do you see the driver?" Maksim asked. "Is it a man? What does he look like?"

Daniel checked his rearview. "His headlights are no longer blinding me, but these"—he gestured toward the station's exterior lights—"are reflecting off his windshield."

"Maksim?" Fear cascaded through Kat's features. "It's Vladimir, isn't it? He's found us."

Maksim slipped his hand into hers. "I'm here, and I won't let anything happen to you."

A tear spilled down her cheek. She sniffled, nodding.

Daniel parked at the entrance. "Kill the lights," Maksim said. "Keep the engine running."

Daniel executed to the instructions.

Maksim returned his attention to Kat. "I need you to get out of the car and enter the store. *Without* appearing panicked or worried." His gaze fell to her shorts. "As you move toward the entrance, slow down enough to dig in your pocket, but do not stop. We want the driver to see what you're doing, but I don't want you to remain exposed."

"Wh-what if he shoots me?" A tremor took hold of Kat. "Maksim—"

"He's not going to shoot you." *He's going to shoot me.* Maksim nearly spoke the thought aloud. He didn't—she was frightened enough—but he genuinely believed his assessment. Vladimir wouldn't kill Kat until he had possession of her inheritance. What he believed to be *his* inheritance. Maksim, on the other hand, served no purpose and could thus be eliminated.

Maksim rested a hand on Kat's knee. "But just to be safe, it's best to keep moving even as you search in your pocket."

"What am I searching for?" She touched her pocket. "I-I could pull something out. Someone's phone?"

"Take this." Maksim pulled out his wallet. As he opened the top, a blue and white glimmer snagged his attention.

He angled the wallet, ensuring Kat couldn't see the ring, and handed her a five and a twenty. They were euros rather than lei, but he hoped the driver wouldn't notice. "It's early, and you need coffee. That's what the cash is for. Once you're inside, pretend to browse and stay *out* of view."

"They stopped at a pump," Daniel said, sliding another peek into his rearview.

"They?" Maksim had to restrain himself. "There's more than one?"

"No. I'm sorry." Daniel cleared his throat. "No one has exited the car. I meant 'they' in the general sense."

The amendment did little to ease the pressure bearing down on Maksim.

Daniel unlocked the doors, and Kat grabbed the handle.

Maksim reached out. "Hey." His voice brought Kat's head around. Fear shone through in her blue eyes. "I'm right behind you," he whispered. "Go."

Kat grabbed the handle and pushed. The door didn't budge.

Madă stopped praying. "It is locked," she said, pressing the unlock button. At least, Maksim had assumed that was the button she'd pressed.

Kat's door remained shut and locked.

"We had this issue earlier," Daniel said. "I think the safety lock is engaged."

Maksim frowned. Before he could speak up, Daniel opened his door and climbed out. He smiled broadly—*too* broadly for five thirty in the morning—and opened Kat's door. She was visibly shaking as she stepped out. Daniel didn't seem to notice, sweeping a dramatic hand toward the store. That combined with his overly bright demeanor made the whole thing utterly unbelievable.

Maksim fought the urge to face-palm.

Kat checked her pocket as she'd been coached—but she was trembling so badly she dropped the money. Then she dropped it again. And again.

Maksim groaned. *Damn me. Devil take me.*

After what felt like an eternity, Kat entered the store and disappeared from view.

Daniel dropped into the driver's seat. He was smiling as if nothing out of the ordinary had happened. And when he discovered Maksim glaring, his expression went blank. *"Ce?"* (What?)

Maksim clenched his jaw. *"Do not exit this vehicle until I tell you it's safe to do so. Do you understand?"*

Daniel's confusion heightened. *"I should not have exited the vehicle?"*

Maksim ignored him and stepped out. The car that had followed them was an Audi A4, white, new. He could only see the side due to the way the pumps had been erected; and since the car had tinted windows, he could hardly detect the figure in the driver's seat.

He yanked out his wallet, pretending to check for cash, and wandered into the store. He didn't see Kat offhand and returned to the front.

"Are you looking for your wife?"

Maksim spun toward the clerk. *"Excuse me?"*

"Your wife? Or is she your sister?" The woman motioned toward the back of the store. *"She went to the toaletă."*

"Thank you." Maksim relaxed into a smile. *"I'll wait for her here."*

"Am înțeles." (Okay, I understand.)

Maksim pretended to browse magazines on a rack. The front door chimed, and someone entered. Maksim jolted to attention as an overweight man, middle-aged, sauntered toward him.

No. He was headed for the register. Maksim's tension rounded down when the clerk expressed familiarity. *"Did you just leave from work now?"* the woman asked.

"Yes, I'm done," the man said. *"How is your father? Is he well these days?"*

The two spoke slowly, elongating their words and singing

them together—a common trait among Transilvanians. This man couldn't be one of Vladimir's henchmen.

The thought passed through Maksim's mind the very moment he registered a crash. The clerk and cabbie halted their conversation. *"Well now, what's this about?"* the clerk asked, craning her neck.

Maksim raced to the back of the store and discovered Kat on her hands and knees, surrounded by Romanian chocolate bars. A metal display lay beside her.

"I cut the corner too fast." Her attention moved to the toppled display. "My shoulder—"

"It's all right." Maksim knelt beside her and began scooping up candy bars. "When I said stay out of sight, I didn't mean in the WC."

"I-I got nervous. I didn't know where to go." She pushed herself up and grabbed the rack. Maksim helped her, then froze when the front entrance chimed.

Kat clutched his arm. "Someone's coming in," she whispered.

He examined their surroundings. "Did you by chance see a window? Any kind of backdoor?"

"I don't know. I wasn't paying attention."

He pulled her along, believing there might be an employee entrance or break room, when a familiar voice halted them. "It's okay," Daniel called out. "Everything is okay."

Maksim snapped to attention. His eyes grew wide as Daniel hurried up the aisle. "She's a woman," Daniel said. "Nothing nefarious about her."

"I told you to stay in the—" Maksim processed what he'd heard and straightened. "She?"

Daniel nodded, and Maksim's thoughts spiraled.

"You're sure it was a woman?" Maksim demanded. "When did you see her?"

"Just now. She exited the car, and she looked normal. Like a normal person. I believe she ran over something." Daniel stooped, gathering chocolate bars. "She was checking under her car, inspecting the tires."

The way Daniel phrased his explanation resonated with Maksim in a very specific way. She *was* checking under the car. Not "is."

Maksim launched across the store. The cabbie who'd been chatting with the clerk was ambling toward the entrance. Maksim followed him out, and the bright exterior lights smacked him. Coolness hung in the air, and something else too —dread, a sense of foreboding.

The Audi was gone.

CHAPTER
THIRTEEN

06:49 (6:49 AM)

LAYERS OF PINK, yellow, and orange broke across the horizon. Birds fluttered, perching on trees and singing a sunrise melody. Maksim paced Mircea's laundry room. He was speaking with Daniel, working out a contingency plan.

His original plan had been to hit the safe deposit box in Belgrade, then he and Kat could hitchhike to Germany from there. But if Vladimir knew they were in Sibiu, he might anticipate Serbia for exfiltration.

"Let's forget Belgrade." Maksim raked at his hair. "Kat and I head south instead, through Bulgaria, and I can hit my safe deposit box in Skopje. It's a small cache, but I have another in Kotor that would be enough to supplement. So we go to Macedonia first and then swing around to Montenegro—"

"One moment... Skopje?" Daniel's arms fell at his sides. "I thought that was Arben's territory."

"It is, which is why Vladimir wouldn't expect it. We would be safe in that region."

"Safe from Vladimir," Daniel countered. "Not safe from the Albanian mafia."

Kat had been leaning against the washing machine, nervously sipping coffee. "Wait, what?" She set her mug down, splitting a wide-eyed stare between Daniel and Maksim. "The Albanian mafia?"

Maksim held up a hand. "You would be fine."

"And you?" Daniel asked.

"It's risky, all right? I admit that." Maksim dragged his fingers forward, combing his hair in the other direction. "But it may be less risky than taking a route Vladimir would—"

Movement upstairs contended for Maksim's attention. He stilled himself.

"It's Levi," Daniel assured him. "This is about the time he wakes up."

Footsteps shuffled down the stairs, and then Levi's tall form and gray hair appeared in the kitchen. He noticed their group in the laundry room and hurried to the open doorway. "I saw something. A car."

Madă gasped.

Maksim tensed, his adrenaline spiking. "Where? What did the car look like?"

"It's silver. Some type of sedan."

"Silver? Not white?"

"It looked silver to me." Levi motioned for everyone to follow him. "I was getting ready for my morning walk"— he cut through the kitchen—"when I recalled Mircea telling me about a set of urban trekking poles he has. I've not been able to look for them because they're in the room Brandy and her beau were sharing." Levi crossed into the living room and then cut right, heading up the staircase.

Maksim, Kat, Daniel, and Madă trailed him.

"When I realized their entourage was gone, I let myself into the room, intending to check the closet. As I passed the window, I looked out and saw the car."

"Did you note the license plate?" Maksim asked.

"It was too far." Levi kept the overhead light off as he entered the room and positioned himself beside the window. "There it is, just down the street. I'm certain I've never seen it before."

Nighttime evaporated under the glowing sunrise, and Maksim could easily make out the car in question. "You're right. It's silver," he said, stationing himself across from Levi. "And I've never seen it before either." He threw a glance to Daniel, who had stopped behind him. "You?"

Daniel shook his head. "Do you think it could be related to the cheating husband? He may have another mistress. Perhaps he instructed her to park somewhere different."

"A new mistress, in a new car, on a day we happened to be tailed?" Maksim flagged him with a look.

Daniel sighed. "I see your point."

"I can't tell the make or model," Levi said. "Can anyone else?"

"Škoda Superb," Maksim replied. "But that was definitely a white Audi we saw earlier."

"Earlier?" Levi blinked out a surprised look. "So this is the second unfamiliar car you've seen?"

"The second in one morning. The driver of that car was female, and she appeared to be tailing us." Maksim held a hand toward Daniel. "May I borrow your phone?"

Daniel passed him the device.

Maksim opened the camera and turned off the flash. Keeping to the side of the window, he held the phone up and zoomed in. "Red plates."

"Huh?" Kat inched forward, trying to get a look. "Like license plates?"

"Precisely." Maksim tapped the round button and the camera snapped. That was the only indication he'd taken a photo. There was no flash. He showed the photo to everyone. "Typical license plates contain black digits. These are red, which implies a special type of registration. They're usually reserved for rentals."

"Or dealer plates," Madă said. "I have seen car dealers use red plates."

"In this instance, I believe it's a rental." Maksim snapped another photo, this time of the windshield. He zoomed in on the image and pointed at white stickers. "This is where rental companies typically place their registration stickers."

"I don't remember the Audi having registration stickers." Daniel inspected the photo. "That has to mean this is someone else, yes? A rental couldn't be changed out so swiftly."

"It could, but a second tail is the more likely scenario. But why would they rent a car?" Maksim mumbled the last part, more to himself. None of Vladimir's men would have been stupid enough to rent a car.

Would they? Surely not.

"Is that… hold on." Daniel took the phone. He squinted, staring at the image on his screen. Maksim had snapped a photo of the windshield, but the driver could be seen as well. "This is her."

Maksim snapped to attention. "Who?"

"Our friend in the Škoda. It's the same woman we saw at the petrol station." He held the phone toward Madă. "Yes?"

Madă squinted, then shook her head. "I cannot see her face."

"No, but you can see her, uh…"

Everyone waited for Daniel to finish. He merely gestured toward the photo. The woman had lowered her visor, blocking any view of her face, but that did nothing to hide her physique. Maksim had to mentally brace himself to keep from staggering. He recognized the curves of her body, the leanness of her arms, the lines of her neck.

Romanian women, even those with a progressive fashion sense, were known for dressing modestly. This woman wore a skintight low-cut shirt that revealed yet another attribute Maksim recognized. His thoughts spun, landing on a single name that blew through him like a storm. *Gabriela.*

When it became clear that Daniel was referring to the driver's curvy figure—and to the low-cut top, which was difficult to ignore—Madă's confusion lifted in surprise before tightening into a glare.

Daniel cringed through a tense chuckle.

Kat observed their exchange. Her attention shifted to Levi, who was biting down on a smile, and then to Maksim, who was *not* smiling.

Kat tilted her head, brow creased… but then a glimmer of understanding twinkled behind her eyes. Her stare swung to Daniel's phone. She grabbed the device and studied the image.

Maksim pulled the phone away. "Don't."

"It's her, isn't it? The dancer from the club." A tremble entered Kat's voice, and Maksim watched the light in her eyes fade. She looked like someone had knocked the wind out of her.

Perfect. This was just goddamn perfect.

"You know this woman?" Levi asked.

"Yeah." Maksim passed the phone to Daniel. "She worked for Ștefan."

"What would possess her to rent a car? Her name is going to be tied to the rental paperwork."

"She doesn't own a car, and she wouldn't necessarily know not to rent one." Maksim stole another glimpse of Kat. She was hugging herself tightly, protectively. Betrayal had left its mark on her, and those old wounds oozed with grief.

"How do you know she doesn't own a car?" Levi pressed. "Why wouldn't she know—"

"We need to go. Before more of Vladimir's people show up." Maksim wrapped an arm around Kat and pulled her along. She let him, but not with her usual fervor. Not with her usual *trust*.

The realization slowed his descent down the stairs. He thought to remove his arm, but he was afraid to let her go, as if she might evaporate into thin air.

He commanded his emotions to obey and released her. "Is your bag ready?" he asked as they reached the ground floor.

She met his gaze. The uncertainty that flickered across her face struck him in the heart. *She's not going.* That was Maksim's first thought as he read her expression. At the very least she was having doubts.

He went to repeat himself when he registered movement. His head turned toward the kitchen. The noise had stemmed from somewhere beyond that. Someone had entered the laundry room.

He made eye contact with Daniel. "Did you lock the door?"

Daniel was coming down the last two stairs. "Which door?"

Maksim squeezed a fist. Daniel had parked near the back gate, and they had all entered via the laundry room. If they had failed to lock the back door…

The footsteps quickened. Maksim reached for his pistol and realized it wasn't there. *It's in the duffel.* The duffel was upstairs, in the room he and Levi were once again sharing, and he didn't have enough time to retrieve it. The assailant was in the house.

His attention shot to a block of knives on the kitchen counter. He yanked out the two largest and grip-switched them into a downward chambered position, holding the handles tightly in his fists. He then stationed himself between the kitchen and the living room.

Madă whimpered from the staircase. Levi pushed past everyone and positioned himself, fists raised, next to Maksim.

The intruder passed through the laundry room and angled for the kitchen. Kat shrieked. Maksim and Levi tensed, ready for action…

Mircea—*not* an intruder—appeared. His attention jumped to the knives, and the man stumbled backwards. *"Oh, doamne."* (Oh, Lord.)

Maksim dropped the fighting stance.

Levi raced forward. *"Mircea. We're sorry. We had a scare."*

Mircea held up a hand. *"The apology isn't necessary, my friend. But please, I must tell you—I was nearly to my job when I noticed I had forgotten my work badge. As I returned to the neighborhood, I noticed a car I have not seen before."* He aimed the comment at Maksim. *"I have been watching for unfamiliar vehicles as you said."*

"*Was it a silver Škoda?*" Maksim asked. "*Parked down the street?*"

"*Yes, and with a woman inside. The windows are dark, and I couldn't see well inside.*"

"I noticed her, too," Levi said. "*Only minutes ago.*"

"*She was not there when I left for work. Perhaps she just arrived.*" Mircea turned to Maksim. His eyes flashed toward the knives, and Maksim made his way to the knife block. "*I continued past the house and circled to the other street. That is why I entered through the back gate.*" Mircea directed his attention to Daniel. "*I saw your car. I'm parked behind you.*"

"Did you see other cars?" Maksim homed the knives in their appropriate slots. "*Anything else suspicious?*"

"*Only the car. Nothing else.*"

"*Thank you for telling us. You should go to your job now.*" Maksim stopped in front of him. "*Tell your boss you had to return for the badge, nothing more.*"

Mircea nodded and continued through the kitchen, through the living room, and up the stairs.

"What's going on?" Kat joined everyone in the kitchen. "I-I didn't understand that exchange."

"False alarm," Maksim said. "Mircea saw the same car."

"This is astounding." Levi moved to the kitchen table. "As many resources as Vladimir has, why would he send one woman who doesn't own a car to tail you?"

"She doesn't have direct access to Vladimir. And even if she did, he would never permit her—" Maksim rubbed a hand over his cheeks, down around his chin. His eyes grew distant, pensive.

"What?" Levi asked.

"Vladimir would never permit her to rent a car while conducting business for him."

"So?"

"That means she may be here unsanctioned."

"How so?" Levi dragged a chair out and parked himself there. "Is that even possible?"

"I've been following news reports since my misadventure in București. The men who attempted to flee were apparently detained for questioning. Some were found to be in possession of illegal firearms, drugs. Others had warrants for their arrest. I guarantee that tied up Vladimir's most immediate resources."

"But Vladimir has innumerable resources," Daniel said, joining Levi at the table. "Does he not?"

"He does… in theory. But he faked his death last August, and Ștefan was the only person who knew he was alive. Everyone else, even his closest associates—even I—believed him to be dead. It's been nearly a year that people have dealt solely with Ștefan. Now the word is out that Ștefan is dead while Vladimir is alive."

"And that Émilien is in police custody." Daniel snorted a laugh. "There's no telling what they've heard about you—that you're wanted by your dead uncle, that you're finding ways to have his people arrested."

"And this woman in the Škoda is trying to… what?" Levi rested an elbow on the table. "Fill the vacuum while Vladimir is busy reorganizing?"

"Something like that. She's ambitious, and when Ștefan was alive, she was actively working toward advancement in—" Maksim caught a glimpse of Kat.

Pain glistened in her eyes. Maksim's gut twisted.

"The point is," he continued, turning his back, "that woman is nobody right now. But if Vladimir hears she tracked us here, she'll become a somebody very quickly, and she knows that. We need to deal with her before she routes our location to the right people. Those who do have access to Vladimir."

"How do we know she hasn't done this already?" Madă asked. "And what about Mircea? We can leave, but he lives here. Will he be in danger?"

Footsteps treaded down the stairs. Mircea appeared with his employee badge, and everyone fell silent. *"Is everything okay?"*

"We're trying to figure that out," Maksim replied in their native language. *"Will you let us know if you see anything else that's suspicious?"*

"Of course. And I won't permit the driver of the Škoda to notice me." He waved. *"See you all at dinner. I hope to hear what you have decided."*

Maksim's dread sank. Mircea would *not* be seeing them at dinner. Not Maksim anyway. But what about Kat?

Madă pricked Maksim with a warning look. "Mircea should be more aware of the danger," she hissed in English.

"I know, I know." Maksim rested his fist dead center against his forehead. "We need a plan that includes his safety. But for the moment, he will be safe at work."

"What can we do about the woman?" Daniel asked. "Should we confront her, hope to scare her away?"

"A confrontation won't keep her away. She'll simply park somewhere else."

"Or change rentals again," Levi pointed out.

"And the local police?" Daniel said. "What if we call 112 and report a suspicious vehicle?"

"You could. I'm not sure you'll want to." Maksim wiped a hand down his face. "You would have to selectively edit a host of information and then keep your story straight afterwards."

"What information?"

"Where Kat and I have gone, any and all information I've shared with you, any crimes you know I've committed. You would be looking at falsifying a police report as a best-case scenario. Criminal conspiracy at worst."

"I see." Daniel shifted. "Perhaps we can devise another plan that doesn't involve the police."

"I hope so."

Kat stayed quiet during their exchange. She reverted to hugging herself, glancing between the kitchen and the living room. Picking up a tail could be unnerving. The fact that this particular tail had slept with Kat's ex—a covert op coordinated by Ștefan to ensure Kat traveled to Romania alone—made this far more personal.

That had to be the core of why she was upset, why she felt so betrayed. Maksim hadn't even known Kat when he'd been involved with Gabriela. There had been no betrayal by him.

Then why do I feel guilty? He'd been asking himself that a lot lately.

"We need a plan," Levi said. "Some way to deal with our new friend. But I think we would all agree that Kat and Maksim must make their escape while they can." He pumped up a thick gray eyebrow. "Yes?"

Daniel gave a firm nod. "Levi is right. If you two are going to Frankfurt, the time to leave is now."

"Daniel." Madă's features widened. "We spoke of this. You said you didn't want them to go off together."

"Ideally, they would come with us, my love, but Kat needs to claim that account, and Maksim can help her do that."

Madă then proceeded to say all the things she'd been thinking. The things she and Daniel had been discussing in private, apparently.

Going away wasn't wise.

Going away wasn't safe.

Going away wasn't the proper thing to do because Maksim and Kat weren't married. This seemed to be the biggest issue for Madă, actually. It was likely a concern for Daniel as well, but he did his best to calm his wife.

Maksim shifted his attention to Kat, intending to silently apologize. Her expression remained dull, lifeless.

She turned away and entered the living room. Maksim listened as her footsteps drifted toward the guest room in the basement.

CHAPTER
FOURTEEN

MAKSIM KNOCKED on Kat's door.

There was a short delay, followed by a meek "yeah?" It sounded like she'd needed a moment to collect herself.

He nudged open the door. Kat stood at the foot of her bed, zipping up her backpack. "Hey," he said.

She sent a fleeting glance. "Hey."

"Are you all right?"

She let another delay unfurl, checking the front pocket of her bag. She pulled out her passport and immediately put it back. "I'm… fine. Just been a stressful morning."

"I'm sorry for that—and everything else." He leaned a shoulder against the doorframe and crossed his arms. "I'm sure you've noticed that Madă is very traditional in her thinking. Daniel is as well, but he's a bit more understanding about… modern nuances."

"They didn't have a problem with Brandy and Dave sharing a room." Kat spoke this plainly, almost blandly, without looking up.

Maksim was about to broach the topic of Gabriela, assuming that was the real reason Kat was upset. He stopped himself. Had he misread that? Was *this* the real reason—feeling judged or perhaps smothered?

"Daniel and Madă have good intentions," Maksim said slowly. "But I'm like a son to them, so they feel differently when I'm involved. They're more protective."

"Are they protecting you?" Her eyes flicked toward him. "Or me?"

Three counts passed before Maksim's brain processed what he'd heard. The insinuation stung.

"You don't have to come with me." He walked forward. "I would understand if you no longer want to."

Kat said nothing. She simply tightened the straps on her backpack and then double-checked for her passport.

Maksim closed the gap. "Once we leave this house, we'll be committed. There's no turning back."

"I know." She dragged the backpack off the bed and winced. "Probably need to find a roller suitcase. This thing is going to be a pain to carry."

Maksim took the bag and returned it to the bed. Then he cupped her cheek and ran his thumb along the cheekbone. Bruises dotted her chin, neck, forehead, along the side of her eye. But her cheek remained clear, as if nothing had been permitted to leave a mark—not since the night Émilien had struck her.

Maksim's heart hammered at his remembrance, and a dire need to protect Kat—almost as powerful as the desire to be with her—rose up in him.

Kat covered her hand with his. Her breaths sped up, her chest rising and falling. But then she turned her head, breaking the connection. "Maksim, I was thinking—"

Footsteps approached from upstairs. Maksim discerned the gait as Levi's, and a soft knock rapped at the door seconds later.

Levi stood in the open doorway. "I'm sorry to intrude. Daniel was explaining your dilemma to me."

"About our—" Maksim hesitated, unsure of "we" and "our"

even applied anymore. "About the route?" he amended, feigning an air of casualness.

"Indeed. He said you're unsure if you should leave the country by way of Serbia or Bulgaria." Levi paused. "He mentioned Skopje. You have a safe deposit box there?"

"Yeah." Maksim broke away from Kat. "I suppose Daniel mentioned the complications I may face by entering North Macedonia."

"He may have." Levi rocked back on his heels. "I hope it's all right that we were discussing it. He's concerned, obviously, as am I."

"If it's just me, I have no problem going by way of Serbia. But I may not have enough cash for both Kat and myself."

"Are we talking about luxurious living or bribing border guards?"

Maksim sighed. "I'll give you one guess."

"All right, but what if you didn't have to bribe anyone?"

Maksim flagged Levi with a questioning look.

Levi peered past him and addressed Kat. "Did you know your father and I watched illegal movies during communism?"

"No. I mean, he always loved movies, but what he watched in Romania never came up."

"Romanians were allowed two hours of television time during the week, and we were only permitted to watch State-sanctioned shows. Whatever served the Party. But"—Levi sang the word—"your father knew a man who smuggled banned items into the country, including VHS tapes. He loved American movies, especially comedies, and my wife and I were subjected to many such films while she was yet alive. I didn't have the heart to continue watching them after her death."

"I'm sorry for your loss," Maksim said, and Kat echoed the sentiment with a nod.

"I'll have to tell you what happened, another time perhaps." Levi started up the stairs and gestured for Kat and Maksim to join him. "The reason I'm telling you this," he said as they ventured up the steps, "is because the man who sold him the VHS tapes used a smuggling route between Naidăș and Bela Crkva."

"Bela Crkva." Maksim slid past Kat and came alongside Levi. "That's on the Serbian side of the border. Not far from Belgrade."

"You know your geography." Levi relaxed into a smile as he crested the top of the stairs. "The smuggler ran a pharmacy in Naidăș, a village on the Romanian side. It was a family business before the communists took over, and, interestingly enough, the family was forced to continue running it since none of the other villagers were pharmacists. What Kat's father gathered—what he explained to me all those years ago—was that the family decided to use the pharmacy as a front for their smuggling oper-ations. Illicit goods would come through Belgrade, then Bela Crkva, and would be delivered to this pharmacy in Naidăș. Various family members would then sell to their contacts in București."

"And my dad was one of those contacts?" Kat asked.

"He certainly was. Not many people had money to spare for illicit items. Your father managed because of *his* father. Vasile's position in the Nomenklatura, his proximity to Ceaușescu, allowed Nicolae to get away with more than most people."

"I think I see where you're going with this." Maksim angled for the kitchen. Daniel hadn't moved from the table. "May I see your phone?"

Daniel looked up from the screen. "You can, but I've already found information about the pharmacy." He passed the phone to Maksim. "The courts restored the property to that family six years ago."

Maksim studied the news story Daniel had found.

"I believe traveling to Naidăș is your best bet," Levi contin-ued. "If the family does still own and operate that pharmacy, they'll surely know the old route to Bela Crkva. There's a lot of forest in that region, and if you could find a map—or a guide—there would be no need to take the official border crossing."

"What if they don't own the pharmacy?" Kat asked. "They might've sold it or closed down."

"Then perhaps someone else can assist. Though I wouldn't go around advertising that you're purposefully avoiding the official checkpoint."

Maksim skimmed the six-year-old article while mentally running through scenarios. "We would likely be on foot. That could be strenuous." He looked at Kat. "Would you be able to handle that?"

"I-I'm not sure." Her attention darted between Maksim and Levi. "What's the topography like? Are we talking mountains? Plains?"

"Hilly on the Romanian side," Levi said. "Flatter as you reach Serbia. However..." He wrinkled his nose. "There is a river. Some sections may be as shallow as a stream, but there could be others that are rather deep. You'd have to ask a local where to cross."

Kat's shoulders sagged. "Great."

"There's another flight to Munich," Maksim suddenly said.

Everyone's attention swiveled to him.

"It leaves this afternoon, and you'd arrive in time to catch up to your friends."

Several sets of eyes shifted toward Kat.

"Daniel could take you to the airport," Maksim pressed. His comment received another round of silence, and he raised both eyebrows. "Right?"

"Oh. Yes." Daniel stood up from the table. "I'm happy to."

Maksim eased closer, forcing Kat to look at him. "I wouldn't be able to see you off, and I don't know when I could be in touch, but... it's okay if you've changed your mind." The statement ricocheted through him, leaving pulses of pain wherever they touched. He wanted to be with her. But only if she wanted to be with him as well.

Her attention circled the kitchen, landing on Levi first and then Madă and Daniel. "I think maybe everyone's right. Maybe it's not a good idea to go off together." She lowered her gaze. "The sooner I get home, the sooner this can be over."

A sharp pain mushroomed in Maksim's rib cage. She wanted this to be over—of course she did—and he wanted her to be safe. That didn't make her answer hurt any less.

He throttled his emotions and opened his mouth, ready to profess that she was right. Her next statement halted him. "But I have to go to Frankfurt."

Surprise held him in place.

Daniel skirted the table. He didn't stop until he was standing in front of Kat. "Your father gave his life to see that Vasile's wealth went to you and not Ștefan. It's perfectly understandable that you feel the need to claim what's rightfully yours, and we will be praying for you if and when you decide to do that." He hesitated. "We will support and pray for you no matter the course you decide, but if the trip is limited to Germany, that would certainly ease our minds."

"We're concerned for your safety," Madă said. "And for your heart. We only want to protect you." She pivoted toward Maksim. "Both of you."

"Are you certain about this?" Maksim asked. "Because if you are, we have to leave now."

She pushed up a smile. It was weak, and she still couldn't hold his gaze, but she managed a nod. "As long as you can get me home from there."

"I should be able to—barring any extenuating circumstances of course. Even if such circumstances arise, I'm certain I can devise a contingency plan." Maksim raked at his hair. "All we need is an international airport with direct flights to the US. The city doesn't matter. You can always book the Atlanta flight after you're stateside."

Daniel rested a hand on Maksim's shoulder. "I know you can do it, son. We believe in you."

Madă walked forward and embraced Kat. "I'm sorry, dear. I didn't mean to become upset." She took Kat's face in her hands.

"We want you both to make good decisions. To be well and safe."

"I know. I appreciate that." Kat made her second attempt at a smile. She was more successful this time. "My dad would appreciate that, too."

Madă, teary-eyed, wrapped her arms around Kat before doing the same for Maksim.

He hugged her back. *"Te iubesc, mamă."* (I love you, mama.)

"How are we getting to the border?" Kat hoisted her backpack onto her good shoulder. As she seated the strap, she sent a hopeful look to Levi.

"I would love to take you, but I must oversee the plan for dealing with our friend in the Škoda."

"Oh. Sure." Disappointment filtered into Kat's demeanor. "That makes sense."

"I cannot go either." Madă wiped the dampness from beneath her eyes. "Mircea is my cousin, and I feel responsible for his safety." She gestured toward Daniel. "We have more relatives and friends in Sibiu. I could search for another place to stay."

"That would probably be best," Maksim said. "At least until Levi can figure out a solution for—" He stopped short of speaking Gabriela's name. "For our other problem," he finished.

Madă scooted past him, angling for the living room. "I'm going to pack a bag for Mircea. He can come with us until it's safe for him to return home."

"I suppose that leaves me." Daniel held up his keys. "Who's ready to go to Naidăș?"

———

THE E-81 STRETCHED into the distance as Daniel, Maksim, and Kat traveled west. Transilvanian towns sprinkled the landscape, but much of the region consisted of countryside, filling their journey with huge swaths of nothingness.

A lot of farmland. And transponder towers.

Lorries—what Kat referred to "eighteen-wheelers"—rumbled in the right lane. Daniel passed them, going a decent speed, though not too fast. They couldn't afford to get stopped. But they couldn't afford to waste time either.

Daniel had fueled up the night before. His Dacia had a fifty-liter tank, and Maksim estimated they would only need about sixteen liters of petrol to reach Naidăș. So they could drive straight there, without stopping, and Daniel could make the return trip as well.

He hadn't liked that idea. In fact, he'd resisted when Maksim mentioned it. "Four hours there and back?" The sides of Daniel's mouth sank. "No stopping for rest or food?"

"You could, but you would have to be cautious, especially if Levi involves the police. If the authorities become aware of *my* presence—"

"How would they become aware of your presence? Levi isn't going to mention your name."

"And what if Gabriela mentions my name? Hm?" Maksim rubbed his neck. "The police could question her, and if *that* happens, you won't want any eyewitnesses linking you to me."

"Oh, Maksim. I know there are risks." Daniel glanced at his passenger. "I'm prepared to face the consequences."

"Are you prepared to go away to prison?" Maksim met his stare. "The idea of being separated from your wife, potentially for years, doesn't bother you?"

"It does. It would." Daniel focused on the road. "I suppose erring on the side of caution won't hurt."

"Hey, so…" Kat's voice stemmed from the back seat, and Maksim twisted around. "I can't figure out this phone." She held up the flip phone Maksim had given her. "How do you text?"

Maksim hid a smile and held out his hand. "Here. I'll show you."

He pointed out the letters that corresponded to each number on the keypad and explained how to cycle through them. "For T, you'll press and hold the 8 key." He demonstrated. "For U, press and hold the same key, but after the T appears, you'll press 8 again, and that will cycle you to the next letter. For V, it's the same thing but you'll press the 8 key twice."

"That makes sense. Here, can I…?" She reached for the phone. Her stomach gurgled as he passed the device to her. Red splotches bloomed in her cheeks. "I, um, guess I'm pretty hungry already."

"I'll buy snacks at the pharmacy, but we may have to wait until we're across the border before we can have a proper meal."

"How much longer?"

"We just passed the dinosaur geopark," Daniel said, checking the clock on his dashboard. "That puts us one hour and thirty minutes from Sibiu."

"Two and a half hours to go," Maksim said. "Thereabouts."

Kat sighed, dragging her backpack onto her lap, and laid her arms across the top. She used her forearm as a chin rest, her gaze drifting toward Maksim. "It's going to be a long day, isn't it?"

"Yeah." He faced forward. "It is."

CHAPTER
FIFTEEN

11:32 (11:32 AM)

THE CAR DIPPED HARD, jarring everyone.

"Ow."

Maksim dragged his attention from the hilly landscape. Kat had been holding her backpack, and as Maksim turned around, he found her lifting her head, her eyes squinty. Pink lines scored one side of her face like she'd been using the backpack as a pillow.

"Sorry about that," Daniel said. "Our infrastructure isn't the best in these rural parts." He kept his focus on the one-lane road in front of him. "We're, uh… here." He gestured at their surroundings.

Kat peered out her window. "We're in the middle of nowhere."

"Yes, well, it's a small village." Then he muttered, "Very small."

A large hill with brush and trees filled the view on their left. Dilapidated farm buildings sprinkled the scenery on their right;

beyond those, a series of hills rolled into the distance. The road was paved but not kempt, and potholes threatened to shake something loose every twenty meters.

Daniel hit another one and winced. "It's been many years since I've visited a village of this size."

"How close are we to the official checkpoint?" Kat asked. "Should we be concerned?"

"The official border crossing is on the highway," Daniel replied. "We're three kilometers south of that."

"Is that close enough to encounter border police?" Her voice strained.

"It could be." Maksim reached for his duffel on the floorboard. "But this area is heavily wooded, which will provide cover."

"You could potentially bribe the police, too," Daniel said. "That sort of thing is almost unheard of in the cities these days, but in rural areas like this, where people are struggling..." He punctuated the thought with a shrug.

Maksim didn't comment. He had about thirty-five grand on him—enough to buy himself out of a bad situation—but he wasn't sure if that would be enough for him *and* Kat. Further, he'd given his Glock to Levi, leaving Maksim with only a pocketknife if things went sideways.

He felt exposed without the Glock, vulnerable, but he had his reasons for giving it to Levi. He just hoped that had been the right call.

Daniel followed the craggy pavement to a small bridge that crossed a drainage ditch. They continued through a grove of trees and then started toward a larger bridge that connected two sides of a river.

"Is that the Danube?" Daniel motioned ahead.

"The Nera, which is part of the Danube." Maksim craned his neck, trying to glimpse the water. The river ran wide and deep. Too deep to cross on foot. Tension coiled in his stomach.

Cement posts with rusted-out rebar lined both sides of the

forthcoming bridge. The structure was long but extremely narrow, offering enough space for exactly one compact vehicle.

"What if someone on the other side needs to cross?" Kat asked. "We'll get stuck."

"Not to worry," Daniel said. "The locals are accustomed to this lifestyle. Should someone else need to cross, they'll see us and wait." He looked at Maksim. "My parents grew up in a village like this. Did I ever tell you?"

Maksim shook his head.

"Șercaia, near Făgăraș. We took family trips there every summer, visiting my grandparents." Daniel's expression turned wistful. "I grew up in a small town, mind you, but not as small as Șercaia. Oh how happy I was when I finally went to university in Brașov. The 'big city.'" He chuckled. "That's where I met Madă. She and her family are from Brașov."

"I did know that part. Only because of the—" Maksim stopped short of saying "the ring" when he remembered Kat was in the back seat.

Daniel waited for him to go on.

"Because of the story you shared," Maksim revised, "about Madă's family and how their property was taken by the communists."

"Ah, yes. The dark days." Daniel peeked at Kat through the rearview mirror. "Our house was used as a police station during the Ceaușescu regime."

"What?" Kat shifted in her seat. Maksim didn't turn, but the movement indicated she had straightened. "Your house—the house where you guys live now—was a police station?"

Daniel nodded. "They were called the *miliția* back then. It's something of an inside joke—the *miliția* became the *poliția*, only changing the first two letters and nothing else. The chiefs, officers, procedures, standards all remained in force until much later. Some high-ranking *miliția* and *Securitate* linger in the police today."

"But... how did this happen? And why? I can't even picture your house as a police station."

"When everything was nationalized, the state could evict families at will, move other people in, force multiple families to share a single home, tear down people's homes. You name it, and the regime did it. Our house is in a good location—near the old city without being *in* the old city—and someone in the government decided it was an ideal place for the station. The neighborhood didn't look the way it does now, nor did the house. Everything was very rundown when Madă's family regained the rights five years ago."

"*Five years ago*? I thought the revolution was in eighty-nine."

"It was. The courts have been hearing property rights cases since the nineties, but many thousands are not yet settled. Some estimate in the hundreds of thousands."

"What about your family?" Maksim asked. "How long before their property was returned?"

"It hasn't been. Our case is yet to be heard."

Kat gasped from the back seat.

Maksim matched her surprise with a widened expression. He hadn't realized he knew someone in the backlog. Anyone associated with Ștefan—those who'd been in his good graces or were owed favors—could have their cases expedited easily enough. Similarly, Maksim had seen cases thrown out or moved to the end of the line—for those *not* in Ștefan's good graces, especially those who owed him money.

Maksim wondered if he could have done something for Daniel and Madă when he'd had the chance. They likely wouldn't have accepted his help, being that other people's cases would have been pushed back, but he wished he would have known while he'd been Ștefan's *mâna dreaptă* (right hand) and had the power to do something.

"My family's story is akin to this pharmacy you'll be visiting," Daniel was saying as they neared the bridge. "My grandfather was a farmer, and because of his skillset, his family was permitted to stay in their home. Daily life didn't change much as I understand, but they did lose the rights to their equipment. And the property. And they weren't allowed to eat what they harvested after a certain point in the nationalization process. Rather, they weren't supposed to, but I'm certain they snuck extra food when they could."

"Isn't that feudalism?" Kat asked. "Where there's a lord of the manor and the people that live there are the serfs?"

"In essence. Except under communism, the government is the lord and the citizens are the serfs." His gaze returned to the rearview. "They never tell people that part when they're recruiting for the Party." His attention slid to Maksim. "My grandparents were proud communists until times grew hard and the government failed in its promised benevolence."

"I didn't know most of that," Maksim said. "About your family, I mean."

Daniel remained upbeat, but a hint of pain cut into his smile. "Now you do."

They reached the bridge, and Daniel slowed to a crawl. The structure bore their weight, but the creaks and groans were unnerving. Maksim rolled down his window, and the sounds heightened.

He listened past that, wondering how fast the current flowed. His ear detected slow-moving water.

After they reached the other side, Daniel resumed a more reasonable pace. The road widened, though not much, and they continued through a gauntlet of brick and stucco homes. Some of the buildings had newer aluminum roofs; most had traditional terracotta tiles so old they had faded to a dusty brown.

Kids chased each other outside one of the homes. A woman carrying a bag of groceries stopped to fuss at them. The sidewalk broke off into dirt and crumbly cement, and the kids were playing in the mound. "...*This is where the dogs defecate. You are going to be ill,"* the woman was shouting. *"I'm going to inform your mother!"*

The kids ignored her, kicking and flinging the dirt at each other.

Another local sat beneath the overhang of a house. The elderly man kept a watchful eye on Daniel's car.

"I think we're supposed to turn here." Maksim pointed ahead and to the right.

"I hope I can remember the way out." Daniel took the turn. "I very much hope I can find my way to Sibiu."

"You didn't bring your phone?" Maksim asked. "What about the one I gave you? The one that works like a burner."

"Madă is using the burner to make calls. I decided to leave mine behind as well since we don't know how that woman in the Škoda found us." Daniel tilted his head. "I was wondering… how is it that you know her? Were you her handler?"

"No." Maksim directed his gaze out the window. "I knew her from the club."

"I was curious because… well, if she was a friend, I wondered if you had mentioned something about staying with us. Could that be—"

"I've never mentioned you or Madă," Maksim snapped, though he hadn't meant to. "Not to Gabriela, nor to anyone in Ștefan's operation."

"It wasn't an accusation, son." Daniel tightened his grip on the steering wheel. "I was only thinking of ways she may have discovered us." He hesitated, seeming to measure his words. "I know you would never say anything intentionally. I know how careful you are. But anyone can slip up and say something in passing."

Maksim had didactic memory, an ability that allowed him to remember things down to the smallest detail. He would have provided this as his defense—except that he'd been drunk the night he'd slept with Gabriela. He didn't *think* he would have been stupid enough to mention Daniel or Madă…

but he also shouldn't have been stupid enough to sleep with her.

And so he said nothing. Not as a defense, nor as a confession.

Kat had gone quiet in the back seat, and Daniel joined her. Maksim retreated into the silence, desperate to escape the tension that radiated in the car. He couldn't bring himself to look at either of them.

A dull red supermarket filled the next corner. The road forked, and Maksim pointed to the left. Daniel followed the turn. Trash littered the drainage area that ran beside the decrepit sidewalk. A church cordoned off by a metal gate loomed on their left.

"There. The building with the green trim." Maksim pointed. "I think that's it." There was no *farmacia* sign, but confirmation came in the form of a green pharmaceutical cross and an herbal leaf painted on the building.

Instead of a sterile-looking glass storefront, this pharmacy had been converted from a basic stucco building. The windows had lockable shutters that were currently propped open as morning bled into afternoon. The entrance door had likewise been propped open.

"Keep going."

They passed shops, a barber, and multiple vacant-looking buildings before Maksim gestured. "Park there."

Daniel pulled over as far as he could and then eased his right-side tires onto the curb. The car lifted, and he managed to leave enough space in case other cars needed to pass. Currently there were none.

He killed the engine. "Why so far?"

"So that the pharmacy owner, or whoever is working, cannot identify you or your vehicle." Maksim checked the passenger-side rearview. The town's dusty sidewalk stretched in the reflection. "This is far enough that he shouldn't be able to catch your plates."

"And what's your plan?" Daniel split a curious look between Maksim and Kat. "Two tourists seeking an adventure?"

"Close." Maksim turned to Kat. She wiped away her emotion, the stunned expression on her face, and met Maksim's stare. "You're an American tourist whose late father was from Romania. You came here to reconnect with your roots and wanted to visit some of the places he spoke about."

"I can do that," Kat said. "I mean, it's basically true."

"The closer we stick to the truth, the easier we'll be able to remember the details. We're going to use Levi's story about the VHS tapes. Just pretend like it was your *father* who shared that information with you. This needs to be a nostalgic venture—you heard these stories growing up, and now that you're older you must visit the place that helped your father fall in love with American movies. I'm your guide and translator. You found me through a tourism agency and hired me to bring you here. A taxi from Timișoara dropped us off."

"Got it." Kat unbuckled her seatbelt. "Anything else?"

"Don't give any indication that we're looking to avoid the official border crossing, nor that we're in any sort of danger. Any money that changes hands will be done under the auspices of gratitude in helping you feel more connected to your deceased father."

"They likely won't speak English," Daniel said. "So just smile and be pleasant and let Maksim do most of the talking."

"Wait until the topic of money is discussed," he continued, pulling out his wallet. "Let the owner or myself bring it up. When that happens—" Regret gnawed at him as the ring came into view. He shoved the feeling aside and forced himself to focus. "When that happens," he tried again, "you'll have to be the one who makes an offer." He handed the euros to Kat. "So that the exchange appears authentic."

Kat took the money. "I offer all this?"

"Yes, but make it realistic." He slapped the wallet shut a little harder than he'd intended. "That's a thousand. Start lower, go higher, and if it sounds like more will get us what we need, act willing but reluctant. You'll have to pretend you need a *bancomat* as well."

Kat leaned back and stuffed the money in her pocket. "That's an ATM, right?"

"It is. We don't really need one, but carrying any more cash will appear suspicious. If the price goes higher than what you have there, just say you need to withdraw more. While appearing reluctant." Maksim focused on Daniel. "What about you?"

Daniel touched his pocket. "I have the cash you gave me earlier."

"I meant how you're feeling. Are you good to drive back?"

"Ah, well, I am tired and could use a coffee."

"Try to get clear of this border region before you stop. Anything small that looks family-run should be fine. Avoid chain petrol stations or shops. Look for CCTV cameras like I taught you."

Daniel smiled. "I'll do it."

A goodbye pressed forward on Maksim's tongue… but then he changed course. "I'm sorry for how I reacted a moment ago. My connections to old colleagues are tangled, and—" He hesitated, realizing Kat was listening. But in a sense, the explanation was for her, too. "They're tangled," he continued, "and the woman, Gabriela, is part of that. I hope to God I never said anything that would now endanger you, Madă, or Mircea. But if I did, please forgive me."

Daniel wrapped his arms around Maksim and pulled him in for a hug. *"Tati."* (Dad.) Maksim spoke with genuine affection, matching Daniel's embrace.

Daniel squeezed harder, his shoulders beginning to shake. *"Fiule." My son.*

Maksim fought the onslaught of tears rising in him.

Daniel pulled away and wiped his face. "Kat," he said, turning toward her. "Take care of him." He reached for Maksim's hand. "Take care of each other."

Kat worked a smile onto her face. She looked like she was about to cry as well.

"We need to go before we draw too much attention." Maksim pushed open his door and stepped out. Kat grabbed her backpack and met him on the sidewalk.

Daniel started the car and pulled forward. He drove slowly, passing several more decayed buildings, then turned left at the next cross street.

Maksim led Kat toward the pharmacy.

CHAPTER
SIXTEEN

STALE HEAT GREETED them inside the *farmacia*. Sweat accumulated beneath Maksim's long sleeves, and part of him wished he'd worn a tee. That wasn't happening today. Short sleeves exposed Maksim's scars, and the scars exposed his weakness—his own personal "Achilles tendon."

Until he knew who he was dealing with, he wasn't going to reveal anything that could be perceived as a weakness.

His attention zeroed in on a video camera mounted in the corner. He noted the camera's age—old, probably from the early 2000s—and there was no red light or any other indication the device was recording.

A tall guy, thirtysomething, with dark hair and a lean form manned the counter. He was holding his phone, doomscrolling from the looks of it, and he had a hard time tearing his zombified stare from the device.

Kat offered a friendly wave as she unloaded her backpack. The guy jerked in surprise and watched the bag settle onto the filthy floor.

Maksim grimaced. She clearly hadn't realized her faux pas, and she was struggling physically, so he decided not to say anything.

"Hi. Uh, *bună ziua*," she said, oblivious. *"Sunt,* um…" She pivoted toward Maksim. "How do I say 'my father was Romanian' again?"

Maksim's brow furrowed—but then he realized she was playing up the "I'm with my tour guide and translator" bit.

The pharmacy worker piped up before Maksim could respond. "I speak English," he said through a heavy accent.

"Oh, perfect. Because my Romanian is—" She made a playful chopping motion. "Definitely should have learned when I was younger, but my dad didn't, um…"

The guy watched with a bland stare.

"Anyway, my dad was Romanian and I'm visiting my roots. Reconnecting, I mean. With my roots. *His* roots." She cleared her throat. "He was from here."

"Who is your father?" The guy's dense black eyebrows lifted. He sounded genuinely curious. "He is from Naidăș?"

"Not from *here* here. From Romania." She bit her lip and sent another glance to Maksim. "Sorry, I'm a little jet-lagged."

"Her father had a connection to your town." Maksim set his duffel on the floor, careful to keep one boot under it, and eased into a pleasant smile. "He lived in București, but he knew someone from your village, a longtime friend who helped him obtain certain goods from the West." Maksim paused, waiting for the clerk's reaction. "VHS tapes," Maksim added when the guy gave no response.

"My dad loved eighties movies," Kat said, inserting excitement into her speech. "He told me all kinds of stories about how he used to get them from this friend of his during communism—"

"American movies were banned during communism." The guy's curiosity drained from his expression as he immersed himself in the phone. "There's a restaurant in our town," he said without looking up, "but it's not great. You will find more touristic places in Timișoara."

"That's where we just came from." Kat frowned, her cheerfulness dimming. "I-I wanted to come *here* specifically because, well, I wanted to see the town he used to talk about. Also… I guess I was hoping I could find his old friend."

The guy pinned her with a glower.

"Is that person still alive?" Kat forced a smile as a stream of sweat chased down her face. "Do you happen to know?"

"Apparently, the man her father knew ran this pharmacy," Maksim explained. "It was a family business before the communists took over."

The guy tilted his head, eyes searching them—Maksim first and then Kat. "Who are you exactly?"

Panic struck Maksim. He hadn't warned Kat against using her real name.

He did his best to conceal his alarm. "Florin," Maksim said casually, hoping Kat would catch on that she needed to change her name as well. "I'm with Timișoara Tours."

"Liz." Kat walked forward and stuck out her hand. The clerk wrinkled his nose. "I know this probably sounds weird," she said, withdrawing. "An American comes in here, asking for the owner of the pharmacy—"

"My family owns the pharmacy," the guy said flatly.

"Oh." Kat fidgeted. "Well, you don't seem old enough to be the guy my dad talked about. Could that have been *your* dad or maybe your grandfather?"

The guy set his phone on the counter and squared up to them. He tilted his head, eyes brimming with suspicion. "What do you want from my family?"

"*Listen, friend.*" Maksim switched to Romanian, coating his words in warmth. "*I'm sure there aren't many tourists who pass through here, but apparently her father*"—Maksim let his gaze flick to Kat—"*died not too long ago. This seems to be her way of dealing with the grief.*"

The guy's scowl didn't lessen per se. But he didn't tell them to get the hell out either.

Maksim pressed forward with the explanation. "*She's*

desperate to find a way to learn more about these stories he told her." A shrug. "*She paid to have me bring her here, and she knows there could be more expenses involved.*"

"*Expenses for what?*"

"*An adventure. Nothing too crazy. She just wants to see the old smuggling routes that helped bring her father the movies he loved.*" Maksim held up both hands in surrender. "*I understand if you aren't interested. But she paid me a lot.*"

The guy directed his stare to Kat.

"It's official." Kat laughed tensely. "My Romanian is *really* terrible. Anyone wanna fill me in?"

"You want to see the old smuggling routes?" the guy asked.

Her eyes flashed toward Maksim. He was hanging on to that easy smile of his, and she took the cue. "Yep! YOLO, as they say."

The crease in the guy's forehead deepened. Maksim had heard the expression but feigned confusion.

"YOLO? You only live once?" Kat picked nervously at a cuticle. "That's why I'm here. I'm about to start college, and it's my last chance to do something like this for a while."

The clerk switched to Romanian again. "*How much did she pay you?*" He was talking to Maksim.

"*One thousand.*"

The guy harrumphed. "*One thousand lei?*"

"*Euros.*"

He straightened. "*One thousand euros? Only to bring her here?*" A glimmer twinkled in his eyes. Maksim knew the look well. They had him. "All right, one thousand euros." He flitted a casual hand between them. "Each."

Nemernicul ăsta, Maksim thought. (This scumbag.) He suppressed his disdain with a blasé shrug directed at Kat. She didn't have an immediate response, so he said, "It's your call."

"Mine?"

"I'm not paying for myself. That would leave me with nothing."

"Oh! Right. I would be paying for both of us. That's fine." She chuckled. "I mean, it's a bit steep, but... YOLO." She touched her pocket. "I just need one of those *bancomat* machines."

"There's a *bancomat* inside the supermarket." The guy checked his phone. "I'm off work at fifteen thirty. Be here by then. I will not wait for you."

"Great! No, we'll be here."

"What's your name?" Maksim asked.

The guy stared back, seeming to debate if he should answer. "Bogdan," he said finally.

"Nice to meet you, Bogdan. And thank you." Maksim picked up his duffel and nudged Kat. "Come on. I'll help you navigate the *bancomat*."

Kat shouldered her backpack, and they exited the pharmacy. "Fifteen thirty," Kat whispered as they headed up the sidewalk. "That's three thirty this afternoon, right?"

"Mm-hm." Maksim settled into a relaxed stride, his pace casual as he observed their surroundings. "Orthodox church," he said, pointing at the structure on their right.

"Huh? Oh." Kat traced his line of sight. "We're acting like tourists, aren't we?"

"Nailed it."

The buildings on their left created a long swath of shade while those across the street sat under the burning midday sun. Kat kept her attention on the shaded side. "I wonder if they have any shops. Sunglasses and a hat might be nice."

"Let's go to the supermarket first. We'll buy snacks for the excursion, then we can hit the restaurant Bogdan mentioned."

"Okay, but—" She adjusted her backpack. "I really need a better way to carry this thing."

Maksim zeroed in on the bag. "Is your shoulder bothering you?"

She nodded, tugging on her t-shirt and stretching the neckline. "I thought if I carried it on my good shoulder I'd be fine, but this shirt is kind of scratchy. Doesn't help that I'm sweating like crazy."

"I don't mind to help." He shouldered his duffel and reached for the backpack.

She handed it over. "Thanks. Sorry."

"It's not a problem for now, but I'd prefer to keep my hands free for the excursion. In case Bogdan tries anything." That was partly the reason. The other part involved his scarred arm and damaged shoulder. He kept that part to himself. "Do you have another shirt? I'd rather not go traipsing through town on a shopping spree."

"I have a tank top." She skirted a jagged section of sidewalk. "It'd be more comfortable, but I still have stitches. Wasn't sure I should expose those to the elements."

An older woman shuffled out of her house. She was carrying a broom and proceeded to sweep her doorstep and then the side-walk. Dust kicked up before she noticed Kat and Maksim.

She paused and stared. Kat hurried past. Maksim smiled and offered a polite greeting in Romanian. The woman replied, sans any smile, and waited for them to move along.

As the supermarket came into view, Maksim noticed a sting flare up in his shoulder. With only a laptop and a few clothes, Kat's backpack wasn't at all heavy. But it felt heavy to him. Heavier than it should have.

He pushed the pain aside and homed in on the splotch of dull red at the next corner. Maksim gestured in that direction, and they crossed the narrow street and entered the supermarket. Dust, must, and a strangely sweet smell waited for them inside.

Maksim beelined for the snack aisle and found a scattering of junk food. He would have preferred protein bars, nuts, anything relatively healthy that could withstand the heat. Instead he got corn puffs and pretzels.

"Oh my gosh." Kat picked up a shiny red plastic bag.

"Those will likely melt," Maksim said. "They're—"

"Sour candies." She fingered the crinkly bag. Her gaze

lingered, her expression traveling somewhere far away. To a memory if Maksim had to guess.

"We can get them."

"Hm?" She dragged her stare from the shiny red bag.

"Those candies." He gestured. "We can get them, but they may not hold up well."

"Um… yeah. Okay. If you don't mind?"

"Not at all. Come on."

She held on to the candies while they meandered toward the front. There was only one register. It was large, yellowed, and looked older than Maksim. He exchanged pleasantries with the clerk, and as he was asking about the local restaurant, he thought to inquire about something else. *"Does the restaurant have a clean WC? My friend has an injury, and she may need soap and clean water."*

"I don't know about that." The clerk scanned their snacks. *"But there is a hotel next door to the same restaurant. Cazare Banat. The owner keeps her place very clean."*

"We aren't staying the night."

"No?" Her gaze drifted to Kat. *"This hotel would be very inexpensive for an American."*

Maksim bagged the snacks—everything but the sour candies, since Kat seemed reluctant to part with them—and they made their way into the broiling heat. The restaurant Maksim had inquired about occupied a small building less than one hundred meters from the supermarket.

A hearty aroma beckoned them, but Maksim continued past the restaurant and stopped in front of the building next door.

"What's this?" Kat studied a sign. "Cazare Banat?"

"*Cazare* means accommodation. It's a hotel."

"I thought we were going to eat."

"We are." He held up her backpack. "But if we get a room, we can leave our bags, *and* we'll have a place to rest for the next few hours. How does that sound?"

"Actually…" Kat shielded her eyes, her attention trailing

over the two-story stucco building. "Not having to carry our bags sounds pretty great. And I'm tired." She looked at him. "Would I have time for a nap?"

"We'll make time."

The hotel had three rooms, and all of them were vacant. So when Maksim and Kat strolled up to the front desk, the owner didn't press too hard about the required identification.

"We are very hungry and tired, and I'm not certain where our passports are at this moment." He showed her the large duffel. *"Please, madam. I will pay extra if you will allow us to eat and rest. I'll bring you our passports later."*

She happily accepted the extra fifty Maksim offered and then pointed them to a staircase. *"Your room is upstairs. The bathroom is in the hallway."* She handed him the key.

"May we have two?"

The woman smiled. *"After you bring your passports."*

Maksim thanked her and proceeded up the stairs. The old wooden steps creaked under his weight plus everything he was carrying—his duffel, Kat's backpack, the bag of snacks.

Kat carried the sour candies. She didn't realize her error until they had already reached the room. "I didn't mean to— Maksim, I could have carried something."

"You're fine. It's been a long day." He passed her the bag of snacks and slid their room key into the door handle.

He twisted, making several rotations until the lock disengaged. Then he pushed open the door. A double bed had been pushed against the wall. Across the room, a TV hung from a wall mount directly beside a window.

Maksim dropped their bags on the bed and positioned himself alongside the window, peering through the lace curtains. The street they'd taken from the supermarket appeared below. They were directly above the hotel's entrance.

Kat was taking in the room when Maksim turned around. She noted the TV, a wooden desk, and then the bed. Her attention shot to Maksim. "There's only one."

"It's yours." He motioned toward the bed. "The bathroom is in the hallway. Unfortunately, she would only give us one key, and I'm afraid I'll have to bring it with me."

"Where?"

"I'm going see if the restaurant does takeaway. That way you can rest a bit more."

"Oh, okay, that's… actually perfect." She perked up. "Do you think the restaurant serves *mici*? That'd be easy to picnic."

"They should, or the Serbian version, *ćevapi*. Do you like flatbread?"

She perked up and nodded.

"*Ćevapi* is served with Balkan flatbread. *Mici* will likely be served with fries or traditional bread." He unzipped his duffel. "You're good with any of that?"

"Any. All of the above."

He snatched a tee from his duffel and peeled the long-sleeved shirt off his sticky, overheated body. Thick scar tissue, so much paler than the rest of him, appeared in his line of sight.

He ignored the severely marred skin and shook out his tee, giving his arms and chest an opportunity to breathe. As he moved his bag onto the desk, he noticed Kat's eyes on him. Specifically on his abs.

He grinned, slowing his transition into the tee. "Well?" His eyebrows jumped. "What's the verdict?"

She met his gaze, and a rosy hue mushroomed in her cheeks. "S-sorry, I—" Her gaze drifted again, this time to his chest. "I noticed you're bruised."

"Ah." He pushed up a bland smile. "Courtesy of Drago and Émilien. Who knew I made such a good punching bag?" Maksim ran a hand over his damaged chest, then over his neck and jawline—bruises he felt but couldn't see without a mirror. The black and blue marks ached, but they were nothing compared to the damage his former colleagues had done to his arm and shoulder. The same arm and shoulder that carried his scars.

Kat squinted, reaching out. "I can't believe I didn't notice this last—" She caught herself and lowered her hand.

Maksim climbed into the shirt while he waited for her to go on. She didn't, so he finished for her. "You didn't notice the bruises… last night? You mean, during our midnight rendezvous?"

Her blush deepened.

"Your room was dark, and your eyes were closed most of the time." He grinned. "Otherwise I'm certain you would have noticed."

Her embarrassment ruptured. She turned on her heel and crossed to the window.

Maksim tugged on his sleeve, pulling it down as far as he could. The scar tissue covered his upper arm, and t-shirts did a poor job of hiding the marred skin. But as long as he didn't run into Bogdan, the weather was too damn hot to care.

Kat studied the sheer curtains on the window. "Are you dressed?"

"Almost." He tucked in his shirt and straightened his belt. She didn't make a move until he strolled up behind her. "Would you like to talk about what happened last night?"

She peeked up at him. "I didn't plan that. Just so you know."

"I didn't either." He took a breath. "I've been in the habit of checking on you at the hospital, and that's what I was doing. I went down there to—"

"Can we talk about this later? Maybe after I take a nap?" She brushed past him. "I'm so tired."

He had a feeling she wouldn't be up for it later, but he let it go. "I brought a first aid kit." He sifted through his duffel. "Alcohol pads, gauze, ointment. It's all in here." He handed her a small nylon bag. "In case you need to treat your shoulder."

"Thanks."

"Do you need to use the bathroom before I leave? There's only one key, unfortunately." He showed her the room key. "You're welcome to come with me—"

"I'd rather stay here." Her shoulders sagged. "Maksim, I have to rest or I won't be able to make the excursion."

"I understand, but—just to be clear—you will be locked in."

She frowned. "I won't be able to get out? What if there's a fire?"

"Then I promise to come rescue you." He winked, and her blush made its second surprise appearance. "In all seriousness, I did ask about a second key. The woman said there isn't one."

"It's… whatever." She flopped onto the bed. "I'll be fine 'til you get back."

He started to pull the door shut.

"Don't take too long, okay? Please?"

"I won't." He closed the door and inserted the key. A few twists later and he had the room locked up and was descending the creaky stairs.

SEVENTEEN

MAKSIM BALANCED two colas on top of a pizza box, which didn't actually contain a pizza. This box was full of *mici* and *ćevapi*.

He slid the room key into the door and twisted. "Good news." He pushed open the door. "The owner's wife is Serbian, so they had—" He quieted himself. Kat was curled up on her side, hugging a pillow. He registered her soft steady breaths—a sound he'd grown to recognize from his nights at the hospital.

He locked the door and left the key in the handle. Then he set the food and drinks on the desk and fished out his burner phone.

13:48

One hour and forty-two minutes before their meet-up with Bogdan. He needed to eat but didn't want to start without Kat. She needed to rest, so he decided to leave her be and get a little rest himself.

He yanked out his wallet and tossed it onto the bedside table. Then, with his boots on, he eased onto the bed. The temptation to lie down clawed at him, but he resisted. If they needed to bug out, he had to be ready.

But they *wouldn't* need to bug out. They were safe. Safer than he'd felt in a long time. Was this what Spain would be like? Feeling relaxed and... free? Free to wear a t-shirt when he wanted, to come and go from a hotel without worrying about Vladimir.

This was only a taste, he realized, a foreshadowing of what was to come. But it was real, and he longed for more.

His attention moved to Kat. She had replaced her t-shirt with a spaghetti-strap tank top that exposed her scar. He leaned in. Fresh scar tissue ran vertically along her shoulder blade. The stitches were no longer necessary, and they may have been the source of her discomfort, especially if she'd been wearing a scratchy t-shirt.

He knew all about that.

Maksim pulled himself upright and leaned against the head-board, which was so thin he could feel the wall behind it. He ignored any discomfort and reviewed the plan.

Leave the hotel by 15:15.

Be at the farmacia by 15:25.

Make sure Kat already has the cash for the handoff.

Make sure you're wearing the other shirt. He was *not* looking forward to being out in the heat in long sleeves, but he wasn't taking any more risks today.

Maksim rehearsed a handful of evasive maneuvers—an instance where Vladimir's men showed up in town, another where they surrounded the hotel—but these thoughts faded under the sense of security he was experiencing.

Soon he drifted off to sleep.

———

*M*AKSIM *FOUND himself standing in his apartment.*

Wait... his apartment? Was he dreaming?

He was, and he realized it as some other version of himself barrel through the front door. That version was carrying a leather duffel and chucked it.

The duffel landed on the living room floor and skidded. "Ughhhhh!" He slammed the door and began pacing. He cursed himself, his life, the men who had killed his parents, even their dead relatives for birthing murderers into existence.

Maksim watched all of this in amazement—like watching a movie while being part of it. He tried to get his other-self's attention, but that version couldn't see him. Like he wasn't even there.

He moved to the couch and sat down. This was a memory, he realized, and he recognized some of the utterances he heard, particularly about Kat. Maksim had been with her in Brașov, attempting to solve a scavenger hunt created by her late father. The clues had led them to a letter that revealed his true identity.

Nicolae Brațiu, son of the infamous billionaire Vasile Brațiu. Vasile had done horrendous things as a high-ranking member of the Communist Party. He'd been an elite, a member of the Nomenklatura, and had lived richly while the working class suffered. Vasile had authorized the deaths of many and the imprisonment of many more. His was the name associated with Pitești, an experiment of torture and horrorism initiated by the KGB and their prodigies, the Securitate.

This monster, Vasile Brațiu, was Kat's grandfather.

Maksim watched his other-self go to the door. Ștefan stood on the other side, appearing concerned. "I received your message. I had my driver bring me right away."

Maksim opened the door wider and invited his cousin—the man he'd always thought was his cousin—to enter.

Ștefan ambled into the apartment. "I like what you've done with the place," he said, letting his cool gaze wander over the furniture. He didn't seem to notice Maksim—the Maksim watching all of this from the couch.

"So." Ștefan faced Maksim's memory self. "Did you solve the mysterious scavenger hunt?"

"Yes, yes."

Ștefan's eyes lit up. "And?"

Maksim watched his other-self battle with what to say. With what not to say. He remembered that internal battle well. It had happened less than two weeks before, and he remembered, word for word, what his other-self was about to say.

"You were right. Kat's father, Nicolae, knew the Traveler."

"I suspected something was amiss. Oh, Cousin." Ștefan placed a hand over his heart. "When I received that intel—"

"From where did you receive it?" Maksim crossed the room in two strides. He moved so swiftly Ștefan rocked back a step. "How did you receive the information? From who?"

Ștefan observed the lack of space between them, and Maksim remembered himself. "Forgive me." He took a measured step back. "I'm very upset by all of this."

"I can understand why." Ștefan inspected his fingernails. "The source wishes to remain anonymous." His stare flicked toward Maksim. "I hope you can understand."

Maksim watched his other-self clench a fist. "Do I have a choice?"

Ștefan's mouth curled into a smile. His eyes remained dull, mirthless.

Maksim guffawed and moved to the window. His apartment was on the eighth floor, far above where anyone could see in, but paranoia prompted him to discreetly peer out. The city stretched around him, beginning with the next-nearest high-rises and then rolling into smaller and smaller buildings.

Darkness drew his attention to the sky. His brow creased, and the Maksim on the couch, the one who'd been sucked into this memory, knew what his other-self had just seen: storm clouds. But Romania had been experiencing a drought and heatwave, and many months had passed since a rainstorm had come through.

"What of the scavenger hunt?" Ștefan sauntered closer.

Maksim's other-self released the blinds. Fury had burned a scowl into his features, and he looked like he was about to spew everything to Ștefan.

One blink and the look vanished. "The scavenger hunt led to the Traveler."

Ştefan straightened. *"You found the Traveler."*

"No. But that was the point of the whole thing. The man is in hiding, and—" Maksim blinked away another wave of fury. *"Kat's father wanted her to find him."*

The anger—the rage—Maksim had been suppressing seemed to swell up in Ştefan. His eyes tightened along the edges. Fire ignited in his features, but his voice remained cool and calm. "And where was the Traveler to be found? What did the scavenger hunt say?"

Maksim watched his other-self hesitate. "The clues directed Kat to return to the university. The information is there."

Ştefan, his features expectant, took a measured step forward. "Where?"

"What do you mean 'where'? How am I expected to know?" Maksim threw up his hands. They fell at his slides with a loud **slap!**

Ştefan gritted his teeth. "When are you accompanying her to the university?"

"I'm not. She's going home."

The fury that had been bubbling below the surface suddenly exploded. "WHEN?"

"Her friend is purchasing a ticket for her. That's all I know." That was a lie. Maksim had known much more than that, but something wasn't right about all of this. He rubbed his forehead. *"We had an argument. She said she never wanted to see me again."* Another lie. *"That's when she told me she was going home."*

"You were supposed to finish the scavenger hunt!" Ştefan aimed a threatening finger at Maksim. *"That was the deal!"*

"We did finish it! I told you—"

"But you didn't find the Traveler!"

"What is your interest in my parents' murderer? After all these years, after dissuading me from pursuing him, why do you want to find him now?"

Ştefan looked away. "The Traveler must know something," *he muttered.* "Yes. He knows."

A flash of light seeped in from between the blinds. Thunder cracked, and an electrical charge hummed in the apartment. The lights flickered.

Maksim shot a look to his other-self, who was already racing to the window. He watched his other-self's face pale and knew instantly what he was thinking. He remembered the epiphany as the first raindrops splattered his apartment building. Ștefan had been using Kat to find the Traveler. But why?

Maksim jumped up from the couch. For the first time since finding himself in this memory, he spoke. "You have to warn Kat," he said to his other-self.

Instead of responding, his other-self directed his attention to Ștefan. "Forgive me. What can I do?"

"Nothing." A tremor moved through Ștefan's answer. "Do nothing, Maksim, until you hear from me." He leveled a fiery look. "And do not expect that your debt is paid. It is not."

His other-self nodded. "I understand, Cousin."

"He isn't your cousin!" Maksim grabbed his other-self and shook him. "You have to warn Kat. Call her. Now. While there's still time!"

His other-self gave no acknowledgment, no indication that he'd heard any of that, and Maksim could do nothing as he watched Ștefan leave.

SHRILL VOICES RATTLED MAKSIM AWAKE. His eyes fluttered open, his ears tuning into a conversation about... celebrities? The people sounded far away, and he wondered if he'd been sucked into another dream.

A *pop* and *hiss* roused him a degree more. His eyes broke open the rest of the way. He was still sitting up, still leaning against the headboard. Kat, no longer asleep, sat cross-legged at the foot of the bed. She had the takeaway box open and was about to take a drink of her cola.

Maksim's attention shifted past her. The conversation he'd heard was celebrity gossip TV. The glammed-up hosts sported big hair and even bigger attitudes as they argued over the most prolific Romanian actors. As their conversation heated up, Kat pointed the remote at the TV and lowered the volume. Her head swiveled toward Maksim, and she gave a little jump. "You're awake."

"Just now." He rubbed his eyes. "And not fully."

She scooted backwards, bringing the food with her. "I didn't know Romania had trash TV."

"Mmm, yeah." Maksim stretched, careful not to overextend his bad arm. "We have the best trash TV in Europe."

She held the takeaway box toward him. "Hungry?"

"Thanks. I'll have some in a moment." He glanced around. "How long have I been—?" Reality came crashing down. His eyes widened. "What time is it?"

"Two thirty last time I checked." She picked up her burner phone and checked the time. "Two forty-one. Fourteen forty-one?"

He relaxed against the headboard. "We need to leave here by fifteen fifteen."

"Three fifteen. Got it." She reached into the box. "The *mici* is pretty good."

"That's the *ćevapi*." He pointed at the thicker pieces of rolled meat. "That's the *mici*."

"I probably would have liked the *mici* more if there'd been mustard." She grabbed the other cola and held it toward him. "I looked but didn't see any sauces. Just flatbread and sodas."

"The restaurant didn't have plastic ramekins." Maksim accepted the drink. "I asked the owner to dump mustard on the *mici*. He must have forgotten."

"I'm just happy to have something to eat. Speaking of which." She tilted the box toward him. "You should definitely have some before we go."

He set his cola aside and reached toward the box. As his fingers plucked a piece of *mici* from the pile, the lid came down and swatted his hand. He recoiled.

"*If* you think you can get it." Kat arched an eyebrow. "I'm totally kidding... or am I?" Her other eyebrow joined the first, both of them flying high as if to dare him.

Maksim smirked. She clearly had hold of the lid, ready to fling it down on his hand. "That's all right." He relaxed back. "I'm good for now."

"Aw." Her smile fell. "You're no fun."

Maksim watched and waited. As soon as she had a piece of flatbread, he lunged and snatched it from her. The bread was in his mouth before she could react.

"Mmm." He chewed. "You're right. Delicious," he said with his mouth full.

She laughed, and he found himself enamored by the melody. Had he heard her laugh like this before? Surely he had.

"Okay, okay. I've had enough bread anyway," she said, patting her stomach. Her denim shorts drew his attention, and he followed the lines of her legs—down to her thighs, along her calves, all the way to her bare feet. Her close proximity didn't escape his notice, and he had to look away to keep from undressing her in his mind.

"You seem to be feeling better." He reached for his cola, which sat on the bedside table, and cracked open the lid. "I gather you slept well."

"I did. And waking up to the food—"

The celebrity gossip show ramped up, cutting her off. The hosts were on their feet, shouting and pointing at each other. A brawl was about to ensue.

Kat grabbed the remote and lowered the volume to mute. "Just eating takeout and watching TV makes me feel…"

He swallowed his first gulp. The room-temperature liquid burned going down. "Normal?" he hedged, speaking past the fizz. He didn't particularly enjoy cola, but it would work in place of coffee.

"Exactly. I can't remember the last time I felt normal. It had to be before my dad died, so… six months ago?"

"I've never known normal." Maksim let his attention drift over the TV, the food. "But this seems like a good start."

Her entire face glowed under a smile. "Even in spite of our…?"

Maksim tilted his head. "Our impending and very illegal border crossing?"

"Yeah. That." She reached for her phone and checked the time again. "Could you help me with my shoulder before we leave? I've been letting the injury breathe, but it's still bothering me."

"It's the stitches." Maksim set his drink on the bedside table. "They shouldn't be ready to come out yet, but they are."

"Dr. Rhyland said the same thing." Kat wrapped an arm around herself, reaching for the spot. "She was supposed to remove the stitches today."

"I've self-removed plenty of stitches in my life. I'm happy to remove yours in Belgrade."

She lowered her arm. "Not now?"

"We need suture scissors. I could potentially get those from the pharmacy, but I don't want Bogdan to know we're dealing with injuries."

"I guess I could wear this top for the excursion." She looked down at herself. "It's not great for hiking, but it's better than the T-shirt." She set the takeaway box aside and went to climb over Maksim. Her attention was on her backpack, not him, but he became completely and immediately aware of her.

He grabbed her waist and tugged.

"Oh!" She landed in a straddle across his legs, and he watched her blush spread like wildfire.

His gaze followed the curve of her neck, brushing along her bare shoulder before moving to her collarbone. "This doesn't cover much," he said, taking a swath of the tank top between his fingers. The material was thin, fitted. More of a sleep top in his estimation.

She said nothing, her chest rising and falling.

Maksim released the fabric and reached up. The tip of his finger hooked one of the spaghetti straps, and he plucked. "I don't think this would be good for an excursion."

"It's the only one that doesn't… rub." She whispered the response as he secured her hips and dragged her closer. Her knees bumped the headboard on either side of him, and she inhaled a soft gasp.

He drew her in, parting his lips, tilting his head. Her breaths quickened, and Maksim knew they were about to share a passionate kiss that would very likely lead to more. Anticipation sparked within him.

The moment their lips connected, the very moment he allowed his desire to ignite, Kat wedged both hands against his chest and launched herself up and off the bed. Her landing was off-balance, and she staggered to the desk. "I might have another shirt. Maybe." She yanked open her backpack and started digging. "I-I'll look."

Maksim stood. "Hey," he whispered, coming alongside her.

She kept digging.

He brought his hand to rest on hers, halting the search. Her eyes flashed toward him, and he spied a tear skidding down her cheek. "Kat, what's wrong?"

"Nothing. I just—" She wiped away the dampness and focused on the bag. "Can I look for my top, please?"

He removed his hand but didn't otherwise move.

She dug until she found a light gray tank. The straps were thicker, but the material was as thin as the black number. "I normally wear a sports bra under this one." She inspected the top. "I don't think I can handle a sports bra today. Not until the stitches come out."

Maksim took the light-gray material between his fingers. "Everything will be much more visible under this." He was no longer being playful but serious, and he was only agreeing with what she herself had admitted.

For some reason, she tensed. He noticed but didn't expect what came next. "Did you tell Gabriela how to dress, too?"

Her response hit him like a bucket of ice water. Three beats passed before his brain processed the accusation. "I never dated Gabriela." Maksim wasn't sure why he'd proffered the information. Kat knew Gabriela had been a one-night stand, nothing more.

Well, not much more.

"But if you *had* dated her, would you have told her not to

wear things that were too revealing?" Kat leveled a hard stare. "Probably not."

"We're about to traverse wild terrain, and we'll be with a guy who's a bit of a bastard as far as I can tell." A muscle ticked in Maksim's jaw. "Forgive me for expressing concern."

"And why are we in this predicament again? Remind me?" She squared up to him. "We were perfectly safe in Sibiu until *your* side chick"—she shoved a finger in his chest—"decided to show up and ruin everything."

"She was Ty's side chick, not mine. Kat, I didn't even know you back then." He took possession of her hand—not roughly, but not gently either—and pulled it away. "You *chose* to come with me, despite knowing there would be danger." He guffawed. "But it's not the danger that scares you, is it? It's me." He pointed at himself. "I'm the danger."

Confusion splintered her features. "That's… ridiculous."

"Is it?" His eyes tightened along the sides. "Every time I do something wrong, every time you learn something unsavory about me, it confirms all those fears you've had. All the things Brandy has been warning you about."

Understanding glistened in her eyes. Or were those tears? She stiffened her bottom lip, which was trembling, and shoved the gray top into her backpack. "You don't know anything." Her voice broke over the words, and another tear escaped.

"I *do* know." He took hold of her, with both hands this time, and spun her around to face him. "I know because I care for you, and when I think on the matter too deeply, when I consider how vulnerable my feelings make me, it's terrifying." The admission jarred him. He pressed on, bringing himself eye-level. "The status quo would have been easier for me. But I don't want easier. I want you. I'm here with *you*."

She tried to pull away. He reeled her in.

"If we were going to be with Levi or Daniel or any other trustworthy man, I would have no problem with what you wear.

But I don't know Bogdan, and I have nothing but a pocketknife and a list of physical hindrances should things go sideways."

Worry eclipsed her features. She dragged herself out of his grasp and stationed herself by the window. It wasn't until her shoulders began to shake that he realized she was weeping.

Everything within him longed to go to her—to hold her, comfort her, most of all to protect her—but the sting of rejection held him in place. His pride whispered that he couldn't handle another blow, so he made his way to the bed. "There's no turning back." He parked himself on the mattress and settled his elbows on his knees. "We have to go with Bogdan. "

"Why didn't you bring the gun?"

"Because if there's any chance we'll encounter border police, I could be shot and killed, and *you* would be incarcerated. Vladimir would have access to you in the justice system here." A hesitation. "There's... another reason as well, something I haven't shared." He clasped his hands, head bowed, and exhaled a heavy sigh. "Levi intends to plant the pistol on Gabriela, around her vehicle, so that bystanders will see it and call the police. Until then, I feel better knowing he has a weapon in case—"

Maksim didn't finish, but he didn't have to. Kat knew which "in case" he'd been referring to. "You have a lot of people to protect."

His attention shot to her.

"That's why I'm thinking I should go home after Germany." She hugged herself. "One less person for you to worry about."

A sharp pain entered his chest. If she went home, he may never see her again. She couldn't return to Europe, and whether he could fly to the States remained an unknown.

But she would be safe.

But *he* would be gutted.

"Pick a top. Whichever you want." Maksim stood. "We need to head out."

CHAPTER
NINETEEN

15:26 (3:26 PM)

BOGDAN WAS ALREADY SHUTTERING the windows when Kat and Maksim arrived. Maksim smiled. Kat fidgeted, trying not to mess with her injury. She'd worn the t-shirt she'd been wearing earlier, and the fabric was unforgiving.

"Do you have the money?" Bogdan asked.

Kat pulled out a stack of cash that had been folded in half.

"In here." Bogdan glanced both ways and motioned for her to come inside.

Maksim followed them to the doorway, resisting the urge to insert himself further. Kat was playing her part. He had to play his.

Kat held the money toward Bogdan. He stared for a long moment, head tilted. "You count it," he said eventually.

She counted out the banknotes—two thousand euros in all. Maksim noticed the way Bogdan leered at her, and every fiber of his being tensed. *Let it go.*

But then another part of him whispered, *Watch your back.*

Bogdan took the money and motioned for Maksim to enter. "Close the door."

Maksim crossed the threshold, pulling the door shut, and Bogdan waited patiently before giving his next command. "Remove your shirts. Empty your pockets."

Maksim went static. "Excuse me?"

"I need to make sure you are not carrying weapons." He gestured at Kat. "You too."

"She isn't carrying a weapon," Maksim said. "I can assure you."

Bogdan narrowed his stare. "What assurance can you give me?"

"I've been with her for two days."

"And what about you?" The guy folded his arms. "How do I know *you* aren't going to attack me?"

"Are you kidding?" Maksim huffed a laugh. "I would be fired. My boss would be furious."

Bogdan buckled down on his glare.

"But I'm happy to prove that I have no weapons." As Maksim untucked his shirt, his attention shifted to the video camera mounted in the corner. The device hadn't been operational earlier, but now a red light glowed. The camera angle had been adjusted as well, pointing directly at Kat and Maksim.

The bastard had planned this.

Maksim propped his duffel against the wall and began unbuttoning his shirt.

"Open it all the way." Bogdan gestured. "I want to see your waistband."

Maksim worked his way to the last button and then opened the shirt. Bogdan twirled his finger, and Maksim did a slow 360.

"Slower," Bogdan barked. "Lift your shirt in the back." A hesitation. "Stop. What's that?"

Maksim reached into his back pocket and pulled out his pocketknife. "I always bring this on excursions."

"Leave it there." Bogdan nodded toward a shelf and then focused on Kat. "Now for you."

Maksim was setting his knife down. His eyes flashed toward Kat, who stood frozen.

"Do it," Bogdan rumbled.

"Don't." Maksim moved fast, stationing himself beside Kat. He kept his eyes on Bogdan. "She will *not* be required to lift her shirt."

"You think you are a tough guy?" Bogdan pursed his lips. "That you don't need to follow my rules?"

"She doesn't have anything. You would see it." Maksim nudged Kat. "Turn out your pockets."

Kat pulled out the linen material. The pockets of her jean shorts were empty.

"That will be sufficient for her." Maksim rebuttoned his shirt and tucked the tails. "This is inappropriate and puts my job at risk. Either you're taking us or you're not. Which is it?"

Bogdan snorted. "You can't fault a man for being cautious, can you?"

Maksim's disdain oozed. He let it show with a narrowed stare.

Bogdan shrugged and angled for the entrance.

Maksim grabbed his duffel. He considered swiping the knife as well, but his thoughts reverted to the camera. Bogdan may have stationed someone in the back. The person could have been watching the feed. One call or SMS to Bogdan, and Maksim would be busted. The pocketknife, though useful, simply wasn't worth the risk.

Bogdan locked up the pharmacy, stored the keys in his pocket, and started up the street. Kat and Maksim dogged his heels.

They continued past the supermarket and veered onto a narrow road lined with one-story houses. Many of the structures were in disrepair, and stacks of roofing materials dotted the sidewalk.

The sun cooked them from above and below, the heat radiating off the pavement, and sweat poured from every crevice of

Maksim's body. He'd worn the long-sleeve to hide his scars, but there'd been no hiding the bruises on his chest.

He ran through cover stories to explain the injuries. A motorcycle accident seemed most logical. He could speak with authority on the matter, and since he had other scars from a real bike accident, he could always make a joke about needing to give up the hobby.

Unfortunately, Bogdan never asked about the bruises. He never said much of anything.

They crossed a footbridge that traversed a ditch, and a large hill covered in greenery appeared before them. Maksim brought up the rear of their line, and he'd been watching Kat struggle more and more with the backpack.

She tried one strap over her good shoulder.

Both straps over both shoulders.

Holding the backpack at her side.

Holding the backpack with both hands in front.

Maksim was about to step in when she stopped in her tracks. He came up behind her. "Would you like me to carry it?"

She didn't acknowledge him.

He took hold of the backpack but couldn't pry it from her grip. Then he noticed that her attention lay on the hill ahead. He realized why. "We're not at Village Ksorba."

Her attention moved to him.

"We're going to Serbia," he whispered as Bogdan turned around. Kat's attention roamed in that direction. Her expression remained blank. "Kat." Maksim touched her arm.

Her eyes returned to him. "I was remembering—"

"I know." Maksim took the backpack from her. "But we need to go." His gaze flicked toward Bogdan. "Right now."

She swallowed, nodding, and they continued up the road.

Villagers dotted the road, their voices blending with the crunch of footsteps that trekked past them. No one dared sit or stand in the sun. Even the town's stray dogs had enough sense to stay in the shade. *Only we're foolish enough to be out in this.* Maksim kept the thought private.

The houses grew distant behind them as their path inclined. The craggy sidewalk disappeared as they took a gravel road around the right side of the hill.

A mini hatchback approached from behind. The vehicle barely fit, and Bogdan motioned for Kat and Maksim to scoot over. They did, but it was such a tight squeeze the passenger-side mirror bumped Maksim's hip.

The car disappeared a moment later. "Is this one of the old routes?" Maksim asked. Bogdan didn't have an immediate response, so Maksim tried again. "I wasn't expecting paved roads—"

"Because it's *not* one of the old routes." Bogdan cast a surly look over his shoulder. "We are getting there, okay? We have to cross the highway first."

Panic jolted Maksim. Daniel had said the highway led to the border checkpoint. How close were they to that? Was there a risk of border agents patrolling?

Maksim had no way to know and no way to ask without giving away their real plans. *Damn me.*

The highway appeared as they crested the hill. After winding their way down, they found traffic moving in both directions on the two-lane road.

Maksim held his breath, watching. So far, none of the vehicles looked very official—a yellow van, two Dacias, another hatchback.

Bogdan let the vehicles pass before crossing over. Maksim and Kat did their best to keep up. "I can carry my backpack," Kat said as they reached the other side. "For a little while."

"I'm all right for now." Maksim pumped lightheartedness into his tone even though the pain in his shoulder had begun to smolder. "I'll let you have a turn soon."

Kat didn't seem to know what to say. "Um, how much further do you think?"

"Good question. Let's ask our fearless leader." Maksim figured Bogdan could hear them, but he amplified his voice as part of the ruse. "About how much farther?"

"Why? Are you tired?" Bogdan was trekking alongside the highway and sent a glance over his shoulder. "We're going there," he said dryly, pointing at two o'clock.

Maksim spied a dirt road that led into a forest.

"Think you can make it without needing a break?" Maksim posed the question to Kat but asked loud enough so that Bogdan could hear.

She panted. "I… think so."

Maksim quickened his pace—as much as he could with both bags—and caught up to Bogdan. Kat did the same. Well, she tried, but it wasn't long before she'd fallen behind again.

Vehicles cruised past, swirling up dust and hot air. Still no government vehicles. They needed to get off this highway before their luck ran out.

They cut over when the dirt road spanned to their immediate right. A green hill filled the horizon, and the trees around them grew thicker as they walked.

The hum of engines faded behind them, and the trio entered a canopy of green. The forest air was cooler, more tolerable, and as Maksim fanned his shirt, the sweat on his face, neck, and arms began the process of drying. "I'm guessing this is it," he said, pretending to be amazed by their surroundings.

Again, Bogdan had no immediate reply.

"Is there anything you can tell us about this particular smuggling route?" Maksim pressed. "Do you know if this is the one that was used to bring the VHS tapes?"

Bogdan chuckled. "You can stop the acting."

Maksim and Kat shared a look. "We're not acting," Maksim said, lengthening his stride. "I told you. I'm supposed to be giving a—"

"That's far enough." Bogdan wheeled around, and Maksim froze as the barrel of a pistol appeared.

Bogdan tightened his jaw in resolve and took aim at Maksim.

CHAPTER
TWENTY

MAKSIM'S MOUTH TUMBLED OPEN. Where the hell had this guy gotten a handgun? Gun ownership was heavily restricted in Romania. Those who qualified for a license typically had hunting rifles. Gun collectors might have black powder rifles.

Only the police carried handguns. *And criminals.*

Maksim's brain shifted into overdrive. The pistol was a .22, something along the lines of a Walther PPK. Twenty-twos didn't have much stopping power, and he considered a direct assault. He would likely be shot—multiple times—but he felt sure he could overpower this asshole.

And then what? The question plucked at his logic. What would Maksim do after he overpowered Bogdan? Kill him? That would be a surefire way to have Interpol up his ass for the next twenty years.

He could tie Bogdan up, but that would be a very temporary solution—only until someone noticed his absence—and would likely result in a phone call to the police. Bogdan could provide descriptions of Maksim and Kat. Hell, he had video of them now.

Maksim swore.

"Did you really expect me to believe that ridiculous story about the VHS tapes?" Bogdan's mouth curled up along the sides. "You must have thought I was stupid. The stupid boy from the little village."

Maksim opened his mouth to answer.

Bogdan cut him off. "What kind of tour guide brings a bag that large on an excursion like this?" His attention moved to the duffel strapped to Maksim's shoulder. "Drop it."

Maksim lowered duffel. He did the same with Kat's backpack and then raised both hands.

Bogdan tipped his gun toward the duffel. "Open it."

Maksim hesitated.

"Did you not hear me?" Bogdan tightened his grip, training the weapon on Maksim. "Open the bag," he said slowly.

The duffel contained several items of great importance—the cash, the hardware wallet, Maksim's leather wallet with more cash, three of Maksim's passports, Kat's passport…

A jolt of panic shocked Maksim's system. The lockbox was in his duffel.

Maksim maintained eye contact as he unzipped the bag. The lockbox was a top priority, as were the passports. Then there was the cash—roughly thirty grand earned through grueling enforcer work. He'd risked his life and spilled his blood to save up that money. The thought of losing it made him nauseated.

But he did have cash in his wallet. And there was half a mil waiting for him in Belgrade.

His plan formed quickly. He spread the bag open, revealing his clothes first and then the cash.

Bogdan's eyes ballooned. "I knew it. You're running away from something. From some*one*." His thick, unkempt eyebrows flew high. "This is an elaborate scheme for crossing into Serbia. You must be a thief like those dirty communists." He aimed the pistol at Kat. "And you? Are you his accomplice?"

Maksim straightened and stepped in front of her in a single swift motion. "Do not point that at her."

"I knew you two were together. Not at first, but when I told her to lift her shirt, I could see how much it bothered you. And those bruises." Bogdan flitted the pistol toward Maksim's chest. "You were in a fight."

"You caught us." Maksim forced a smile. "So why don't you take the money and let us go."

"Close the bag. Toss it to me." Bogdan pointed at the ground in front of him. "Here."

Maksim hesitated. The lockbox was irreplaceable. And so was…

Madǎ's ring! The sapphire solitaire was in his wallet, which he'd stored in a folded-up pair of pants in the duffel. *Goddamn it!*

"Listen, friend—"

"Do it!" Bogdan's grip tightened on the pistol. "Do it or I will kill her and make you watch!"

"I'm trying to help you."

"You think I won't do it? I will *bury* you out here where no one will find you." Bogdan held the pistol steady. An amateur always revealed their inexperience with shaky, unsteady hands. Bogdan was unhinged. But he was not, by any means, an amateur.

Maksim detected Kat's touch. She clutched his shirt, whimpering.

"Take the money," Maksim repeated. "We're not going to put up a fight. We just want to be on our way… but we won't get far if you're caught."

Bogdan's face had twisted with rage. His features ironed out as he processed the statement. "I won't be caught if you're dead."

"That's not what I meant." Maksim gestured over his shoulder, indicating the direction they'd come from. "How many people saw us walking through your village? How many saw *me* carrying this bag?" He flagged Bogdan with an eyebrow. "What will happen if *you* return with the same bag? How many old-timers still have the communist mindset of informing on their neighbor?" Maksim glanced at the duffel. "How many would suspect you were paid for something—whether a service or something illicit—and decide *they* want this money?"

Bogdan hadn't thought of that. Maksim could tell by his surprised expression. "Okay," Bogdan said, his tone much more conciliatory. "What are you suggesting?"

"Take the money. All of it. I'm simply asking to keep our bags, which have our clothes, some food." He thumbed at Kat. "Her father really did die, and we have some of his trinkets in the bag."

Thoughtfulness tinged Bogdan's expression—and yet, he didn't seem fully convinced. Maksim had one more card, and he decided to play it.

"I'll give you everything you need to access my crypto wallet."

Bogdan's eyes lit up. "Crypto?"

Maksim nodded. "May I?"

Bogdan readied himself with the pistol. "If I suspect you are reaching for a weapon—"

"No weapon. I swear." Maksim knelt slowly and fished out the hardware wallet.

Bogdan snorted. "That's not a crypto wallet."

"It is." He lobbed the device, which landed with a *plop* at Bogdan's feet. "We cashed out, but there are reserve funds."

"How much?"

"Seven thousand. A little more."

A glimmer sparked behind their captor's eyes. He glanced at the device. "Are you lying to me?"

"I'm not. But even if I were, you'll have more than thirty thousand in cash."

"Thirty thousand." Bogdan gawked. "*Euros?*"

Maksim nodded. "You wouldn't want to risk all that money by killing us, especially since we can't report the money missing." A pause. "You do realize that, don't you?"

Bogdan narrowed his stare. "No. I don't." His lips quirked. "Convince me."

"*If* we contacted the police—and we're not going to—they would demand to see our passports, and they would realize we don't have exit stamps for Romania. We'd be facing jail time." Maksim tipped his hands as if to say *See? Why would we incriminate ourselves?*

Bogdan pursed his lips in a pinched smirk. "It's a deal, then. I let you live. I keep the cash."

"And the crypto wallet. I'll give you the PIN and passphrase. Then please, let us go."

Bogdan scooped up the device and took three giant steps backward, putting more space between himself and Maksim. Bogdan found the power button and pressed it. The screen lit up, casting a soft glow onto his harsh features.

Maksim gave him a numeric PIN and then a longer passphrase—a mix of letters, numbers, and symbols. Bogdan entered everything and examined the screen. "Where are the funds?"

"On the blockchain."

Bogdan flashed a look that was one part disbelief, two parts confusion.

"Crypto is stored on the—" Maksim sighed. "Never mind about that. Just know that the information you need for *accessing* the funds is saved in the device. Now that you have control of the wallet, you'll have control of the funds." Maksim went step by step, explaining which ledger to download, how to connect the wallet to the app. "You can use a computer or a mobile device. You'll also need this." Maksim stooped and, without breaking eye contact, felt around in his bag.

He found the USB cord and tossed it.

Bogdan rubbed a hand through his hair the way Maksim did, except the guy looked utterly deranged. He reined in his excitement and cleared his throat. "You." He looked past Maksim. "Bring me the cash."

Kat released Maksim's shirt. He turned and found her stepping out from behind him. "No."

"You! Shut up!" Bogdan aimed the pistol at Maksim. "You. Woman. You are going to gather the money and bring it to me, or I will shoot your boyfriend."

Kat placed a hand on Maksim's arm, her expression fearful but determined. Then she knelt and gathered every last bit of cash she could find.

"Is that all of it? Show me."

Kat opened the bag wide and shifted the clothes around.

"What's that?" Bogdan pointed the pistol at something.

Kat reached for the item, and Maksim's stomach bottomed out. Silently, in his mind, he swore with every curse he'd ever heard or known. Outwardly, he remained stoic.

Kat's hands trembled as she withdrew the lockbox. Everything she needed for claiming her inheritance was stored in the small metal box, and Maksim added himself to the list of curses. He could have copied the information down, kept the notes somewhere safe. At the very least, he could have memorized the most important details. Why hadn't he?

Because the lockbox belonged to Kat, not him, and he hadn't wanted to insert himself into her financial affairs. But he could have made helpful suggestions.

Bogdan's bushy black eyebrows converged—but then a look of understanding crossed his features. "Your father's?"

Kat nodded.

Bogdan trained his gaze on the lockbox. He wanted it— whether out of curiosity or greed Maksim couldn't tell, but this man wasn't going to let them keep it. Maksim, not knowing what else to do, exchanged the silent swearing for a prayer Daniel had taught him. He closed his eyes. *Holy art Thou, O God. Through the Theotokos, have mercy on us.*

"My father is dead, too." Bogdan's confession sent a flutter of surprise through Maksim. He opened his eyes.

Kat swallowed, clearly nervous, and managed a weak smile. "I'm sorry for your loss."

Bogdan stiffened his chin, shoulders straightening. "Bring me the cash. The box, too."

Kat's expression fell. She collected everything, which turned into an armful, and circumnavigated the duffel.

"Slower." Bogdan leveled the pistol at her, and Maksim nearly climbed out of his skin. *Bastard.* He pictured himself racing forward, snatching the pistol, and shoving it into the guy's smug mouth and down his throat.

But a blanket of calm descended. He closed his eyes again. *Doamne, miluiește.* (Lord, have mercy.) That was all he could muster.

Kat slowed her pace. Maksim watched the tremor in her hands consume the rest of her body. He almost said something positive, reassuring, but didn't want to startle Bogdan. *Lord, have mercy.*

Kat stopped an arm's length from their captor and handed over the cash, which Maksim had divided and rubber-banded in preparation for their journey. Bogdan shoved the stacks into his pockets. When those were full, he stuffed the remainder in his underwear. There was a bulge about him, even with his shirt untucked, but the average person likely wouldn't notice.

The lockbox rattled as Kat held it toward him. Maksim couldn't see her face, but he heard her sniffle.

Bogdan eyed the metal box. Then, to Maksim's amazement, the guy scooped up the USB cord and pushed past Kat. "Out of my way."

He aimed the pistol at Maksim, giving a wide berth, and walked backwards. "Border is that way." He jerked the pistol in the direction they'd been going. "To the left of the next hill. Beyond the river."

Maksim kept his mouth shut and his hands raised.

Bogdan continued until he reached the edge of the forest.

Then he launched into a sprint, glancing over his shoulder every five to ten steps. Maksim didn't budge until the scumbag had disappeared down the dirt road.

TWENTY-ONE

"ARE YOU ALL RIGHT?" Maksim walked beside Kat as they made their way through the forest. Daylight broke through the trees in the distance, and the hill Bogdan had mentioned became visible.

"You mean besides having a PTSD response because we're in a forest with a guy who's waving a gun around?" Kat's voice trembled. "Apart from that, I'm great."

"I'm sorry. I knew the guy was shady, but Romanian business owners aren't exactly in the habit of carrying handguns."

"What are we going to do?" She reseated her backpack. "Maksim, he took your money."

"It's fine."

"No, it's not!" She stopped. "Thirty *thousand* euros? Really? How are we supposed to get to Germany?"

"It was a lot. I know." He adjusted his duffel, ignoring the nausea still sloshing around in his stomach. "But putting up a fight would have led to nothing but trouble for us." He reached for her backpack. "Plus, I didn't give him everything."

Her tension deflated. "You didn't?"

He gestured, indicating they should continue. "I always keep a thousand in my wallet," he said as they cleared the last trees.

"That will be enough to get us to Belgrade. And not that it matters, per se, but the passphrase I gave him was for a decoy wallet. The primary is hidden, and he'll have access to significantly less money in the decoy."

"Oh." She cleared her throat. "How much less? I mean… how much do you have in crypto?"

Maksim's mouth angled up. "A lot, and I'm going to hit my cache in Belgrade. As I said, we'll be fine." He used his hand as a visor, shielding his eyes from the furnace overhead, and observed their surroundings. "Bogdan mentioned going around a hill." He nodded toward a green slope. "I'm guessing that's it."

"He mentioned a river, too, but not how to cross."

"Levi said some parts are shallow. Perhaps we'll wander across such a spot."

"I hope so." She reached for her injury. "Maksim, my shoulder hurts."

His shoulder hurt as well. But all he said was "Try to hang in there."

They skirted the hill and made good time doing so. But when the river appeared, reality dashed their hopefulness to pieces. This wasn't a creek. It was a micro delta, deep and wide, with tree groves lining the other side.

Disappointment slinked through Maksim. There was no way to cross with all their belongings. They had to find a shallow section.

Maksim carried their bags to a large tree twenty meters from the riverbank. "Stay here."

"Why? Where are you going?"

"To find a better crossing point. Hide behind this tree while I'm gone. Anyone sees you, just say you're hiking and that your guide went to relieve himself." Maksim set the bags down. "Keep to this side. You'll be hidden from the river, though it won't help if someone spots you from the forest."

"What if…" She fidgeted. "What if Bogdan finds me?"

Maksim was checking the direction of the sun, trying to

orient himself. His attention returned to Kat. "You don't have to worry about that, *dragă*."

"But—"

"I promise." He stood in front of her. "Bogdan is busy counting his loot and accessing the decoy wallet. He's not worried about us."

She scanned the tree line and sent a worried look toward the river. "So then border police are our main concern?"

"They're our *only* concern." He took her hand and gave a reassuring squeeze. "I'll be fast. You won't even know I'm gone."

"'Kay."

He refocused on the present task. The checkpoint was north, which meant he needed to go south. Down river. To the left.

He broke into a jog. "I'll be back," he called over his shoulder. Kat responded by parking herself on the duffel and leaning against the tree.

Maksim quickened his pace. The river moved lazily on his right, widening the farther he ran. Lush greenery filled the opposite bank.

He kept going.

The river narrowed in one section. Then it narrowed some more. Pebbles ran along both banks, and the forest sat back from the water's edge by fifty meters. This helped the area feel less marshy—precisely what he was looking for. Entering and exiting would be easier here, and although he couldn't discern the water's depth, the crossing would be quick and painless even if they had to swim.

Maksim sprinted the whole way back—a solid eight hundred meters. "Everything okay?" he asked, his head on a swivel while he worked to catch his breath.

"No signs of police," Kat said. "I was listening for voices, boat motors, anything."

"Good." Maksim grabbed his duffel. "Can you swim?"

"It's sort of a requirement where I'm from." She pushed up. "But I was hoping I wouldn't get my clothes wet."

"I'm not certain of the depth, but the spot I found is narrow." He beckoned her. "I have a solution for the clothes."

———

"Nuh-uh. No way." Kat stared at the crossing. "I'll have to take off my clothes, and I told you. I'm not doing that."

"Then wear them." Maksim stripped off his shirt. "Personally, I'm not going to."

"What about our bags? My laptop is in here."

"I'll carry the bags across. Then I'll come back and help you."

She lowered her backpack to the ground. "What if the water is so deep you *can't* carry them?"

He leveled an annoyed look. "What do you want me to do? Hm? We don't have a lot of options." He stripped down to his boxer briefs and carried his clothes and boots toward the water. "I'll cross first, and then we'll know the depth."

As soon as his feet hit the pebbles and rocks—before he reached ankle depth—he winced and backed out. "I'm going to wear my boots," he amended, returning to where he'd started.

He donned the boots without socks and laced them. The end result looked utterly ridiculous. He *felt* utterly ridiculous.

Maksim gathered his clothes and proceeded to the riverbank —188 centimeters of pure flesh concealed only by his underwear and boots. He might as well have been walking around in a loin cloth. Pale, crinkled skin covered the right side of his body— from the top of his shoulder, down his upper arm, along his ribs and back, and all the way to his thigh. The bruises showed. So did the tan lines on his forearms. His tribal band, which he loathed for what it represented, shouted its existence from his left arm.

But at least his feet wouldn't hurt when he entered the river.

"We never speak of this." He held up a stern finger to Kat, who had been drinking him in—and not in the way he would have liked. "I mean it. I don't want to hear any jokes, not a thing."

She hugged herself, biting down on a smile, and nodded.

Pebbles crunched beneath his boots as he entered the river. Cool water reached to his knees… his thighs… his waist… his chest.

He lifted the clothes over his head and continued forward, pushing through the slow-moving current. "I think this is as deep as it gets." He turned toward Kat. "Top of my chest."

"That's basically the top of my head."

Maksim delivered his clothes to the opposite bank. He returned for the bags next. The riverbed was as rocky as the shore, and he was grateful to have the boots even if he looked like an underwear advertisement gone wrong.

Maksim decided to take both bags at once. The quicker they could get across, the less likely they would encounter a river patrol.

He hoisted the duffel onto his good shoulder while the backpack rested on his weaker, injured shoulder. Back across he went.

The river followed him out each time, his boots waterlogged, but he carried on and stored everything on the opposite bank.

"Let's go," he said as he returned to Kat. "We can't linger."

"Okay, but…" She wrung her hands. "How did it feel carrying both bags like that? On your shoulders?"

"The weight wasn't balanced, so the load felt unsteady a couple of times." He shoved a wet hand through his hair. "Why?"

"I thought maybe you could do that again. You know"—her expression turned pleading—"with me?"

He stalled. "Carry you on my shoulders?"

"I really don't want to get my clothes wet, and you're already…" She gestured in his direction. Her gaze fell to his crotch, and her eyes widened.

He looked down. His manhood showed through the boxer

briefs, which were pale blue and soaked through. A flush of heat crept into his neck and face. He really did look like an idiot.

"I've done it before at pool parties." Kat pointed her gaze skyward. "And I have decent balance. You'd just have to squat low enough so that I can climb on."

"Fine." Maksim rolled his eyes. "Whatever it takes to get you moving."

Kat exhaled her relief. "Thank you."

"Don't thank me until we're on the other side." He cast a worried look upriver. "Your legs will be submerged, so you'll probably want to remove the shoes and socks."

She yanked off her shoes and used them to store the socks. Then she tied the laces and draped the shoes around her neck.

"Ouch," she said, following Maksim to the entry point. He looked down and saw her toes curling. "I can't go any farther."

He widened his stance and dropped into a squat.

She hitched her leg, trying to swing it over him. His broad shoulders hindered each attempt. "Use this." He patted the top of his thigh. "Like a step."

Kat stepped up and swung her leg around. Fire ignited in Maksim's shoulder as her leg found its home. He sucked a sharp breath.

"Are you okay?"

"Fine." He gritted his teeth. "Let's go."

She brought her other leg around and secured it over his other shoulder. The fire lessened as her weight evened out.

"Ready?" he asked, sending any residual pain into the background of his mind.

"I… think so."

He held her legs and rose to standing. She wobbled, and he took a step forward to steady them. That made her wobble even more. "You need to balance," he said.

"I'm trying."

"Extend your arms."

He felt her tip forward again.

"To the sides!"

The wobbling stopped, and a sense of balance came from the top down. He took a measured step. Then another. "Entering the water."

Her legs tightened, her bare feet pressing against his ribs. This put pressure on his bad shoulder, and the fire ignited. He gritted his teeth and suffered through it, unwilling to risk another wobble.

Cool water reached to his thighs... his boxer briefs... The depth had reached his navel when Kat nearly toppled off.

Maksim widened his stance, reclaiming the balance they'd lost. "What are you doing up there?"

"Hang on. Maksim, hang on." She lowered her hand and smacked his upper arm several times. "Stop moving."

He stilled himself, his boots resting on a layer of river rock.

"Do you hear that?" A pause. "It sounds like a motor," she whispered, "but I can't tell where it's coming from."

Panic rocketed through Maksim. He swayed. Kat gasped, swaying with him.

Maksim caught himself and took his next step. Then his next. Kat's toes, feet, and ankles became submerged. His ears had detected the motor, but he couldn't tell where it stemmed from. There was no bridge that he could see, no way for anyone to drive down there.

It had to be border agents. Likely in a patrol boat.

"Come on, come on," Kat whispered. "We're almost there."

"Working on it," he said, jaw clenched.

They reached the other side as the roar of the engine grew louder. Maksim checked both directions. Still nothing in sight, but the sound was definitely growing louder.

"Oh!" Kat jostled up top. "There's a road. Maksim, I can see it."

"Where?" Maksim couldn't turn his head, so he focused his attention north instead. "Show me."

Kat pointed toward their eight o'clock—behind and to the left. "I think we're hearing a car."

Maksim rotated his upper body as much as he could. As much as he dared. Trees lined an area off to the left, and he observed sections of pavement beyond the greenery. A road, hidden by the tree line, appeared to run parallel to the river.

Movement blurred on the other side of the trees.

"Well?" Kat said as the motor faded. "You think they could see us through the trees?"

"I'm not certain. They didn't appear to be stopping, but—let's focus." Maksim faced forward and continued. River rocks crunched under his boots. Hot air replaced the cool water as he carried Kat onto the bank.

He stopped beside the bags and squatted. "Step down onto my duffel," he said, releasing her left leg.

Kat slid off on that side and pulled her other leg around. Maksim did his best to balance, hold, and catch various parts of her until her foot found his thigh and then the bag.

Maksim gathered his clothes. "We have to move. Hurry."

Kat fumbled with her shoes.

"Skip the socks," Maksim said. "We'll regroup in the forest."

She shoved her bare feet into the shoes and grabbed her backpack. Maksim gripped the short handle of his duffel, and they raced for the tree line.

PART THREE

CHAPTER
TWENTY-TWO

19:49 (7:49 PM)

THE COMING sunset layered the sky in deepening shades of gold. Traffic buzzed in all directions at Zeleni Venac, a neighborhood in central Belgrade, and the stench of fumes and hot pavement saturated the air.

Maksim and Kat sat in the back of a city bus, waiting for their stop. They'd never made it to Bela Crkva. They hadn't even made it to Serbia when they first crossed that river, something they only learned after encountering an elderly farmer driving a horse-drawn carriage.

Maksim recalled how the man had lifted a tan, weathered arm and pointed, directing them to a dirt road they would have missed otherwise. *"Go there. Follow the path. It will take you all the way to the border."*

"We have an urgent matter in Belgrade," Maksim had said, *"and we don't have time for border checkpoints—if you understand my meaning?"* Maksim followed up the explanation with a fifty-euro

banknote, and the farmer divulged a plethora of helpful information—what to look for at the crossing, how to reach the nearest Serbian town.

More importantly, the man had explained some key places where border police might be and how to avoid them.

"Go to Kusic," the man had said. *"The village is south and west of where you will cross. You can hire an unofficial taxi"*—the farmer paused dramatically—*"if you understand my meaning."*

"Mulțumesc frumos." (Thank you very much.) Maksim handed him another fifty. *"You never saw us."*

"Saw who?" The farmer pocketed the cash and flicked his reins. The horse started forward, pulling the rickety carriage up the dusty road.

The bus lurched, tethering Maksim to the present. Kat sat next to him, exhausted and sunburned as she ate her melted sour candies. They had claimed the seats in the far back, placing their bags on either side of them. This gave them the entire row... and a bit more privacy.

Kat leaned forward, trying to glimpse the city outside.

"Don't." Maksim gripped her shoulder. "CCTV cameras."

Her mouth sprang open. "Maksim, we're on a bus. They have CCTV onboard."

"Not here. Not yet." He examined their surroundings, watching all the passengers coming and going. "The Serbian government is working with a Chinese company on a mass surveillance project. 'Safe City' as they call it. They've managed to outfit some, not all, of the neighborhoods with cameras, and the buses are planned for 2020."

"Next year." Kat hugged her backpack. "Wow. So... how are we getting where we're going? Do you know where all the cameras are?"

"I know some. The place we'll be staying is safe, but getting there is another story." Maksim eyed the crowded bus. Nobody appeared to be paying attention as he pulled the duffel onto his lap and fished out the ball cap he'd bought in Bucureşti. "CCTV cameras are usually mounted up high to capture the broadest scope of vehicular and foot traffic. Wearing this cap and keeping my head down will prevent any cameras from gleaning my image. So if any of Vladimir's people are using facial recognition—"

"Wait. Facial recognition?" Kat blinked. "Who are these people? The CIA?"

"Vladimir has moles in strategic industries. Not the CIA, but European intelligence. All he would need is one person running facial-recognition software, scanning and cross-referencing footage from across Europe, and the system would detect us."

Kat's eyes widened. "I don't have a hat. What am I going to do?"

"I have an idea, but we should hurry. Our stop is coming up." Maksim gestured toward her backpack. "May I?"

She passed it to him.

"How many black tops do you have?" He unzipped the backpack. "Offhand."

"Two t-shirts and the tank top you hate."

"You mean the *sleep* top?" He slanted a look. "I don't hate it."

She bit into one of the candies. "Seemed like you hated it."

The temptation to argue swelled. But he ignored the comment and pulled out the two black tees. One had graphics that bled through to the inside. The other was plain black.

"Put this on, but don't slide your arms into the sleeves as you normally would." He handed her the shirt.

She took it. "So just… around my neck?"

"And your shoulders. If you can."

She did exactly that. The shirt draped her precisely as he had envisioned. Well, except for the shirt sleeves, which stuck out. He tucked those inside themselves, flatting them, then pulled out the infamous tank top.

"Do the same with this one."

She followed his instructions. "Now what?"

Maksim did his best to tuck the straps inside the top. They were stubborn and kept poking out. "Take your hair down."

She dragged the rubberband out of her hair, and her black curls flopped down in a sweaty, frizzy bunch. He tucked her hair under the fabric and then pulled the rear of the tank top up and over her head. This drew the front section to her chin, but that didn't matter. Her head—nay, her conspicuous hair—was covered.

Maksim scanned the bus as the latest wave of passengers located their seats. Several stood, holding on to the yellow safety bars. "This is a diverse city, and it's not unusual for Muslim or Orthodox women to be seen with their heads covered."

"Do they usually wear dirty jean shorts?" She presented her legs.

"You're right. That will garner attention." He rummaged through her backpack. "Do you have pants?"

"I have workout leggings. They go below my knee, but they're tight."

He found the leggings. "Keep these at the ready. I need to figure out one more component."

The bus eased forward in bumper-to-bumper traffic. Maksim didn't go near the window, but he knew they had already crossed the Danube and were now traveling through the gauntlet of glass towers and brick apartments on Braće Jugovića. They were nearing their stop.

Maksim swapped the backpack for his duffel. Black clothes weren't his thing, but he did have one item—a knit long-sleeve shirt he wore during the autumn. *Not anymore*, he thought as he unfolded the long-sleeve. "Can you stand?"

Kat rose, reaching for the nearest safety bar. Maksim took his hands and wrapped them around her waist. She inhaled a sharp breath, recoiling, but he continued with the makeshift measurements. He'd have to stretch the neckline, and the realization spurred a sour expression on his part. But it was just a shirt and Kat's safety was of far greater importance.

"What?" she asked.

"Nothing." He grabbed hold of the neck and tugged. The seams gave, enlarging, and then he tucked the long sleeves inside the shirt. "See if you can fit this over your shorts."

Kat glanced to and fro and then stuck her feet through the neck. With a bit of wiggling, she managed to drag the neckline up to her butt.

Maksim gripped the neckline again and yanked hard. Perhaps too hard. The seams tore, leaving the fabric in a droopy, pathetic-looking state. "Try again."

She was able to pull the neckline over her derriere, her hips, and all the way up to her waist. "It's not going to stay up." She showed him the saggy "waistband."

"Tie a knot." His watchful stare swept over the passengers. "You need to put those tights on now. We're nearing our stop."

"I can't take my shorts off here."

"You can with my shirt covering you." He pointed. "Do it behind those last two seats."

"Maksim—"

"Everyone is just trying to get where they're going. People are listening to music, reading, SMSing, scrolling social media." He gathered the tights and placed them into her hands. "Do it gradually, part by part, until they're on. Then prepare to disembark."

Kat attempted to execute the instructions. A guy looked their way at one point. Maksim stood, pretending to stretch while stepping in front of Kat. Either the guy saw nothing or he'd been in his own world, because he didn't glance their way again.

Their bus proceeded through a tunnel, and as the space on either side of them opened up, the stone buildings transformed into a mix of Art Deco and Neoclassicism.

"This is us." Maksim pointed ahead. They were stuck behind another bus, making it impossible to see out the front, but he knew to stand up when the trendy shops of Zeleni Venac appeared.

Passengers angled for the exit. Maksim grabbed his duffel and motioned for Kat to follow him. "Keep your head down," he whispered. "Pull the tank top around your face as much as possible. Try to cover your mouth and chin."

Kat tucked and pulled as the crowd pressed forward. The doors opened, and people poured out.

Maksim led the way, squeezing between bodies while hauling his duffel. Kat shuffled after him, carrying her backpack and clutching the waistband of her makeshift skirt.

"Stay two to three paces behind me," he whispered. "Keep your phone out and pretend to be reading a text."

Kat nodded, shouldering her backpack.

Maksim took his turn disembarking. When he glanced back, he saw Kat letting a woman go ahead of her, then a man, then she put her head down and started after him.

He focused forward, striding up the sidewalk. Trendy local shops occupied the ground level of several stone buildings— similar to București's neoclassical buildings, but with Belgrade's own flair. The hum of traffic, dotted with periodic honks, filled the air.

A pang of regret plucked at Maksim's stomach. Belgrade had always reminded him of București. He'd left his hometown not even a week ago and already he was homesick.

Pedestrians hurried along the sidewalk, some of them offering a wide berth when they noticed Maksim with his duffel. He nodded in thanks each time and then hung a right at the main entrance to the Design District. The area looked like it should have been pedestrian-only, but a slew of cars and work vans crowded the space, making it difficult for pedestrians to move about.

Maksim stalled beside a van and pulled out his flip phone. The brim of his cap covered his face as his head swiveled left, his eyes searching for Kat.

A Muslim girl outfitted in a black *hijab* and a frumpy, odd-looking *abaya* appeared. That was what Maksim perceived at this distance. In reality, it was Kat in disguise.

She kept her head down and her eyes focused on her mobile as she carried her backpack into the Design District. Maksim smiled to himself. "Not bad," he said to himself. Kat followed instructions well—for the most part—and she was tenacious. It wasn't professional level, but she had done better than most people would have under such stressful circumstances.

She positioned herself behind a crowd gathered outside a traditional Serbian restaurant. The people had just exited and were saying their goodbyes. Two of them smoked beside a planter that had been converted into a giant ashtray.

Kat blended in and scanned the vicinity. She zeroed in on the van, and her gaze connected with Maksim's. He replied with a wink.

Relief shone through in her eyes, and he watched the heaviness of fear lift off her. She ducked her head, pulling the makeshift *hijab* around her face, and started toward him. He skirted the van and made his way to a long ramp that led to the upper level.

The Design District had once been a bustling mall. Now abandoned, many local businesses had begun to set up shop in the former stores. A handful were run of the mill—a travel agency, an Army surplus store—but many had blossomed into fashion boutiques, art galleries, and artisan shops.

Some of it was a bit froufrou for Maksim's taste, particularly the stores that sold organic everything, but there were also swaths of unrenovated mall space. Vacant storefronts, crumbly walkways, and graffitied walls dominated these unoccupied areas. A spiral staircase, once elegant, was now rusted out and cordoned off by massive cement blocks.

Maksim climbed the ramp at a brisk pace. A mural covered an entire wall on his left, splashing vibrant colors across the drab building. The hum of traffic grew distant behind him.

He turned left at the top and slowed, allowing Kat to catch up. An arched entryway led to a set of stone stairs trimmed in traction strips. Maksim rolled his eyes. The traction strips were for safety, yet the stairs hadn't been maintained in decades. So he could break an ankle, but at least he wouldn't slip.

He stepped inside the alcove and waited.

TWENTY-THREE

FOOTSTEPS SHUFFLED CLOSER, THEN STOPPED. "MAKSIM?" Kat whisper-called his name.

He leaned out, revealing himself, and she followed him into the shadowy stairwell. "Watch your step." He pointed at a broken stair with a huge chunk of stone ripped out. "And here."

She circumnavigated the hazards and followed him to the second story. "These are locked at night." Maksim pointed at a rusty metal gate ahead of them and another on their left. He continued through the one on the left. "I have a key. Rather, I will. So don't panic if you happen to look outside and see the gates closed."

"Why would I panic?" She adjusted her backpack. "You're not going somewhere, are you?"

"I'm going to pick up our dinner and—"

Kat waited. "And?"

He abandoned the "run an errand" he'd nearly appended to his answer and checked his phone instead. "And today is Sunday. Our options will be limited."

Kat's brow pinched. "In a capital city?"

"Serbia is predominantly Orthodox. The same is true in

București. Many places are closed. Those that are open will be closing early."

"Oh."

Clay tiles spanned the walkway on this level. Maksim and Kat followed the path, bypassing a long section of glass windows that had once been a storefront.

Something inside drew his attention. The store was still vacant, but a ladder, tools, and paint equipment indicated renovations had begun. Likely a new shop, the latest addition to the Design District.

A sign hanging on the door confirmed his suspicions. *Uskoro se otvara*. (Opening soon.) Maksim frowned.

"Something wrong?" Kat had stopped beside him.

"This is going to be a shop. The sign says they're opening soon."

"That's not good?"

"Not for me." He gestured, and they continued up the walkway. "Up to this point, there haven't been any shops in this part of the mall. Businesses typically set up camera systems. Not all, but if they're in a section like this, without any other shops, they probably will." He yanked his cap off and dragged a hand through his sweaty hair. "This was bound to happen at some point. I suppose I was hoping for later rather than sooner."

"So this place *was* a mall." She reached for the guardrail on her right. Tempered glass had been installed between the balusters, and she let her hand slide over one of the panes. Her attention shifted to the abandoned storefronts around them. "I've been wondering."

"It started with about twenty designers in 2014." He donned the cap. "Growth has been steady but relatively slow. Until recently."

Kat shuffled along, keeping hold of her makeshift *abaya*, and inspected the street-style globe lamps installed along their path. Graffiti marked some of the orbs while others had become havens for dust and cobwebs.

"Most of those don't work," Maksim said, "which makes this area pretty dark at night." He gestured at a two-story building that sat back from the mall. "That's a call center, so no lights will be on over there tonight, and not much light emanates from those apartments." He gestured at a set of high-rise tower blocks. They were massive, designed in the Brutalist style, with hard lines and straight edges.

Kat marveled at the giants, their facades weathered and worn, exposing ragged cement underneath the paint. "How long are we staying here? And where, exactly?"

"Here."

She turned as Maksim swept his hand toward a glass storefront. Horizontal blinds covered the top half, stopping at waist level, and flattened cardboard had been taped along the bottom. The door was glass as well, the commercial kind with a push bar across the front.

Kat's jaw fell slack. "We're staying in an abandoned store?"

"It looks abandoned, but it's a loft apartment."

"Whose?"

"Mine." He guided her to his other side. "Go ahead and ditch the disguise. I don't want my property manager asking too many questions."

She blinked, clearly not understanding, but peeled off the outfit piece by piece.

Maksim moved to the guardrail and leaned over, trying to catch a glimpse of the bar below. The door stood open, but the outdoor tables hadn't been set up.

He was about to go down when a lanky form exited the bar.

Viktor balanced a cigarette between his lips while carrying a café table. Maksim let out a sharp whistle. The guy looked up, and a flash of surprise knocked him back a step. He put the table down, checked his surroundings, then held up a finger to wait.

"Is that your property manager?" Kat stuffed the clothes into her backpack. All but the long-sleeve.

"It is. He owns that bar, so he's able to keep an eye on the place."

"Makes sense." Kat held the shirt toward him.

"You should keep that. You may need to use it again." He leaned on the guardrail, watching in the direction of the stairwell. "Don't say anything while Viktor is here."

"Why? You don't trust him?"

"I trust him enough to give him the key to my place. But the less we say, the better off we'll be. Less is more."

Viktor appeared at the entrance to the stairwell. He hustled past the vacant storefronts, keys in hand, and crossed to where Maksim waited.

Kat set her backpack down and withdrew to the corner.

Viktor greeted Maksim in Serbian. *"Gospodine Vuković. Kako ste?"* (Mr. Vuković. How are you?)

Maksim had a Montenegrin passport under the name Luka Vuković. He'd purchased the apartment under that name, and that was how Viktor knew him.

Kat, however, didn't know.

Maksim had intended to tell her about his alternate identities—among other things—but with their future uncertain, he had decided against it. He simply couldn't afford to burn more identities if she said something to the wrong person.

He sent a fleeting glance her way. She had settled her forearms on the guardrail while she studied the nearby high-rises. Apparently she hadn't discerned anything out of the ordinary.

Maksim focused on Viktor. *"Dobro, dobro. Hvala. Kako ste?"* (Good, good. Thank you. How are you?)

Viktor answered with another *dobro* and passed the keys to Maksim. *"A new club has opened. They call it Kulture with a K."* He gestured down below. *"I don't mind the loud music, but too many of their customers come to my bar by mistake. I give directions many times per night."*

"Sounds like a good marketing opportunity." Maksim answered

in Serbian, but with a Montenegrin accent, adding dialectical *y* and *j* sounds where Serbs left them out.

"What do I know about these things? I am a bar owner, not a marketing professional." Viktor transferred his attention to Kat. *"Is this your girlfriend?"*

"A friend. We've been traveling." Maksim stepped in front of her, cutting off Viktor's line of sight. *"Have you experienced any problems since my last visit? Seen anything unusual?"*

"Not that I can think of." Viktor reached into his pocket and pulled a fresh cig from the pack. *"Everything has been normal."*

"You haven't seen anyone loitering?"

"Not by your apartment." He mumbled the answer, the cigarette pressed between his lips. *"They are adding a new shop there."* He glanced toward the storefront Maksim had noticed earlier. *"Contractors visit, but I've only seen them very recently."*

"Good. You still have the telephone number I gave to you?"

"Da." Viktor flicked his lighter and placed his cigarette to the flame. The tip burned.

"Well then, if you see anyone come around, don't hesitate to leave a voicemail at that number. And thanks for these." Maksim held up the keys. *"I'll send extra to your account as soon as I can, a bonus since there's more activity lately."*

"Thank you for that, but I haven't been paid yet for the month." He blew out a breath of smoke. *"I don't mind that it's late. I assumed you were busy. You can pay me when you can."*

Maksim was about to unlock the door. He froze. *"You weren't paid?"*

"Ne." (No.)

Maksim's instinct, the sixth sense he'd developed, tingled. He always paid Viktor on the first of the month, and this month had been no different.

Had it? He thought back.

He'd been in Brașov on the first. With Kat. They'd been working on the scavenger hunt. It was a Saturday night—early Sunday morning, technically—and he recalled the late hour at which he'd initiated the transaction. Banks sometimes did scheduled maintenance on Sundays, and he had specifically wondered if perhaps he should wait until Monday.

But there'd been a lot going on, so he'd gone ahead with the transfer after all. Perhaps it had failed. It must have.

"Come see me if you need anything," Viktor was saying as he took a drag of his cigarette. *"You and your friend can come by the bar for a drink."*

"Uh, thanks. And please, take this." Maksim broke open his duffel and fished a fifty out of his wallet. *"Just until I can sort out this problem with the bank. I'm going there tomorrow."*

Viktor thanked him and ambled toward the stairs.

"Everything okay?" Kat folded her arms. "Was he asking a lot of questions or something?"

"Uh, no. Not exactly." Maksim eased past her. "We were talking business," he said, unlocking the door. "Nothing to be concerned about."

"Then why do you look like that?"

He sent a sideways glance. "Like what?"

"I don't know. Like something's wrong."

"Something *is* wrong." He pushed open the door. "My payment didn't reach him, and I was trying to work out why the transfer would have failed." He grabbed his duffel and ushered her inside. "But then I remembered what happened, so…"

"So nothing to do with Vladimir?"

"Vladimir was faking his death at that time, so nothing to do with him, and I was on good terms with Ștefan as well." Maksim shrugged. "The system likely failed in some odd way. It happens occasionally."

Her next breath escaped with relief. "So we're safe."

"We need to stay vigilant, but yes. Safe enough to stay for a few days, rest, regroup." He took her backpack and set it on the table in the breakfast area. "This is the kitchen. Refrigerator is there."

Kat let her attention sweep over the sink, the stove, and then the counter that stopped beside a narrow white fridge.

"This was a hostel," Maksim explained as he crossed the room. "So the bathroom is divided." He opened a door. "Toilet is in there." He shut that door and opened another to the right of it. "Shower is there."

Her stare blanked as she walked forward. "Is this what they mean by 'water closet'?" she asked, inspecting the shower.

She wasn't wrong. This shower in particular looked like a closet. Americans were accustomed to shower curtains around a tub or glass enclosures around a shower pan. Some Europeans designed their bathrooms this way as well, but many took the minimalist approach. No enclosure. No pan. Just a straightforward, walk-in style. That was how Maksim's shower had been designed, the floor sloping ever so slightly toward the drain.

"How do I...?" Kat couldn't seem to piece together her question. "When I take a shower, is there, like, a way to keep the water contained?"

"Shut the door." Maksim shut it as if to demonstrate.

"Yeah, but won't water still get everywhere?" She looked down. "It's bound to seep out, right?"

A broom, mop, and floor squeegee stood propped in the corner. He grabbed the squeegee. "The drain is built into the floor and—" His attention moved from the shower to the squeegee and then trailed up the wooden handle. "I know this setup isn't the greatest, but it's an older building, and the hostel had to make do with the confined space."

Kat's confusion heightened—but then she straightened, like an epiphany had landed on her. "Oh! No, I just meant..." She readied a smile. "This place is great, and the setup makes total sense—separating the shower and toilet. Then the hostel guests could still use the bathroom while someone was washing up. You and I can do that, too. I mean—" A hint of rouge touched her cheeks. "Like, if you have to go to the bathroom, you won't have to wait on me. In case..." Her rambling trailed off.

"It's pragmatic," he said, filling in the gaps.

"Exactly." She snapped her fingers and pointed between the bathroom facilities. "I like it, actually. It'd be nice if we had something like this at Brandy's house." She nodded, more to herself it seemed. "Anyway, I'll try not to make too much of a mess when I shower."

"Even if you do, I don't mind."

She stilled herself. Her eyes found his.

They held each other's gaze for a lengthy moment. Maksim had been looking forward to this part of their journey, to the privacy they would have together, but now he wasn't sure what to think. In a sense, things between them had become stiff, clunky—and yet having her here felt natural despite a thread of awkwardness woven in.

"You would have liked my apartment in București." He re-homed the squeegee to its spot in the corner. "The place was nice, more modern, with a fantastic view. I had it professionally designed and decorated." His attention trailed over the kitchen. "I couldn't do that here."

"Yeah, but… I really like this place. It's not what I'm used to, but different is fun." She took a step toward him. "I mean it. It's neat how you turned a hostel into a loft apartment." Her gaze lifted. "But if there are no bedrooms and we have to sleep down here, I might be disappointed."

He chuckled and cut over to the spiral staircase at the back of the kitchen. "I kept all the beds from the hostel, so you can have your pick."

Kat started toward the staircase.

"Mind your head." Maksim placed himself beside a stair that reached head-level. "I added these after a handful of encounters myself." He ran his hand over a foam casting molded to the underside of the stairs. "The staircase is metal. And sturdy. The foam hurts less, but I wouldn't call it soft."

"So don't flood the bathroom, and don't knock myself out on the stairs." She gave a thumbs-up. "I got this."

He hoisted his duffel and grabbed her backpack, then they wound their way to the loft. "I usually sleep here," he said, laying his duffel next to a single bed pushed longways against the left wall. "You can take one of the bunks"—he motioned toward two bunk beds across the room—"but if you take the other single, we can share the multi-outlet. The wall outlets are otherwise hard to reach."

She hung her backpack on one of the bunk posts, which Maksim perceived to be a "no thanks," but then she parked herself on the second single. "I lost my cable."

Maksim squatted in front of his duffel. "For your laptop?"

"Mm-hm." She stifled a yawn and relaxed against the wall. "I think it went missing at Village Ksorba."

"Perhaps it's with my money." He pulled out a fresh set of clothes. "My money that was taken from the village. Not the money Bogdan made off with."

"It's a lot to keep up with at this point." She watched him reorganize his things. "I'm sorry about that again. This whole thing is getting pretty costly for you."

"It won't matter after tomorrow." He grabbed his toiletry bag. "When the banks open, I'm going to close out that safe deposit box and I'll be set for a long time."

"I'll pay you back for everything. As soon as I can access my own funds, I mean."

He looked at her.

"Vasile was a billionaire, and thirty-five thousand euros won't put a dent in that."

He braced his knees and pushed himself to standing. "Kat—"

"I'll pay you for this too—getting me here, taking me to Germany." Her attention drifted over the room. "I'm so grateful, and I really am sorry for everything you've had to sacrifice."

The single beds formed a straight line, end to end. Maksim crossed to her bed in a single stride and squatted in front of her. "I mean this wholeheartedly. It's not an affront to your generous offer." He reached over and placed his hand on hers. "You don't owe me anything. Not for this. Not for Germany."

"Okay, but… Maksim, it's a lot."

"It's also the noble thing to do, and I hope you'll let me do it as a friend rather than some kind of business arrangement." Before she could answer, his eye caught a glimpse of deep gold sunset through the shutters. "I need to get going." He stood and checked the time on his phone. "I have a few minutes to spare. I'm going to use them on a quick shower."

Kat pushed up from the bed. "Can I come? I'll wear the outfit."

"That's a bit risky with the number of cameras going up." He offered an apologetic smile. "Why don't you stay here and rest? I won't be long, and you'll have extra privacy when you shower."

She flopped onto the bed. "I guess you're locking me in again."

"I'm sorry. It's in your best interest as well as mine." He nodded toward a bookshelf. "I may have books in English. And here." He stepped over to the nearest window and jimmied the shutters. Not-so-fresh air and warm sunshine streamed inside the room. "In case you need a change of scenery."

Maksim gathered his clothes and toiletries. He spied her passport, and a thought occurred to him.

Kat meandered toward the bookshelf. Maksim was about to ask if he could borrow her passport, but he knew that would inspire questions about where he was going and why. He wasn't sure if he could disclose that. Not until he talked to Miro.

With a hint of reluctance—and a massive dose of guilt—he pulled her US passport from the duffel and slipped it into his pocket.

"Hopefully there's not a fire while you're gone." She tilted her head, reading through the spines of each book. "Did you know there are 387,000 home-structure fires every year? That's in the US, as of 2018, but I bet it happens here, too."

Maksim stood. "If there *were* a fire, those shutters dislodge easily. You can climb out, make your way onto the roof, and then jump down to the walkway out front."

She straightened. "Are you serious?"

He smiled. "Call me if you smell smoke. Viktor should have a spare key, otherwise he has tools that can break the storefront window." Maksim stopped beside her and grabbed one of the books. "Have you ever read *Barnaby Rudge*?"

"Never even heard of it." She examined the cover. "We read a lot of Dickens in school, but only his uberfamous works."

"This one is good, and it's in English." He passed her the book. "I found it at Shakespeare & Company. It's a famous book-shop in Paris."

"Paris?" Her eyes sparkled. "Is the book set there? I've never been."

"It's set in London."

"Oh." Her mouth turned down. "I've been to the airport there."

"Now you can visit the Victorian-era version." He turned away. "I have to get going or I won't make the *ćevapi* place." He carried his clothes to the staircase. "I mean it. Anything happens, just call."

She waved, stationing herself on the bed, and opened the book. He watched her expression grow pensive, her eyes shifting left to right as she read.

Confusion flickered through her features. She looked up. "I thought you had to go."

"I am. Rather, I do." His mouth settled into a smile, his mind reeling with how wonderfully normal all of this felt. "Sorry, I was… thinking." He turned, still smiling, and descended the spiral staircase.

CHAPTER
TWENTY-FOUR

20:51 (8:51 PM)

MAKSIM DEPARTED IN A FRESH TEE, jeans, and his ball cap, keeping his head down as he exited the Design District. He turned right and hurried up the sidewalk. Apartments loomed while the sights and sounds of the city buzzed, a hive of humans all working and going about their lives.

He hooked right at Kolarčeva and proceeded past a number of restaurants. He had one *ćevapi* place in mind, a takeout window all the locals considered the best in town. It'd certainly been the best he'd ever tried, and after the way Kat had reacted to that mediocre *ćevapi* in Naidăș, he was dying for her to try this one .

Too bad it's going to be cold. There wasn't much he could do about that. After picking up their dinner, he had to go see Miro.

Maksim hustled, following the street as it turned into Makedonska. A glass building rose on his right. A casino filled the corner on his left. His bank was on this road, but he wasn't going that far tonight.

Traffic motored past in waves and then trickles as cars veered onto a side street. He kept his gaze lowered at the next major intersection, which was packed with shops and restaurants—and cameras—and he made it his mission to find another side street as soon as possible.

Dusk settled, and the neighborhood blinked to life as he hurried up the busy sidewalk. Storefronts glistened around him. A sign on his left glowed green. APOTEKA. (PHARMACY.) He suddenly remembered that Kat needed suture scissors. He'd have to find a pharmacy later, one that was closer to Miro's. *Not on a major street.*

After some zigzagging, Maksim found himself on Skadarska, a street that led to Stari Grad (Old Town). Parked cars lined both sides of the street, trimming the drivable space to one lane. He raced down the hill. Familiar high-top tables and barstools dotted the sidewalk. This particular *ćevapi* place always had a line, sometimes around the corner. Tonight it did not.

Maksim arrived at the takeout window as the last customer— a food-delivery person—walked away. The guy set his order in a cube-shaped thermal and mounted his motor scooter.

"Dobro veče." Maksim panted, out of breath. *"Kako ste?"* (Good evening. How are you?)

The worker manning the takeout window made a slicing motion at his neck. *"Zatvorena."* (Closed.)

"Please. I'm supposed to order dinner for my girlfriend. She's visiting from out of the country, and I promised her the best ćevapi in Belgrade." Maksim inserted a pleading expression. *"Our bus was late."*

The guy leveled a disbelieving look. *"Where is your girlfriend from?"*

The question sounded innocent enough, but Maksim had spent enough time there to know better. *"She's Romanian. We had a very difficult journey, and her first ćevapi was disappointing. I'm determined to change her mind."* One more heartfelt expression. *"Please?"*

The man, who was likely the owner if Maksim had to guess, slanted a look. It was Sunday. He probably wanted to get home to his family, his friends, his video games or whatever else he had planned. Instead the man told his cook they had one more order.

The cook questioned him. The owner explained, and his employee merely shrugged and retied his apron. He was still wearing his chef's beanie—a type of skull cap with a mesh top— as he lit the grill.

"Fifteen minutes," the owner said.

Maksim pressed his hands together in thanks. *"I'm very sorry to arrive so late."*

The owner waved him off. *"Had you said your girlfriend was American, this may have become a different story."*

This was Maksim's reason for saying Kat was Romanian. The 1999 NATO air strikes—seventy-eight days of straight bombing campaigns—had left bitterness in the hearts and minds of Serbs. Fast-forward twenty years, and the people had not forgotten.

Maksim ordered, including an extra *ćevapi* wrap for Miro, and stood to the side, relishing the hearty aroma that filtered into the twilight. The neighborhood was quiet, despite the apartments that loomed over both sides of the street, and Maksim watched the lights of each ground-floor restaurant go out until only the takeout window glowed.

The owner came through a side door and began to haul his patio tables inside. The man motioned toward a barstool, indicating Maksim could have a seat.

"I'm good, thank you. I can—" He fell silent as a pair of headlights attached to a white hatchback swung onto the narrow side street. The car pulled alongside the takeout place, and two navy-blue uniforms jumped out. Maksim read the Cyrillic plastered on the side of the vehicle. Policija. (Police.) His initial hope was that the cops had been doing the same as him—trying to order takeout before the *ćevapi* place closed.

The owner's wide expression told Maksim that might not be the case. *"Hi. Can I help you?"*

The female cop adjusted her tactical belt and squeezed

between two parked cars. *"Zdravo, gospodine."* (Hi, sir.) *"Did you see a man run past here?"*

Maksim's insides twisted.

"What do I know? We have been working all day." The owner motioned toward himself and his cook. *"Today is Sunday. We were very busy."*

The cop pivoted toward Maksim. *"And you, sir?"*

Maksim wished he had a cigarette or some other object in his hands. Something that would make him appear more relaxed. *"Uh, no. There was only a food delivery driver when I arrived. He left on a motor scooter."*

The male cop, who'd been behind the female, stepped forward. *"Your accent is different. Where are you from?"*

Maksim redoubled his efforts, inflecting as much Montenegrin as he could muster. *"I'm from Perast, but I live here during the summer. My family owns an apartment in the Design District."* Many cops had a highly developed intuition and could sniff out evasiveness the way K9s could sniff out drugs. Maksim hoped he'd elaborated enough that he wouldn't be perceived as evasive.

The male cop walked forward another step, squinting against the restaurant's bright signage. *"You look familiar to me."*

"I can't imagine why." Maksim answered with a light laugh but then added, *"I've been mistaken for the footballer, Marko Krstović. But he's shorter—"*

"Why do you look like an American?" The man's gaze flicked to Maksim's ball cap.

"I was hiking with my girlfriend." Maksim shrugged, blasé. *"We just returned, and I was in a hurry."*

"They just returned from Romania," the owner snapped. *"They had a difficult journey. Leave him alone."*

Maksim clenched his jaw. He'd never said they were hiking *in* Romania, only that his girlfriend was Romanian. Hopefully he wouldn't be asked for his—

"Passport," the male cop demanded.

Maksim made a show of seeming surprised. *"Wow, I came for dinner, and now I'm being interrogated? I didn't expect this."* He reached for his back pocket roughly, like he was being inconvenienced, while in actuality he was freaking out. He'd brought his passport—Kat's as well—but neither of them had an exit stamp for Romania, nor did they have entrance stamps for Serbia.

Miro was a resourceful guy, and Maksim had wondered if he could help with this problem—the reason he'd brought documents. But he hadn't made it to Miro's yet. So he had two passports, and neither contained evidence of their arrival.

The cop would check for that. When he didn't find it, Maksim would be arrested.

The man extended a hand, waiting. Maksim touched both passports and ran his finger along the edges. Kat's was more frayed than his, which helped him discern between the two.

He left hers in the pocket and went to bring his Montenegro passport forward. Prayers and curses alike jumbled his mind. What else could he do? Run?

His muscles tensed, ready for action.

"Why are you harassing my customer?" The owner inserted himself, leveling the cop with a furious outburst. *"I know this man. He orders from me frequently. The person you are searching for is not here. The police are late again, like always!"* He threw his hands up. *"Why do you harass innocent bystanders? Can you answer me that? It is becoming too familiar to the days of Milošević. You are too young to know, but I remember the abuse of power!"*

"Sir, please calm down." The female cop eased closer.

"I will not!" The owner cranked his volume. *"Last week, one of my customers was pickpocketed. And what happened? Where were the police then?"*

The female cop tried again, holding up a calming hand. *"Sir. Please. I must ask you—"*

The clang of metal against pavement rattled from somewhere down the street. The owner continued his rant while the police went on high alert. *"You heard that?"* the female cop said.

Her partner nodded. *"The noise came from there."* He pointed at a bend in the road.

They hurried to their car, jumped in, and their tires spun as they launched forward. Maksim released the breath he'd been holding.

"I'm sorry that I did not come to your aid sooner." The owner wiped his brow. *"It has been many months, but I remember you now."*

"Last year." Maksim mustered a weak smile. *"You have a good memory."*

"Yes, but you came a lot during that time." The man grabbed a barstool. *"Why have you been away for so long? Did you find better ćevapi somewhere?"*

"I was... in an accident." Maksim glanced at his shirt sleeve. The scars started at his elbow and covered his upper arm.

The man grabbed his head. *"O, strašno!"* (Oh, scary!) *"Did it happen here? The traffic is bad, and the drivers can be crazy."*

"It happened while I was traveling. But I had a good doctor, and I'm okay now."

The cook called out that the food was ready. The owner took the barstool inside and then circled around to the window.

"May I ask a small favor?" Maksim said as the man bagged up the food. *"Can you place the third ćevapi in a separate bag? I'm going to deliver it to a friend. I haven't seen him since the accident."*

The owner beamed. *"You are a good man to think of your friend, especially while you have a beautiful girl waiting for you at home. Your parents must be very proud."* He put his hand up in refusal when Maksim's wallet came out.

"Please. You stayed open for me." Maksim didn't have any Serbian dinar, so he tried to give the man a twenty-euro banknote. The man shook his head, so Maksim deposited the money in a tip jar. *"A gift for your wonderful cook then. Thank you for your kindness."*

The owner placed a hand over his heart and bowed his head

in thanks. The cook tapped his chef's beanie, doing a mini-salute.

Maksim took the plastic bags and backtracked. His normal route would have taken him to the end of Skadarska, but that was the same direction the cops had gone. He could not risk another encounter, and that meant doubling back to Braće Jugovića. It would add five minutes to his walk, and there would be more cameras, but it was the better of the two choices.

He pulled his cap low and trekked up the road. Restaurants cast light all around him, but all he could do was pass through, navigating outdoor patio tables and a swarm of foot traffic while keeping his gaze downturned.

The buildings became a mix of old and new, weathered and restored. The closer Maksim drew to Dorćol—the area where Miro lived—the narrower the streets grew and the more run-down the buildings became. The streets grew darker as well, most of the light radiating from intersections.

Maksim checked his six periodically. More than periodically. So far, he hadn't picked up a tail, but that cop's expression—the way he had recognized Maksim—haunted him.

Twenty minutes later, graffiti wallpapered the buildings all around him. The street transitioned to cobblestone, and his path vectored in a downward trajectory. The plastic sacks bumped his leg, crinkling as he turned into a courtyard. Tower-block apartments sprouted up.

Maksim slipped through a rickety metal gate and straight-lined for the entrance. An intercom hung from the wall. He pressed a button at random, and a ringtone peeled through the janky speaker.

A woman answered. She sounded elderly, sleepy.

Maksim hung up and pressed another.

"Da?" This voice was male, young, and distracted. A movie played in the background.

Perfect.

"Dostava," Maksim said. *"Namirnice."* (Delivery. Foodstuffs.)

A buzz rattled the speaker, and the door clicked open. Maksim slipped inside, and a motion detector activated, lighting the entryway. He dashed up the stairs, boots scuffing against the cement. Each time he hit a landing, the motion detector answered by turning on the lights.

Progressive trance flowed from down the hall. Maksim followed the music… past the other apartments… past a cracked hallway light. He stepped up to the last door and gave a friendly double knock. He didn't hear anything in response, so he knocked again. A shuffle of movement stemmed from the other side—then nothing.

Maksim raised his hand a third time.

The door flew open. A scrawny guy with shaggy hair, blood-shot eyes, and an unkempt goatee gawked from the doorway. Miro's bushy eyebrows lifted high, making room for his widening expression. "Whaaat the—"

"Delivery." Maksim held up the bag with his friend's food. "Can I come in?"

TWENTY-FIVE

"LET ME UNDERSTAND THIS," mumbled Miro—a.k.a. Miroslav Jovanović, the hacker known as Nostradamus Unauthorized—through a mouthful of *ćevapi*. "You are not dead, obviously, and also your uncle is not dead—"

"Vladimir is not my uncle."

"Whatever. Neither of you are dead. Only Ștefan?" Miro stared, expression blank, as he chewed his food. "Because of antipersonnel mines?"

Maksim nodded.

"In *Romania*? Bro." Miro swallowed and shook his head. "I didn't know other European countries had landmine problems."

"Neither did I." Maksim had shared an abbreviated version of what happened at Village Ksorba. He *hadn't* explained why anyone had gone there, nor did he mention Kat, but he did share enough to explain how Ștefan had died.

"Vladimir blames me. But I'm telling you, Miro, I had nothing to do with it." Maksim paced in front of his friend's gaming rig. Three 4K monitors spanned the length of his desk. "Ștefan turned on me. *He* was going to kill *me*, and then he himself detonated the mines that killed *him*."

Miro sat there, looking bewildered. All he managed to say

was, "Bro." In addition to being a hacker, Miro was a serious gamer with many of his virtual friends living in the West. He had a knack for accents and colloquialisms, and Maksim could always tell when he'd been spending time with Brits versus Aussies versus Americans. Presently, he sounded like a SoCal surfer with a Slavic accent.

Maksim navigated candy wrappers, chip bags, and takeout sacks that littered the floor. He used his boot to nudge a soggy lump of something. Whatever it was had been there a while.

Miro studied one of his screens, reading through a chat he'd pulled up. "People are talking about what happened," he said as he scrolled. "What they *think* happened—the fate of the Răzvan clan, who's going to fill the power vacuum. Look at this." He switched to the center screen, entered a command, and launched a darknet message board. "They're placing bets on who will take over the Răzvan territory."

Maksim leaned in. "What are they saying?"

"Many say Arben's clan, but some are speculating that Émilien will rise up." Miro focused on Maksim. "You said Émilien is in jail?"

"For the moment. If and when he gets out, he'll become Vladimir's right hand."

"So then he *won't* be taking over the operation." Miro smirked, fingers flying over the keyboard, and joined the chat.

> **4nope_str0_damus1:**
> 1 bitcoin says emilien is not your guy. any
> takers?

The responses poured in…

> **jedimindtrikk:**
> ill take that bet.

> **silly_shad0w_w@lker:**
> me. source says your wrong.

h0lla@ya_boi:
ohhhh shit just got real!!

inc0gnit0m0de:
i'm in. you better pay up.

One response in particular snagged Maksim's attention.

IV_3.1415cr1me:
what ya kno, ?

"Ivy," Maksim whispered, noting the moniker; though, even if the user had been anonymous, he could have guessed who it was based on the Cockney-style rhyme. Technically she hadn't finished the rhyme, but that was what made it Cockney.

Historically, this type of rhyming slang had been codespeak for the traders in London's East End. When the bobbies started to catch on, the Cockney had been shortened, eliminating words and at times whole phrases. Those fluent in the slang understood what the missing pieces were based on the first part of the rhyme.

In the case of Ivy's comment, "kno" rhymed with "Miro." But instead of calling him out, she'd left that part blank, making his name implied. Only Miro would realize she was talking to him.

Miro worked with Ivy, so he knew all of this. He grinned and typed a response.

4nope_str0_damus1:
whoa whoa whoa wouldnt you like to kno...
bro!

He chuckled, proud of his rhyme, and moved his pinky to the Return key.

Maksim caught his hand. "Don't."

"But—"

"You cannot say anything that will give me away." Maksim straightened. "You've already said too much."

Miro sat back. "I have said nothing."

"People can read between the lines, Miro." He gestured toward Ivy's comment. "You think she didn't perceive that you have inside information? She will want to know who it's from."

A bright *ping* pealed through the speaker. Miro glanced at the direct message. "Ohhh." He grabbed his head and sent a wide-eyed look to Maksim. "It's her."

Maksim brought himself eye level with Miro. "I came here at great risk to myself because you're one of the few people I trust." He grabbed hold of Miro's shoulders, and the gaming chair swiveled. "Vladimir could be waiting for someone to slip up, to give some indication they've seen me, heard from me, spoken with me—"

"You think Vladimir is watching?" Miro's eyes widened. "Does he know my handle?"

"Ivy knew it." Maksim straightened. "You have to respond to her."

"What? No!"

"You must."

"And what do I say?" Miro grimaced. "I... I don't know, Maksim."

"Not answering would be suspicious." Maksim turned the chair back around, squaring Miro with his monitors. "Act casual. When she inquires further, say you saw someone talking about Émilien on a message board. She'll want more details, so you'll need to be coy. Tease her about taking the bet."

Miro exhaled a sigh that expanded his cheeks. "I'll try." He opened the message.

IV3.1415crlme:
hru

(translation: How are you?)

"What do I say?" Miro asked.

"Whatever you normally say."

His expression turned thoughtful. "I can't remember. Maybe no one ever asks."

Maksim rolled his eyes. "Do you have any other messages you could check?"

Miro opened another window and pulled up his DMs. He scrolled through one thread and then another, searching for how he'd responded to other people.

Another message pinged.

> **IV3.1415crlme:**
> hru
>
> ?

She'd added the question mark and nothing else.

Miro swore. "I know someone just asked me that. What did I — Oh! I remember." He returned to the thread with Ivy and typed his answer.

> **4nope_str0_damus1:**
> stfu

He paused, then added another line.

> ... punk!

Maksim rubbed his forehead. *Shut the F up* wasn't exactly what he had in mind, but at least it was genuine.

> **IV_3.1415crlme:**
> funny, mate. i see what ya did there.
>
> now, wuz this about emilien?

Miro fleshed out a response and then waited for Maksim to give his approval.

> **4nope_str0_damus1:**
> saw someone talking about him on a message
> board. seems he's *ahem* indisposed.

Maksim's eyebrows converged. "That doesn't mean what you think it means."

"What? Indisposed?"

"Use 'incapacitated'."

Miro made the change and hit Return. Ivy replied with another question mark.

"I don't think *that* means what you think it means," Miro muttered, typing his next response.

> **4nope_str0_damus1:**
> u kno my engleski is rubbish. whats the word
> for 'in jail'?

> **IV3.1415crlme:**
> wtf! r u serious, mate?

> **4nope_str0_damus1:**
> thats what i heard. guy deleted his comment
> after. i figured he was wrong... or he was right
> and knew he shouldnt have said that. catch
> my whiff?

> **IV3.1415crlme:**
> it's 'drift' you twat
>
> whereabouts u see this?

> **4nope_str0_damus1:**
> like im goin to tell u ;) whats the matter, i.v.?
> scared to put your € where your big beautiful
> dirty british mouth is?

Miro paused before hitting Return. "Too much?"

"I don't even know anymore." Maksim straightened. "Just send it."

Miro hit Return, and Maksim could almost sense Ivy's eye roll.

IV3.1415crlme:
piss off

A system-generated notification appeared, and the green dot next to Ivy's handle lightened to dull gray.

IV3.1415crlme has left the chat

Miro relaxed, kicking his feet up, and clasped both hands behind his head. "I think that went well."

"Let's hope so." Maksim hadn't finished the statement before his pocket buzzed. He assumed it was a message, but the phone kept buzzing. He pulled out the device. The number to Kat's new burner appeared, and a ray of panic flickered within him.

He flipped open the phone and pressed it to his ear. "Yeah?"

"Thank God you answered."

"Of course I answered." He squeezed between two desks, both of which were piled high with junk. "What's wrong?" he asked, putting distance between himself and Miro.

"I thought something happened to you." Fear glimmered in her voice. "You've been gone for two hours."

"I had to make a couple of stops." His attention fell to a box of cables. "Power supply," he said, reaching into the box.

"Huh?"

"Didn't you need a power supply? For your laptop?" He pulled out the cord he'd noticed. A sticky substance coated the wire, and he wrinkled his nose. "For your laptop?"

"Oh." Her fear morphed into understanding. "Yeah. I do."

"A lot of places are closed. I didn't have many options."

"What about dinner? Is there anything open at this hour?"

"I've already picked up dinner—"

A guffaw in the room interjected. Maksim's attention flew

toward Miro, who was gawking wide enough to swallow a ballistic missile.

Maksim gave the hacker his back and lowered his voice. "Listen, there are people around. I'm almost done. This is my last stop."

Plastic and paper crinkled from across the living room. "Is *this* dinner?" Miro sang, holding up the bag with Maksim's order.

"Who is that?" Kat asked.

"A guy at this shop." Maksim pulled his phone away and switched to Serbian. *"Set that down. Now."*

Miro dropped the bag on his desk and raised both hands in surrender.

"I'm about to leave," Maksim said into the phone. "Then I'll be going straight home. All right?"

Three beats went by. "Um, sure. Be careful."

"I will." He closed the phone, disconnecting the call. Was it just his imagination or had she sounded strange there at the end?

His brain needed a second to catch up. She'd been responding to that last exchange, the way he'd said "then I'll be home." He hadn't meant it in any particular way, but perhaps he should have been more careful with his words.

Miro must have been thinking the same thing because his expression widened. "Going *home* to your girl, eh? Wow." He scooped up his dangling jaw. "Bro, I thought you were over Marie."

"I am." Maksim shoved the phone into his pocket. "That wasn't Marie."

Miro gasped, covering his mouth. "What the f—?"

Maksim held up a stern finger. "I know what you're thinking. And no, we're not talking about this. We can't. *I* can't."

"She's hiding from Vladimir, too, isn't she?" Miro lowered his hands. "Damn."

"Speaking of which, do you remember that virus you built for me?" Maksim made the perilous return journey through

Miro's living room. "That should be hitting someone's system soon."

"Oo, who's the lucky ducky?"

"Vladimir's men."

Miro's expression widened again. "Brooo. That's checkmate right there!"

"Not yet. Some of them were arrested, so there may be a gap before you can pull any data. But I need you to be watching. SMS this number if you see anything."

Miro woke up his phone and plugged in the telephone number Maksim spouted off. "This is how I contact you now?"

"Temporarily. I need to set up a laptop that can handle all my apps, specifically a custom VoIP. You don't happen to have a spare lying around, do you?"

"None that work." His eyes shifted toward the cluttered desk. "I'm not traveling much these days. But you can check the computer shop at Cara Dušana. They open tomorrow at ten."

"Do they have hardware wallets?"

"For your crypto?" Miro's expression soured. "Maybe? But I would order from the manufacturer."

Setting up a hardware wallet was a secretive process, requiring information only the user should have. Scammers had learned to hack the system by creating realistic replicas and selling them as new. Even reputable shops had been fooled, their inventory tainted with scam versions of what should have been trusted brands.

Miro was right. The only way to ensure a device's security was to order from the manufacturer.

"You can have the wallet shipped here," Miro offered. "I swear I won't touch the parcel."

"The problem is that I may not have time." Maksim shoved a hand through his hair. "I was planning to leave later this week, but I'm wondering if we should take off sooner."

"Where to?"

Maksim settled an earnest smile on his friend. "I can't tell you that. I'm sorry."

Miro shrugged. "Your uncle wants to kill you. I understand keeping secrets."

"He's not my uncle," Maksim repeated for what felt like the eight-millionth time. "But with all the cameras going up, I could use suggestions for exfil."

"Exfiltration from Belgrade to… where? You cannot tell me." Miro pushed back from his desk and kicked his feet up. A half-empty chip bag toppled, spilling the contents.

"We're going west. I can tell you that."

"You and your girl, huh?" Miro grinned, bouncing his shaggy eyebrows. "By 'west,' do you mean America, or something closer? Bosnia? Croatia? Italy?"

"Any of those would work."

"You cannot take the passenger trains. Too many cameras." He massaged his chin scruff. "My cousin runs a tour company in Sarajevo. They bring day tours here, but only on certain days. Perhaps he could give you a ride during one of their return trips." He grabbed his phone.

"I'm not sure that would work. We don't have exit or entry stamps."

"You snuck into Serbia? You bad boy." Miro snorted a laugh. "But you know, maybe it's not a problem. I'll ask."

"I suppose we could hike. That's how we came from Romania."

Miro shot up straight, his feet landing with a *thud*. "Do you want to join Ștefan in the afterlife?" Miro made a *pfff* sound. "Every time the EU says they have cleared more mines, some hiker goes off and finds another, losing a foot, a leg. Croatia is the worst, but the border with Bosnia is second."

Scratch that idea. "All right, then what else?"

"There are cargo trains. They go everywhere, all over Europe." He did a search and clicked on the first website. "See here?" He pointed. "Belgrade to Rijeka, departing two to three times per week. We figure out the train, discover the schedule, what kind of cargo it's carrying…"

"Can you look into that for me?" Maksim grabbed the plastic sack with his takeout. "Please, Miro? I'm late."

"Yeah, yeah. Go be with your girl." Miro's mouth slanted up. "But you owe me."

"I did bring you *ćevapi*."

"Then *I* owe *you*." Miro stood and held up a hand. Maksim gripped it and tugged, their hands clasped in solidarity. "I'll SMS with best options."

"And you'll keep an eye on that server the virus is linked to?"

"You'll know the moment I get a hit." He held up his phone. "I have a new number, too. Be watching for the code word so you know it's me."

They didn't have a code word per se, but Miro had knack for fabricating creative phrases. The more ridiculous they were, the better mood he was in.

Maksim shook his head, fighting a smile. "I'll be watching." As he reached the front door, he remembered the power supply he was holding and held it up. "Any chance I could have this?"

CHAPTER
TWENTY-SIX

23:47 (11:47 PM)

MAKSIM PASSED through the shadows of the Design District. Most but not all of the work vehicles were gone, which left him a bit more conspicuous to CCTV cameras and prying eyes, though he appreciated the veil nighttime provided.

He came through the stairwell and found the gates locked, precisely as he had told Kat they would be. He adjusted the plastic sacks he was holding—three in all—and dug out his keys. The gate groaned, metal clanking, as he let himself in.

He secured the padlock and did his best to blend with the shadows. A neon glow radiated from Viktor's tiny, no-name bar, but the light didn't reach to this level. The lights from the new club, however, did. Techno thumped, dampening the voices below.

Glass shattered, echoing into the night. Shouts went up.

Maksim reached the end of the walkway and peered over. Two men tossed their cigarettes and started toward each other. A well-built man in slacks and a sleek jacket raced forward, attempting to break up the fight. The club's name burned over the chaos, a fiery red that added a hellish glow to the entrance.

Kulture

Dread dropped anchor in Maksim's stomach. Viktor's clientele consisted of friends, family, and a handful of barflies. Clubs tended to draw a different crowd, particularly drug dealers and organized crime. *If* someone in organized crime wasn't already running the place.

It was only a matter of time before the police began investigating. When they did, Maksim's apartment would be in their purview.

Maksim shifted his attention to the no-name bar on the ground level. Viktor had stepped into the doorway, cigarette ablaze, as a finely dressed couple approached. Viktor anticipated the clubbers with a bland expression and pointed them in the right direction.

The fight ramped up, the shouts becoming more animalistic. Fists connected with bone, and the couple hurried to the railing that wrapped around Viktor's bar, trying to see what was happening on the sublevel.

Maksim gripped the to-go bag and strode for the apartment. He'd been planning to call Daniel, curious to hear what happened with Gabriela, but that wasn't going to happen. His apartment had to go dark before the police showed up.

He unlocked the door and let himself in. As he twisted the key, relocking the door from inside, another door in the apartment closed.

He spun to find Kat padding away from the bathroom. "Sorry to be the bearer of bad—" His attention traveled to her bare legs, and his statement evaporated. She was wearing the sleep top and panties. Nothing else.

"What?" She traced his gaze and then gasped. Not a small gasp indicating surprise, but a very large, very loud gasp that expressed shock.

She shuffled backward, groping for the bathroom door. When she didn't find the lever, she switched gears and darted for the stairs. Maksim caught a glimpse of scrape marks and yellowed bruising on her upper leg, just below her panty line—from where she and Ștefan had fallen down the hill. The scrapes were faint. The bruises were nearly gone. How was that possible?

"I know you're looking," she snapped, attempting to cover her tush.

"Not at that." Not precisely.

She disappeared behind the staircase. "I forgot…" The explanation trailed off into nothingness.

"You forgot I was on my way?" he asked, setting the to-go bag on the table.

"It's hot in here. I forgot I wasn't wearing my shorts." She peered out. "Can you turn around, please?"

Maksim faced the other direction. He registered light footsteps racing up the metal stairs. "We have a bigger concern," he said, securing the lock. "It's a bit more pressing than your cute little *funduleț*—which I've already seen, need I remind you."

"What concern?" Her head appeared at the top of the staircase. "Fundu-what?"

"Nothing. Listen, this is going to sound strange, but we need to eat dinner in the dark." He killed the downstairs light and carried the bags to the staircase. "Are you dressed?"

"Uh… yeah. Now I am."

He began his ascent. His footsteps were heavier than hers, and the metal vibrated under his weight. "Two guys decided to fight outside the club. I don't want anyone to know we're here."

"Viktor knows."

"Yes, but Viktor won't say anything." Maksim crested the top step. He'd been planning to explain more, but the words lodged in his throat. Kat had donned his shirt—the long-sleeve with the stretched-out neck—over her sleepwear. Seeing her a moment ago had been a pleasant surprise, but seeing her like this—in *his* shirt—drove something primal within him.

He wanted her, but more than physically. He wanted her to

belong to him. For *him* to belong to *her*. His mind spun in the direction of the ring. He closed his eyes and made himself take a breath, desperate to order his thoughts.

Lights. Dinner.

"Was this not okay? I thought you said I could have it."

He opened his eyes and found her staring down at the shirt. He shook off the daze, powered forward, and crossed the room with purpose. "I'm not a fan of eating up here," he said, ignoring her question. "But we'll have to." He headed for one of the bunk beds. "The table downstairs is too close to the front door."

"Why?" She tucked her hands inside the oversized sleeves. "Are you expecting someone?"

"I'm concerned about the police." He set the plastic bag on the bottom bunk. "That fight was getting out of hand. I don't want the cops to come knocking, believing they have witnesses to interview."

She straightened. "They'd do that?"

"Depending on the severity of the fight." He paused. "I should probably tell you... I had a run-in with the police."

She sat up. "Tonight?"

"While waiting for our food. They were looking for someone else, and one of the cops asked for my passport. Nothing came of it, but it was a close call. That's probably why I'm feeling extra cautious." He handed her a bottled water, then angled for his duffel. "Thankfully, I have a solution for eating in the dark." He sifted through his bag until he found his headlamp.

After killing the last of the lights, he activated the headlamp and switched the light to red mode. A cone of soft red spilled down his jeans, painting him in an eerie glow. "It's not ideal," he said, returning to the bunk, "but we'll be able to see."

She studied the plastic bag, her hands, her arms. "Looks like we're in a horror movie."

"The police showing up would be worse than a horror movie." He secured his headlamp, tightening the strap, and pulled out the suture scissors. "We'll have to wait until morning to use these."

"The morning?" She groaned and flopped onto the lower bunk. "Maksim, no."

"I'll do it before I go to the bank. I promise."

She slumped against a bedpost.

"Also got you this." He held up the power supply. "Should be the correct one, but I'll need to check your laptop." The unknown substance that coated the wire rubbed off on his fingers. He sighed. "I'm going to sneak downstairs and wash this. And my hands."

Kat stared. "Is it used?"

"It was a small shop, family run." He stripped off the head-lamp and passed it to Kat. "Feel free to get started. The *ćevapi* is made into wraps with onions, cabbage, spicy cheese. There's extra *kajmak* in the bag." He took the power supply and headed for the staircase.

"Hey, Maksim?"

He did an about-face.

Kat pointed the headlamp down and a red dot radiated from her hands. "Be careful. Going down the stairs, but also tomorrow." The red light joggled, presumably as she fidgeted. "That would have been horrible if you'd been arrested. I wouldn't have known what to do."

"You're right. We need a contingency plan." He walked forward and knelt in front of her. "Viktor is your first point of contact here. Anything goes sideways or you suspect something is afoot, you go to the bar. I'll talk to him tomorrow, see if he can have another key made. Until then, I'll let him know you need the spare."

"Okay."

"But you *cannot* leave this apartment. Not for fresh air, not to take a walk. Only in case of an emergency. Anything else is too dangerous, and we cannot risk exposure. Promise me."

"I promise." Her

"I need you to memorize this address. Visokog Stevana 32."

She blinked. "Vis—what?"

"Think of a visor." He held a hand to his head as if to shield his eyes. "*Viso.* Say it back to me. Use your hand."

She copied him. "Viso."

"And *kog*. Think of a cog in a clock." He drew a circle in the air with his finger.

She echoed him.

"Put them together. Use your hands."

"Viso." She did the visor. "Kog." She drew the circle.

"For the second word… think of a female, Serbian version of Ștefan. Stevana."

"Stevana."

"What's the number?"

She hesitated. "Thirty-two?"

He grinned. "Now put it all together."

She did the visor and the cog first and then nodded. "Visokog Stevana 32."

"See? You're a natural." He reached out with his free hand and brushed his thumb along her chin. Her shiver was faint in the red light. Nevertheless Maksim noticed.

Fire flooded him. He tilted his head and leaned in—but her expression, whether good or bad, was unreadable. He withdrew his touch and backed away. Her gaze followed him. "Anything goes sideways with Viktor," he said, "get yourself to that address. Top floor, end of the hall, broken hallway light. Tell him I sent you."

"Who?"

"He'll decide if he wants to share his name. Otherwise just call him 401."

Her expression turned quizzical. "Like… a prisoner number?"

"Not quite." His lips quirked. "I'm going to wash up. Low risk of mission failure."

Maksim took extra care descending the shadowy staircase

and felt his way into the bathroom. He knew the layout of the apartment well enough, but navigating the space in pitch darkness added a new complexity.

His sticky skin pleaded for another shower, but he settled for peeling off his shirt and splashing water on his chest, stomach, and armpits. He fanned himself, cooling his body another degree.

All of this he did without turning on a single light.

While he was downstairs, he decided to peer out the blinds. No flashing lights, no more shouting. Just the drone of techno filtering up from the subterranean club. Perhaps his night had turned around after all. He needed that. He had a big day tomorrow, and everything had to go right.

———

LUNI, 17 IUNIE, 10:12 (MONDAY, JUNE 17, 10:12AM)

Belgrade thrummed on that Monday morning, the sidewalks filled with pedestrians, the streets blanketed with traffic. The sun cooked everything on high, and the overabundance of car fumes stung Maksim's nostrils.

He filtered into the sea of pedestrians and made his way from the Design District to his bank on Makedonska. Sweat accumulated under his new suit, but he didn't break stride. Couldn't. He had a long list of things to accomplish, and he couldn't do any of them until he checked off this first task.

Stone buildings rose up on both sides of the street. A long row of shops stretched on his right, and he glimpsed his reflection in each of the storefront windows—except it wasn't him. It was Luka Vuković, a businessman from Montenegro.

Maksim reached up, fidgeting with a pair of thick-rimmed readers he'd found at a pharmacy. Even at the lowest diopter strength, they added a slight blur to his surroundings, but they were his best option in lieu of the ball cap.

As he passed a boutique, he noticed a bulge in the satchel he was carrying—one more component of his disguise, but this one had a practical application.

Maksim stepped to the side, letting the foot traffic flow past, and opened the satchel. He was using it to store his jeans and t-shirt, and the bag added an official-looking touch to the business attire. Unfortunately, it wasn't very large, and even with his clothes tightly rolled, they added a roundedness to the leather.

He adjusted the clothes as best he could and moved his passport to an outer pocket located on the flap. Then he wouldn't have to open the top to retrieve his identification and thus risk anyone seeing the clothes.

A city bus rumbled up the street, aiming for a set of covered bus stops outside the bank building. Maksim joined a crowd of pedestrians crossing Ulica Nušićeva—Nušićeva Street—and strode alongside the bank's stone and glass multilevel building.

He turned in.

A grand entryway with a sleekly tiled floor opened up before him. The clack of dress shoes echoed, and he prayed no one noticed his chunky motorcycle boots.

A blonde seated behind her glossy reception desk greeted him in Serbian. *"Good morning. How may I—?"* Recognition criss-crossed her lovely fortysomething face. *"Ahh, Mr. Vuković. How are you? What a pleasure to see you again."*

"Jelena. Hello. I'm well, thank you." He stopped at the desk and set his satchel on the floor, giving himself space to relax into the conversation. *"How is your family? Are your children happy to be free of school for the summer?"*

Her smile brightened at the inquiry. *"They are! We will be traveling to the beach, and they are very excited."*

"And your husband? He was starting a new job the last time I was here. How is that going?"

"You are such a busy man. How do you have time to remember these things?" She chuckled. *"My husband is well, and he likes his job. Thank you for remembering us."* She stood and circled around the desk. *"And how is your family, sir? How is business for you? I haven't seen you since a long time."*

"Business is very good. I couldn't ask for more success. But I'm troubled over a recent death in my family."

"Oh!" Her smile fell. *"I'm sorry to hear this. May God give you and your family strength during these days."*

"Thank you. Sadly, I need to close my safe deposit box." He gave a mild shrug while his expression emphasized regret. *"This is a complicated time."*

"I understand completely." She pushed a clipboard with a running list of names and signatures toward him. *"Sign in, please, and of course I will need your passport."*

"Certainly. And thank you many times again for your condolences." He feigned a weak smile and then signed the sheet.

She waited patiently as he retrieved his passport from the satchel and handed it over. She opened the document and cross-referenced his information against the sheet.

Maksim's pulse kicked into high gear. Had he signed his name as Maksim Răzvan? That would have been an amateur mistake, though not impossible commit.

Thankfully, though, he had not made that mistake. He'd created a unique handwriting and signature for Luka Vuković, and he had flawlessly executed both on the sign-in sheet.

Nothing to worry about.

The woman nodded, satisfied, and lifted a pleasant smile to him. *"Please wait here while I find a manager who can facilitate the account closure."*

"Oh, and Jelena?" He reached out as she turned toward a glassed-off admin area. *"My passport?"* He pumped up a playful smile because, obviously, she had forgotten to return the document.

Except she hadn't "forgotten."

"Mr. Vuković, you know I am required to take this."

His brow dipped. She'd never taken his passport before. Signing him in and cross-referencing the names had been the whole of her process.

Realization dawned across her soft, round features. *"Sir, forgive me. I am not thinking—"* She glanced to and fro and then stepped closer, eliminating the space between them. *"We have experienced policy changes since your last visit."*

He tilted his head, wanting to appear curious. Internally he detected the first inklings of panic—racing pulse, increased heart rate. *"What kind of changes? More paperwork?"*

"Government compliance."

His insides sank. *"I hadn't heard about that. I've been busy, and I haven't been keeping current with the news."*

"The news isn't talking about this. I think they've been asked not to." She lowered her voice. *"The government is becoming stricter about overstays."*

"Visa overstays?"

"Overstays for any visitors. Many tourists are coming here, working remotely and benefiting from a life in Serbia—but without paying Serbian taxes. The law changed very recently, but we were told to implement this new practice more than six months ago." She bit her lip. *"I'm not actually supposed to share much of this. I could get in trouble."*

"No, no. I won't speak a word to anyone." Maksim gave the appearance of being cool and composed, but his fight-or-flight was nearing maximum velocity. This had to be the reason for the cop's hypervigilance last night. He'd made a reference to the ball cap, saying Maksim looked American.

Maksim had assumed this was the usual animosity, but perhaps it was because of this new law.

His thoughts snapped back to the present dilemma. The easiest way to determine a foreigner's status was to check the entry stamp in their passport. But he didn't have an entry stamp.

The bank manager would realize that pretty quickly and then… what? Inquire with him further? Call the police?

Maksim was about to ask when Jelena turned away. *"I know you are very busy,"* she said, hurrying toward the admin area. *"I will tell the manager to expedite this process. Don't worry. We will only be a moment."*

MAKSIM CONSIDERED RUNNING AFTER JELENA, snatching his passport, saying he'd be back. A blip of navy blue held him in place.

He leaned against the reception desk, wanting to appear casual, and lowered his glasses. The bank used private security, and one of their guards was patrolling the upper level.

Maksim scanned the ground floor. He didn't see another guard, but that didn't meant there wasn't one. He decided *not* to chase after Jelena—and subsequently make a scene—and instead rehearsed possible explanations.

I watched the border guard stamp my passport. Perhaps the page fell out.

The guard who stamped my passport was having problems with his ink. He must have run out.

Everything he considered sounded utterly ridiculous… until one idea pushed forward past the others. The manager could still report him to the police, but he *might* be able to talk his way out of it. His chances of success were even greater if Jelena vouched for him. He felt sure she would. The only question was whether he would be dealing with her or strictly with the bank manager.

That was beyond his control, so he took a calming breath and mentally rehearsed his explanation. Five minutes ticked by. Ten. Customers filtered in, many of them heading for teller windows. More suits came and went. The guard noted everyone who passed him. Occasionally his gaze traveled to the ground floor.

Maksim pretended to be preoccupied, sometimes checking a make-believe watch, other times checking his phone.

Finally, Jelena hurried through the doors of the admin wing. She was alone, and relief swept through Maksim. But the feeling was short-lived when he saw her empty hands.

"Mr. Vuković, I must ask—" She fidgeted. *"The manager and I cannot find your entry stamp for Serbia."*

"What?" He drew back, feigning shock. *"That's impossible. I saw the guard stamp it."*

"How did you enter... may I ask?"

"Nikola Tesla International of course. The same as always." He spoke as if she should have known that.

"Somehow the page is gone." She grimaced. *"But there don't appear to be any missing pages."*

He pretended to think hard, rubbing his chin, looking all around. Then he gasped and pinned a surprised stare on her. *"I think I know what happened."*

She straightened. *"Do you?"*

"I cannot believe it." He let out a relieved chuckle. *"All this time has passed..."*

"What happened, Mr. Vuković? Tell me, please."

"I lost my passport some months ago. Don't worry. The passport has been replaced." He held up a reassuring hand. *"But I never did find the old one. Jelena, I believe we just found it!"*

"That is wonderful news." Her smile returned, her expression brimming with relief. *"Do you have your new passport?"*

"I certainly hope so." He made a show of being frustrated while he reached into the front pocket of his satchel. There were no other passports in there, but she didn't know that.

"Perhaps the document is inside the bag," she said, stating the obvious.

He grinned sheepishly, pivoting as he flipped open the top. He didn't expect her to be intrusive, but he couldn't risk exposing his rolled-up clothes. That would only further damage his credibility.

He groped, searching, and all the while fear clawed at him from deep inside his rib cage. He needed to access this safe deposit box. He and Kat needed the money. But at this point, he would be happy if he could get out of Belgrade without the bank manager calling the police.

His mind wandered to his phone. He needed to call Kat and tell her to get packed and ready. Perhaps Viktor could drive them out of the city. They could hit one of the smaller towns and catch a bus not yet outfitted with cameras.

But how would he pay Viktor? He was running low on cash, and his last transfer—

Maksim's train of thought derailed. *The account. The failed transfer.* His mouth went completely dry.

"Mr. Vuković?" Jelena stood with her hands clasped. She tilted her head, eyes expectant.

"Forgive me. I must have left my current passport at the apartment." Worry poured through him. *"This has never happened before. Please tell me… is this a big problem? I can't afford any trouble. That's not good for my business."*

"To answer honestly, sir, I don't know. You see, after the manager initiates this process, the system does not allow her to reverse the request. She had already begun to enter your information before we realized there was no stamp."

"My apartment is very close by." He thumbed toward the doors. *"What if I go there and return quickly? Then she can continue entering my information. It will be like nothing happened."*

"That's true." Her heavy mood lifted. *"You can return directly here? She won't be able to exit from the program until she completes the entry."*

"Of course. I will run if I must." And run he would. *"I will need my old passport in the meantime. The Montenegrin government is very strict about this kind of thing. I'll have to submit the passport to them as soon as I return to my country."*

"Serbia is very strict about this, too. Allow me to—" The phone at her desk rang, cutting her off. *"One moment please. That may be the bank manager."*

The tension in Maksim's stomach coiled.

She answered with a smile in her voice, glancing and nodding in Maksim's direction. The person on the other end of the line—presumably the manager—began to speak, and Jelena's eyebrows converged. She turned her back to Maksim, whispering something before going silent again.

Maksim's instinct heightened, taking him from DEFCON 5 to DEFCON 1.

Movement on the upper level drew his attention. He peered over the top of his glasses and saw the security guard speaking into a two-way radio. The man listened to a transmission and then began to scan.

His stare landed on Maksim.

Shit!

Maksim turned, ready to spew the first piece of manufactured garbage that entered his mind, when Jelena lowered the phone into the cradle. The color had drained from her face.

"I have a business call to take. It's important." Maksim yanked out his phone. *"I'll be outside when you're done."*

"I—I'm afraid I can't let you leave, sir."

Another blur of movement dragged Maksim's attention to the stairs. The security guard was on his way.

Maksim focused on Jelena. *"How long have we known each other? Two years?"*

She refused to make eye contact.

"Jelena." He lowered his volume and inserted his most pleading tone. *"Jelena, you can talk to me. Tell me what's happening. Please."*

"Your account has been frozen," she whispered, *"by the Financial Intelligence Unit of the Republic of Serbia."*

His expression widened in alarm.

"We cannot return your passport, and"—she swallowed—*"my manager is required to notify the police."*

His phone sang out a polyphonic ringtone. Someone was calling, but his brain couldn't process anything. Dazed, he backpedaled, angling for the door.

Jelena put a hand out. *"No, Mr. Vuković. Please don't do that."*

"I… must take this call." Maksim pushed open the door as the security guard leapt down the remaining stairs.

"Mr. Vuković!" Jelena's frantic voice chased after him until the door swung shut.

He launched up the sidewalk, sprinting past the bus stops, knocking people aside. A man shouted in Serbian. *"Watch where you're going!"*

Maksim didn't slow down. He needed to find a side street and get to an area with fewer cameras. Storefronts breezed past him until everything was a blur—because of his speed, but also because of the glasses. He wanted to shed them. The jacket, too.

He couldn't. Not until he was clear of any cameras.

A siren pierced the hum of traffic. Maksim threw a glance over his shoulder and found the security guard barreling out of the bank. A cop car, with lights and sirens blazing, approached from the east. The guard waved and pointed in Maksim's direction.

Maksim faced forward and pumped his arms. His shoulder resisted, the muscles refusing to stretch with the movement. He couldn't lengthen his stride a centimeter more.

The injury was officially throttling him. *Damn me! Devil take me!* He scanned his surroundings, searching for freedom. The polyphonic ringtone cried out from his hand. He hit Answer as he sprinted through another wave of pedestrians. "Stand by," he said without placing the device to his ear. He couldn't afford to break stride or slow down.

"Maksim? H-hello?"

Maksim barely registered the frightened voice. It belonged to Kat, but she was whispering.

"Stand by," he said, louder this time. *Think. Prioritize.*

There were no cross streets, but Maksim noticed what looked like an alley just beyond a *trafika*—a Serbian convenience kiosk. He darted across traffic and sprinted toward the alley. Rather, what he thought was an alley. In reality, it was a driveway that forked—a parking lot to the left, an underground garage to the right.

He angled for the parking lot, using it at a cut-through, and entered a complex of high-rise apartments. He sprinted through the courtyard and raced behind one of the buildings. An entire column of balconies stretched above him—not the greatest place to stop, but he needed to orient himself.

Out of breath, Maksim held the phone to his ear. "Kat?"

"Maksim," she whispered, voice quivering. "Someone's at the door. It's a woman. I-I think she's a cop."

Nausea knocked him sideways. This was his worst nightmare come to life, and it was happening in overdrive. "Do not answer the door. Don't say anything or move around in the apartment. Just stay where you are. I'm going to call Viktor."

"Okay." Tears leaked into her voice.

"Put your phone on silent as soon as we hang up. Watch for my call, but don't answer if someone might hear you."

Noise in the background rattled through the phone. Whoever was at the door was banging now.

"Do you remember the plan?" Maksim asked. "Press a key on your phone one time for yes, twice for no.

Silence unfolded, then came the beep. There was only one.

"That's what we're doing," he said. "Copy that?"

One beep. She understood.

"I don't have time to change my ring settings. I know you're scared, but wait for me to call you. I have to go." He closed the phone and darted for the next apartment. His brain started to shut down, yielding to the panic rising in him.

He forced himself to remain calm, to *think*. He'd been on Makedonska, traveling west, and he needed to go north to reach Skadarska. That would be the fastest way to Miro's.

But what about these clothes? He would be easy to spot on the traffic cameras, which the police were surely tapped into by now.

He reached the end of the complex and found himself on the corner of Skadarska and Bulevar Despota Stefana. The siren from earlier had multiplied. He counted three—no, four—and their volume had increased. They were closing in on him.

He aimed for the crosswalk that would take him across the main boulevard. A pizza restaurant sat at the corner, and he knew with certainty there was a back patio. He could run inside, change, and escape out the back…

His newly birthed plan came to a crashing halt. He'd left his satchel at the bank, which meant he had no clothes to change into. Anger at himself, at his foolishness, swelled. *Be calm. You have to work the problem.*

He changed direction and headed toward the only place he could think of—the stretch of Skadarska near the takeout window. He'd walked that street many times. There were no cameras until closer to Stari Grad.

Then another epiphany dawned. *The takeout window.* He sprinted that way. The road curved, putting him beyond the last camera—the last *known* camera—and he was able to strip off his jacket, tie, and glasses.

He tossed everything behind a row of bushes and rolled up his sleeves. The urge to run burned through him. He resisted. The residents of this neighborhood were bound to come out, wanting to investigate the sirens. He couldn't give anyone a reason to suspect him.

The sirens echoed, drawing closer. Paranoia redoubled its grip on him. *The takeout place won't be open. It's not yet noon.*

He pressed on. If they were closed, he would figure out his next step—hiding in an alley perhaps. Hell, he might even be able to break into one of these buildings. That would be a last resort, but one he had to consider. He could *not* let himself be arrested. That would leave Kat vulnerable. More vulnerable than ever.

He imagined one scenario after another—involving corrupt police, Vladimir, Émilien.

A black van sat parked outside the *ćevapi* place. The takeout window was shuttered, but the side door was open. Maksim ducked inside and shut the door. Voices spilled into the hallway from somewhere in the back.

Maksim cupped his mouth. *"Dobar dan?"* (Hello?)

The voices decreased in volume, and Maksim realized someone had been listening to talk radio. Footsteps shuffled his way, and the overhead lights kicked on. The owner appeared at the end of the hall. He saw Maksim, and his brow pinched.

A siren blared, drawing closer. Others remained distant, but this one came barreling toward him. Were they right outside? They certainly sounded like it.

Maksim closed his eyes, waiting. The siren continued past, heading toward Stari Grad. Same direction the police had gone yesterday.

He opened his eyes, releasing the breath he'd been holding.

The owner's surprise collapsed into suspicion. *"Was that for you?"* He was referring to the siren.

"It was." Maksim met the man's stern gaze. *"The police are after me. I think it's related to what happened last night."*

"The police officer who questioned you?"

"I think so, yes." This was the most honest explanation he could conjure. He himself didn't understand why he'd appeared familiar to that cop. Perhaps he'd seen an all-points bulletin for Luka Vuković, who was apparently wanted for financial crimes.

The owner of the takeout place eyed Maksim. *"Why are you here? Tell me what happened."*

"I was running an errand at my bank, and they wouldn't let me access my account. They took my passport and said the funds are frozen."

The owner sighed. *"How can you afford an attorney when you cannot access your money? That is why they do these things. Bastards."*

Maksim neither affirmed nor negated the man's conclusion. *"I have a friend who is well-connected. He can help me."*

"Do you want to call him?" The owner reached into his pocket. *"You can borrow my phone."*

"His telephone number changes a lot, but his apartment is close." Maksim, drenched in sweat, looked down at himself. *"I wondered if you have a spare chef's hat and apron. I can walk to my friend's, and I'll look like I'm getting off work rather than running from the police."*

"And what happens if you are caught?" The man folded his arms. *"The police will come after me and my business."*

"Not if you report me. Call 112. Tell them someone broke into your restaurant and stole the items."

The man slumped. *"You want me to report you?"*

"I want you to be free from legal trouble. All I ask is that you give me enough time to reach my friend's apartment."

"How long?"

"Forty-five minutes. One hour would be better." That should be enough time to reach Miro's and figure out a contingency. Hopefully. *What about Kat?* God, he hoped she hadn't been picked up by the police, but he could figure that out at Miro's.

The owner pursed his lips, his eyes tightening along the sides. A musty odor hung in the hallway. The smell of burnt grease lingered from the night before.

Ten seconds ticked by before the man exhaled a heavy sigh. He gave his head a slow shake, which Maksim perceived to be a "no"—but the man's words contradicted his reluctance. *"I'll give you what you're asking for."* He beckoned to Maksim. *"And we have work pants, too."*

11:48 (11:48 AM)

THE OWNER WENT ABOVE and beyond. Not only did he provide an apron, a chef's beanie, and a pair of work slacks, he also gave Maksim the keys to his van. *"You understand,"* the man said, *"I'll have to report the vehicle stolen."*

"I understand." Maksim lowered his phone. He'd been trying Viktor and Kat, and neither of them were answering. *"I'm sorry again. My girl is tangled up in this, and I have to make sure she's safe."*

"As I said, you are a good man." The man extended his hand.

"Thank you from the heart." Maksim accepted, and they shook. *"Are you able to give me at least forty-five minutes?"*

"I am very busy today, documenting our inventory for the week. Maybe I don't notice the van is gone for many hours"—the man shrugged—*"perhaps the end of the day. Will that be good for you and your girlfriend?"*

Maksim straightened. The van was a golden ticket for exfiltrating the neighborhood. He would have additional cover *and* reach Miro's within six minutes. The longer he had, the better off he'd be. Hell, he might be able to get himself and Kat out of the country before this man made the phone call.

"That's very helpful. I'm so grateful." With that, Maksim grabbed two plastic to-bags full of wadded-up butcher paper—a small but authentic part of his food-delivery disguise—and slipped outside. A moment later, he was cruising up Skadarska.

Residents had been trickling outside, opening their windows, stepping onto their balconies. Navy-blue uniforms and flashing lights encircled an apartment building closer to Stari Grad. Probably the same building those two cops had descended upon the night before. It seemed the police had come to the wrong conclusion.

Maksim's thoughts came full circle. He'd mentioned having an apartment in the Design District. Then an officer—female, according to Kat—showed up at his place. Had it been the same female cop from the previous night?

He lowered the visor the way Gabriela had done in the Škoda and navigated traffic. "Come on," he muttered, redialing Kat. He pressed Speaker and held the phone below the window line. The phone rang… and rang…and rang.

He ended the call and squeezed a fist. *They have her.* Perhaps she had ventured outside. She might have thought the police were gone when in fact they had been lying in wait. And what about Viktor? Had he been arrested, too?

As Maksim considered possible scenarios, his thoughts landed on his duffel, which he'd left at the apartment. Everything of value was in that bag—his Ukrainian passport, Kat's lockbox, his wallet with the last of his cash…

And Madă's ring.

Heaviness landed on his shoulders and spilled into every part of his being, down into his bones. Overwhelming nausea washed through him. After removing Kat's stitches that morning, he'd pocketed his wallet and had started out the door. Something had nudged him to go back. He'd been planning to change at the men's store, after buying the suit, and having the wallet on his person seemed risky. So he'd made his way upstairs and had buried the wallet in his duffel.

The nausea swirled, pushing bile into his throat, and he very nearly vomited right there in the man's van.

Five minutes later, he parked on an isolated strip of road not far from the Danube. It was the kind of place mafia guys parked before dumping a body in the river. There were a couple of abandoned houses, and he'd heard stories of people being interrogated there.

Overgrown brush spilled onto the decrepit sidewalk. Trash scattered the ground on one side of him. Train tracks ran on the other side. Maksim grabbed his phony to-go bags and hopped out. Several apartment blocks loomed in the distance. He ran in that direction, cutting through parking lots and complexes, zigzagging through the most obscure side streets he could find.

Soon, he was standing at the entrance to Miro's building. He pressed the intercom button for Miro's apartment. Miro answered. *"Da?"*

"Delivery. Foodstuffs." It was the same line Maksim had used the night before. This time, he didn't change his voice.

A gasp rattled the speaker box. The door buzzed and clicked open. Maksim darted inside and sprinted up the stairs.

Miro had his front door open, waiting for him. *"Koji kurac?"* (What the dick?) He grabbed Maksim by the apron and dragged him inside. "The police are looking for you," he whispered… and then he noticed Maksim's impromptu disguise. "What *is* this?"

"Is Kat here?" Maksim dropped the fake to-go sacks and swung around to the living room.

Miro followed him. "Who?"

The heaviness threatened to bring him to his knees. "My girl," he said, barely able to choke out her name. "I gave her your address in case anything went sideways." He ripped off the chef's beanie and swore.

"No shit it has! Look at this." Miro flopped into his gaming chair and pulled up something on the web. Luka Vuković's passport photo appeared with a list of crimes he was wanted for. "They're saying you're armed and dangerous."

"Vladimir is behind this. He must be." Maksim stared at the image. "But he didn't know about Luka Vuković."

"Did he know you have contacts in Belgrade?"

"I would assume so, but I have contacts all over Europe." Maksim had gone to great lengths to keep his Luka Vuković identity a secret. He'd had to. That safe deposit box had been the first and most important link in his lifeline.

"You're being charged with financial crimes." Miro spun in his chair and faced Maksim. "Could be a police investigation."

Maksim considered the possibility. "That particular bank account," he said, rubbing his neck, "was connected to a centralized exchange. I've been cashing out crypto for about a year. Perhaps I amassed the funds too quickly."

"Could be. The government is getting stricter about those kinds of things." Miro shoved a hand through his bangs, clearing them from his forehead. The greasy locks stuck straight up. "I've heard rumors about centralized exchanges being investigated, mostly by the US government, but Serbia could be getting in on the action. There's a lot of money to be confiscated."

Maksim tensed. "It's only a matter of time before they link Viktor to me."

"Who?" Miro's head jerked. "Who are all these people?"

"Viktor has been keeping an eye on my apartment. He despises the government, so I don't think he would have reported me." Maksim began to pace within the confines of Miro's cluttered living room. "The police will see I've been transferring money to him. They could detain him for questioning." Perhaps they already had. That would have explained why neither Viktor nor Kat were answering.

"Maybe *he* was being investigated." Miro lifted a lazy shoulder, mouth turning downward along the sides. "I know people who fit that mold—not criminals, but they resent the government. Some get bitten for tax evasion. It's such a small amount, usually for cash they're not reporting, but then bigger fish go down with them." Miro leaned back, hands clasped behind his head. "The guy might have been on a watch list, which would have led the police to your account pretty easily. And with a little more digging—"

"They realized they had a bigger fish." Maksim swore. "I knew I shouldn't have given up my name to that cop. I wouldn't have, but he was demanding to see my passport."

Miro threw up an eyebrow. "There is so much more to this story, isn't there?"

Maksim was about to give him a complete rundown when a soft knock pealed through the door. Maksim silenced himself and gave a signal for his friend to do the same.

Miro tiptoed to the door. "It's a Muslim girl," he whispered, placing an eye to the spyhole, "with a middle-aged Serb."

Maksim bolted across the room and flung open the door. Kat looked up at him, and relief exploded through her features. "Maksim!" She dropped her backpack and flung herself into his arms.

"Kat. Thank God." He wrapped her in a hug. She held him in a death grip, her delicate arms turning to steel around his waist. He relished it, drinking in her presence, experiencing the warmth of her body pressed against his. Her shoulders shook under soft sobs.

He rubbed her back and began to whisper in Romanian, reciting one of the prayers Daniel had taught him. *"Tatăl nostru (Our Father) who art in heaven, hallowed be Thy name. Thy kingdom come, Thy will be done, on earth as it is in heaven..."* He drew her away from the door and motioned for Viktor to enter. His property manager was carrying the duffel, and Maksim feel like crying himself. "You brought my bag."

Kat pulled away, sniffling. "I wasn't going to leave it."

He cupped her cheeks and thumbed away the wet streaks. "We're going to figure this out, all right? Do you believe me?"

She nodded.

"I can't stay." Viktor dropped Maksim's duffel. *"The police came to my home, asking about what I do for you."*

"And?" Maksim said. *"What did you say?"*

"Only that I watch your place. They asked if I keep a spare key. I have this one." He pulled a brass door key from his pocket. *"I said you arrived after being away a long time and that you hadn't brought a key, and so I gave you mine."*

"I think the police tracked down my payments to you. You may need to hire an attorney."

"I thought so after they questioned me." Viktor dragged on a half-smoked cigarette. *"It's not all in the bank. I withdrew many small amounts like you told me. I have enough for an attorney."*

"What are you guys saying?" Kat leaned against Maksim. "Is Viktor telling you that I drove here?"

"She drove?" Maksim's eyes snapped toward Viktor, who nodded. *"Why?"*

"I didn't want the new traffic cameras to detect me, in case the police were watching, so I hid under a blanket in the back seat." Viktor gestured toward the door. *"I need to go. I borrowed my neighbor's car, and I need to return it."*

"I understand." Maksim extended his hand. *"Viktor, thank you to the sky. I will try to be in contact as soon as possible. I don't know when I can send another payment—"*

"No, no." Viktor let out a nervous chuckle as he took Maksim's hand. *"I'm grateful for the opportunity, but I think contacting me will create more problems."* He slipped the key into his pocket. *"Stop by the bar when you can return. I will hide the key somewhere."*

"Wait." Maksim unlatched himself from Kat and dug the flip phone out of his pocket. He opened the device, twisted, and broke the phone in half. "I need yours as well," he said to Kat.

She pulled out her burner phone. She noticed the number of missed calls and did a double take. "Sorry. I couldn't check the phone while I was driving."

"It's better that you didn't." He repeated the process with her phone and handed the pieces to Viktor. *"Wipe all of those down and throw them out somewhere discreet. Not anywhere near here, nor your home. Watch for cameras."*

"I will do it." Viktor shoved the pieces into his pocket and ambled into the hallway. Cigarette smoke formed a trail to the stairwell.

Maksim closed the door.

"Hey, so… I'm Miro." The hacker edged in front of Maksim and extended one hand toward Kat while smoothing his greasy hair with the other. "I suppose Maksim has told you all about me." He summoned a gigantic grin. "It's all true," he sang with a laugh.

"Oh, um… thanks." She shook his hand. "So you're… 401?"

He shot a look at Maksim. "You told her my alias?"

"I never give people your real name." Maksim wrapped an arm around Kat and led her into the living room. "Proceed with caution," he said as they circumnavigated Miro's desks and a great deal of trash. Somehow, the place had grown dirtier since the night before. "Miro, we need a plan and fast. Have you been able to research those freight trains?"

"No, but I have something better." He grabbed his phone and accessed his photos. "I was going to send this to you, but I knew you were using that clamshell."

"Clamshell?" Kat mouthed to Maksim.

"He means the burner phone," Maksim said at a normal volume. "Those flip styles are great for text-only messages, but they don't handle images well."

"Bro, look." Miro launched a photo on his smartphone and showed Maksim. "See?"

"What am I—?" Maksim realized the answer before he had finished the question. He snatched the phone and expanded the photo. A Republic of Serbia exit stamp had been inked onto white copy paper. "It's dated for today," Maksim said.

"Yes, it is." Miro flopped into his gaming chair. "Grab your chopsticks, my friends. The sushi roll is about to hit the soy sauce."

14:29 (2:29 PM)

MAKSIM AND KAT waited outside the Western City Gate, a thirty-five-story twin-tower-block wonder of Brutalist architecture. Straight lines defined the main structures of these interconnected buildings, while the towers themselves were bookended by cement cylinders, adding contrast and tension to the Communist-era design.

"What's taking him so long?" Maksim wiped the dash clock, attempting to clear what he'd assumed was dust. The substance smeared, and he groaned. *"E un porc."* (He's a pig.)

"What's that disk at the top?" Kat leaned into the front and pointed at a circular structure crowning one of the cylinders. "Is it a radio tower? I think I see antennas."

Maksim kept his head on a swivel, glancing all around in search of police. But he knew, without looking, what she was talking about. "It was a revolving restaurant."

"Wow. So you can get a 360-degree view while you eat."

"It's been closed since the nineties. The revolving mechanism never worked."

Kat sank into her seat. "Oh."

Maksim watched a vehicle approach. He and Kat were waiting in Miro's car, which sat parallel-parked outside the towers. Maksim had adjusted the driver-side visor so that it lay flat against the side window. His visor was down, blocking anyone's view from the front.

He tugged on the chef's beanie, pulling the fabric around his ears, as the car cruised past. Not a cop car. "Thank God," he muttered.

Something jostled in the back seat. Kat was rolling down her window.

"No," Maksim said. "I told you we can't do that."

"But it's so hot." Kat peered over the top of her sunglasses—courtesy of Miro. She'd worn the makeshift "hijab" and was plucking at the fabric to fan herself. "He's been in there so long."

"The rear windows have good tint. We need to make use of it." Maksim twisted around. "Perhaps I should sit back there, too."

He braced the front seats, about to crawl through, when a lanky form with shaggy hair exited the left tower. The courtyard was about as unkempt as Miro, with overgrown weeds and droopy bushes, but Maksim discerned his friend through the unpruned greenery simply by observing his gait and mannerisms.

Miro examined his surroundings with covertness the average person wouldn't have caught—eyes scanning, head unmoving, posture totally relaxed. The guy may have seemed like a bumbling idiot, but he had incredible street sense and a keen ability to read people. Not to mention the fact that he was a brilliant hacker, one who appreciated white- and gray-hat activities more than the black variety—though, Miro *and* Maksim had executed their fair share of black-hat operations. There was no denying that.

Miro stuffed his hands into the light jacket he wore, and Maksim discerned the shape of his and Kat's passports through the fabric. "He has them."

Kat let two beats pass. "Was there a chance he wouldn't?" Confusion glimmered in her voice.

"There's always a chance of something going sideways." Maksim unlocked the car as Miro reached the door.

"Boom." Miro whipped out the passports and passed them to Maksim. "Houston, we have lift off."

"You're a lifesaver." Maksim leaned back and shoved his passport—the *Ukrainian* passport—into his front pocket. He slipped Kat a glance, wondering if she'd noticed. He probably should have told her about his cover identities, but he couldn't afford to burn this one, so he was erring on the side of caution. "Here." He held her passport toward her.

She reeled in her stare from the towers. "Thanks," she said, accepting the navy-blue document.

"Awww." Miro clasped his hands and divided a giddy smile between them.

"*Miroslav.*" Maksim gestured toward the road. "*Our time is low, and our luck is thin.*"

"Meh." Miro flitted his hand toward Maksim. "My cousin is still giving his tour. They won't depart for Sarajevo until 15:00."

"Yes, I know. From Republic Square." Miro's passport guy lived in Novi Beograd—New Belgrade—an urbanized neighborhood across the river from Central Belgrade. Far away from Republic Square.

Miro pulled out his phone. His face widened. "Oh, damn!" He anchored his key and twisted. The Yaris purred to life.

"You cannot speed." Maksim tugged on his seatbelt. "Go with the flow of traffic. Don't stand out, but also be vigilant."

"Roger that." Miro pulled onto the road.

Winding their way through the Blokovi—an area known as "the Blocks"—didn't take long. But they turned the page on that chapter when they crossed Branko Most (Branko's Bridge), leaving New Belgrade behind.

The road funneled them into a gauntlet of multilevel stone buildings. These buildings towered over the area, though not nearly as much as the Blokovi. Buses stacked the right lane. Traffic in the left lane moved forward, and Miro darted into the space. They made progress for all of thirty seconds and then rolled to another stop.

"There." Maksim pointed to the right.

Miro zipped toward the space, but another car anticipated the move and lurched forward. Maksim slammed a hand against his window. "Stopstopstop!"

Miro braked. A honk blared.

Kat and her backpack flew forward. "Oof!" She landed on the console, between the front seats, and her backpack landed on the gear shift.

Maksim helped her. "Seatbelt," he said, holding on to her bag. "You," he barked at Miro. "Pay attention."

"I am!" Miro proceeded in the left lane. "I'm being vigilant."

"Vigilant is not aggressive."

"I know, but look at the time! It's—" He rubbed the dash clock. The greasy substance smeared some more. *"Prokleto."* (Damn it.)

"Maybe you should clean your spaces sometimes." Maksim slanted a look. *"Do you clean your ass?"*

Miro lifted his arm and dipped his head, sniffing. His mouth turned down. *"I could use a bath maybe."*

Maksim snorted.

"What? I've been busy." Miro pumped the brakes, edging behind another car. He glanced at Kat. *"You let yourself stink in front of your girl?"*

Maksim rolled his eyes.

"You still shower twice every day?" Miro grinned. *"Maybe she is inspiring three times. Does she help wash your asscheeks and reach all the places you can't find?"*

Maksim narrowed a glare at his friend. *"Ćuti.* (Be quiet.) *Drive."*

Miro giggled and continued to edge forward.

Traffic was stop and go through Zeleni Venaci. Finally, the road opened up on the other side of a tunnel

"Get ready." Maksim passed the backpack to Kat. *"Where do we go to meet your cousin?"* he asked Miro.

"Kod konja." (By the horse.) Miro dipped into his pocket and yanked out his phone.

"What is the time?"

Miro was in the middle of dialing. He glanced at his screen, and his eyes widened. Maksim snatched the phone and swore.

"What?" Kat's voice pinched. "It's after three?"

"Fifteen eleven." Maksim glared at Miro. "Three eleven p.m."

"Do not worry. I am calling him now." Miro followed the road as he dialed. A monotone ring pealed through the speaker. A voicemail answered and Miro swore.

"I don't think there's on-street parking around the square," Maksim said. "Do you know? Where would the tour company park?"

"Parking garage?" Miro hung up and redialed. "On-street parking somewhere else? Maybe they walked to Republic Square. But it would have to be the yellow or green zone, right?"

"You don't know?"

"I don't drive unless I'm going outside the center." Miro pressed redial. "Look, we're almost there." He flitted a finger. "That's the square up there. Beyond those—"

"Zdravo." (Hello.) The man's greeting rattled through the phone speaker.

Miro gasped and switched to Serbian. They exchanged brief pleasantries before getting to the crux of the matter. Maksim's blood pressure began to rise. First, the man said they had already left. When Miro offered to meet them somewhere, the story changed and supposedly there was no more room.

"How is there no space?" Miro demanded. *"I spoke to you last night very late!"*

"We received two more tourists. I wasn't expecting them. The van is very crowded."

"What's going on?" Kat unbuckled her seatbelt and leaned forward. "Maksim?" Her voice quavered, and Maksim felt like he might lose his mind.

She was afraid. And he couldn't do anything about it.

"Miscommunication." His expression softened to a smile. "We'll get it sorted."

"You think Miro could drive us... wherever? To our next destination?"

"He doesn't know any border guards, *dragă*. Perhaps the stamps are good enough, but we won't know until we arrive."

Her shoulders sagged, but then her expression lit up—not with excitement. With a thought. She flipped through her passport, and her pale face turned a shade whiter. "Oh my God," she whispered in a peep.

"What?" Maksim stiffened, officially on high alert. "The stamps are bad?"

"There's no exit stamp for Romania."

Maksim dug out his passport. His last stamp had been entry into Serbia. There was no exit stamp for Ukraine. He inserted his hand into Miro's space and covered the phone. "We don't have exit stamps."

Miro jerked. "What? Are you certain?"

Maksim showed him. Miro split his attention between the road and Maksim's passport. Maksim flipped through the pages.

"Check the last page," Miro said.

Maksim blinked. Meanwhile Miro's cousin was shouting through the phone. *"Are you there? Hello? I'm disconnecting."*

Miro switched to Serbian and told him to wait. "Check the last page," he repeated to Maksim.

Kat gasped from the back seat. "Mine's on the last page."

Maksim flipped to the very last page in his passport. Sure enough the Romanian exit stamp was there. "Why would your guy do this? It's nowhere near the others."

Miro shrugged. "Why does that matter?"

"Because it could raise suspicion with the border guards."

"My cousin knows the border guards. One of them."

"I think I know why he did that," Kat said.

Maksim twisted around. She was flipping back and forth between pages.

"The stamps are slightly different." She returned to the last page and placed her finger next to the exit stamp. "Look at the red ink," she said, showing Maksim. "And the font… something about it is different, too."

Maksim flipped to the last page in his passport. Sure enough, the red ink had a pinkish hue. The font was thicker, blockier.

"That's good!" Miro shifted into first and pulled forward. "Then the new stamp isn't near the old one. They will be more difficult to compare."

Miro's cousin spoke through the speakerphone. *"How much will you send if I agree to take your friends?"*

Miro looked at Maksim.

"A bitcoin," Maksim said. "Kat can sit on my lap if he truly doesn't have extra space."

"You're sure?" Miro whispered.

"As long as you can cover me. I'll hit you back as soon as I access my wallet."

Miro repeated what Maksim had said. The other end of the line went silent, then the man said, "One bitcoin each plus whatever the border guard requires."

Miro flagged Maksim with both shaggy eyebrows. "Twenty thousand euros?"

"What choice do we have?" Maksim tipped his head back. "Unless you want to drive us to the border."

"I won't know any of the guards if something goes wrong."

"Yeah. I know." Maksim gestured for Miro to go ahead.

"I guess it's not so much in the scheme of things." Miro layered a positive tone over the comment, but Maksim wasn't feeling it. How much money had he lost? He couldn't even remember. He wasn't sure he wanted to.

"You should go to the horse," Miro said. "I'm stuck in this

line"—he frowned at the bumper to bumper traffic—"and I don't think my cousin will wait."

Maksim turned to Kat. "We're going on foot."

She grabbed her backpack. "It was nice to meet you, Miro. Thanks for sharing your real name." She managed a smile. "I like Miro more than 401."

"And what about you? I think you could use an alias." He grinned. "Kitty Kat. Katmobile. Katnanigans. Katalytic Konverter."

"Katnanigans, maybe. Kitty Kat, not so much."

"I like her," he said in a whisper that was directed at Maksim but loud enough for Kat to hear.

Kat chuckled. Maksim rolled his eyes.

"Watch out for my boy here." Miro was talking to Kat now. "Teach him how to relax a little."

Maksim pulled him in for a brotherly hug. "Thank you."

"I would not do this for anyone else. Not anyone. *Any*one."

"I know. I have no way to express my deep gratitude. One hundred bitcoin wouldn't suffice."

"Just don't get caught." Miro observed the immediate area. "I don't see any police."

Maksim pushed open his door and circled around. Kat climbed out, and they darted to the opposite sidewalk. Mannequins dotted the exterior windows of several shops. Maksim shouldered his duffel, ignoring the pain and exhaustion in his body, and launched into a run. Kat dogged his heels.

The horse—a.k.a. the Prince Mihailo monument—stood front and center in Republic Square. The bronze figure on horseback held out a regal arm, finger extended, and pointed east. Some people claimed he had been pointing toward Serbia's future. Others joked that he had been directing the Ottoman's to the exit. As Maksim ran toward the statue—toward freedom—he realized Mihailo's finger pointed in the direction he and Kat had come from.

Foreboding filled Maksim. The statue wasn't alive. Prince

Mihailo wasn't *actually* pointing at something—and yet, it felt that way, as if there were a message for Maksim, some warning he needed to glean.

Go back? Or… someone was coming?

Reality crashed down. Maksim raced past the tourists taking selfies around a red #belgrade sign. A Neo-Renaissance building topped with three domes loomed over the plaza, creating a classical, polychromatic backdrop. Maksim stopped beside the horse. Voices hummed all around him, blending with the buzz of traffic. Many people traversed the square, but he didn't see a tour group offhand.

Kat joined him, panting. "Where is he?"

"I don't—"

"Are you Maksim?"

Maksim spun toward the sound of his name. A nondescript Serb—not particularly tall or short, neither skinny nor large—approached from the other side of the statue.

Maksim nodded. "It's me. I'm Miro's friend."

"I'm Ivan, his cousin." Ivan beckoned for Maksim and Kat to follow him. "We must go. The tour group is already in the van, waiting."

21:56 (9:36 PM)

IVAN HADN'T BEEN LYING about the van being full. Maksim and Kat rode in the very back, sitting on a bench seat that left little legroom and zero space for Maksim's duffel, which had to be crammed into the aisle.

And that wasn't the worst of it.

They took an alternative route to Bosnia in order to cross at a certain checkpoint. The road was rough, and the journey became a twisty, hellish nightmare after that. Maksim vacillated between extreme thirst and wanting to vomit. One of the tourists *did* vomit. As the smell diffused, the other passengers began to dry heave.

Maksim managed to wrestle his stomach into submission. Kat could not, however, and ended up retching into a plastic bag she'd found in her backpack. He had nothing to offer her. No water. No medicine. Not even a little bit of comfort. Each time he wrapped an arm around her, trying to console her—or at least keep her from bouncing around—the van hit another pothole, and their heads would crash like cymbals.

They finally made a pit stop, and Maksim was able to purchase bottled waters, a sports drink to share, and motion-sickness pills. Kat refused any food. "Not hungry," she mumbled, holding her stomach and turning away from the snack aisle.

Maksim skipped the snacks as well and opted for a second pill.

The Dinaric Alps alternated between lush and rocky while jutting in all directions. Sarajevo was nestled in the heart of the mountains, and eeriness tiptoed through Maksim as late afternoon yielded to evening. The sun disappeared behind the peaks, and the remaining daylight cast a dull gray covering over the land. He watched the night press forward until only a pale glow hovered over the landscape. But that, too, evaporated as the inky blackness spread into a thick, even layer across the sky.

The lights of Sarajevo glistened as they approached—a million candles burning into the darkness. The city radiated inside the valley while bits of gold light trickled up into the mountains. Their van continued toward Baščaršija—the Old Bazaar—and as the pavement roughened into cobblestone, the van finally—*finally*—rolled to a stop.

"Here we are," said Ivan from the driver's seat. "Beautiful Sarajevo."

Movement succeeded his announcement as the tour group gathered bags and opened doors. Kat had fallen asleep on Maksim's lap, using her backpack as a pillow. He nudged her awake.

"Thank you for indulging me as we tried this new return route," Ivan continued. "The views are excellent, but perhaps the roads aren't optimal."

A smattering of thank-yous circled through the van. One person piped up about how amazing the views had been. Another muttered, "Next time I'm flying."

After everyone had piled out, Maksim and Kat peeled themselves out of the back seat and made their exit. Ivan helped Kat as she stepped down. "So how do you know Miroslav?"

"Long-time friend." Maksim was being purposefully evasive and appended a yawn-and-stretch to the answer, hoping Ivan would catch the hint.

He did not. "And where are you staying the night?"

"We don't have a place yet." Maksim observed Kat, who was hugging herself in the cool night air. She swayed, and he steadied her. "I know there are hotels down in the Old Bazar. But if you know of any hostels or guesthouses, that would better-suit our budget."

"I do know of one, and it's included in your tour package." Ivan started up a cobblestone hill and motioned for his stowaways to follow him.

"Sorry, what tour package?" Maksim called.

"The one Miroslav purchased for you." The man motioned again, not stopping to wait.

Maksim understood now. The hefty payoff Miro had arranged was the "tour package."

"Can you carry your backpack?" Maksim whispered to Kat.

Kat nodded, and he was grateful. Exhaustion oozed from every pore in his body, and he didn't think his shoulder could handle one extra iota of weight. He had to wear the sling tonight.

Golden lights draped restaurant patios near the peak of the hill, forming a bubble of warmth in the darkness, but Ivan departed from the path and entered the shadows.

Maksim went on high alert. "Where are we going exactly?"

Ivan's outline formed a dense shadow in the darkness. "My apartment," the man replied. "All I have is a sofa to offer, but it's yours if you want it." A pause. "I didn't believe this arrangement to be legitimate when Miroslav contacted me. I certainly didn't expect to receive two bitcoin out of it. I asked, believing you would tell me to get lost. Never did I expect you to say yes."

"Miro will pay you soon." Maksim situated the duffel on his good shoulder. "I'm going to repay him as soon as we reach our destination."

"But he already did pay me. I saw the transfer come through." A smile entered the man's voice. "It's a lot of money. He must trust you a lot."

"We've known each other for a long time."

"I'm under strict instructions to care for you as I would family, and so I welcome you into my home to rest for the night." Maksim's eyes adjusted, and he saw Ivan point toward the ground. "Exercise caution here. There are stairs."

Maksim detected rough pavement scraping against the sole of his boot. He extended a foot, trying to feel his way, and discovered the first stair. "Careful," he told Kat.

She answered with a tired sigh.

"My wife has made *begova čorba*. It's a creamy chicken and okra soup, very good, and I welcome you both to enjoy a bowl with me."

"Thank you." Whether from exhaustion or caution—perhaps both—Maksim continued to keep his answers polite and succinct.

After ten minutes of climbing, they reached an apartment with a flickering exterior light. Ivan stooped to unlace his shoes, then opened the door. A vegetable-rich aroma filtered outside. A woman—presumably his wife—called out. Ivan answered, and movement stemmed from what must have been their bedroom.

The woman appeared a moment later, wearing an *abaya* and *hijab*—authentic ones, unlike what Kat had worn in Belgrade. Maksim could only assume she must be Bosniak (Bosnian Muslim).

Maksim paused at the entryway. He wasn't as familiar with the Bosnian dialect of Serbo-Croatian, and the Bosniaks had different dialects beyond that. So he greeted the woman very simply and in his practiced Montenegrin accent.

She smiled and nodded, standing off to the side. Her eyes

glittered with surprise, but she did a good job hiding it from her husband who acted like bringing complete strangers home was perfectly normal.

"The sofa is there." Ivan swept a hand in that direction. The narrow sofa rested in the corner, directly beneath an open window, and a set of heavy lace curtains rustled under a breeze.

The sofa wasn't large enough for him, but it would suffice for Kat. Perhaps he could sit at the far end and rest his head against the wall. His duffel could serve as an ottoman.

A large Persian rug covered the floor. Kat had nearly reached the rug before Maksim caught her arm. "Shoes."

She looked stunned for about five seconds. Maksim bent forward and began to unlace his boots. Her confusion lifted, and she peeled off her running shoes.

Ivan said something to his wife. She nodded and returned to the bedroom.

"Please. Make yourselves at home." Ivan ushered them in and closed the door.

Maksim left his socks on as he freed himself of the motorcycle boots. Then he and Kat made their way to the sofa. Ivan's wife returned with sheets, two light blankets, and two pillows.

She stacked everything on the couch and then steered toward the bathroom. The next time she appeared, she was carrying a towel and a wash cloth for each of them.

"*Hvala vam,*" Maksim said. (Thank you very much.)

"*Molim.*" (You're welcome.) The woman smiled, offered a slight bow, and then ducked into the bedroom.

"How long will you be staying in Sarajevo?" Ivan dragged a chair from his dining room and stationed it by the couch. "I gather you're only passing through?"

Maksim said, "We haven't decided" at the very moment Kat said, "We're on our way to Germany."

Maksim sent her a warning look. She did a double take. "What?"

"Germany," Ivan repeated. "That's very interesting. My friend was just talking to me about Germany."

"We haven't decided yet," Maksim repeated. "We have multiple options."

"There are many wonderful places to go, I suppose, including places in Bosnia. Banja Luka is nice. And Mostar. My company has tours that travel to both places if you need transportation."

"Banja Luka," Maksim said. "Isn't that on the way to Zagreb?"

"It is, yes. I know tour guides who lead day trips from Banja Luka to Zagreb. Let me know if you're interested, and I'll connect you with one of them."

Maksim's thoughts hummed. He hadn't considered hitching rides with tour groups. The idea had simply never occurred to him. Could they do that all the way to Frankfurt?

He envisioned a map and mentally drew mental lines from one major city to the next. When he finished, he felt sure he could find day tours operating between each set of cities.

Sarajevo to Banja Luka
Banja Luka to Zagreb
Zagreb to Ljubljana
Ljubljana to Salzburg
Salzburg to Munich
Munich to Frankfurt

"Now, then." Ivan stood. "May I offer you soup?"

"I'd love some," Maksim replied, and a spark of happiness shone through in his voice. Coming here had been costly, but clearly worth it.

"I would, but… I can't." Kat rested a hand her stomach. "I'm too queasy from the drive."

"Don't worry. There will be plenty left over." Ivan led

Maksim into the kitchen and retrieved two bowls. "So? What part of Germany?"

"As I said, Germany is one of many possibilities."

"Yes, yes. But if you do go, which part are you looking to travel to?"

Ivan seemed harmless, but Maksim had learned too many hard lessons in his life. He couldn't risk disclosing their real plans.

"It's still up in the air, really." Maksim tacked on a smile. "There are too many places we want to see."

"The reason I ask," Ivan said, dipping a large serving spoon into the pot, "is because I know a man who drives a truck, and he often goes to Germany. But he's old and, well, these days traveling is a challenge for him." Ivan spooned the creamy soup into Maksim's bowl. Steam rose, and Maksim's mouth moistened. "This man was telling me—recently, in fact—that he had decided to turn down a contract because he couldn't handle the drive."

"That's... unfortunate." Maksim couldn't tell where Ivan was going with this.

"It certainly is." Ivan filled his own bowl and gestured toward the table. "But I wondered if the three of you could help each other."

Maksim waited to see which chair his host claimed. He then took the other. As he started to dig in, he noticed Ivan crossing himself in the Orthodox manner—head, heart, right shoulder and then left—while the man whispered a prayer. Sarajevo was an interesting place. There'd been great conflict here—wars, genocide, the worst humanity had to offer—and yet an Orthodox Serb could be married to a Bosniak Muslim.

Maksim lowered his spoon and crossed himself, minus the prayer, and waited for Ivan to finish. "I'm not sure I follow your logic," he said finally, dunking his spoon into the soup. "About your friend."

"I was just thinking... Well, let's say he had help driving his truck. Then he could earn some money, which he needs, and you would experience an adventure."

"And how much would this adventure cost me?" Maksim angled up an eyebrow. "Because I'll warn you now that my present resources have run dry."

"I am sorry about charging Miroslav—*you*—so much for this short trip." Ivan glanced toward the bedroom and lowered his voice. "My wife and I need the money. We have business debts, but also one of my employees was robbing me for two years. I only caught him recently." Ivan released a sigh. "I experienced much guilt accepting Miroslav's offer." He met Maksim's gaze. "Truly, I am sorry. I would not have set such a high price except that we need it."

"I'm not offended. I simply don't have much left after our long journey. I'd rather be clear about that up front."

"I appreciate it. And I feel sure my friend wouldn't charge much. He's an honest man, and you would be helping him, too."

Maksim swallowed a spoonful of soup. He couldn't tell if it was the rich, hot creaminess comforting him or the possibilities arising from this conversation. "What kind of truck does he drive?"

"A produce truck."

That was better than a lorry. Maksim wasn't sure he could handle a truck that size, but a produce truck would be manageable. "May I speak plainly?"

Ivan nodded, dabbing his mouth with a cloth napkin. "Please do."

"My girlfriend's safety and well-being are my highest priorities." Maksim cast a glance over his shoulder. Kat was spreading a sheet across the sofa. She met his gaze. "I need to know," he said, focusing on Ivan, "that she would be safe with this man whether or not I was around to intervene."

Ivan chuckled. "Bugi is no danger to anyone." He pronounced the name *BOO-ghee*. "Perhaps to himself sometimes, but only because he pushes too hard when it comes to work. He should be retired."

Maksim's brow pinched. "How old is he?"

"Sixty-nine, turning seventy when the leaves fall. He should have retired four years ago, but his job makes him feel important in a way. As long as he has that truck of his and there are companies willing to hire him, he is willing to carry on." Ivan scooped up another spoonful of soup. "As my father always said, 'willing' and 'able' are brothers—not the same, but related. Bugi is willing. He just may not be able any longer."

"But why? Is he having health problems?"

"His eyesight is a hindrance. He can drive without issue during the daytime, but he cannot see after dark. Deliveries must be made within a certain timeframe, and that becomes difficult without the nighttime driving. He also grows tired quickly and must rest after only three or four hours."

Maksim mulled over the information. This might be a better option than tagging along with tour groups. If any of those people, whether the tourists or the guides, saw a news report about Belgrade, it would put Maksim and Kat in a precarious situation. Riding with Bugi would give them privacy, and continuous driving would take them across Europe in no time. They could be at the German border within ten hours.

"You say he's already turned down that contract for Germany?" Maksim asked. "Would it be too late to change his mind?"

"I'm not sure. He only told me this yesterday, and I've been gone all day today." Ivan picked up his empty bowl. "So then you *are* going to Germany?"

"Ultimately, yes," Maksim relented. "If we can." He scanned the room, in search of a clock. "Is it too late to call your friend?"

MARTI, 18 IUNIE, 00:12 (TUESDAY, JUNE 18, 12:12 AM)

MAKSIM PULLED the knit blanket over himself and rested his head against the pillow he'd situated between the wall and the top of the sofa. Kat had been chilled with the window open, so he'd closed it about an hour ago.

He drew the lace curtains aside. Ivan's apartment lay under a siege of darkness, making a nightlight of the pale moon and the bits of gold that trickled up into the mountains.

Kat's bare feet shuffled, bumping Maksim. They moved again, this time finding the underside of his leg. Her toes entered the space between his hamstring and the sofa and began to burrow.

"Are you still cold?" he asked in a whisper. Ivan and his wife were asleep in the next room, and he didn't want to wake them.

"A little." Her melodic voice, with its usual warm cadence, had weakened to a sleepy waltz. She was exhausted. So was he.

He used his free hand to gather his blanket and lay it across her. He didn't have much leverage with his arm bound in the sling, and he ended up more or less tossing the knit blanket in her direction.

She sat up, freeing her feet. "That's yours."

"I don't need it."

"You might." She attempted to spread the blanket over his legs. Moonlight filtered through the curtains, casting a soft haze across her. Her black curls were bundled high with only a single lock left unsecured. The strand cascaded along her slender neck and down her back.

She was wearing "the sleep top he hated"—how she'd begun to refer to it—and his eyes shifted toward the marred skin that ran vertically along her shoulder blade. "How's the injury?"

"It's… okay. Better since you removed the stitches." She drew her leg in, sitting on it, and draped her own blanket across her lap. "The muscles are weak, so whenever I carry my backpack, there's like a… I wouldn't call it pain, but more of a…"

Maksim waited. "Pinch?" he said finally.

"Kind of. Yeah." She rotated to face him, and the moon set her face alight. "How's your arm?"

He tipped his head back. "Truthfully?" he said, closing his eyes. "I should have been wearing the sling more."

"Is it that same kind of pinch I feel in my shoulder?"

"More of a fire smoldering beneath the surface. Tonight it's a bit of a bonfire." His jaw tightened. "Whenever this happens, everything—muscle, skin, bone—I can never seem to put out the flames."

"That's because of your scars?"

"Partly." He inhaled deeply. "My muscles and tendons are trying to heal, and the nerve damage amplifies the pain." He tugged on his sleeve and ran a hand over the warped, crinkled skin. Heat flared. "Exponentially, at times."

"I didn't realize… I mean, I knew that was why Drago and Émilien—" She cut herself off.

Maksim might have pressed her, might have even finished

the sentence—*why Drago and Émilien had beaten the hell out of him at Village Ksorba*—but tonight he said nothing.

A soft, cool touch made contact with his upper arm. He opened his eyes and found Kat resting a hand on his scars. Heat smoldered, intensifying… but the coolness of her hand stifled the flame. The sensation spread, moving across his upper arm and around to his biceps and triceps.

He inhaled a breath, and the same coolness filled his chest and lungs. "That feels amazing."

She placed her other hand to his shoulder. The scenario repeated—first with the smoldering, then with the coolness. He began to relax. "How are you doing that?"

She didn't give an immediate answer, and as her eyes caught the moonlight, the irises radiated in a bright, burning blue.

He opened his mouth, intending to describe the phenomenon, but then his attention shifted to her hand. Moonlight glistened over a deep shade of sapphire blue.

He straightened, disconnecting himself from her touch. "How did you find that?"

"What?" She sounded genuinely confused.

"The ring." Maksim gaped at the sapphire solitaire on her finger. The halo of diamonds glittered. "That's Madă's ring."

"I know. You told me the story." Her attention drifted to the sapphire. "But you said I was supposed to have it." Doubt flickered through her features. The blueness of her eyes dulled. "You… you gave it to me."

"I didn't." Maksim's mind raced. "And I never told you the story."

"You did. You said the ring belonged to Madă's grandmother and that Daniel dug it up from the garden." A quaver entered her voice. "I-I must have been confused. I thought you wanted me to wear it."

He pushed a hand through his hair, mind racing. *Had* he given her the ring? Was it possible he'd forgotten?

No. They'd been on the run. He had nearly been arrested in Belgrade.

Something moved in the dark. A dense shadow, even blacker than the room, drew closer. Maksim bolted upright. "Who's there? Ivan?"

Silence answered.

"I'm sorry. Here." Kat tugged at the ring. "I-I must have misunderstood."

Maksim thought to stop her, but the shadow was drawing closer. The figure stepped into view, and Maksim detected a rugged face and silver hair. This was *not* Ivan.

The man's imposing frame towered over Kat, and the fire in Maksim's shoulder reignited.

"Behind you!" Maksim lunged, intending to throw himself in front of Kat. An invisible force crashed into him, lifting him off the sofa and hurling him against the wall. His back hit first, then his head.

He collapsed onto the floor.

"I'm sorry, Maksim."

Kat's voice shook him out of the daze. He lifted his head and watched as Vladimir hauled Kat from the couch. She screamed, thrashing, but couldn't break the steely hold.

"Let her go!" Maksim tried to push himself up. He collapsed with each attempt, held down by an unbreakable force. His limbs felt heavy. His vision crossed.

Kat continued to fight, to struggle, as her frightened stare locked with his. "I'm sorry. Maksim, I'm so sorry."

"No!" He grunted, trying again to push himself to standing. Thick, warm liquid oozed from his head and spilled down his face. Blood. *His* blood. Pain rocketed through him, through every fiber of his being. The fire hit him like a back blast, and a scream tore through him.

Vladimir laughed—a cold, mirthless chuckle—and dragged Kat into the shadows. Her blood-chilling cry split the stillness, reverberating in the room and echoing all around him.

Something hit the floor with a metallic *ping*. The sapphire ring tumbled into the hazy light. Maksim's eyes flashed from the ring to the darkness. "Kaaaaat!"

———

HE AWOKE with a jolt that launched him to his feet. He had no sense of time or place—only that he needed to give chase—and as he took his first step, his feet caught on something.

His duffel. He'd been using it as an ottoman, which allowed him to sit at an incline while he slept. Same way he'd been sleeping in the hospital.

Except he wasn't in the hospital. He was in Ivan's home.

He hit the floor with full force, a *thud* shook the space around him. The floor creaked. A nearby lamp rattled. Pain mushroomed in his left arm, which he'd used to catch himself. His other arm was trapped in the sling.

"Are you okay?" Kat hurried over from the dining area. "Maksim?"

He pushed himself up and grabbed hold of her with the same voracity he'd experienced at Miro's.

"It's okay." She hugged him. "Everything's okay. We're safe."

His brain caught up to reality. He released her and gathered himself, taking in his surroundings. Ivan sat at the dining room table, his mouth slightly agape. His wife stood to the side, holding an *ibrik*—Turkish coffee pot—while looking horrified.

"Forgive me." He pushed a hand through his hair. "I was… startled."

"I think you were having a bad dream." Kat touched his arm. Unlike the dream, the coolness did not come and put out the fire. "You fell pretty hard. Are you hurt?"

"No. I don't know. Maybe." His attention darted to the window. Someone had opened it, and a cool breeze drifted inside. He walked that way, inhaling deeply. Hints of wood and coal blended with the earthy aroma in the house. Slowly, his fight-or-flight began to diminish.

Kat eased beside him and slid an arm around his waist. He wrapped his free arm around her, pulling her closer.

"We're going to make it," she whispered.

He looked at her.

"Bugi called the German company first thing this morning. They never found a replacement driver for the delivery." She smiled up at Maksim. "He's going to take us."

Maksim longed for a rush of relief to flow through him. But all he felt was dread.

"He knows back ways," Kat whispered, "and he actually prefers that. So we won't be going through major cities."

"How do you know that?"

"I'll tell you later." Her eyes flicked in the direction of their hosts. "Dzana made Turkish coffee," she said, her volume returning to normal. She guided Maksim away from the window. "Come have some."

"Bugi has to pick up the delivery in Dubrovnik," Ivan said as Maksim and Kat approached the table. "That's going to add time to your trip, and he's on a deadline. Please enjoy some coffee while you can."

Ivan's wife—Dzana?—set a place for Maksim. He lowered himself into the chair and tried to scoot forward. The effort was weak with his arm bound by the sling.

"She made baklava," Kat said. "Look."

Maksim's attention shifted to the flaky slabs of phyllo dough, their tops crusted in honey and crushed nuts.

Kat sat on his left and slipped her hand into his. "I guess maybe you didn't sleep so great, but I did, and I had this amazing dream that we made it to Germany."

Maksim sat back as Dzana poured thick, black coffee into his espresso cup. "A dream?" he repeated, feeling stunned.

"Yep. A good one for once." Kat released his hand and pulled her chair closer to the table. "I really think everything is going to be okay."

Dzana placed a piece of baklava on Maksim's plate and made hand gestures to eat and drink. He smiled in thanks and took a sip of the coffee. The earthy blackness roused his senses, drawing him farther away from the nightmare.

"Delicious, isn't it?" Ivan said. "Just wait until you try the baklava. My wife makes the best in Sarajevo." He repeated himself in the Bosniak dialect, and his Dzana's smile broadened with a blush.

She held the coffee toward Kat.

"Yes, please." She turned to Ivan. "But I'm going to need some of that water."

Ivan passed it to her. "Turkish coffee is very strong. But that's why we like it, right?" Ivan checked his watch. "Bugi cannot drive into our neighborhood with his truck, so we'll have to walk down to the main street." Ivan hesitated. "If you still want to go, of course."

Kat turned to Maksim and nodded. He didn't agree immediately, and she reached for his hand again. Her soft fingers glided until her palm came to rest against his. She gave a reassuring squeeze.

"I… suppose it's our best option." Maksim thought of something else. "Actually, I need to purchase mobile phones for us." He glanced at Kat. "In case we need them during the trip."

"Mm." Ivan chewed a bite of his baklava and dabbed a napkin to his mouth. "There's a shop very close to where you'll meet Bugi. I'll show you."

MARŢI, 18 IUNIE, 10:05 (TUESDAY, JUNE 18, 10:05 AM)

IVAN WALKED Maksim and Kat to a modern café on Ulica Telali (Telali Street). Most places didn't have disposable cups, but this one did, and they all agreed that to-go coffees would be good for the long trip.

A plaza full of shops and restaurants funneled pedestrians to the Sebilj, an 18th-century Ottoman-style wooden fountain, and then to Sarajevo's world-famous bazaar. The lights they'd seen the night before belonged to the thousands of homes that fanned out from the city center. Those houses filtered up into the mountains that wrapped the city in a protective cocoon.

"Where's that mobile phone shop?" Maksim set his duffel on the floor. His shoulder strained, and then he realized… he'd been carrying the bag with his bad arm. Confusion blinked through him. He rarely used that arm, especially for heavy items, yet he'd carried the duffel all the way from Ivan's place.

"Outside and to the right. Just past the Sebilj." Ivan moved to the front-facing windows and pointed in that direction. "Would you like me to go with you?"

"I'd prefer you stay with Kat."

"I'm happy to." He made his way to the coffee bar and greeted the barista.

Maksim pulled a ten from his wallet. He was low on cash, and the ring was beginning to show more. He needed to figure out another place for that.

His mind rewound to the nightmare. The memory made him shudder.

"Black?"

Kat's voice snagged his attention. He snapped the wallet shut. "Sorry?"

"You want your coffee black?" She eyed the banknote. "Will that be enough for two?"

"Here, yes. They'll give you convertible marks as change." He passed her the ten. "Stay in the café. Even if Bugi comes, please do not go outside."

"We can't sit on the patio?"

The fear Maksim had experienced in the nightmare swelled. Vladimir's face flashed in his mind. He shook his head. "Please, Kat. Just until I'm back."

"I'll go outside if Bugi arrives," Ivan offered, pushing up a smile. "And the coffees are on me."

"That's not necessary," Maksim said. "You've helped us tremendously already."

"No, no. Miroslav sent extra, and I insist."

"Thank you." Maksim planted a kiss on Kat's head. Rather, on her *hijab*. She was wearing a proper one today, paired with a long black abaya—gifts from Ivan's wife—and topped off with the sunglasses Miro had given her. Maksim wore his ball cap.

He left the café, turned right, and veered into the foot traffic flowing toward the bazaar. The mobile shop was three doors down.

Maksim entered and addressed the young man stationed at the counter. *"Dobro jutro."* (Good morning.) *"May I see your most basic smartphone?"*

The guy had no problems understanding Maksim's Montenegrin and pulled a phone from behind the glass case.

"How much?"

"One fifty-nine." The 159 was in convertible marks, and it was an abbreviation. In reality, it was 159,000 or about eighty-two euros.

"Do you have the clamshells?"

"I have this." The guy showed Maksim a minimalist, open-faced phone. "Push-button," he said in English through a heavy accent. *"Fifty-nine."*

Fifty-nine thousand convertible marks was about thirty euros.

"Two, please." Maksim pulled out his wallet. *"You can activate them?"*

The guy nodded and started the process, adding SIMs and powering them up. *"They have fifty percent power,"* he said blandly. *"One hundred minutes is the minimum. Includes one hundred SMS messages."*

"Good. Can you change the language to English for one of them?"

The guy lifted a surprised stare to Maksim. *"Engleski?"*

"It's for a friend."

The guy continued through one phone and then the other. Maksim leaned outside, keeping his head down and his cap low. People milled about the plaza, capturing photos and drinking water from the Sebilj.

Everything was calm, peaceful. Why did he feel so disturbed?

"Ready," the guy said from the counter.

Maksim paid—seventy euros in all—and shoved both phones straight into his pocket. The guy bagged the boxes, which contained the power supplies and manuals, and handed those over. Maksim thanked him and left.

Ivan and Kat were waiting in the café when Maksim returned. Maksim's duffel and Kat's backpack sat on the floor.

"There you are." Ivan stood.

Kat joined him, handing Maksim a large coffee in a paper

cup. "I got iced coffee," she said, showing off her clear plastic cup. Her coffee swirled light brown with only a few chunks of ice.

Maksim allowed himself to smile—a real, genuine smile—for the first time that morning. "Very modern."

"That's what I said!" Ivan shook his head. "The things people think of these days."

"What's the world coming to?" Maksim's smile gave way to a light chuckle. Sleeping in a stranger's home and not having any form of communication must have stirred his paranoia. He certainly felt better now that he had the phones.

"What'd you get?" Kat asked. "Can I see?"

Maksim reached into his pocket. "They tried to sell me a smartphone, but I know how much you love these." He passed her the minimalist phone, and she looked like she might cry. "I'll get us smartphones soon," he promised. "For now, this was all our budget would permit."

"Speaking of budget." Ivan dipped into his pocket and removed a wad of cash in different currencies—convertible marks, Serbian dinar, euros, and even a few US dollars. Tips from his tour business if Maksim had to guess. "I thought you might be able to use this for food along the way."

"I have cash set aside for that," Maksim said. "We'll be fine."

"I understand. But I meant what I said about Miro sending extra. He did, and I have more than I need to cover my business expenses." He nudged the bills toward Maksim. "I'll have enough to pay all my debts even without this."

"Thank you." Maksim shuffled the cash, organizing it by currency and then amount. He had the banknotes folded neatly, all facing the same direction, by the time Bugi arrived.

"There he is now." Ivan peered outside. "I see his truck."

Maksim had expected a modern produce truck, the kind with a metal enclosure and cargo door. But this was a converted pickup truck, an old one, with wooden planks custom-built around the bed to add vertical space. He and Kat grabbed their things, and they all three hurried across the street.

"There won't be a place for him to park," Ivan said. "We'll have to say our goodbyes now. Oh, and you should know Bugi doesn't speak English."

"I'm sure I'll manage with Serbian. Though I may struggle if he's leans heavily on any of the dialects."

"He does, and it's a lesser-known dialect called Old-Shtoka-vian. I can understand him because I've been living here long enough, and some of the older generation still speak it. But for many young people, it's difficult." He finished as the produce truck pulled alongside the curb.

An elderly man with a sprinkling of missing teeth leaned across to the passenger side and jostled the door open. The man was all smiles and beckoned them to get in.

Maksim hesitated, unsure if he should hug Ivan. He wanted to. Before he could decide, Ivan pulled him in. "I'm sorry for whatever struggles you're facing, but please know your circum-stances have been a lifeline to us. My wife and I are tremen-dously grateful."

Maksim hugged him back. Kat embraced him with an awkward side hug, trying to keep her *hijab* from falling off, then she hauled herself and her backpack into the truck. Maksim climbed in after her and stuffed his duffel on the floorboard. Ivan shut the door and circled around to Ivan's side. A car pulled behind them, but, surprisingly, the driver didn't honk.

Ivan waved at the person, then he and Bugi had a brief exchange. Ivan was saying to take care of "these kids." The old man laughed and replied in a strange dialect that evaded Maksim's ear. "Old-Shtokavian," Maksim said aloud, commit-ting the name to memory. He'd have to research the dialect after he found a smartphone.

The two friends wrapped up their goodbyes, and Ivan waved one more time. "Bugi will give you my telephone number. Please call me if you need anything."

"We will." Maksim waved as Bugi pulled onto the road.

The old man began to speak and didn't stop even as they proceeded onto the curvy roads that led into the mountains. Maksim caught bits and pieces, but the overall meaning was lost.

Kat leaned in. "What's he saying?"

"Honestly, I don't know." Maksim kept listening. "Something about Dubrovnik. And the load we're picking up? I think he's talking about the produce, but he must be using different words, because it doesn't make sense."

"Does that worry you?"

Maksim focused on her. "What?"

"That we can't communicate with him."

Maksim considered the question. "Not especially. Ivan was speaking in Bosnian, and the old man understood him. As long as he can understand me, we'll figure out the rest."

Kat's lips quirked. "So you're feeling better then?"

"I am. A bit." He relaxed against the seat. "I suppose everything is working out after all."

"Not just working out." She peeked up at him. "We're going to make it."

"We're going to make it," he repeated, leaning in to the positive mindset—but he also knew they had a very, very long road ahead of them.

Germany
C
Aus
Switzerland
Slov
Italy

Dubrovnik, Hrvatska (Croatia)
Ukraine
Slovakia
Hungary
Romania
Croatia
Bosnia and Herzegovina
Sarajevo
Belgrade
Naidăș
Sibi
Serbia
Montenegro
Dubrovnik
Kosovo
Bulgaria

Germany
Cz
Aust
Switzerland
Slove
Italy

Domžale, Slovenija (Slovenia)
Ukraine
Slovakia
Hungary
Romania
Croatia
Sibiu
Bosnia and
Herzegovina
Belgrade
Naidăș
Sarajevo
Serbia
Dubrovnik
Montenegro
Kosovo
Bulgaria

Germany
C
Grödig
Aus
Switzerland
Slove
Italy

Grödig, Österreich (Austria)
Ukraine
Slovakia
Hungary
Romania
Sibiu
Croatia
Bosnia and
Herzegovina
Belgrade
Naidăş
Sarajevo
Serbia
Montenegro
Kosovo
Bulgaria
Dubrovnik

Germany
C
Saarbrücken
Grödig
Aus
Switzerland
Slov
Italy

Saarbrücken, Deutschland (Germany)
Ukraine
Slovakia
Hungary
Romania
Sibi
oatia
Bosnia and
Herzegovina
Belgrade
Naidăș
Sarajevo
Serbia
Montenegro
Dubrovnik
Kosovo
Bulgaria

CHAPTER
THIRTY-THREE

MIERCURI, 19 IUNIE, 16:47 (WEDNESDAY, JUNE 19, 4:47 PM)

MAKSIM HAULED a crate of tomatoes from Bugi's truck and carried them to a pallet. Sweat gushed down his body, soaking his hair and glossing every centimeter of his skin. Exhaustion weighed heavily on him, but he pressed on even as the pallet truck operator sighed and checked his watch. The distribution center was closing in thirteen minutes, and there were still several more crates to unload.

Their trio had departed from Sarajevo the previous morning. Bugi drove to Dubrovnik—only four hours away—but when they arrived at Gruž Port, Maksim and Kat had realized their assistance would be needed. They didn't mind to help, but the task proved challenging for Kat—partly because of her weakened shoulder, but also because of her clothes.

Ivan's wife had gifted her with an open *abaya*, a light robe with an open front, which Kat had layered over her normal clothes. This permitted her to shed the robe whenever possible—

while riding in the un-air-conditioned truck for instance, or while helping load produce—but the *hijab* could not be removed due to her big, curly hair, which was far too conspicuous to expose. She'd grown lightheaded while loading olives and had struggled to recover in the Mediterranean heat.

That left Maksim and Bugi to finish the job. Bugi was fast for an old man, but not fast enough for their timeline. All the other pick-ups had happened that morning. Their trio hadn't arrived until late afternoon.

Then mishap number two happened.

One of the other trucks had broken down on the way to Dubrovnik. The driver had been trying to fix the problem, but when he couldn't, he called the German company, who then called Bugi. The caller spoke in broken Russian with a German accent—which was strange and confusing but allowed Maksim to understand what was going on.

"Vy govorite po-russki?" Maksim had said after Bugi hung up. (Do you speak Russian?) *"This is how you can speak to me. I'm fluent in Russian."*

Bugi waved him off. *"I don't speak Russian."*

Kat leaned in. "What's going on?" Her question was barely audible over the rumble of the truck.

"He said he doesn't speak Russian. But he said it *in* Russian, and the person who called was speaking in broken Russian."

Kat frowned. "That's weird."

"Russian is close enough to Serbo-Croatian that he likely understands the basics." Maksim proceeded to explain what had happened and why they were making a U-turn.

So back to the port they went. All three of them loaded the truck with more produce from Greece. Bugi and Maksim handled the tomatoes, which were in large wooden crates, while Kat carried cucumbers in lighter plastic crates.

From Dubrovnik they drove to Domžale, Slovenia—fourteen kilometers north of Ljubljana—and then to Grödig, Austria. From there, they took the "back ways" Kat had made reference to. The journey should have taken them through Munich, but instead they traveled past Chiemsee—a freshwater lake in Bavaria—and through the mountainous countryside more than sixty kilometers from the city. They circumvented Stuttgart in the same way, following a route that took them thirty kilometers south of the city.

The roads were narrow, winding through the Bavarian Alps, and the truck used more petrol for the journey. But there was a good reason for Bugi's knowing—and preferring—this route. Kat explained everything on the way to Slovenia. "Ivan told me that Bugi has been getting stopped for inspections." She stood in the petrol station's coffee area, blowing on her coffee. "Apparently it happens a lot, usually when cops notice the Bosnian license plates. They take advantage since he doesn't speak their language, and he ends up with frivolous citations."

Maksim, who was getting his own coffee, snapped to attention. "Citations?" He punctuated the question with a lengthy scan of their surroundings. A young guy with a bored-out-of-his-mind expression was manning the cash register. Bugi was outside, walking around the truck.

There were no other vehicles. There was barely any traffic on the road.

"Why didn't you tell me this before we left?" he demanded, focusing on Kat. "I would have passed on Ivan's offer."

"I know. That's exactly why I didn't tell you." She lowered her paper cup. "Ivan said the inspections were only happening in the cities, which was why Bugi mapped out a back way to Saarbrücken. The route takes longer, so he wouldn't have made the deadline driving solo. He will with us, though."

"Hopefully." In Maksim's mind, he added, *And hopefully we can get there without being stopped.*

Bugi's voice snatched Maksim out of the memory. The truck was empty, and the old man was waving for him to come on.

They had met their deadline. With four minutes to spare.

Maksim loaded the last tomato crate onto the pallet, and the pallet truck driver started the machine. A *beep beep beep* alerted passersby that the vehicle was backing up.

Maksim watched the man drive the load to the far back of the massive distribution center. Very little space remained—probably because everyone else had already made their deliveries.

Bugi called out again, this time from inside the truck. Maksim jogged over and slid in beside Kat, who had taken up her usual seat in the middle. Maksim fought with his duffel, finding space for his legs and feet, and yanked the door shut.

The truck rolled forward.

"Any idea where we're going?" Kat had stripped down to her workout tights, which she had folded above her knees, and a t-shirt. To her credit, she hadn't removed the *hijab* or sunglasses.

"I'll ask, but there's no guarantee I'll understand him." Maksim switched to Serbian. Bugi had no problems understanding, but his answer, as predicted, evaded Maksim.

After several attempts, Bugi sighed. *"Hotel,"* he said sharply through his Bosnian accent.

"Okay." Kat grimaced. "Even I understand that one."

"Yes, but he was explaining more. From what I pieced together, we're going somewhere to sleep—not a hotel, but something in that realm. I didn't understand the word he used. I believe he was saying the German company paid for it."

They pulled out of the distribution center's parking lot, turned left, and cruised through the industrial park. After crossing a bridge, they followed a highway alongside a river until Bugi veered off. This road took them through town.

Maksim pulled his cap low and helped Kat fix her hijab. "Keep your head down."

She had her gaze lifted, her eyes on a row of modern buildings painted in alternating colors. She sat back and ducked her chin.

Worry clawed at Maksim as they bypassed the town and continued onto another road that led out of the city. He checked the position of the sun. They were heading north by his estimate, and the realization caused him to sit straight. *"Are you taking us to Frankfurt?"* He posed the question in Serbian and then repeated himself in Russian.

Bugi answered in Old-Shtokavian. He enunciated a bit more, emphasizing key words. From what Maksim gathered, they were *not* going to Frankfurt. Just to whatever hotel Bugi had mentioned.

"Guesthaus!" Bugi suddenly burst out. His eyes brightened as if he'd finally remembered the word.

"Guesthouse?" Kat repeated. "Is that where we're staying?"

"Apparently." Maksim let his gaze drift over the lonely landscape. They had passed through the town in a matter of minutes and already wilderness stretched around them.

They continued through a village with two- and three-story buildings that reminded him of French villages he'd seen. A handful of homes had been designed in the half-timbered style, but the rest had normal facades, their structures comprised of sand and limestone. Some appeared to be made of cement.

The guesthouse was in Jägersfreude, a village on the outskirts of greater Saarbrücken. Bugi began to prattle on about something, gesturing toward their surroundings.

Maksim conveyed what he could to Kat. "I think we're staying out here because of his distaste for being in cities."

They turned right, entering a residential neighborhood, and ascended a hill. Houses dotted both sides of the narrow street. Another turn led them onto an even narrower street. Bugi parked outside a two-story beige house with a slate roof. Matching sun-drenched windows offered an open view of the ground floor and the first story. Smaller attic windows adorned the second story.

Maksim popped the handle on his door. *"This is where we're sleeping?"*

Bugi slanted a look and gave an answer that sounded like he was speaking to a five-year-old. Maksim got the gist. As he and Kat gathered their things, Bugi pulled a plastic bag from behind his side of the bench seat. Maksim recognized the logo plastered on the bag—a chain supermarket originating in Romania, but the name had been changed to something more Slavic.

"Was that all he brought?" Kat asked, hoisting her backpack.

Maksim's mouth tipped up. "As if we've brought much more."

"True."

Bugi shut his door and led them toward the guesthouse.

Kat stayed beside Maksim. "How's your arm?" she asked.

Maksim dragged his attention from their surroundings. He'd been searching for cameras. So far he hadn't seen any. "My arm?"

"And your shoulder. Just… how are you feeling?"

His mind flashed to the dream, and confusion splintered his thoughts. His gaze fell to the leather duffel. He was carrying the bag with his right hand. "Fine," he said, switching to his left hand, but not because he had to. His right arm was sore, to be sure, but not sore enough to warrant the exchange. Definitely not as sore as it'd been for the last week. "How about you?"

"Tired. Hungry." Kat sighed as they followed Bugi up a short set of steps. "I can't decide if I want to eat, sleep, or drink more coffee."

"I feel about the same." Maksim looked down at himself. "A shower is in order as well."

"You think this place might have a washer?" Kat plucked at her t-shirt. "My clothes are starting to stink."

"I'll check around once we're inside."

Bugi pulled out his phone—a smartphone, but an older one—and checked a message. Someone must have sent check-in information, because he proceeded to enter a code into the eLock mounted beside the door.

The locking mechanism released, and a high-pitched tone sang out. Bugi pushed through and straight-lined for a staircase. Maksim noted the entrance to a kitchen up ahead. He could make out the stove from this angle but not much more.

Perhaps Bugi would let him borrow the truck for a quick trip to the local supermarket. Then they could prepare something to eat here.

Their trio climbed to the first floor, then to the second. Two dark-wood doors spanned a narrow hallway. Bugi chose the one on the right. Maksim and Kat followed in a line, edging through the narrow hallway with their bags. Maksim had to slouch to keep from banging his head on the slanted ceiling.

This door, like the one downstairs, had an eLock. Bugi entered a code, and the door opened to a large room with two single beds and a bathroom.

Bugi set his shopping bag down beside the first bed and then motioned toward the other, saying something Maksim didn't quite catch. Something about the German company.

"I take it we're sharing," Kat said.

"I think this was the best he could manage." Maksim set his duffel on the floor beside the second bed. "Maybe this was all he could get the German company to pay for. I'm not certain, but I don't mind to sleep on the floor." He hesitated. "Could I shower first, though?"

"Wait, you'll sleep on the floor? You're sure?"

"Would I rather have the bed? Of course. But there's nothing in me, as a man, that would permit me to do that… unless you'd want to share?" He arched an eyebrow. "I could definitely do that."

Kat's cheeks, which were already rosy from the heat, darkened. "Um…"

Maksim chuckled, letting her off the hook, and pivoted toward Bugi. The old man was sitting on his bed, dabbing his brow with a handkerchief. *"We'd both like to shower,"* Maksim said, *"but you're welcome to go first. Will you be taking one?"*

Bugi's answer didn't compute with Maksim, but his actions did as the old man stood and made his way into the bathroom.

"Would you like me to handle dinner?" Maksim asked.

Bugi reached into his pocket and pulled out a wallet that

looked older than he was. He retrieved a stack of euros and held them out.

Maksim took them. *"This is for dinner?"*

"Jok, jok, jok." He said it *yohk, yohk, yohk.* Based on his body language, he was saying no.

"I don't understand," Maksim replied in Serbian. *"What is this for?"*

After several attempts, they resorted to a game of charades. Bugi pretended to lift something and then carry it to the bed. Then he returned to where he'd started, pretended to lift again…

"Oh!" Kat snapped her fingers and pointed. "Unloading crates from the truck!"

Maksim translated into Serbian, and Bugi's head gave a slow up and down. He must have thought Maksim was a complete idiot. Maksim certainly felt like one.

Bugi performed one more reenactment of the loading-unloading and then pulled out the money, splitting it between Kat and Maksim.

"You're paying us?" Maksim tilted his head. *"For helping you?"*

"Jaaaa." He said it *yahhhh.*

Maksim counted the money. One hundred euros each. *"I was expecting to pay you. Ivan said you needed the money."*

Bugi pantomimed receiving a call. He spoke the Russian word for "Germans"—*nemtsy*—and then held up the money while exuding surprise.

"I think the German company gave him extra," Maksim said. "Perhaps for the extra load. He wants to give it to us."

Kat gestured with her banknotes. "Thank you. Um, *hvala.*"

"Hvala vam," Maksim said. (We thank you.)

Bugi shook his head, mumbling, and carried his plastic bag into the bathroom. The door closed behind him, and the shower kicked on a moment later.

"I'm going to investigate the kitchen." Maksim started across the room. "Cooking in will be worth the extra effort, but only if we can keep the shopping simple."

"Can you look for a washer and dryer?"

Maksim doubted there'd be a dryer, but he promised to check and headed downstairs. A chalkboard with instructions—written in English and German—welcomed guests to use the kitchen, but Maksim didn't find much in the cabinets. No oils or seasonings, only a few small pieces of cookware.

He frowned and backtracked, intending to search for the washing machine. As he exited the kitchen, he noticed a hall table with a basket full of pamphlets and brochures. He shuffled through them. Many contained information for touristic activities, including a day trip to Frankfurt. He kept that one, laying the others down, but then another pamphlet drew his attention.

He grabbed it and returned to the room. "Look what I found," he said, charging in. He hadn't thought to knock. Perhaps he should have.

Thankfully Kat wasn't undressed apart from the *hijab*, which she had draped across the top of a chair. "You don't mind if I open this window, do you?" She tugged on the lever, and the window opened wide. "It's really hot in here."

"You're lucky I'm not superstitious." His mouth twisted into a playful grin. "Other Romanians would never permit that."

"Why?"

"*Mă trage curentul.* It means 'the draft is pulling me.'" Maksim came alongside the window and peered out. Residential homes stretched around them, the neighborhood sloping down to the village below. Nothing alerted him to the presence of police. Had they really made it all the way to Germany without any more incidents?

The nightmare he'd had in Sarajevo buzzed in his memory. He peered outside again, searching for unusual activity, cars, people. Anything that might indicate someone had followed them. Again, he perceived nothing. Only the quiet stillness of the neighborhood.

"I don't get it." Kat followed his stare. "Is 'the draft' pulling you now or something?"

"In Romania, people widely believe that you'll become sick from moving air. That's why many Romanians don't roll down their car windows or open the windows in their homes."

"*What?*" Kat staggered to the bed and plopped onto the mattress. Her mouth hung open. "My dad never liked opening windows."

Maksim ambled closer. "You never knew why?"

"I thought he was being… him. There were so many things about him I'd always found strange. But since he never talked about Romania, I just assumed *he* was strange." Her gaze traveled to the open window. "I called him a weirdo when I was a kid. He never got offended, but… I think it hurt his feelings, like maybe he wanted to explain more but couldn't."

"I'm sorry." Maksim joined her on the mattress and rested a hand on her knee. A rogue tear snaked down her face.

She sniffed, swiping at the dampness. "What's that?" Her stare landed on the pamphlets in Maksim's other hand.

He passed her the first one. "That's a day tour to Frankfurt. As long as they're operating, we'll have a ride to the city. With what Bugi paid us, we may have enough for a private tour, which would be better than going with a group."

Kat glanced at the tour brochure before homing in on the other. "Is that dinner?"

He passed her the pamphlet. "Local pizza place. They deliver."

She studied the images of pizzas and calzones. "I love pizza." Her tone hit like a condolence message for a death in the family. In a way, Maksim supposed it was. Perhaps her father loved pizza as well. Perhaps she was remembering a time when they'd had pizza together.

Maksim scrambled for a way to boost her mood. "We can order whatever you want. You pick the toppings."

She lowered the pamphlet. "Why are you so nice to me?"

A faint smile touched his lips. "Kat, you know why."

"Because you think of me as your girlfriend?" She watched

his smile slip and averted her gaze. "I heard you call me that. When you were talking to Ivan."

He *had* called her that, hadn't he? He'd let Miro call her that as well. But the truth was, he didn't have a clear label for their relationship. Based on her conflicted expression, neither did she.

"Am I?" She pinned him with a genuinely curious look. "Your girlfriend, I mean."

"I don't know what to call... this. Us. There's a very large equation to solve between my circumstances and yours, and I have no idea where to begin with that."

She nodded as the flow of water from the bathroom tapered off.

"Let's wait for Bugi before we order," Kat said. "I'll eat anything except anchovies, but he might be pickier."

"Fair enough." Maksim pushed up from the bed. "I never did search for the washing machine. Let me go do that and then I'll come up and play charades until we figure out what he wants."

"That should be fun." A smile tempted the edges of her soft pink lips. "Hey, Maksim?"

He was across the room and had the door open. "Yes?"

She stood. Her hair spilled in long, frizzy, messy cascades as she crossed the room. When she reached Maksim, she lifted up onto her tiptoes and planted a kiss on his jawline. That was about as far as she could reach without requiring him to stoop. "Even if Bogdan had taken the lockbox, all this would be worth it because I've gotten to know you." Before Maksim could think of an appropriate response, she slid her hands around his waist and wrapped him in a hug.

He hugged her back. "I care about you," he whispered into her hair. "Deeply."

"I know."

Bugi shuffled out of the bathroom, fully dressed in a pair of checkered pajama bottoms and a dingy undershirt. He barely acknowledged them as he flopped onto his bed.

"I'm going to look for that washing machine." Maksim

repeated himself in Serbian, and Bugi replied with a halfhearted wave. "I'll only be a moment," he whispered to Kat, pressing a kiss to the top of her head.

She tightened her hold. Her natural smell mixed with sweat and road trip filtered into his senses. He likely smelled like trash to her, but he didn't let that deter him as he tucked a finger under her chin and lifted. Their gazes intertwined. Her blue eyes shined in the late afternoon light, her lips beckoning him. He might have taken them up on the offer, but Bugi's presence dumped a barrel of ice water on the otherwise intimate moment.

Kat surely felt the same way because she broke away and wandered to the window. "Can you leave the door open?"

"Yeah." He exhaled a long breath and raked at his hair. "I'll… be right back."

JOI, 20 IUNIE, 07:34 (THURSDAY, JUNE 20, 7:34 AM)

BUGI WAS DRESSED and ready to go early the next morning. He was ranting about something while he paced the room and motioned for Maksim and Kat to hurry.

Maksim shoved his sleep clothes into the duffel. He was annoyed but only slightly. Bugi could only drive during the day, and he had a very long way to go. Nevertheless, it would have been nice to have a heads up.

"Where are we going?" Kat whispered, stuffing her clothes into the backpack.

"I'm going to ask Bugi to drop us off at a café." Maksim zipped his duffel. "We can stay there while we wait for the tour company to open." He gripped the strap and hoisted the duffel onto his bad shoulder—which was holding up surprisingly well despite his night spent on the floor.

Well, most of the night. He'd spent about thirty minutes on the bed before he and Kat realized—for two entirely different reasons—that sharing wasn't the best idea.

Kat shouldered her backpack. "Ready."

Maksim took one look at her. "Your *hijab*."

"Oh. Right." She grabbed the *hijab* and stretched the material over her head while Bugi spoke from the doorway. Maksim held up a hand for him to wait.

"Sunglasses?" Maksim asked.

Kat dug them out of her backpack and met Bugi at the door. Maksim followed.

"Do you know of a café in the town?" Maksim asked when they were downstairs. He expected a *ja* or *jok*—yes or no—but Bugi responded with a lengthy answer, ushering them out of the guesthouse.

Maksim tried again as they traversed the walkway that led to the truck. *"We need to go somewhere while we wait for the tour company to open. Could you take us to a café?"*

Bugi stiffened, stopping in front of the truck. His accent thickened as he gestured toward the guesthouse, then the street, then Maksim and Kat.

Kat gasped. "Do you think something happened?"

Maksim turned a furrowed brow toward her. "Like what?"

"I don't know. Maybe it's not safe for us to be here. I-I saw him scrolling through his phone last night. What if he saw a news report? Or what if Ivan did. He could have SMSed Bugi."

Panic rocketed through Maksim. He approached Bugi. *"Please tell me… did we do something wrong?"* He studied Bugi's response closely—and it was not a response someone would have even if they were trying to hide the fact that they had heard something unfortunate about their guests.

No, the response was pure confusion. Bugi asked an indiscernible question that Maksim perceived as *What are you talking about?*

Maksim tried again. *"Is there a reason you want us to leave so quickly?"*

Again, confusion.

"Did we do something wrong? Please tell me simply—yes or no."

"Jok!" (No!) Bugi sounded horrified at the suggestion.

Maksim inhaled deeply, filling his lungs with relief. So the old man wasn't trying to get rid of them. *"Then you must be in a hurry because you have a very long drive ahead of you. Is that right?"*

Bugi bounced his head from side to side, as if debating. Maksim perceived his answer to be something along the lines of *not exactly* or *that's not such a concern.* So if the man wasn't trying to get rid of them and he wasn't concerned with the long drive, what—?

"… Frankfurt na Majni."

Maksim snapped to attention. He hadn't caught the rest of what Bugi had said, but he'd heard the last part. *"Frankfurt am Main,"* Maksim repeated. *"The city?"*

Bugi rolled his eyes. *"Ja, ja, ja."* He tapped his truck and motioned for them to get in. He continued to prattle on as Maksim opened the passenger side and let Kat climb in.

She set her backpack on the floorboard. "Did I just hear him say Frankfurt?"

"Yes." Maksim squeezed in.

"Is he taking us?"

Maksim relayed the question in Serbian.

Bugi smiled the way an adult might when a child draws stick figures. *"Jaaaa. Razumiješ."* Yeeesss. You understand.

Relief washed through Maksim. He tipped his head back and exhaled a laugh.

"What?" Kat asked.

"Yes." He looked at her. "He's taking us to Frankfurt."

Kat squealed and threw an arm around Bugi. He recoiled, waving her off. The old man continued talking while he turned the truck around. He pointed toward the north and then toward the south—not at anything in particular, but as if debating something. Perhaps he had been debating whether to help them or to return home.

Apparently, he had decided on the former. They were going to Frankfurt.

———

THE DRIVE SHOULD HAVE BEEN two hours, but, true to form, Bugi took back roads. They also had to stop outside Wiesbaden so that Maksim could run two errands.

"I have an idea," he'd said, pointing Bugi toward a mobile phone shop. "But I'm going to need a smartphone and a gift card."

"What kind of gift card?"

"You'll see."

The smartphone had been the easier of the two errands. The process worked the same as the mobile phone shop in Sarajevo, and Maksim walked out with a newly activated smartphone twenty minutes later.

The gift card had been more challenging. He was specifically looking for a gift card to one of the ride-sharing services that operated in Frankfurt. After four stops and a bit of fussing from Bugi, Maksim asked if he could use Bugi's credit card to purchase a digital version of the gift card online. The old man agreed, and Maksim paid him in cash.

Fifteen minutes later, Maksim had the ride-sharing app connected to a new email, freshly set up, with the digital gift card redeemed to the account. A one-hundred-euro credit appeared on the dashboard of the ride-sharing app.

Kat watched him. "Okay, so what's the plan?"

Maksim told Bugi they could continue and then focused on Kat. "Kopernikus was one of the clues in the scavenger hunt, and I'm betting Vladimir knows that. We have to assume he has a surveillance team watching Kopernikus-Bank, just like he did for my apartment."

"Why? Vladimir wasn't even at Village Ksorba. How could he know about that clue?"

"Ştefan had a satellite phone while we were out there, and he had possession of the clues overnight." Maksim's thoughts grew distant, dragging him into the events from two weeks ago. "I'll never forget the way he withdrew that piece of paper from his pocket—when we were on the hill and he was trying to open the lockbox. I knew him well, and I can tell you, definitively, he had been mulling over the information, piecing together the puzzle."

"But are you sure Vladimir would know 'Kopernikus' was a reference to a bank? *This* bank that we'll be going to?"

"Even if I wasn't sure, we must approach this with the utmost caution. We *must* assume Vladimir has surveillance team in place."

She glanced at the new smartphone. "I'm guessing your plan involves ordering a ride-share?"

"That's how we'll pass through the area so I can do some reconnaissance." He opened the app. "This ride-sharing company offers a black-car service." He navigated to the About section and read the description. "High-end, black cars driven by professional, top-rated drivers with these amenities guaranteed —air conditioning, satellite radio, and tinted windows."

Understanding sparked behind her eyes. "The tinted windows will keep us hidden."

"Precisely. There is a risk we'll be on camera inside the vehicle, but those types of videos are mostly for reference purposes— in case the driver is robbed for instance. The camera wouldn't be linked to a centralized database."

"My friend Dave gigs for two ride-sharing companies. He has a camera installed, and he deletes the video at the end of every shift. *Unless* he encounters a problem."

"See? All we have to do is not create any problems for our driver." Maksim thought of something else, something he probably should have shared sooner. "I'm going to make a list for you. These are things you'll want to be thinking about today, but they're helpful for everyday life as well."

"What kind of list is it?"

"Here. I'll type it out." Maksim opened the memo pad on his phone but then hesitated. He needed his phone to map out routes, devise exit plans.

He unzipped his bag and dug around. Had he brought a notebook? Pen? Anything?

"Do you have a pen and paper?" He posed the question to Bugi, who flitted his finger toward the glovebox. Maksim popped it open and pulled out a spiral notebook full of addresses, delivery information, and a plethora of scribbled notes.

He found a blank page and went in search of a pen. His hand came into contact with thermal paper. He realized what he'd discovered, and his insides froze solid. Bugi had a stack of tickets —from a whole host of countries—stuffed in his glovebox.

Maksim shot a horrified look to the driver's seat. Bugi steered his eyes from the road long enough to see what Maksim had found. The old man shrugged.

"Ohhh myyy gooosh." Kat grabbed a handful of tickets and read the cities stamped on each one. "Salzburg. Paris. Munich. Munich…" She flipped to the next ones. "Munich. Munich."

Bugi snatched the tickets and tossed them toward the glove compartment. Maksim returned them to their home and said a silent prayer that he would get through today without being sent to prison.

Then he thought of a second prayer—that Daniel and Madă would be praying for them today, too.

He grabbed the pen, which was buried under the tickets, and jotted down the most important rules for Kat to remember. He paused, thinking through each one, deciding on the simplest ways to convey each message. When he finished, he ripped out the page. "I want you to memorize these. Rehearse them to yourself the rest of the trip. Recall is most difficult under duress, so they'll need to be second nature in case something goes sideways."

Kat took the paper.

<u>Maksim's Rules of Survival</u>

1: Be aware.

2: Be discreet.

3: Think logically.

4: Listen to your instinct.

5: Always be ready.

6: Avoid unwanted attention.

7: Assume you're being tailed.

8: Note every possible exit.

9: Assess every possible threat.

10: Never <u>ever</u> reach the second location.

Maksim opened a browser on his phone and searched for Kopernikus-Bank. He entered the address and went into Street View, surveying the area around the bank. He followed the street all the way up and down and then branched off to side streets, and all the while he placed himself in the mind of whoever might be running this op for Vladimir. How would a surveillance team remain incognito in Frankfurt's busy financial district? Maksim figured out how *he* would have done it, and then he ran through those scenarios one at a time.

He had to be ready for anything. He *was* ready. But was Kat?

12:16 (12:16 PM)

"TWO GUYS. There. At that bus stop." Maksim pointed ahead as the ride-share driver eased forward in traffic. Skyscrapers towered over the financial district, deflecting sunlight and heat across the vast stretch of concrete.

Kat squinted, trying to see out the front window. "How do you know they're not just waiting for the bus?"

"I can't say for sure, obviously, but look at their position." He nodded toward Kopernikus-Bank—ahead and to their left. "That bus stop is directly across the street. So they can sit there and watch the building all day without rousing suspicion."

Kat sat back. "I guess it is kind of strange that they're wearing suits. Would businessmen ride the bus in Germany?"

"Anything is possible, but also nothing is *im*possible." Maksim nudged her. "Stay behind that seat. I don't want them looking this way and getting a clear view of you through the windscreen."

Kat shifted behind the passenger seat. "Do you see any others?"

Cars crawled along both sides of the street. Pedestrians scurried in all directions. Even women in high heels moved at double speed, flying across the sidewalk to hail taxis or beat the crosswalk.

Maksim scanned, searching for anything unusual. He locked onto something and pointed. "See that man? He's standing by that cluster of electric scooters. To the right of the bank building."

"I see him."

"He has his phone out, like he's checking something, and every so often he grabs one of the scooters and does a brief inspection." Maksim waited. "There. He did it again."

"But why? What's he doing?"

"Making it look like he's trying to rent a scooter. Or perhaps that he's debating renting one."

"Maybe he really is. He might be trying to download the app."

"Then why does he keep looking around?" Maksim sat back. "He's watching for someone."

"He could be meeting someone."

Their car moved forward, the ride-share driver navigating thick traffic, as Maksim locked onto the next tango. "Male, mid thirties, restaurant patio." Maksim pointed. "See how he's holding that newspaper? He isn't reading it. He isn't even looking at it."

"He's looking around like the scooter guy." Kat frowned. "They're watching for someone."

"They're watching for *us*. Those are Vladimir's men."

Panic spread through her features. "How do we get past them?"

"I don't know, *dragă*. I'm still working that out." He continued his visual sweep.

An alleyway ran between the bank and a red-brick building,

and Maksim spied a motorcycle parked at the entrance. The driver wore his helmet and was seated on the bike, ready to go—and yet he had just lit a cigarette.

"Tango. Over there, on the bike."

Kat followed his stare. "How can you tell?"

"He's mounted, helmeted, but he's not going anywhere." Maksim lifted his gaze toward the sky. Gray clouds had been forming all morning, but not enough to stifle the summer heat. "You know as well as I do he's roasting in that helmet. Why keep it on to smoke a cigarette? Unless he's been told to stay ready."

"He's looking around, too. Like the other men."

"We are almost to your destination." The ride-share driver spoke in choppy German. He was Arabic, late fifties, and he didn't sound like he'd been in the country for long. *"Do you prefer to walk?"*

"*Alles gut*," Maksim said. (All is good.)

The man shrugged. He didn't seem to be wondering what they were talking about, but perhaps he already knew because he'd been listening.

"Sprechen Sie Englisch?" Maksim asked, keeping his tone friendly and conversational.

"Nein." The man rolled forward while more traffic piled up behind him. *"I come from Beirut, and we speak Lebanese and French. I am learning German."*

Maksim smiled and switched languages. *"May I speak with you in French? It's a beautiful language, and I'm fluent in speaking and understanding."*

The man's eyes lit up in his rearview. *"Oui, s'il vous plaît."* (Yes, please.)

"What's your name?"

"I'm called Amir."

"Are y'all speaking in French?" Kat interjected.

"We are. He's not fluent in German, and he doesn't speak English. Well, supposedly doesn't speak English. I should probably test that." Maksim paused, thinking. Then he said, "Elephant ass."

Kat sent a sideways look from across the back seat. The driver didn't flinch.

Maksim tried again, amplifying his volume. "A tiger eating an elephant. A whale, shark, and crocodile battle to the death."

Again the driver showed no reaction, his gaze drifting over the traffic and trailing up the buildings.

Kat's mouth hung open. "What the hell is going on?"

"I want to make sure he hasn't understood our conversation. I don't think he has." Maksim zeroed in on the bank building. The shiny structure sprouted up from the concrete, a Goliath that towered over the tallest buildings in the financial district.

His attention reverted to the restaurant. Could the tango reach Kat from that outdoor patio? If so, he would have a clean getaway via the alley that ran along the right side of the bank. Amir continued to roll forward, and Maksim was able to look straight down that alley. The path ended at the next street, a major road that ran parallel to this one. The perfect escape route.

Maksim's attention roamed to the tango on the bike. That alley was their secondary line of defense. If the target ran, the motorcycle could swing in.

A black luxury town car traveling in the opposite direction pulled up to the bank. Maksim's window was tinted, but he withdrew by instinct. Someone exited from the back of the town car and stepped up onto the curb.

This wasn't another tango. It was a woman.

The town car pulled away, revealing a lean form in a long gray pencil skirt, white blouse, and black stilettos. She slid a designer purse onto her arm, seating the handle at her elbow, and sashayed toward the bank. A clean part ran down the center of her head, her hair sleek and knotted in a low bun.

A blur flashed in Maksim's periphery. The guy on the motorcycle had tossed his cigarette and was twisting the ignition key. The guy on the patio sat straight, folding his newspaper. The scooter guy stepped to the side, stationing himself outside a shop.

"Maksim." Kat twisted around, keeping to the side, and pointed to something outside the back window. The first men they'd seen—the ones at the bus stop—had risen to standing. One of them stepped off the curb, holding a hand up to stop traffic.

Maksim followed their line of sight to the woman. She was taller than Kat, and her hair was straight and brown rather than black and curly. Nevertheless, she had aroused suspicion.

"They think she's me," Kat whispered.

"Yes. And they're ready in case they're right."

One of the men at the bus stop reached for his ear. He bowed his head, as if trying to listen, and fidgeted with something. They had comms.

Maksim leaned across the back seat and peered out Kat's window. His attention trailed up the building that stood across from the bank. This one wasn't nearly as tall, but it was tall enough to post overwatch. He recalled the events that had happened in București, specifically the gut feeling he'd had about the sniper. Would Vladimir dare to carry out an assassination here, in the middle of Frankfurt, with so many bystanders?

He would. Maksim knew he would... except Kat wouldn't be the target. If she were, Vladimir would have simply hired a hitman, who would have carried out the job stealthily. No, hers was a capture order. That was the reason for these men, their stakeout, why they'd been posted so near to the bank's entrance.

If there was a sniper, it was for dealing with Maksim.

The traffic light turned green, and Amir straightened to attention. Traffic began to roll forward, drawing Maksim and Kat away from the ambush awaiting them.

"We can't do this." Maksim focused forward. "It's too dangerous."

"What?" Kat angled her body toward him. "But we've come all this way—"

"We've come all this way, and what a waste it would be if things turned tragic now." He wiped a hand down his face. "Getting you in the building is high risk. Getting both of us in there is damn near impossible."

"What about disguises? That worked for you in Bucharest."

"Vladimir will be expecting that now." He flitted a hand in the general direction of the bank—behind them and to the left. "You saw how they responded to that woman."

"Look. There she is." Kat unbuckled her seatbelt and twisted all the way around, staring out the back window. The woman had exited the bank and was sashaying toward the curb. She faced traffic and craned her neck, lifting her sunglasses.

She was looking for someone. Probably her driver.

Maksim scanned. He spotted the town car pulling onto the main road from a side street.

"Maksim?"

He swiveled and found Kat staring at him, her expression thoughtful. "I think I could do that."

"Do what?"

"Look like her."

His eyes tightened at the corners. "No. Absolutely not."

"But I could. All I'd have to do is—"

"*Monsieur?*" Amir peeked at his passengers through the rearview mirror. "*Your destination is close.*"

They didn't have an actual "destination," but the app had required one, so Maksim had entered an address farther down the street.

"*Is it possible to change the route?*" Maksim asked. "*We need to return to the starting point. Forgive me. We've forgotten something important.*" Maksim added the last part when the man's expression turned quizzical.

The explanation seemed to satisfy him. "*You can change the route, but only through the app. It must be done before I reach the arrival point.*"

Maksim pulled out this phone.

"What are you doing?" Kat asked, oblivious to the exchange. "What did you say to the driver?"

"He's taking us to the starting point. I have to update the route."

"What?" Kat lunged for the phone. He switched the device to his other hand. "Maksim!"

"Bugi is waiting. I'll ask him to drop us off somewhere, perhaps in the same village where we stayed last night. We can regroup and try again tomorrow."

"We won't have this chance tomorrow. Please, just listen to me." She scooted across the seat, bringing their legs flush. "Gray skirt, white dress top. The purse was black and matched her shoes. She walked like a model. I can do that. I can recreate her."

"Those men are too close to the bank. If they recognized you—"

"They wouldn't."

"But if they *did,* they would have possession of you within seconds and with *two* possible escape routes. Kat, I wouldn't be able to stop them. Even if I tried, I guarantee they have a plan for taking me out." Maksim copy-pasted the address from the original pickup point and added it to their route.

Amir's phone pinged from the front. He gave a thumbs-up.

"Hear me out. I'm begging you." Kat touched his shoulder. He remembered the dream, and his eyes flashed toward her hand.

The ring wasn't there, but he'd half expected it to be.

"When they saw that woman," she whispered, "they went on high alert but ultimately didn't apprehend her. Right?"

"Because they had comms. I saw one of them messing with his earpiece."

"So someone told them to stand down. Why?"

"Obviously because the woman wasn't you."

"Okay, then what would happen if the same woman showed up a second time?" Kat paused, letting the question take root. "Think about it," she continued slowly. "Do you really believe

—be honest—they would scrutinize her as much a second time?"

Her logic throttled his next argument. The cogs in his mind began to turn. She was right. They wouldn't scrutinize her as much. Not if she showed up in the same car.

His gaze circled through the interior of the ride-share. The *luxury* ride-share. It wasn't as large as the town car, but it was a high-end sedan—black, clean, and well cared for.

His attention slid to Kat. She wasn't the right height, but high heels would make up the difference. The woman had been rail thin, while Kat was more muscular, her body curving along her hips and thighs. But with the right clothes…

"No," he said—except he didn't sound as convinced this time.

"Maksim, I can do it. I did it in the dream. It was scary, but I was in some kind of disguise, and I walked right in."

"Look, the psychology is accurate. It's perfect social engineering, and the situation could very well play out in our favor. But it may not"—he gave her a once-over—"and we don't have the resources to outfit you."

She looked down at herself. Maksim had made her strip off the *hijab* and *abaya* before their driver had arrived. He'd had a Middle Eastern name, and although there was a chance he wasn't Muslim, Maksim hadn't wanted to risk offending him or causing a scene.

The last-minute change had left Kat in jean shorts and a t-shirt with colorful graphics splashed across the front. Maksim would need thousands to make Kat look like that woman, and he only had a few hundred left. Apart from the clothes, she would need a wig, and where would they find *that*?

His thoughts spun. He squeezed his forehead, attempting to ground himself. "We don't have the funds for this. The clothes would have to be designer—"

"No, they wouldn't."

"They would. Knock-off brands are evident to people who live in the lap of luxury. Even the bank personnel would notice."

"What about a thrift store? Someplace that might carry designer clothing at a discount?"

Maksim yanked off his cap and raked hard at his hair, down to his scalp. The sensation soothed him as the city breezed past his window. He felt like he could breathe again now that they were out of the financial district.

"Maksim, please. *Please.*" Kat tugged on his hand, trying to get his attention. "I know you don't think much of my grandfather, and I know how you feel about the inheritance. It's just money, right?"

"It *is* just money." His stare connected with hers. "Your life is worth infinitely more."

"And what about my dad's life?"

"His as well."

"Then he died for nothing." Tears leaked into her voice. Defeated, she released him. "All of this—everything he and Vasile and Popescu did—was for nothing."

Maksim massaged his chin. His multi-day stubble scraped, contending with the roughness of his callouses. "Your father had good intentions," he said finally. "Your grandfather likely did as well. That doesn't mean you should follow in their footsteps."

"I'm sorry, but… I don't accept that. I can't." The tears spilled over and skated down her beautiful pale cheeks. She reclaimed his hand and squeezed. A tiny pressure entered his palm and vibrated through his being. "I don't want their deaths to be for nothing. I don't want Vladimir to win."

Maksim tipped his head back, settling against the headrest. "Vladimir only wins if he gets what he wants."

"No. He wins if we're afraid. And you know what?" She swiped at the wet streaks. "Ștefan is dead, but he'll win, too. Maksim, I don't want them to win."

Her determination crashed into him. He *was* afraid—not for himself, but for her. He was protecting her… and yet Vladimir had managed to instill fear in his heart, his mind. Even his dreams.

He redirected his eyes, watching the buildings grow smaller. All the while, his mind raced with things that could go wrong with Kat's plan.

"Please," she whispered. "Maksim, please."

His gaze flicked to his phone, which he held in his left hand. "I don't know how we can pull this off." He swallowed. "But I'll… search for thrift shops."

Her hold on his right hand tightened. "Thank you."

"Don't thank me yet." He did a search and skimmed the results. "We could visit every thrift store in the city and still not find what we need. Bugi drove me to four different shops earlier, and none of them had what I was looking for. It's a crapshoot."

"At least we can say we tried."

"Yeah. We can say that." He dragged his focus away from the phone and took note of their surroundings. "Perhaps we could ask—" He fell silent as a flash of yellow snagged his attention. The neighborhood was mostly residential with businesses occupying the ground level. One such business was an electronics shop. Stationed outside that shop was a bright yellow ATM.

But not just any ATM. A bitcoin ATM.

Maksim leaned forward. *"Excusez-moi."*

Amir's attention flicked to the rearview.

"Would you mind to let me off at that shop?" Maksim thumbed over his shoulder. *"I will only be a few minutes, and I'll tip extra for the delay."*

"I can only do this when the request is made through the app."

Maksim reopened the app. *"So add another stop?"*

"Yes, of course. People use our service for important errands, therefore the app allows multiple stops between the origin and the destination. But you must enter the address."

Maksim searched for the shop's address and discovered it was a chain electronics store with several locations throughout

Frankfurt. The store was a trusted brand in Germany. *Trusted* being the keyword.

He added the stop, and Amir's phone pinged.

"Parking is difficult here, monsieur." Amir eyed a long row of parked cars. *"It's okay to circle the block until you are finished?"*

"Yes, it's fine. Merci beaucoup."

"What's going on?" Kat asked.

"Errand. A quick one." He waited until the car came to a stop, then pushed open the door.

Kat grabbed him. "What kind of errand?"

He nodded toward the bitcoin ATM. She tilted her head, dividing a perplexed look between him and the bright yellow—but then Maksim watched as the epiphany sparked.

Her mood brightened. "This is going to work. I know it."

THIRTY-SIX

14:41 (2:41 PM)

KAT AND MAKSIM hurried from their final stop. A logo depicting Sock and Buskin—the comedy and tragedy masks—plastered the storefront window on their left. THEATER MODE. The place was a costumery shop run by theater students and aficionados.

Kat tugged at her wig, ensuring the cap was secure. It was thanks to the overzealous clerk, who had been eager to assist with Kat's "first big role." The woman had assumed that role was for a play. Maksim and Kat hadn't contradicted her.

As Amir's car came into view, Kat did one more outfit check. She was already dressed, down to the purse and heels, and she gave herself a once-over. "You think it's close?"

Maksim had been scrutinizing her every step of the way. With the clothes they'd found at a high-end shop—plus the blond wig wrapped in a low bun—she held a striking resemblance to the woman.

Except for the high heels. Kat hadn't been able to stay upright in stilettos, so they had settled for a heel that was slightly thicker.

"Do the walk," he said.

Kat hooked her arm through the purse and sashayed up the sidewalk precisely as Maksim had taught her. Well, shown her. He'd actually demonstrated the walk, which had felt ridiculous, but she'd been struggling to execute the motion up until that point.

She must have taken excellent mental notes, because her current execution was flawless.

Satisfied, Maksim led her to the car. *"This is for you,"* Maksim said, passing one of his shopping bags to Amir.

"It's a gift?" The man pulled out a black chauffeur's hat. *"Why?"*

"It will look more official since my girlfriend is conducting important business at the bank."

Amir nodded and donned the hat.

The smaller buildings of the West End gave way to large glass towers. Traffic grew dense, and they found themselves stuck in another long line, this time traveling in the opposite direction. The same direction the woman had been traveling earlier.

Maksim turned to Kat. "We're getting close. Let's go over the plan one more time. From the beginning."

"Amir pulls up to the curb, and I wait for him to open my door. I don't get out before that. I have the purse in my right hand and then slide it onto my forearm after I'm on the sidewalk."

"Yes, and try to keep your hands closed as you do that. Not in fists, but loosely." He showed her. "Your fingernails can't be seen with the naked eye, but the overwatch will have equipment. Best to hide that trait in case the woman wore her nails in a color that would be noticeable." Maksim indicated for Kat to continue.

"When I step out, I need to appear flustered, like I've lost something, but without looking around. Keep my head down."

"Exactly. Your purse is a prop. Use it. Pretend to search

through it for the missing item. Don't appear frantic. Just harried."

"Right. Harried." Kat angled her shoe toward Maksim. "You think they'll notice the heels are thicker."

"They're not that much thicker, and nobody will notice anything if you carry yourself the way you've been practicing."

"What about the bank employees?" She touched her wig. "You think they'll say anything since I look different from my passport photo?"

"Women change their hair all the time. You can always say you wanted a different look for summer." He peeked inside her bag. "Where are your new sunglasses?"

She pulled them out. The woman's sunglasses had been large and oval, but Maksim hadn't noted how large, and Kat couldn't remember how oval. "I'll make sure these are on before Amir opens the door."

"And you have everything you need to access the account?"

Kat had finally transferred the account number and passcode onto a sheet of paper. She dipped into the purse and pulled out the sheet.

"Take this." He handed over his smartphone. "Don't contact anyone you know. I'll be making a way for you to do that soon."

She seemed hesitant to accept the device. "Are you sure you don't need it? I don't mind taking the flip phone."

"Oh, no. It would be unseemly for an heiress to use a clamshell." He gave into a grin—but then his expression turned serious. "I've programmed my number into the phone. Call me if you suspect anything is amiss."

"What would you do? I mean—" Uneasiness settled into her features. "Maksim, there are so many of them."

"I would find a way to get to you. And if they had you, I would chase them to the ends of the earth and beyond." He answered firmly but matter-of-factly. Earnestly. It wasn't difficult to sound like he'd meant every word, because he did. And she could tell.

Emotion filled her eyes. "You'd do that for me?"

"I would do it one hundred times. One million. Whatever it took." He reached over and caressed her cheek. "But that's not going to happen today, is it?"

She shook her head, sniffling, and a single tear slid out.

Maksim brushed the dampness away and then cupped her cheek. She closed her eyes, nuzzling his palm. Unspoken words —hers, his—hung in the air, and a slow, serrated ache penetrated his rib cage. The temptation to call this whole thing off drew deathly close, and he had to break the silence before it broke him. "I have to go now."

She opened her eyes. "Where? Why?"

"I can't be in the car when you're dropped off. Someone will see me."

Fear flickered through her expression.

"I'll be just around the corner. It's a strategic location that gives me access to what I believe is their getaway route." He let his smile shine through. "Trust me on this. It's the perfect spot. All right?"

She firmed up her trembling jaw and nodded.

"Remember the rules—be aware, be discreet, trust your instinct. Those are important." He lowered his hand. "But your primary focus is getting inside that building." He switched out his ball cap for the fedora he'd bought at the costumery shop. "When you're leaving, don't walk outside until you see Amir. SMS me after you're inside and again when you're about to leave."

"Okay. I will."

"Amir, can you turn here please?" Maksim pointed at a side street. *"I intend to wait at a café while my girlfriend accomplishes this very private errand."*

Amir answered in the affirmative, giving a thumbs-up, and took the turn. Maksim had seen the café while researching the area. Sometimes those images were outdated, but he was grateful to find that the café still existed.

Amir let him off at the curb.

"Return here as soon as you deliver her," Maksim said.

"Oui, monsieur."

Maksim stepped out and circled around the car. A variety of businesses, including a few seedy sex shops, lined the street. Restaurants and cafés dotted the commercial spaces in between.

Kat lowered her window as Maksim stepped onto the curb. "Sunglasses," he reminded her.

She slid them on.

"Stay focused. Be on guard, but appear relaxed." He hesitated. "Kat, I—"

A car stopped behind them and gave a little honk. Amir rolled down the side passenger window. *"Monsieur?"*

Maksim swallowed what he was about to say. *"Do not reenter your vehicle until she is inside the building,"* he told Amir. *"If anyone approaches her, your job is to intervene. Redirect them. See that she gets inside."*

"As you have told me. I will do it."

Maksim gestured toward Amir's phone, which was mounted on the dash. *"Any problem, large or small, call the telephone number I gave to you. Don't wait. Don't SMS. Just call."*

"Oui, monsieur."

The car behind them honked a second time. Amir rolled up the windows and pulled away, drawing Kat away with him... and subsequently stealing the breath from Maksim's lungs. He collected himself and headed toward the café's patio area. The fedora gave him better coverage than the ball cap, but he kept his head down anyway.

A bubble of German voices hovered over the patio, the patrons conversing and enjoying their drinks. Maksim claimed a table in the far corner. Sunlight poured over the awning, a pale waterfall that spilled onto the sidewalk. Car fumes saturated the air.

He studied everyone who passed by, keeping his eyes pealed for Vladimir's henchmen or police. Beyond that, he could do nothing. Kat was walking into the lion's den while he waited one full city-block away.

He clasped his hands, elbows resting on the table. He couldn't be with Kat for the drop-off, but perhaps he could listen for anything out of the ordinary—shouts, tires screeching.

Gunfire.

His adrenaline spiked at the thought. He closed his eyes and strained to listen. He could almost hear the buzz of traffic on the other road, and as he thought of Kat, he swore he could feel her nervousness.

His pulse sped up. His breaths grew shallow.

"Don't be afraid," he whispered. His pulse answered with a jump.

He mumbled a tiny piece of a prayer Daniel had taught him. The words came to him in Romanian. *"Yea though I walk through the valley of the shadow of death, I will fear no evil, for Thou art with me."* Maksim paused. *With her,* he amended silently. *If this prayer is real, then may God be with* her. *Protect* her. *Help* her.

The noisy café drifted into the background… and then the background drifted, too. The sounds evaporated until a thick veil of silence cloaked him, filling his ears and leaving behind a slight ring. The sound grew louder, sharper, before morphing into a high-pitched whine. The smell of dust and grit floated through his senses. He didn't understand what was happening, only that the noise was beginning to drown out everything else, including his thoughts.

But he needed to be able to hear, and to think, in case something went wrong. And then something *did* go wrong.

An explosion rocketed in the distance, breaking the stillness, reverberating the air. Another explosion followed. Kat's familiar voice reached him. The volume was faint, but the terror that filled her scream was clear. So clear, it shook him. *"Maksiiiiiim!"*

———

His eyes shot open. He pushed back from the table, toppling his chair. A waitress froze. Her customers gasped.

Maksim examined his surroundings. His hearing had returned. He could hear the buzz of traffic, the tinkling of silverware inside the café; though, the patio area had gone deathly quiet as everyone stared. What the hell just happened?

He scooped up his chair and slid it under his table. *"Bitte verzeih mir."* (Please forgive me.) He ducked his head, checking that the fedora was pulled down, and zigzagged between the tables.

A familiar form came into view twenty meters from the café. Amir had parked and was climbing out of the driver's side. He waved.

Maksim jogged over to him. *"What happened? Where is she?"*

"We were there." He angled his body toward the main road. *"I took her to the bank as you said."*

"You saw her go inside?"

"Of course, monsieur." Amir blinked. *"As you said."*

Maksim yanked out his phone, struck by a sudden case of time blindness. He had no idea how long he'd been at the café. Five minutes? Ten? It couldn't have been more than fifteen… could it?

The time read 15:25.

A monochrome envelope showed he had ten new messages. A burst of adrenaline fired as he flipped open the clamshell.

K
I'm in

There are weird letters on the phone keyboard

Wth is ß? What letter is that?!

I think english should bring back the double dots over vowels.

Did you know those are called diacritic marks?
The double dot is a trema. Just looked it up.

> über
>
> naïve
>
> daïs
>
> I did not know coöperative is supposed to have a trema???
>
> Got to go. Bank prez coming. ❤

He exhaled a relieved laugh. She'd made it. She was inside the bank.

"Monsieur?" Amir came around the car and opened the back door. *"Do you want to wait in here?"*

16:53 (4:53 PM)

AMIR PROMISED to heed the same instructions for Kat's pickup—open the back door, wait for her to enter the vehicle, and step in if anyone approaches her.

Please, God, don't let anyone approach her.

Maksim returned to the café for the duration of the pickup. It was the safest option and better than loitering on the sidewalk. The waitress hesitated upon seeing him, but he apologized profusely and said he'd had a long journey. *"I nodded off while seated at the table. When I awoke, I forgot where I was."* He actually *did* believe that was what happened. He couldn't explain the incident otherwise.

The woman's mood improved after hearing this. *"An espresso will solve your problem, I think."*

"I agree," he said, and she happily brought him the order.

He barely touched his coffee as he waited for Amir to return. Five minutes felt like five hours. Then ten minutes ticked by. Fifteen.

He kept his phone out the entire time, reading and re-reading the last messages Kat had sent.

> **K**
> I see Amir. He's stuck in traffic.
>
> Ok. See you soon. ❤

These had come through sixteen minutes ago. Had she ventured outside prematurely? Perhaps she had tried to intercept Amir while he'd been in traffic. She wasn't supposed to, but people did strange things under pressure. More often than not, they failed to follow through—either because they couldn't remember the instructions or because they made a poor judgment call.

Maksim should have known better. He shouldn't have let her attempt this ruse.

He typed a reply. Cycling through each letter on this push-button piece of trash was torture.

> **M**
> everything ok?

He held his breath, waiting, listening. He didn't dare close his eyes this time.

A monochrome envelope appeared. He opened the message.

> **K**
> We're pulling up.

The car appeared within sixty seconds of her message. Maksim left cash on the table and resisted the urge to sprint. As he opened Amir's back door, he half expected Vladimir's henchmen to be waiting on the other side. They could have apprehended Kat on her way out. They could have stolen her phone…

But the men weren't in the car. Only Kat and Amir.

"What do you think? Off or on?" She touched the wig. "My scalp is sweaty, but I wasn't sure if I should—"

Maksim flung himself into the back seat, yanked the door shut, and pulled Kat in for a kiss. Their mouths connected, but her seatbelt restrained her. His fedora got in the way as well. Nevertheless, his lips lingered—an invitation rather than a demand. "I'm so relieved," he whispered, breathless, "that you're safe."

He registered a *click*, and Kat's seatbelt slid off. She reached out and slowly removed the fedora, revealing damp, matted hair beneath. Maksim raked at the mess while Kat set his fedora to the side. His attention followed the hat until he realized she was leaning in, her face mere centimeters from his.

She tilted her head and closed the gap. Their lips met, and white-hot electricity sparked. This wasn't a kiss like she'd given him last night—quick, innocent, filled with uncertainty. No, this kiss was full of passion, like she'd been aching to do this for a very, very long time.

He slid his hands around her waist and hauled her to his side of the back seat. Her lips, the softness they radiated, stoked the flame within him, while the eagerness of her touch set it ablaze. She gripped his shoulders, pulling herself closer. He grunted as her fingers slid up his neck, to his face, and then found their way into his sweaty hair.

He opened his mouth wider, desperate for more of her. Their tongues grazed, and his hunger ignited into a bonfire. The car began to move, but the world around him grew distant as he fell deeper... and deeper... and deeper into the kiss.

One thousand thoughts inundated his brain. Some of them bent toward paranoia—that they were still in the city, that they could still be in danger—while others involved strategic calculations for getting alone with her. But the one thought that landed and stuck was the ring. The blue sapphire, so close to the color of her eyes, flickered in his mind.

Suddenly, the fire lessened, replaced by the coolness he'd experienced in the dream. Except this was real, and the sensation rolled through him in soothing waves. *I love you.* The words filtered into his mind from somewhere hidden, a place he hadn't known existed. He did love her. Beyond comprehension.

Then the timbre of her voice, the melody of its cadence, floated through his mind. *I love you, too, Maksim.* The way she said his name was unmistakeable. She had spoken the words without actually saying them aloud. How?

Stunned, he broke away, panting. She stared at him, her lips pink and swollen.

They stayed that way for a long time, their gazes intertwined. Maksim wanted to know if she felt the things he'd been feeling, if she'd heard the things he'd heard. He desperately wanted to know if she really did love him, but he hadn't the slightest clue how to ask.

"*Monsieur?*" Amir's voice reeled Maksim's attention toward the front. Their driver was suppressing an embarrassed grin, his eyes focused forward on the traffic ahead. "*Shall I deliver you to the original location? The place where I first picked you up today?*"

"*Yes, please. Actually...*" Maksim grabbed his phone, which had toppled onto the floorboard along with his hat. "*Allow me to send a message to our friend. I need to make sure he's there.*"

"*Oui, monsieur.*"

"*Do we need to do this through the app?*"

"*No, monsieur.*" Amir pulled out the large tip Maksim had given him. "*Thank you very much for this. I will take you wherever you want to go.*"

———

19:12 (7:12PM)

Bugi, Kat, and Maksim rumbled along in the truck. Maksim had the window down, his elbow resting lazily on the sill. His other arm held Kat as she leaned against him.

The old man was supposed to be waiting on the outskirts of the city. He'd decided that wasn't far enough, however, and when Maksim messaged, asking where to go, Bugi had replied with a single word.

Bugi
Kelsterbach

Amir was familiar with the village and had offered to drive them there. Maksim tried to give him extra for petrol, but the man had kindly refused. *"I am happy because I made good money today. I have a new professional look"*—he gestured at his chauffeur's hat—*"and I helped your girlfriend."* The man inserted a sly smile and added *"Your wife?"*

Maksim had smiled, thanking him, but didn't remark on the addendum. How could he? He didn't understand any of this.

"Where is Bugi taking us?" Kat asked, interrupting his thoughts. She had changed into her normal clothes plus the *hijab* and sunglasses.

"Saarbrücken."

"We're going back?" She removed the sunglasses. "Like, to the same guesthouse?"

"I believe so." The answer leaned toward a question. "From what I gather, the German company paid for two nights. Or possibly for two rooms." Maksim shook his head. "Bugi definitely held up two fingers when I tried to clarify."

"Two *rooms*?" Kat whispered the question, her voice breathy and tinged in longing. Maksim responded by fortifying his hold. She snuggled closer and planted a lingering kiss on his jawline.

From his core to his extremities, his entire body buzzed.

Thick forest walled in both sides of the highway, hiding the inbound sunset until the road led them west. An earthy fragrance of pine, dirt, and leaves floated into the truck while shades of orange spread themselves like a blanket over the horizon.

Maksim angled his face into the wind. Most Romanians would have rolled up the window, afraid of the dreaded *curent* (draft), but he wasn't afraid of it. He wasn't afraid of anything. Not here. Not now. Not ever? He wouldn't go that far, but Bugi's truck had been their magic carpet, and he was going to enjoy the ride as long as it lasted.

Kat's *hijab* flapped in the constant rush of air. She removed the stretchy fabric and tucked it into her backpack. "Whatcha thinkin' about?"

"Me?" Maksim shrugged. "Nothing much. Just wondering how to get that second room."

She snorted a laugh.

"I should have a solution soon. I'm on the brink." He angled a grin in her direction. "Why? What are *you* thinking about?"

"I don't know." Her answer came shyly, as if she were embarrassed to say.

"You're thinking about the second room, too, aren't you?"

"No." Her smile broke through.

"You are. I knew it." He winked, and she rolled her eyes. "Tell me, is it my manly, sweaty, end-of-the-day smell that most attracts you? Or the he-hasn't-shaved-in-four-days look?"

"Can't it be both?" She eased out of the playfulness and slipped into a sober expression. "Actually, I was wondering… Where are you going after this? I know you haven't wanted to share those details, but—"

"Catalonia." He answered without pause or hesitation. Likewise without any doubt.

"Catalonia?" she repeated. "You mean, Spain?"

"Some people would say no, but… yes, technically Spain. I'm heading to a town on the Costa Brava."

Kat made a *hm* sound, her expression thoughtful—not unlike the expression she'd exuded in Frankfurt when she had concocted that brilliant-but-reckless plan of hers. "Are there any major cities near that town?"

"Near enough, I suppose. Within driving distance."

"And… do you know if those cities have airports with direct flights to the United States?"

His pulse came alive. His full attention landed on her.

"There's one major city in the region, and the airport has direct flights to New York and Miami."

Silence hung between them for several minutes. The hot air sweeping through the truck caught a tendril of Kat's hair and drew the curls loose. "Have you thought about how you're going to get there?" she asked, tucking the tendril behind her ear.

"Thought? Yes. Decided? No." His plans had changed when Kat decided to go home. Traveling solo wouldn't require the same rigor, and Maksim wasn't going to make the trip harder or longer than necessary. But… *was* he traveling solo? He didn't imagine she would inquire unless—

"How long will it take you to get there?" She rested her head against his chest. "To that town in Catalonia."

"Saarbrücken is on the French border." His heart drummed. "A day or two through France, and then Catalonia is right there." He gestured with his hand. "Right across the border."

She repeated the *hm* sound.

His heart abandoned the drumming and outright thrashed. "Is there any particular reason you're asking?"

"No." She paused. "Maybe."

Excitement sparked within him. She wanted to go. At the very least she was thinking about it. "It's going to be a lovely journey, and it would be nice to have a travel companion."

"Travel companion, huh?" She peeked up enough to reveal her smile. "How are you planning to find one of those?"

His mouth twisted, fighting a widening smile. "I have options—newspaper ads, social media posts. I'm sure Miro could post a PSA on the darknet."

Kat arched an eyebrow. "That seems kind of risky with Vladimir hunting you down."

"It certainly would be." Maksim sighed dramatically. "I'm in quite the conundrum."

"Well…" She nuzzled him. "Maybe I could help you out."

He swallowed. "Really?" His question came as a whisper.

"Really. I mean, maybe." She paused. "I'll have to think about it, and my brain works better after food."

"I thought you were going to say 'after second room.'"

She snorted a laugh. He could have sworn she muttered "that too" but he couldn't be sure.

"All right, so then what's for dinner? Pizza from the same place, or should we try something different?" He withdrew his arm and held out both hands, palms facing up. "The sure thing we know we'll enjoy?" He raised one hand higher. "Or be adventurous?" He lowered that hand and raised the other, tipping the scales. "You pick."

"Gosh, that's a tough one." She faced forward, bringing herself shoulder to shoulder with him, and slid her hand into his. "But I think I might be feeling adventurous."

Her playful tone added layers of meaning to the answer. Maksim understood her, perfectly, and a smile dawned across his lips. "Yeah?" he whispered, lacing their fingers.

Her gaze drifted to the tree line, then to the road before them. Her eyes rested in that direction for a lengthy moment, and then she settled her smile on him. "Yeah."

Want more?

Want more access to Kat and Maksim's world? Unlock bonus scenes, character cards, top secret cover art and more. You'll receive a collection of FREE GIFTS just for checking it out…

Access your FREE GIFTS

www.patreon.com/EllisKPopa
Look for FREE FOR EVERYONE. It's pinned at the top.

Can you help us out?

Reviews are incredibly helpful. Ellis and the artists who work on the series would be grateful for your rating or review.

www.Linktr.ee/ReviewFLD

THE FLD TEAM

A heartfelt THANKS to everyone who helped bring *First Light of Dawn* to life. Some of you are new; others have been here from the beginning. Whatever your mile-marker in this journey, I want you to know how grateful I am for your encouragement and support.

Early Readers

Andy Krahling
Bethany Oakes Wisdom
Bob Fendt
Jacob M.
Jenny Coyne
Joshua T.
Liv A.
Nevaeh K.
Nicole Williams
Rebecca Castro
Skylar W.
Vinné B. Crimmes

Technical, Geographical & Linguistic Consultations

Alice Moon

Brian E.
Christian R.
Jacob M.

Creatives

Adrijus at Rocking Book Covers - standard edition covers
Jonna Blankenship - maps
Kilex Ka - opening illustration
Nicole Love - story-themed slides & reels
RedXDesigner - book trailer

Editing & Proofreading

Patrick Weill - editing, proofreading & foreign language
Crystalle at Victory Editing - proofreading & final checks

ABOUT THE AUTHOR

When Ellis isn't writing, you might find her exploring Belgrade's Design District, taking cover in Tirana's Bunk'Art museums, or planning her next research trip to the Balkans. Her latest obsession is post-Soviet Romania during the Communist era, and she's working on a suspense series set in that time period.

If you enjoy books and travel, she'd love to connect with you on her Substack, The Wandering Author.

Substack.com/@EllisKPopa

For a more immersive experience, you'll want to check out her Patreon channel, Disappear Here. Joining gets you special agent status + top secret clearance to bonus scenes, story art, reada-longs, audiobook listenalongs, and so much more.

Patreon.com/EllisKPopa